With a faraway look, Seth brushed cake crumbs off his hands and lay back in the grass, lacing his fingers behind his head. "It's been a lovely picnic, Doc," he said.

"I wish you wouldn't call me Doc. My name is Rachel."

"Okay," he said. He leaned up on one elbow and smiled. "I'll call you Rachel if you'll quit calling me Sheriff." He sat up and took her hands in his. "Would you get mad if I kissed you?" he asked.

"You kissed me last week," she whispered, her heart racing. "Why do you want to kiss me again?"

"Because you're beautiful and all I've wanted to do since you stepped off that stagecoach is . . . kiss you."

Rachel closed her eyes against the intensity of his gaze. Then his lips were on hers — firm, warm, gentle. It was a kiss unlike anything she had ever experienced, and as his mouth caressed hers, she felt giddy and lightheaded. His lips were soft and his skin smelled like sunshine.

Feeling her lean into him, Seth buried his hand in her hair, gently stroking the back of her head and drawing her closer. As their kiss deepened, he felt rather than heard her sigh of pent-up passion. "You're beautiful," he murmured into her hair. "So beautiful . . ."

JANE KIDDER
PASSION'S FEVER

ZEBRA BOOKS
KENSINGTON PUBLISHING CORP.

To David —
my Seth Wellesley

ZEBRA BOOKS

are published by

Kensington Publishing Corp.
475 Park Avenue South
New York, NY 10016

First printing: December, 1991

Printed in the United States of America

Chapter One

"Stage is comin'! Stage is comin'!"

As the horseman galloped down the dusty street shouting his news, the crowd that had been gathering all morning surged forward in anticipation.

A robust woman in her early fifties elbowed her way to the front of the throng and began barking orders like a general assembling troops for battle. Betsy Fulbright was the mayor's wife and took her role at official town functions very seriously.

"Now, move back, everyone! Sadie, get your kids out of the way before the stage runs them down. Will! Tom! Hoist that banner up. Where's Seth?" Scanning the crowd and not seeing the man she sought, Betsy planted her hands on her ample hips and shouted, "Ben! Go get the sheriff. He should be here when the stage pulls in. Martin? Martin, come over here. You're the official greeter. Now, places everybody . . . and, for heaven's sake, smile!"

A huge banner proclaiming, "Welcome to Stone Creek, Dr. Richard Noyes" flapped noisily in the warm spring breeze.

"I do hope we have his name right," a small woman at the front of the crowd fretted. "The handwriting in his letter was so hard to read. I'm still afraid his first name is Robert."

"Nonsense, Nancy," Betsy argued. "I definitely could

5

see an *R,* a *C,* and an *H.* It has to be Richard."

"I hope you're right," the small woman answered still a bit worried. "It would be awfully embarrassing if we had his name wrong on the banner."

"It's not wrong," Betsy answered positively. "It's Richard." Again scanning the large crowd, she shouted, "Martin! Martin Fulbright! Will you *please* get over here?"

A short, balding man bustled importantly to the front of the throng. "I'm right here, dear. Just calm yourself. Everyone is where they should be."

"Except Seth," his wife muttered. "Ben, did you tell the sheriff the stage is almost here?"

Before Ben could answer, the door to the sheriff's office opened and the man in question appeared. As if on cue, every woman's head turned toward the sound. "Oh, Mama," a teenage girl whispered, "isn't he the most handsome man you've ever seen?"

Her breathless observation was met by a sharp, reproving look from her mother. "Hush your mouth, Sarah," the mother whispered back. "Someone might hear you and it ain't at all ladylike for a young girl to be gawkin' at an older man."

"But, Mama," the girl protested. *"All* the girls are gawkin' at him!"

Before the smitten girl's mother could admonish her further, the westbound stage careened around the corner and thundered down Main Street. A hush fell over the crowd as the moment they'd waited for had at long last arrived. The driver brought the six galloping horses to a shuddering halt and looked around in surprise.

"Expectin' the president, folks?" he quipped as he jumped down. " 'Cause if you are, I'm afraid you're in for a disappointment. All I got in here is one little lady."

A collective groan of disappointment rippled through the citizenry of Stone Creek. Betsy wrung her hands in dismay as she quickly pondered the possible reasons for their guest of honor's non-appearance. Had Dr. Noyes missed the stage? Or, God forbid, had he changed his mind? No, Betsy silently assured herself, he surely would have let them know if he'd changed his mind. Maybe she had misread the arrival date in his letter. After all, his writing was almost illegible. Yes, that must be it. She'd just find the letter and take a closer look. Maybe he'd said April 17th instead of April 7th. She'd run over to her house and get the letter before the crowd dispersed so she could clear up this confusion and save her reputation as the town's premier social organizer.

Wheeling her considerable bulk around, she collided with a petite, dark-haired young woman who was just stepping down from the stage. Remembering her manners, she looked at the pretty girl and said, "I'm so sorry, Miss. May I help you find someone?"

"Well, yes, perhaps," answered the girl, repositioning her small hat where it had been knocked askew by Betsy's charge. "I'm looking for Mrs. Martin Fulbright."

Betsy looked at the young woman in surprise. "I am Mrs. Fulbright. And you are . . ."

"Dr. Rachel Hayes," the young woman finished for her. "I believe you are expecting me."

For the first time in anyone's memory, Betsy was at a complete loss for words, and judging by the startled gasps from the crowd behind her, she was not alone. Struggling mightily to regain her composure, she thrust out her hand and stammered, "Of . . . of course. Rachel Hayes. *Doctor* Rachel Hayes . . . oh, my word!"

Rachel stared at the woman in complete bewilderment, noting at the same time the shock and dismay rippling through the crowd. Looking around for a clue as to what was making everyone act so strangely, her gaze was drawn upward to the huge banner over her head.

"Welcome to Stone Creek, Dr. Richard Noyes."

She sucked in her breath, her insides knotting with a sudden rush of understanding. There, above her, was her answer. They were expecting a man!

Whirling on Mrs. Fulbright, she gasped, "Dr. *Richard Noyes?*"

"Well," the matron sputtered, clapping her hand over her heaving bosom, "your handwriting . . . naturally, we just assumed . . . I mean, your writing looked like it said 'Richard Noyes'!"

"I see," Rachel murmured, the enormity of this old buffalo's poor eyesight suddenly gripping her. "I'm sorry for the confusion. I know my writing isn't the best. . . ." Her voice trailed off lamely and Mrs. Fulbright, who was by now quite undone, pivoted on her heel and threw a pleading look at her husband.

Mayor Fulbright cleared his throat and moved purposefully forward, his welcoming speech securely in hand. Wiping his brow with a large handkerchief, he launched into his speech. "On behalf of all the citizens of Stone Creek, Dr. Noyes . . . er, Hayes. . . ." His sentence was never finished, however, as a loud, childish voice from the back of the crowd chimed, "Hey, Ma, I thought it was a man who was comin' to live at Sheriff Wellesley's."

"Hush, Jimmy!" came a swift, embarrassed response. A nervous titter ran through the crowd as Rachel flushed in mortification and Betsy looked as if she might faint.

"I think," said Mayor Fulbright, "that it would be a good idea if we dispense with my welcoming remarks and Dr. Hayes, Mrs. Fulbright, Sheriff Wellesley and I adjourn to our home to discuss this situation."

Trying desperately to salvage some modicum of dignity, Rachel turned toward the stunned crowd and stammered, "Thank you all for coming today. I understand that my handwriting led you to believe I was a man and I'm sorry if my sex has come as a shock to you. But," she continued, her voice gaining strength as she drew herself up straighter and threw the crowd an unflinching look, "I want to assure you that I'm a fully trained physician and I'm eager to establish my medical

8

practice here in Stone Creek. I hope all of you will stop by my office in the next couple of weeks so we can become acquainted."

The crowd was absolutely silent, scandalized by the young woman's use of the word "sex" and aghast that she seriously planned to set up a medical practice in their community. Even the children were silent, not understanding what was going on, but knowing instinctively that it was something of huge import.

Suddenly, Sheriff Wellesley detached himself from the gaping throng and strode purposely toward the embarrassed young woman. "How do you do, Miss Hayes," he said pleasantly, extending his hand, "I'm Seth Wellesley, the sheriff. If you'll come with me, I'll walk you over to the mayor's home."

"It's Doctor Hayes," Rachel corrected, turning to face the speaker. Her words died in her throat, however, as she stared up into the most perfect example of potent masculinity she'd ever beheld. He was huge, with a massive chest and shoulders that stretched the fabric of his cotton shirt. During her studies, she'd come in contact with hundreds of men, but she had never seen one as handsome as this rugged westerner. He was blond, his hair streaked almost white in places. It was very thick and he wore it much longer than was fashionable in the East. But despite its length and heaviness, it looked soft and shiny and Rachel was certain it would feel like silk if she touched it. And his face almost defied description. It was chiseled; the bronze skin drawn tightly over prominent cheekbones and a straight, narrow nose. There were tiny lines radiating from his eyes which attested to a life spent in the sun. His mouth was full, almost sensuous, but the sculptured lips and strong, assertive chin promised a bold masculinity.

"Sorry," he smiled. "May I escort you, *Doctor* Hayes?"

With a weak nod, she allowed him to lead her down the street. As they rounded the corner onto Second Avenue, she allowed herself another covert glance at her companion. Even his profile was perfect, like some ruler on an ancient coin. So engrossed was she in her inspection that she nearly stumbled, causing the bulging muscles of the arm she held to brush lightly against her breast. Startled, she took a hasty step sideways to break the contact. She shot another quick look at him to see if he had noticed their brief, intimate contact, but apparently he hadn't. He was squinting in avid concentration at something in the distance.

Chiding herself for a ninny, she dragged her gaze away before he caught her staring at him like a love-struck girl. But her subtle perusal had already been noted. As Seth purposely stared off at the horizon, every fiber of his being was aware that the town's new doctor was looking him over very thoroughly, and not in the way a doctor examines a patient.

He swallowed hard and made a valiant attempt to break the heavily charged silence. "Are you really a doctor?"

Rachel stopped walking and turned to face him, all thoughts of his handsome looks gone. "Yes, Mr. Wellesley, I am. I am a graduate of Boston University Medical School in Massachusetts."

"Were you in a special program for just girls or did you get to attend classes with the men?"

Rachel shot him an indignant look. "I took every course the men took. There were no "special classes for girls." I don't know if you've ever heard of Boston University, Sheriff, but I can assure you, it's a highly respected institution of learning."

"Oh, I've heard of it," Seth answered, "I have two older brothers who are graduates and a younger brother who took a degree there and is now studying law at Harvard."

Rachel's eyebrows lifted in surprise. "Really? What is his name? Perhaps I know him."

"Adam Wellesley," he supplied. "But, I don't think you'd know him. He's quite a bit younger than you are."

She threw him a sharp look, wondering if this comment was meant as an insult to her advancing age and spinster's status. But, seeing no trace of malice in his direct gaze, she answered, "You're right. I don't know him. I shouldn't have expected to, I guess. The university is a big place and, besides, I've been training at a hospital for the past year."

"A woman's hospital?" he grinned.

Rachel had had enough. Stopping, she planted her hands on her hips and said, "Mr. Wellesley, despite what you think, I am a competent physician. The fact that I am also a woman has no bearing on that competency. I have assisted in surgeries and sewn up wounds resulting from everything from carriage accidents to barroom brawls. I have treated people with scarlet fever, diphtheria, typhoid, and smallpox. I have delivered babies. In short, I am as experienced and as competent as any male physician who might have answered your advertisement."

"Very impressive," Seth conceded. "But this isn't Boston, Miss Hayes. This is Kansas and there isn't a self-respecting man in Stone Creek who will come to you for treatment . . . including me."

"Really!" she snorted. "And just why wouldn't you seek my services?"

"Because, frankly, ma'am, I just wouldn't feel right having some girl checking me over in my longjohns." A low chuckle rumbled in his chest. "At least not in a medical sense."

Rachel yanked her arm out of his. "I beg your pardon, Sheriff, but I must insist that you refrain from barroom humor in my presence."

"I'm sorry," he said contritely, but a smile still hovered. "What I'm trying to say is that unless you want a medical practice limited to treating only ladies' ailments, you've come to the wrong place and you might as well get back on that stage right now."

Rachel faced him squarely and shook her head. "I'm

11

sure that given time, everything will be fine," she said with far more confidence than she actually felt. "I've met with this kind of bias before, but as soon as the men in Stone Creek see how I handle my cases, they'll come around."

"Want to bet?" Seth challenged.

Unwilling to take the bait, Rachel remained silent.

They walked a little further in silence until, finally, Rachel could stand it no more and asked the question that was roiling within her.

"Sheriff, do you know why we are having this 'meeting' at the Fulbright's?"

"Yeah, I think so," he nodded.

When it became obvious that he wasn't going to say more, Rachel stopped and turned toward him, her voice heavy with annoyance. "Well, why?"

Seth paused too, and looked at her as if she wasn't very bright. "Because you're a woman," he answered matter-of-factly. He started walking again, seemingly oblivious to her rapidly rising temper.

"This is ridiculous," Rachel seethed, trotting to catch up to him. Suddenly she stopped again, reaching out to catch his sleeve in an attempt to slow his breathless gait.

With a sigh, he halted and wearily turned toward her. "Now what?"

Rachel's voice was very quiet. "You don't think they're going to send me back, do you? I mean, without even giving me a chance?"

"I don't know, Miss Hayes. Why don't we keep walking long enough to actually *get* to the Fulbright's and maybe we'll find out."

Then, taking pity on her when he saw her woebegone expression, he added, "They're not unreasonable people, Doctor. Your being a woman is just a . . . a . . . well, I don't really know what, but, I'm sure everything will work itself out, one way or another."

"That 'another' is exactly what I'm afraid of," Rachel muttered.

Seth grinned and tucked her arm back into his.

They reached the mayor's house just as Martin and Betsy Fulbright pulled up in their buggy. Helping his wife down from the high seat, Martin turned toward the couple and puffed, "Now, let's all go inside and discuss how we're going to solve this little peccadillo."

"That's the word I was looking for," Seth whispered, "peccadillo!"

Rachel threw him a withering look and walked swiftly up the steps in front of him, unaware of the smile that crossed his face as his gaze followed the slight sway of her hips.

Chapter Two

A half hour later, Seth, Rachel, Betsy, and Martin sat in the Fulbright's parlor sipping tea and staring at each other. They had exhausted every conceivable topic of small talk and were finally faced with having nothing left to discuss except the subject which none of them knew how to bring up.

After a long, uncomfortable silence, Martin cleared his throat and said, "Well, I guess we need to decide what to do next."

Rachel looked at the strained faces around her and shook her head. "I'm afraid I don't understand the problem. I realize my being a woman has come as a surprise to you, but I really don't see what difference it makes. You wanted a qualified physician — and you have one. I don't think anything has changed just because of my sex."

Betsy's eyelids fluttered at Rachel's casual reference to *that* word again and Martin shook his head sadly. "I'm afraid, my dear, that a great deal has changed."

"But, what?" she asked, exasperation creeping into her voice.

"For one thing, the living arrangements we had set up for you are now completely inappropriate."

"And what arrangements were those?"

Seth chuckled. "We planned to have the doctor live in an extra room in my house."

14

"Are you married, Sheriff?" she questioned.

"No."

There was a slight hesitation as Rachel digested this distressing news. She was tired, she was dirty, and, with each passing moment, she was feeling more and more apprehensive. But, above all, she was determined. "Is the room separate from the rest of your house?"

"Well, yes," he conceded, "it's off the kitchen."

Vastly relieved, she spread her hands in a gesture of appeal. "Then, there isn't a problem, after all," she said.

"Oh, Miss Hayes," Betsy gasped, "you can't be serious! It is out of the question that a young, unmarried lady would live under the same roof as a bachelor. Absolutely out of the question."

Undaunted, Rachel turned to Seth again. "Is there a door between your living quarters and those you set up for the doctor?"

"Yes," he answered, amused at her stubborn perseverance, "there's also a private entrance from the outside."

"And do these doors have locks on them?" she prodded.

"Yes, ma'am."

Rachel nodded and turned toward Betsy. "Mrs. Fulbright, from what Sheriff Wellesley says, it sounds like there is ample privacy between the two residences. In Boston, I lived in an apartment building that had many people of both sexes living under one roof. Living arrangements of this type are very common and perfectly proper in the East."

"But, my dear," Martin interrupted, "we keep trying to tell you, this is not the East. It's unheard of for such an arrangement to take place here."

"Mr. Wellesley," Rachel asked, "do you have a problem with my living in your spare room?"

Seth sat back in his chair and gazed at Rachel appraisingly, more than a little impressed by her logic. In fact, he was impressed with everything about this self-

15

assured little woman. He had spent the last several minutes studying the play of emotions that crossed her face as Betsy and Martin Fulbright laid a full measure of their pompous morality on her. His respect had grown with each passing moment as she deftly parried all of the Fulbrights' narrow-minded arguments. He had always been attracted to intelligent, down-to-earth women and this little lady had those qualities in abundance. It also didn't hurt, he admitted to himself, that she was extraordinarily pretty and had a body that was so curvy that he felt hot just looking at her. The way she'd stared at him as they'd strolled down the street had made him feel like he couldn't draw a deep breath. Now, watching her dark eyes spark with indignation and her tight bodice rise and fall as she struggled to remain composed, his throat again felt like it was closing. He shifted uncomfortably in his chair and forced his mind back to addressing her question.

"No, ma'am," he answered politely, "I don't have any problem at all with you moving into that room."

"Seth Wellesley!" Betsy exploded. "I can't believe you're condoning this scandalous proposition! What will people think? This is a good Christian town and we will not tolerate anything less than the highest standards from our civic officials."

All three of Betsy Fulbright's chins were trembling in indignation and, at a loss as to how to placate the outraged matron, Seth turned to her husband for support. Martin did not fail him.

"Now, Betsy," Martin said in his most conciliatory tone, "don't you think that what's most important is that Stone Creek finally has a doctor? We've worked so long to bring a physician to our town and today we have finally triumphed. If we have to bend the rules a bit to make our dreams for Stone Creek come true, then so be it. Don't you agree, my dear?"

Betsy was completely nonplussed. "Why, I hadn't thought of it like that. Do you really think that Miss

Hayes living in the same house as Seth will be accepted by the ladies in town?"

"Do you really think it's the ladies' business where she lives?" Seth asked quietly.

Rachel threw him a grateful look, thinking that perhaps her earlier opinion that he was as narrow-minded and provincial as Betsy Fulbright was unfair. Her insides relaxed a little and she began thinking of the handsome sheriff with the engaging smile and laughing blue eyes as something close to a saviour.

Martin leaned over and patted his wife's plump hand. "I think the women of Stone Creek will be so grateful to have a doctor to treat their ills that they will forgive her just about anything."

"Now, just a moment," Rachel interrupted, her ire again sparking. "I want to make something perfectly clear. I am not going to start a life here feeling that I have to be "forgiven" for anything. I came here because Stone Creek needed a doctor and I felt I could fill that need. But, if you aren't willing to accept me, I will leave on the next stage. I'm sure there are other towns that need the services of a physician and I would not dream of imposing myself on a community that doesn't want me."

Seth grinned, his opinion of Rachel Hayes rising another notch. The ladies of Stone Creek should be damn grateful to have a woman of such conviction in their midst. She would undoubtedly make them a fine doctor. Of course, he was disappointed that Rachel wasn't a "real" doctor, but at least the ladies would have someone to help them through the trials of childbirth and minor family afflictions. That in itself was a start, and perhaps, in a few years, they would be able to entice a real doctor to come and join little Miss Hayes.

Betsy and Martin Fulbright were speechless in the face of Rachel's vehemence. Gaping at each other, Martin finally took the situation in hand and said in a pleading voice, "Please, Miss Hayes—"

17

"It's *Doctor* Hayes!" Rachel snapped.

"Ah, yes, Doctor Hayes. Please don't get the wrong idea about us. We don't want you to leave. It's just that, well, your being a woman *is* a shock and it will take some time for all of us to adjust. Certainly you can understand that."

Rachel rose from her seat and picked up her reticule. "Yes, I can understand that," she relented, "but I'm sure that, given time, you won't regret my coming to Stone Creek. Now, if you will excuse me, I would appreciate it if Sheriff Wellesley could show me to my quarters. I am very tired from my trip and I have a lot of unpacking and organizing to do if I am to open my office in the next few days."

"Of course! Of course, Dr. Hayes." Throwing Seth a look of profound relief that the interview was at an end, Martin bolted to his feet and enthusiastically propelled Rachel toward the front door.

Seth glanced at the still-speechless Betsy, then followed Rachel and Martin to the door. Nodding his thanks for the tea, he put his hand lightly on Rachel's back and escorted her out of the house. He could feel the tension radiating through her stiff body and a wave of compassion swept over him. "Well, I guess you showed them, Doc," he laughed.

Suddenly, all of the anger and disappointment drained away and Rachel started to laugh too. She laughed until she was doubled over and tears ran down her face. Finally, gasping and wheezing, she leaned against the astonished sheriff and blurted, "All the way across the country, I was wondering what this day would be like, but I never, *ever* dreamed it would be like this."

Seth smiled and shook his head. "Things are the way they are. But you've only won the first round, you know. You're still going to have a long, uphill pull before you're really accepted."

"I know," she nodded, sobering. "But at least I have you. Thank goodness for that. After the way you talked on the way to the Fulbrights', I was surprised that you sided with me. I thought you felt the way they do, but I can see now that you're different."

Seth stopped walking and looked at her for a long moment. "Don't get the wrong idea about me, Doc. I'm *no* different than they are. Like I told you before, I won't be one of your patients. If I need a doctor, I'll still go to Wichita—and so will the rest of the men in town."

She stared at him in astonishment. "But, why? You defended me back there! I thought you'd changed your mind."

Seth's expression was tight. "No, Dr. Hayes, I haven't and I won't. I defended you because I don't like narrow-minded people dictating where other people can or cannot live. I also don't like prudish old biddies who assume that just because a woman takes a room in a man's house there must be something going on between them. No one thinks that when a man rents a room in a boarding house, and I don't think this is any different. But as far as you being a doctor, I don't care where you went to school or how good your marks were, women don't belong in medicine. They should be at home, raising up some kids and being taken care of by a man."

Rachel was devastated. "You're right, Sheriff," she said, disappointment heavy in her voice, "you *are* no different than the rest of them."

"Things are the way they are," he repeated. "Anyway, it really doesn't matter about me not using your services. I never get sick."

"But, you're saying that if you got shot, you wouldn't come to me for treatment?"

"Not unless I was unconscious and somebody dumped me at the door to your office," he admitted.

"Maybe I *am* making a mistake by thinking that I can practice medicine here," she muttered.

"Better think about it then, Doc, before you bother unpacking all those trunks I saw them take off the stage."

For an endless moment, an oppressive silence hung between them. Finally, Rachel's chin lifted and she looked Seth squarely in the eye. "No, Sheriff, I'm not leaving. I'm going to stay here in Stone Creek and prove to all of you that you're wrong about women doctors."

Seth couldn't help but admire the look of fierce determination on her face. "Okay," he nodded, "but don't say I didn't warn you. I hope they taught you how to perform miracles at that school of yours because that's what it's going to take to change people's minds—including mine."

"I'll do it," she said firmly. "You just watch me."

Noticing how the sun was glinting off Rachel's glossy dark hair, Seth could think of nothing he'd like better than to spend some time "watching" her, but he prudently kept his thoughts to himself. Instead, he grinned and said, "Yeah, I'll just do that."

They walked along in silence until they arrived at a large, two-story clapboard house surrounded on three sides by a wide veranda.

"Here we are," Seth announced, sweeping his arm in a wide arc. "The entrance to your office is over here." As he guided her around the side of the big house, he dug in his pocket, pulled out a key and presented it to her.

Despite all that had happened that day, Rachel felt a thrill of excitement shoot through her. Her own key to her own office! All the years of study and struggle were finally going to pay off. It made everything that had come before worth it. Beaming at Seth, she unlocked the door and swung it open. To her surprise, she was met with a small waiting room with a settee and an end table in it. Walking through a connecting door, she stepped into the examining room and gasped with pleasure. It was exactly as she'd always dreamed it would be. At one end of the room there was a desk. It was far from new, but had been polished to a high sheen and was large and serviceable. A chair had been pushed under it and another, smaller chair for patients sat on the opposite side. At the back of the room was a table covered with a clean piece of linen. A surgical table, Rachel thought with delight, walking over to it and running her hand lovingly over the clean linen drape. Ringing the edge of the room were counters with glass-fronted cabinets built over them and a small sink in one corner. It was everything a doctor's office should be and obviously, the people in town had gone to a great deal of trouble and expense to provide it. Smiling broadly, Rachel turned toward Seth and murmured, "It's perfect, Sheriff. Did you do this?"

He shook his head. "Not entirely. Isaac MacDougall who's a carpenter built the cabinets, and Ty Ecklund who owns the general store donated the desk; actually, just about everybody in town had a hand in something. Nailing things in place, painting . . . the ladies cleaned and scoured everything. Come over here and I'll show you what else they did."

Walking across the office, Seth opened another door on the far wall and ushered Rachel into the pretty little bedroom. A brass bed stood against one wall with a fresh feather tick on it. Clean white sheets gleamed in the late afternoon sun. The bed was covered with a bright patchwork quilt and two puffy pillows were plumped invitingly against the headboard. Beside the bed sat a small nightstand with an oil lamp gracing it. A bureau stood against the far wall next to a curtained-off area that served as a closet. There was a washstand near the window with a flowered pitcher and basin sitting atop it. Starched chintz curtains hung at the window and a huge braided rug covered the highly polished floor.

"Oh, Sheriff," Rachel exclaimed, gracing him with a radiant smile. "What a beautiful room! How kind of everyone."

Seth was embarrassed by her effusiveness, considering the manner in which the town had greeted her. "Yeah, well, I'm glad you like it. I'm going to go down to the office and get some of your bags so you can start getting settled. Is there anything you need before I go?"

"Well, actually, um, yes," she faltered, "I need the . . ."

"It's out back," he supplied quickly. "We'll have to come up with some arrangement about who uses what when so we won't get in each other's way. It shouldn't be a problem, though. I'm not home much."

Rachel looked at him in surprise. "Why not?"

Seth shrugged. "Most of time I'm either at the office or out on the trail chasing after some outlaw."

"And do you always get your man?" she asked, casting him a sidelong glance.

"Do my best, ma'am," he answered, grinning with a flash of white teeth.

"I'll bet you do," she smiled.

His heart hammered against his ribs as he was again hit by the blinding beauty of that smile. Backing toward the door, he said abruptly, "Gotta go," and bolted through the portal. Rachel looked after him, slightly bewildered by his hasty exit, but too excited by her new surroundings to give it much thought.

Seth strode down the boardwalk toward his office, thinking that he'd probably made a terrible mistake by encouraging little Dr. Hayes to move in. While sitting at the Fulbright's, he had thought that having Rachel Hayes under his roof might be a pleasant diversion. Now he wasn't so sure. The last thing he needed was the distraction of a beguiling woman so close at hand. Too many good lawmen met their end because their minds were on their wives or sweethearts and not on the desperado they were chasing. A man's commitment to the law had to be total, and Seth's was. Kansas in 1884 was a wild and lawless area, but in his jurisdiction, settlers lived in relative safety and the bank in town had never been hit since he had assumed his post. There was no room in his life for love or marriage and he didn't think there was a woman alive who could make him feel differently, although more than a few had tried.

Although the ladies of Stone Creek thought the Sheriff was oblivious to his good looks, he wasn't. He knew he was handsome. A man couldn't look in his shaving mirror every day and not know whether the face that stared back at him was appealing. Since he'd come to Stone Creek, many women had thrown themselves at him and although he was no saint, he'd taken only what they'd willingly offered and had never made promises he knew he wouldn't keep.

Rachel Hayes, however, had affected him unlike any other woman. She was gorgeous. She was also disturbingly sensual with her luminous dark eyes and soft, expressive mouth. Although slim, her body curved everywhere it should and she had high breasts that thrust impudently forward, just inviting a man's touch. Physically, she was everything that even the most discerning man could possibly want in a woman, but she was also much, much more. She possessed the most dangerous and compelling attraction a woman could have. She had substance. Wit, intelligence, courage — substance.

And that scared the hell out of Sheriff Wellesley.

Chapter Three

"Would you like some company, Dr. Hayes?"

Rachel looked up from her bored perusal of the Dallas House Restaurant's menu. "Why, yes," she smiled in pleased surprise, "I'd be delighted. Please, sit down."

The cheery-looking, gray-haired woman slid into the chair opposite her and said, "I'm Victoria Andrews. I own the Dallas House."

"I know," Rachel nodded, "and may I say, you serve excellent food here."

"Well, you should know," Mrs. Andrews laughed, "you've eaten here every day since you arrived in town, haven't you?"

"Yes," Rachel confirmed.

"What's the matter," Mrs. Andrews prodded, "won't Seth let you use his kitchen?"

"I don't know whether he will or not," Rachel admitted. "I haven't seen him since the day I arrived."

"That's because he's gone."

"Gone?" she asked in bewilderment.

Mrs. Andrews nodded. "I heard he got word from the Federal Marshal that Clint Brady hit a bank in Omaha and was headed this way. I think he took off to track him."

"Who's Clint Brady?" Rachel asked.

"Just about the worst outlaw to ever hit these parts.

24

He's got a gang holed up somewhere in eastern Colorado and they range across three states robbin' banks and trains. I don't know how many men they've killed in the last couple of years—even a couple of lawmen."

"And Sheriff Wellesley went after them alone?"

"Yes," Mrs. Andrews sighed, "Seth's like that. He don't seem to have any fear for himself and he's ruthless when it comes to trackin' outlaws and bringin' them in—usually slung over the back of a horse. I've said it a hundred times if I've said it once that he ought to take a posse with him when he goes after thieves and murderers, but Seth does things his way. He's a private one, that man is. No one really knows much about him."

"Has he always lived in Stone Creek?" Rachel questioned.

"No," Mrs. Andrews responded with a quick shake of her head. "He's only been here about three years. The town advertised in the *Denver Post* for a sheriff and he answered the ad. We know he comes from somewhere in western Colorado and that he was a sheriff there too, but that's about it. Then there's that house of his. He moved into town and built that big place right away. Had furniture shipped here all the way from New York, too. We thought he must have a family somewhere who was comin' later, but he didn't. He's lived there by himself all this time and he still isn't married. Don't think he ever will be by the looks of things."

"What makes you say that?" Rachel asked, leaning forward as her curiosity mounted.

"Why, he never pays the slightest attention to any of the girls in town, except to be polite. And with those looks of his, he could have his pick of anyone he wanted. They're all just dyin' for him, but Seth don't even seem to notice, 'cept for Etta Lawrence, the school marm. She's been sparkin' him goin' on two years now, but nothin's happened. I say if he hasn't proposed yet, he's not gonna. She better set her sights on somebody else or she's gonna end up an old maid, sure as I'm sittin' here."

"Maybe Sheriff Wellesley prefers a solitary life," Rachel suggested.

"Honey, there ain't a man on earth really *wants* to live alone. They just think they do till some woman shows 'em different. And with Seth's good looks and brains, well, he should be raising up a bunch of fine sons just like him. But, so far, none of the girls have been able to get close enough to him to show him just how good marriage could be. And when he does take a little time for himself, he goes to Wichita. He ain't gonna find any women in that wicked place fit to build a future with. Of course, it's none of my business so I don't say nothin' to him. When he comes in here, I just cook him one of those big steaks he likes so much and hope that someday he'll realize he could be getting fed like that every day if he'd just settle down like a grown man should."

Rachel smiled at Mrs. Andrews' earthy opinions about life and love, thinking how embarrassed the sheriff would be if he knew what the gossipy old lady was saying about him. "Well, I can tell you one thing, Mrs. Andrews, if Sheriff Wellesley ever does get married, his wife will have to be some cook to rival you."

Victoria Andrews beamed and rose from her chair. "Thank you, honey. That's right nice of you to say. I better get back to my kitchen before that flighty niece of mine burns it down. I just wanted to say howdy-do."

"It was a pleasure to meet you," Rachel said sincerely, "and, if you ever need any medical attention, don't hesitate to stop by."

"Thanks for the offer, honey," Mrs. Andrews beamed, "but I've never had a sick day in my life."

Rachel heaved a long sigh and returned to her menu.

Four days later, Stone Creek's new doctor stood in the middle of her office and gazed around in satisfaction. Her bags and boxes were unpacked, her medicines labeled and put away, her surgical supplies sterilized and lying on clean linen towels. The pen and blotter her parents had given her graced her desk, her diploma hung on the wall, her engraved wooden shingle swung in the breeze outside. Everything was ready. The only thing missing was patients.

She had been in Stone Creek for eight days and although she'd met many of the town's citizens during her meals at the Dallas House, still no one had come to her office. She tried to reassure herself that the townsfolk were just giving her time to get set up, but deep down, she worried that wasn't really true. Maybe Sheriff Wellesley was right. Maybe Stone Creek wouldn't accept a woman doctor and people would still travel all the way to Wichita to seek medical help.

Rachel found her thoughts drifting, as they had so many times in the past few days, to Seth Wellesley. It seemed that no matter where she went or who she talked to, his name came up. Several women had even been bold enough to ask her what the inside of his house looked like and were surprised and disappointed when she told them she hadn't seen it—except for her own small quarters, of course. She was appalled that the ladies in town apparently thought she spent her time snooping around the sheriff's house. Not that it hadn't been tempting—especially after what Mrs. Andrews had said about the furnishings coming all the way from New York. Much as she hated to admit it, Rachel was as intrigued by the mysterious sheriff as the rest of the women in town and she found herself anxiously awaiting his return.

She was straightening the labels on her medicine bottles for the hundredth time when she heard a wagon pull up at the side of the house. There could only be one reason for a wagon to come around to her entrance. She must be about to receive her first patient! Racing to the window, she surreptitiously pulled aside the curtain and peeked out. A middle-aged man dressed in worn overalls was jumping down from the wagon's high seat.

27

A man! Rachel silently rhapsodized. *What do you think of that, Sheriff? My first patient is a man!*

Walking quickly back to the desk, Rachel sat down in her big chair, not wanting to appear too eager. Folding her hands in front of her, she assumed an expression that she hoped looked competent and professional.

She nearly jumped out of the chair, however, when her office door suddenly banged open, hitting the wall and bouncing back from the force of the blow. The man whom she had seen descending from his wagon staggered into her office, carrying a very large, very pregnant dog.

Rachel bolted to her feet and gaped at him in astonishment as he hurtled across her office and set the Collie on the operating table.

"You the new doc?" he asked breathlessly, pulling off his battered hat.

"Well, yes, but . . ."

"Jessie, my dog here, is havin' puppies and somethin's wrong."

Rachel cast a quick glance toward the whimpering animal. "Sir," she began, "I don't think you understand. I'm not a veterinarian."

"I know that," the man said impatiently, "but havin' babies is havin' babies, right?"

"Well . . ." Rachel stammered.

"Doc, this dog is gonna die if somebody don't do somethin'. Will you help her or not?"

Rachel looked at the distraught man for a moment. "Is this dog your pet?"

"Yes, ma'am. Well, actually, she's my wife's. And my kids'. But Jess is a good herder and I guess I'm partial to her too." His voice trailed off in embarrassment and Rachel quickly made her decision.

"You're right, Mr. . . . ?"

"Johnson, ma'am. Hank Johnson."

"You're right, Mr. Johnson. Having babies is having babies. Let's see what I can do."

28

Hurrying over to the table where the dog lay laboring, Rachel patted her gently on the head and crooned, "Just take it easy, girl. Everything's going to be fine."

As the animal looked up at her with pain-filled eyes, Rachel pushed up her sleeves, washed her hands at her little sink, and went to work. Her gentle examination revealed just what she had suspected. There was a puppy stuck in the birth canal and only by turning it was she going to be able to dislodge it.

"You're going to have to help me, Mr. Johnson."

"Okay," the big man swallowed nervously. "What do you want me to do?"

"Just hold her down. This is going to hurt and I don't want her trying to jump off the table."

Hank Johnson nodded and placed his hands firmly on the dog's shoulders and flanks.

"Talk to her, Mr. Johnson," Rachel suggested. "She knows you and it will make her feel more secure."

"I'm not much good at talkin' to dogs havin' babies," he muttered.

"Do your best," she directed, trying hard to stifle the smile that threatened.

Hank reluctantly leaned forward and whispered into the Collie's ear while Rachel carefully maneuvered the puppy into a better position.

Jessie cried out once and Hank's head jerked around toward Rachel, a stricken look on his face.

"She's all right," Rachel soothed, "I told you it was going to hurt, but she's fine now and the puppy's coming."

Hank mustered a weak smile, looking decidedly queasy as the bloody puppy made its appearance.

Two hours and nine puppies later, Hank and Rachel sat on either side of her desk and sipped the coffee which he had fetched from the restaurant. Judging by the length of time he'd been gone, Rachel suspected that he might also have stopped at one of the town's saloons and had a bit of whiskey added to his, but she kept these suspicions to herself.

Jessie and her nine babies were comfortably ensconced in one of Rachel's empty packing boxes, sleeping soundly.

"Four boys and five girls," Hank beamed, lifting his coffee cup in a toast, "not a bad afternoon's work, eh, Doc?"

Rachel answered his toast with her own cup and smiled. "Not bad at all, Mr. Johnson."

"I'm grateful, ma'am," he said quietly. "She woulda died without you and I don't know how I could've explained that to my kids."

"How many children do you have?" Rachel asked.

"Five."

"Really? And are they all healthy?"

"Most of the time," he responded. "Except in the winter when the croup sets in."

"Well, sir, next time the croup sets in, you bring those little ones to me. And Mrs. Johnson and you come too if anything's plaguing you."

"I'll tell the Missus," he assured her, rising and putting on his hat. "Guess I better get Jess home."

Rachel nodded and rose also, transferring the puppies to a smaller box while Hank carried Jessie out to the wagon and gently laid her on an old quilt.

"Thanks again," he muttered. "I'm beholden to you."

"You're welcome. Just remember in the future that my specialty is really people, not animals."

"If you can take care of people as well as you did this dog, ma'am, you ain't gonna have no trouble at all in Stone Creek."

Rachel thought those were the sweetest words she'd ever heard. "Thank you," she blushed. "If Jessie has any problems, just let me know."

With a quick nod, Hank climbed into his wagon and drove off down Main Street.

Rachel walked back toward her office smiling to herself as she thought about what a wonderful feeling it was to help a creature who needed her. Oddly enough, it didn't matter that her first patient had been a dog. She had alleviated suffering and that was what her goal had always been.

It was late that evening while she was preparing for bed that she heard a sound coming from somewhere in the house. She stopped washing and listened more intently. There it was again. Someone was definitely walking around upstairs, which could only mean that Sheriff Wellesley was back.

A tingle of anticipation raced through her and she hastily threw on a light silk wrapper, just in case he might stop in to say hello.

She wasn't disappointed. A few minutes later she heard him coming down the stairs and walking through the kitchen toward her room. A light tap sounded. "Dr. Hayes, are you still up?"

Forcing herself not to hurry, she walked over to the door and opened it a crack. He was standing with a hand braced against the doorjamb, looking even bigger and more handsome than she remembered. The neck of his shirt was open, exposing a glimpse of bronze skin. He looked tired, but he was smiling.

"Welcome back, Sheriff," she said shyly. "Did you catch your man?"

Seth shook his head. "Nope. Chased him practically to the Colorado border, but I couldn't catch him. I wired everybody between here and Denver though, so maybe the Colorado officials will get him."

"I'm sorry," Rachel sympathized, "it must be disappointing to have to give up."

"Yeah," he nodded, "but I gave him a good enough run that he knows I mean business. I don't think he'll be coming into my territory again anytime soon."

"Was it Clint Brady you were chasing?" she asked.

"How do you know about him?" Seth's voice was suddenly hard and the menace that leaped into his eyes was so terrifying that Rachel took an involuntary step backward.

"Well," she stammered, "some of the people in town were talking about him and —"

"It wasn't him," Seth interrupted flatly. "If it had been, I'd never have given up."

Disconcerted by the sheriff's unaccountable change in mood, Rachel searched her mind for a change of topic. "When did you get in?"

"About an hour ago," he responded, his features relaxing. "I stopped at the saloon for a minute and heard all about what a hero you were today."

"What?"

"The whole town's talking about it. Hank Johnson was in the saloon this afternoon and he told everybody about how you saved that old Collie of his. He wants to give you pick of the litter."

"Oh, this is terrible!" Rachel groaned. "Now, everybody in town probably thinks I'm a vet!"

"Naw," Seth laughed. "You made a lot of friends today. You might even get yourself a patient or two out of this. Surely, every lady in town who's in the family way will be beating a path to your office. If you can deliver nine at a time, I'm sure they'll figure you can handle one or two."

"You find this all very amusing, don't you?" Rachel asked, her voice piqued.

"No," Seth shook his head solemnly. "I think it was a fine thing you did for Hank. That old dog means the world to him. He's had her ever since the family came west. Jessie trekked halfway across the country when she was just a pup. It would've been real hard on Hank if he'd lost her that way. It was good of you to save her."

Rachel smiled, forgiving him for teasing her. "Actually, I was glad I could help. Maybe this will prove to the people in town that I really am a doctor."

"Oh, I don't know about that," Seth grinned, unrepentant. "But everybody's convinced you're one hell of a midwife."

Rachel's shoulders sagged. Obviously, her efforts this afternoon had proved nothing. "Was there anything else you wanted?" she asked in a dejected voice.

Seth was confused at the abrupt change in her tone. She was acting like he'd insulted her when all he'd been trying to do was tell her that everyone in town thought what she'd done was great.

"Well, yeah, there was. I came down to ask you if you want to have supper with me tomorrow night. I know it's not much fun to eat alone and I thought . . ."

"I'd be delighted," she answered promptly, excitement skipping up her spine. "What time?"

"Time?" Seth's brow puckered in confusion. "I don't really know. I generally get home about six o'clock. Why don't I just knock on your door when I get here?"

"Fine," she nodded. "I'll be ready." Again, a fleeting look of bewilderment clouded his eyes, but she didn't notice.

Closing the door, she leaned against it and smiled. Supper out with the handsomest, most eligible man in town. Things are looking up, she thought happily. No matter what happened tomorrow night, the evening wouldn't be a total waste. If nothing else, this engagement should net her some business. Every woman in town would probably feign an ailment demanding medical attention so that they could question her about her date with the elusive Seth Wellesley. But Rachel knew that her excitement stemmed from more than a desire to generate business. After all, he *was* the most attractive man in town and, even though he'd made her angry by insinuating that she was less than a "real" doctor, she was flattered that he had asked her out. She blew out her lamp and climbed into bed, vowing that no matter what the sheriff might say about her medical expertise tomorrow night, she'd not allow herself to become angry. She'd be bright, witty, and sophisticated, no matter what. Seth was an important ally and if she couldn't impress him with her credentials, she'd dazzle him with her charm. After all, there was more than one way to skin a cat!

At six o'clock the following evening, Rachel sat on the edge of her bed, holding her gloves and reticule. She had heard Seth come in a few minutes earlier. He had stopped briefly in the kitchen and then his footsteps had retreated upstairs. For at least the hundredth time, she glanced in her mirror to check her appearance. Her new plum-colored silk gown was beautiful. She'd had it made shortly before leaving Boston and this was the first opportunity she'd had to wear it. The high neck was scalloped with lace which matched a cascade of frills that fell over her hands. The bodice was snug, accentuating her full breasts and tiny waist. The skirt was draped in the front and gathered into a rose-embroidered bustle in the back. Her matching hat was secured into her upswept hair, angling down slightly over one eye. It was a beautiful outfit and Rachel was very pleased with the sophisticated image in her mirror.

She was still smiling in satisfaction when he knocked on her door. Taking a deep breath to still her racing heart, she walked slowly across the room to answer it. The moment she opened the door, however, she knew that something was wrong. Seth stood on the opposite side dressed in a lightweight plaid shirt and a pair of clean, but well-worn levis. Her look of astonishment at his attire was duplicated in the blue eyes staring back at her.

"I think one of us has made a mistake here," he said, his embarrassment obvious. "Did you think we were going out?"

"Well," Rachel stammered, as embarrassed as he was, "I thought that's what you said last night."

"I figured we'd just eat here," he explained. "I heard

you ate out a lot while I was gone and I thought you might enjoy staying in tonight."

"Oh, yes," Rachel agreed hastily, "that would be fine. I didn't know that's what you were planning. I'll just put my things away and be out in a minute."

"You might want to change your dress, too," he advised. "I mean, it's real pretty, but it's a little fancy for eating at home."

"You're right," Rachel agreed again, wishing the floor would open up and swallow her. "I'll change." Quickly closing the door, she turned toward her closet, throwing her purse and gloves on the bed and ripping the hat pin from her hair. Frantically, she worked at the tiny pearl buttons that ran down the back of her dress, wondering how she could ever salvage the evening after such an embarrassing start.

It was a perfectly understandable mistake, she assured herself as she shrugged out of the dress. *How was I to know that the man was going to cook dinner for me?* But, even as she thought this, she realized it didn't make sense. He had just returned from his office and had certainly not had time to fix a meal. Maybe he had stopped at the Dallas House or the Stone Creek Cafe and had something prepared for them. Whatever he'd done, she was pleased by his thoughtfulness. Although she was a bit disappointed that no one would see them together, the thought of an intimate little dinner at home with the handsome sheriff had its own appeal.

After a quick scan of her closet, she chose a peach-colored muslin dress which she knew Seth hadn't seen. She pulled it on and looked at her reflection in the mirror. Although she didn't look nearly as sophisticated as she had a few minutes ago, the soft tones of the dress did highlight her hair and eyes. With a final pat to her coiffure, she opened her door and walked down the short hall that led to the kitchen.

As she stepped into the room, Seth's eyes swept over her in approval. Gesturing toward the counter, he said,

"Everything's ready for you and I've lit the stove. If you want to get started, I'll go down to the cellar and see if I can find a bottle of wine."

Rachel's dumbfounded gaze followed the arc of his arm and for a moment, she just stood and stared at the counter. Sitting on it were two raw steaks, three dirt-covered potatoes that looked like they'd just been dug, and a bowl of peas . . . still in their pods. As the full implication of the uncooked food hit her, she sucked in her breath in indignation and threw him a furious look.

"Is something wrong?" he asked, confused by her outrage. "Don't you like steak?"

"Yes," she replied, struggling to keep her voice even, "I like steak very much — if it's cooked."

"I don't understand," he said, shaking his head. "What do you mean 'if it's cooked'? Did you think we were going to eat it raw?"

"I really don't know," she retorted. "Who did you think was going to cook it?"

"Well," he faltered ". . . you."

"Me," she repeated slowly, crossing her arms over her chest. "Let me see if I understand you correctly. You invite me to have dinner with you and you expect me to cook it?"

Seth knew he'd made a terrible mistake. Running his hands through his hair in agitation, he struggled to come up with a plausible explanation. "I heard you'd been eating all your meals at the Dallas House, so I figured it would be a nice change for you to have something home cooked. Frankly, I can't figure out why you were eating out the whole time I was gone when the kitchen was just sitting here, but I guess that's your business."

"Sheriff," Rachel interrupted, "you never said anything about me being allowed to use your kitchen and I wouldn't presume to enter your house without your permission."

"I wasn't even here," Seth protested. "What difference would it have made?"

"It would have been trespassing," she retorted.

"Trespassing," he snorted, planting his hands on his hips. "The only lock between your room and the kitchen is on your side, so how the hell could it be trespassing?"

"It just is," she insisted. "But it's water under the bridge now, so there's no point in discussing it."

"Okay," he agreed. "So, are you going to make supper or not?"

"No," she said flatly. "I'm not. You invited me. You do the cooking."

"I can't cook," he announced.

"And what makes you think I can?"

"Well, because . . . because you're a woman."

"Of course," she nodded. "Since I'm a woman, I should be able to cook, right?"

"Well, yeah . . ." Seth's voice trailed off and his embarrassed expression suddenly dissolved into smug comprehension. "But, you can't, can you? That's why you eat all your meals out. You've spent so much time learning a man's job that you haven't had time to learn woman's stuff, have you?"

"Whether I can cook or not isn't the point," Rachel argued. "The fact that you just *expected* me to is what I don't like!"

"Well, pardon me, *Doctor,*" he retorted, his voice laced with sarcasm. "I didn't realize that a little cooking was so far beneath you."

A long silence ensued as the two of them glared angrily at each other. Finally, Seth said, "Well, what do you want to do?"

"At this point," Rachel retorted with great dignity, "all I really want to do is go to bed."

Seth couldn't suppress his grin. "Well, I suppose that could be arranged too," he shot back.

Rachel gasped in disbelief. "Oh! You — you are insufferable. You're rude and gauche and I refuse to spend

37

another moment being insulted by you. Good night, Sheriff."

"Aw, come on," Seth called as she stomped off down the hall. "I'm sorry. I was just kidding. Come on back here and I'll cook the damn food."

"No, thank you!" she responded without turning around.

"Are you telling me that after I ran all over town to get this stuff, you're not going to eat it no matter who cooks it?"

"That's right. You cook it, you eat it. I'm not hungry."

"Well, fine!" Seth thundered. "Maybe I'll just go find somebody else to eat with."

"Bon appetit!" she called over her shoulder, slamming the bedroom door behind her.

Long after she had undressed and climbed into bed, she could still hear Seth stomping around upstairs, banging doors and slamming windows.

So much for dazzling him with charm, she thought wryly, staring out her window at the moonlit night. She sighed, regretting her impulsive display of temper. If only he'd just *asked,* she thought self-righteously. I'd have made him a meal that would have knocked his socks off. She giggled at the irony of their argument. The only real extracurricular activity that she had indulged in while at school was to take cooking lessons at the famous Emma Chaffee School of Culinary Arts. Oh yes, Mr. Wellesley, she thought smugly, one of these days when it's *my* idea, I'll make you a meal that you won't forget for the rest of your life!

With a knowing smile, she turned over on her side and, ignoring the hungry rumbling of her stomach, went to sleep.

Seth walked into his bedroom and threw himself down on the edge of the bed, jerking off his boots and hurling them at the wall. "Bratty little bitch," he seethed.

The whole time he'd been out on the trail, his thoughts had kept wandering to the pretty little doctor who had taken up residence in his spare room. Try as he might to forget about her and concentrate on the task at hand, his mind continued to paint images of Rachel: her midnight hair and luminous dark eyes, her sexy little body so elegantly outfitted in her very proper travelling suit, her melodic voice and tinkling laugh. Lying out under the lonely stars at night, his mind had drifted to more erotic visions of his new boarder. What would she look like with that ebony hair tumbling around her shoulders and those full breasts of hers loosed from their confining corset? Seth's blood warmed considerably as his imagination fired his loins.

"Get a grip, man," he told himself firmly. "You're never going to find out." But despite his stern reprimands, his body continued to react to the titillating thought of Rachel Hayes lying naked in his arms, her mouth slightly parted and her breath quickening with desire.

Throughout the entire eight-day chase, his erotic fantasies had been a torture, robbing him of much-needed sleep at night and infuriating him during the day when he realized he was losing track of his purpose. It was dangerous to let his mind wander and he was acutely aware that he was experiencing the same weaknesses that had sent so many of his peers to early graves.

He had been anxious to return home and see Rachel face to face again, confident that her beauty and allure had been much exaggerated in his lusty ruminations. His recent, self-imposed celibacy was becoming a problem and he knew it was time he rode over to Wichita and sought some relief among the many experienced and willing ladies who resided there.

However, the minute Rachel had opened her door the previous evening, all thoughts of the women in Wichita had disappeared. His starved senses hadn't been lying to him out on the trail. She was just as alluring in the flesh as in his imagination. That realization had rocked him to the core and it had taken every bit of will he could muster to stand in her doorway and casually congratulate her on her successful delivery of Hank Johnson's damn puppies. His dilemma wasn't helped by the fact that her hair *was* tumbling around her shoulders and that she was dressed in a light wrapper over an even lighter nightgown—a fact he quickly noted despite the fact that she never fully opened her door.

It wasn't until she became so snobby and high-handed over cooking supper that Seth had felt he could breathe around her. He knew he should be grateful for her haughty little tantrum. It had cooled his raging passions like a dip in a cold river and allowed him to regain his quickly slipping composure.

He was still disgusted with himself, though, for the lack of control he had felt when faced with this little slip of a woman in her bathrobe. He was a mature man, but there was something about Rachel's cool, self-possessed beauty that made him feel like a green kid alone with his first woman.

Well, no more. He now knew her for what she was. A snippy little eastern bitch. He realized now that the self-assurance he had at first found so admirable was nothing more than conceit, and that innocent, wide-eyed expression of hers masked a haughty coldness that, he was sure, no mere man could penetrate.

It was actually a relief to have found out about her true nature so quickly. Now he knew that he could cope with her living in his house without wanting to break down her bedroom door, throw her down on the brass bed and make love to her until she screamed with pleasure.

"Thank God that craziness is over," he told himself. "There's nothing about her that I can't live without. Hell, she can't even cook!"

Chapter Four

It was a beautiful morning. Rachel rolled over in bed, stretched contentedly and looked out at the bright sunshine. Today was the day! She'd waited all week for Sunday to come and she could hardly contain her excitement. Everything was planned down to the last detail.

As long as he goes to church, she thought for the thousandth time. He just has to go to church! There was no sound from upstairs and she uttered a quick word of thanks that Seth was still asleep and she could begin her preparations without him knowing. Barefooted and dressed only in her silk wrapper, she walked into the kitchen and lit the stove. She pulled out flour and lard and began mixing a pie crust, working as silently as she could. When the crust was rolled out, she took the jar of blueberries she had bought at Ecklund's General Store the previous day and began preparing them for a cobbler. As she finished pouring the mixture into the crust, she heard Seth moving around upstairs. She quickly shoved the dessert into the oven and grabbed the coffee pot just as he came through the kitchen door.

Turning her gaze on him, she nearly dropped the pot. He was almost naked, clad only in a towel loosely draped around his waist and another one thrown over one shoulder. The sheer beauty of his body made her

41

feel like the breath had been knocked out of her lungs. With suddenly shaking hands, she set the heavy pot on the counter, and hoping her voice wouldn't betray her, said, "Good morning, Sheriff."

"Morning," he returned, a look of surprise on his face. "I didn't know you were up. I'm gonna take a quick swim in the creek before church."

Nodding dumbly, Rachel tried desperately to look cool and unmoved as she drank in his tousled, sun-streaked hair and sleepy, languid blue eyes.

"I just thought I'd make some coffee," she stammered. "When you get back, you're welcome to a cup."

"Sounds good," he nodded.

Padding across the kitchen, he went out the back door and headed off in the direction of the creek.

Rachel stared out the window at him, awestruck. Never had she witnessed anything as breathtaking as Seth Wellesley's nearly nude body. It was no wonder the women of Stone Creek were falling at the man's feet — he was magnificent!

Turning back to her coffee, she threw a handful of beans into the water. "Quit acting like a ninny," she chided herself. "You'd think you'd never seen a man be-fore." A small giggle escaped as she realized that she never *had* seen a man quite like Seth Wellesley. Oh, wouldn't all the smitten girls in town just die if they could see what their idol looked like without his shirt? Rachel smiled in smug satisfaction, realizing that she'd just been treated to a very private glimpse of the town's most private citizen.

Seth sauntered down the hill toward the creek, a small smile hovering on his lips. His chance encounter with Rachel in the kitchen had finally broken the silence between them and he was relieved. It had been two weeks since their ill-fated dinner and in that time, they had studiously avoided each other. Rachel continued to eat her meals at the Dallas House and he had spent as many hours as possible at the office. Their avoidance of each other had successfully kept them from having further words, but it was an unsatisfactory truce. For some reason, hearing her moving around downstairs made him feel like an intruder in his own home, and he resented it. But, if Dr. Hayes was willing to be civil, he would do his best to get along too. Since they had to live in the same house, it would be nice if they could at least tolerate each other's presence. He just hoped that when he returned from his swim, she would be dressed and have her hair pinned up. It hadn't been easy to act nonchalant when he'd walked into the kitchen and found her standing there in her bare feet with that ebony hair cascading down her back.

Even now, the thought of how her eyes had swept over his near nakedness made his loins tighten uncomfortably. Clenching his jaw against the familiar tension, he quickened his pace and dove into the cold, rushing water with a sigh of relief. But, as good as the water felt, he knew he couldn't linger long. He was meeting Etta at church this morning and services were in less than an hour. Just what I need, he thought wryly, a couple of long, boring hours in church to keep my mind off sin, temptation and barefoot women making coffee in my kitchen!

Rachel glanced quickly at the clock on the kitchen wall. Twelve-thirty. She nodded in satisfaction. Seth should be home from church any minute and everything was ready. Her beef roast was perfectly seared and the kitchen was redolent with the smell of its fragrant juices. The potatoes sat in a fluffy mountain in the warming oven and the green beans Victoria Andrews had given her yesterday were perfectly steamed. She had set two places at the kitchen table, shunning the massive, banquet-size table in the formal dining room. The little table in the kitchen seemed so much more intimate.

43

She was carving the first slice off the roast when she heard the front door open, but her knife stilled and her heart dropped into her stomach as she distinctly heard the murmur of two voices. Seth was talking to someone and that someone was a woman. It had never occurred to her that he wouldn't come home alone. All her plans were going to be ruined, she thought with dismay. Tiptoeing over to the door, she peeked out into the foyer and drew a horrified breath. It was Etta Lawrence! She'd only seen her once before and then from a distance, but it had to be her. Now what? Should she pretend that she was fixing dinner for herself and a guest? Yes, that was definitely the best answer to this embarrassing situation. But, if Seth and Etta stayed at the house, how would she explain it when no one else arrived for dinner? And, what if Seth was angry that she had used his kitchen to cook for someone else after refusing to make a meal for him?

As the couple moved toward the kitchen, Rachel couldn't resist taking another quick look at Etta. The woman was pretty, Rachel conceded. Small, neat and well dressed. Her hair was a rich brown color and, even from this distance, she could see that Etta had beautiful green eyes. With sinking hopes, Rachel quickly ducked back into the kitchen, barely having time to grab her carving knife before Seth pushed open the door. He stopped dead in his tracks and stared at her in astonishment.

"Good afternoon," she chirped gaily. "How was church?"

Seth was speechless. What the hell was the little doctor doing in his kitchen and who was she preparing this feast for?

Etta squeezed past Seth, obviously annoyed to discover that she and the sheriff were not alone. She assessed the kitchen for a moment, then said in a clipped voice, "Church was just fine. I don't believe we've met. I'm Etta Lawrence and you must be Dr. Hayes."

"Yes, I am," Rachel smiled, extending her hand. "I'm pleased to meet you. I understand from the ladies in town that you are a wonderful teacher."

Etta smiled coolly and shook Rachel's hand. "And I understand from Mrs. Johnson that you're a wonderful doctor."

"Oh, yes," Rachel mumbled, "Jessie and her puppies."

The conversation faded and both women looked expectantly at Seth who just stood staring at the half-carved roast and heavily laden table. Finally finding his voice, he said, "Are you expecting company, Doc? Etta and I stopped to pick up some things to take on a picnic but it will only take us a minute."

Rachel thought fast, determined not to be humiliated by this mortifying situation. "Actually, I figured you two might be coming back here and I thought I'd fix you a little something to eat. Why don't you both sit down and I'll finish serving this?"

Etta's eyes narrowed slightly, not believing for a minute that Dr. Hayes had spent her entire morning cooking "a little something" for her. It was obvious that Rachel had had far different plans for who was going to eat this lavish meal and was now struggling mightily to gloss over the situation. Etta couldn't help but be impressed by the other woman's poise. Impressed and scared. In the two years she had known Seth, she had dealt with almost every unmarried woman in Stone Creek making a bid for his attentions. But this was different. The look in Seth's eyes when he gazed at Rachel caused Etta a frightening twinge of apprehension. This pretty little woman holding a wooden spoon and smiling so brightly might possibly pose a threat that Etta wouldn't be able to overcome.

"What an absolutely lovely thing to do," Etta gushed. "Don't you think so, Seth?"

"What?" He dragged his eyes away from Rachel and looked at Etta like he'd forgotten she was there. "Oh, yeah. Lovely."

"It's nothing," Rachel demurred prettily. "I love to cook and when the mood struck me this morning, I just felt I had to indulge myself. Please, sit down, both of you, before everything gets cold."

"Dr. Hayes," Etta smiled thinly, "you must join us. It looks like there's more than enough for three and we couldn't possibly consider eating this beautiful dinner without you. Could we, Seth?"

Seth remained silent, staring at Rachel through narrowed eyes as he digested her comment about "loving to cook."

"*Could* we, Seth?" Etta repeated, a trifle louder.

"Could we what?" he asked impatiently, glancing at her.

"I said, we couldn't consider eating this beautiful meal without Dr. Hayes joining us. Could we?"

"No, I guess not," he muttered, never taking his eyes off Rachel. "I'll get another plate."

Dinner was stilted and endless with Rachel trying valiantly to make small talk, Etta staring nervously at Seth, and Seth ignoring both of them and eating like a trojan.

When they were finally finished with the delicious cobbler, he rose from the table and said, "That was great. Come on, Etta, let's go."

Etta looked at him with a mixture of surprise and relief, but said graciously, "We can't leave Dr. Hayes here with all this mess to clean up."

"Nonsense!" Rachel hurriedly interjected. "You two go on and do whatever you were planning. I'll get this cleaned up in no time."

Etta looked at her dubiously, but said, "Well, if you're sure . . ."

"Absolutely," Rachel responded firmly.

"Thanks for the dinner, Doc," Seth drawled. "It sure does show when a woman loves to cook."

Rachel blushed and quickly turned away, but not before Etta saw the look that passed between them. Her apprehension grew.

Seth grinned at Rachel knowingly, clapped his hat on his head, and took Etta's arm. "See you later," he said, propelling Etta through the kitchen door. "Oh, and don't throw away what's left of that meat. I'll have a sandwich tonight before bed."

Etta's heart sank. Somehow, knowing that he was planning to sit in that kitchen late tonight and eat sandwiches which Rachel would undoubtedly fix made her feel like she wanted to cry.

Seth's casual statement had an entirely different effect on Rachel and as the couple departed, she smiled to herself. Maybe her efforts hadn't been for nothing, after all. Although lunch had certainly not gone as she had planned, Seth's late-night snack posed some definite possibilities. Humming a bright little tune, she turned back to the sink and happily attacked the mountain of dirty dishes.

It was after ten when Seth arrived home that night. Etta had insisted that she fix him supper and had lingered at the table so long that Seth had finally risen and asked for his hat. He liked Etta Lawrence. She was a sweet, undemanding, intelligent woman and he enjoyed her company. But there was no spark—at least not on his part. She was pretty enough, but somehow Seth felt almost brotherly toward her. Not at all the way he felt toward Rachel. All he had to do was look at her and his mouth got dry. He couldn't figure it out. She wasn't really any prettier than Etta and she certainly wasn't as interested in him, but there was something between them that couldn't be denied. And that something was driving him crazy.

He walked into the house and headed straight for the kitchen, hoping she would be there. She wasn't—but a large sandwich sitting on a plate and covered with a napkin was. Smiling at the snack, he bypassed the table and walked down the hall toward her bedroom.

Rachel heard him coming and opened her door and stepped out.

Seth stopped a few feet from her, suddenly unsure of what he intended to say. Rachel waited.

"Hi," he muttered, finally breaking the silence.

"Hello," she responded. "Did you have a nice afternoon?"

"Yeah, it was fine."

More silence. He looked at her, looked at the floor, looked at her again. "Will you come out to the kitchen for a minute? I want to talk to you."

She nodded, surprised by his request, and followed him back down the hall.

When they were seated, he gazed out the window at the black night for such a long time that when he finally spoke, Rachel jumped in surprise. "What was all that about today?"

"What do you mean?" she asked, her expression bland.

"You know very well what I mean. You know, I know, and Etta knows. Why did you go to all that work to make me dinner when the other night you refused to cook what I bought?"

"Because today it was *my* idea," she answered truthfully.

"I thought so." He smiled—a slow, lazy smile that was so appealing that it made her heart pound.

"Where did you learn to cook like that?"

"I took lessons."

"You took lessons?"

"Yes. Cooking is an art and people study for years to become master chefs."

Seth shook his head. "People in the East are crazy. Why don't they just learn to cook from their mothers?"

"Some people's mothers can't cook," Rachel countered.

48

"Everybody's mother can cook!"

"Not mine."

Seth's shoulders shook as he tried to contain his mirth. "You mean your mother was such a bad cook that you had to take lessons from a stranger instead of learning from her?"

"Something like that," Rachel nodded.

"Well, I have to admit, it worked. That was the best cobbler I ever ate in my life."

Rachel felt herself blush and hurriedly rose from the table. "Would you like another piece?"

Seth gazed at her as she moved across the kitchen toward the counter. "Yes, please."

She cut a generous slice of the dessert and set it in front of him. "Do you want anything else?"

"What else you got?"

"Sheriff . . ." she reproved, a blush belying her stern tone, "if there's nothing more you need, I have to go to bed. I have Mrs. Bradford bringing in all four of her children tomorrow morning. Apparently, they all have something wrong with their scalps."

"Knowing the way the Bradfords live, it could be just about anything," Seth warned. "Better not get too close."

"I'm a doctor, Sheriff, I have to get close. It's my job."

He grinned, thinking how much he'd like the doctor to get close to him. Realizing that was better left unsaid, he merely responded, "I noticed your practice is picking up. I've seen a lot of people in and out of your office in the last week."

"You mean a lot of women, don't you?" Rachel asked.

"Well, women are people, aren't they?"

"Oh, Mr. Wellesley," she laughed, "you've said a mouthful there!" Turning on her heel, she started down the hall toward her room. She was almost to her door when his voice called her back.

"Rachel?"

She whirled around, surprised and pleased to hear him call her by her first name.

"Yes?"

"If I take you on a picnic next Sunday to a really pretty place that only I know about, will you fry some chicken and make some potato salad?"

"And will that be chicken for two or three?" she asked archly.

Seth got up from the table and walked very slowly down the hall. But when he reached her, he didn't hesitate a second. He buried his big hand in her long, luxuriant hair, tipped her head back and kissed her . . . a soft, lingering kiss that made goosebumps shoot up her arms. "Two," he whispered. "Okay?"

She stepped back in confusion, disengaging herself from his embrace and groping for the bedroom door handle behind her.

"I have to go now," she whispered.

His eyes swept over her, lingering for a moment on her breasts before they scorched a trail back up to her face. "Yeah, you better," he agreed. Abruptly, he turned on his heel and walked back down the hall, breathing a sigh of relief when he heard her door click shut.

Sitting down again at the table, he toyed absently with his half-eaten cobbler. What was wrong with him? He'd had no intention of asking her to go on a picnic and he could hardly believe his words even while he was saying them. The last thing he wanted was to make her believe that he wanted to start something between them. And then, to top it off, instead of backing out of the impulsive invitation as he'd planned to when he'd followed her down the hall, he'd *kissed* her. He must be losing his mind, he thought, irritably shoving the plate of cobbler aside.

Dr. Hayes was becoming a major problem with her dark, languid eyes and enticing little body. Every time he got near her, he seemed to lose all sense of reason, thinking only of how much he'd like to pull her up against him and kiss her senseless.

Damn it, he raged silently, why did she have to look

the way she did, sound the way she did, smell the way she did? Why couldn't she be like Etta? Safe, predictable, uninvolving . . . Etta understood that they were just friends, that he wanted nothing more from their relationship than an occasional companion for an evening. She made no demands on him and never asked that he give more of himself than he wanted to give. Etta understood him.

Well, he decided, Dr. Hayes would just have to understand too. He'd make his feelings clear on Sunday. He'd just explain that he would enjoy a pleasant, uninvolved friendship with her, but that was all there could ever be between them. Surely, she couldn't be angry with him if he made his intentions clear right from the beginning. She seemed like a rational enough woman.

He pushed back from the table, feeling much better. He was confident that if he was just honest, everything would be fine between them. Just fine — as long as he could keep his hands off her while he told her.

Chapter Five

Rachel put a large, covered plate of chicken into the picnic basket. Everything was ready. Seth was outside, hitching up the horses and as soon as he was done, they'd be on their way.

She was so excited that her hands were shaking. It seemed like a hundred years since the previous Sunday when he'd asked her on this picnic. She hadn't seen much of him during the week. He left for his office before she was up in the morning, and although she would have been happy to fix him supper, he usually didn't come home until she was already in bed. The only real contact she'd had with him had been when he'd stopped by her office on Friday to quietly tell her he had to be out of town overnight but wanted to confirm that she was still planning to go on Sunday. As low as his voice had been, Diane Hagen, the town's worst gossip, had been sitting in Rachel's waiting room and had overheard their conversation. Miss Hagen had wasted no time in spreading the news about their plans, and the speculation about a possible romance between the sheriff and his boarder spread through town like wildfire.

When she'd gone to Ecklund's General Store on Saturday to buy the chicken for the picnic, she'd been stopped by no fewer than a dozen women who'd asked pointed questions about her plans for Sunday afternoon. Rachel had been embarrassed, knowing that anything Seth did caused a furor among the female population of Stone Creek. She didn't want anyone to get the wrong idea about their relationship, especially since she lived under his roof. She'd tried her best to give evasive answers to the prying questions and hoped that she had been nonchalant enough to put out the inferno of gossip that had flared up.

Seth walked into the kitchen, a small smile playing at the corners of his mouth as he looked appreciatively at Rachel's gauzy, lilac-flowered dress. "Ready?" he asked.

Tucking a large linen towel over the top of the basket, she turned and nodded. "Yes, all ready."

They walked out the back door and Rachel halted in surprise, staring at the carriage that awaited them. It was a beautiful little buckboard, the likes of which she hadn't seen since she left Boston.

"Like my buggy?"

"It's wonderful," she murmured. "Wherever did you find this way out here in the middle of nowhere?"

"I didn't 'find' it," he chuckled. "I had it built in New York and shipped out here in pieces."

"You did?" she asked in astonishment.

"Yeah," he replied, his eyes dancing with amusement. "Us rough westerners enjoy small comforts every bit as much as you eastern folks do, you know."

Rachel stared at the buggy in bemusement. This was far more than a "small comfort." The brass appointments alone set it apart from even the luxurious phaetons in Boston. It must have cost a small fortune.

"It's lovely," she murmured, "I haven't ridden in anything this comfortable since I arrived here."

Seth helped her into the lavish conveyance. "Glad to accommodate you, ma'am."

Rachel ran her hand across the plush leather upholstery and wondered, not for the first time, how Seth could possibly afford his lifestyle on a sheriff's salary. His house, his clothing, the horse he rode, and now this. Where did he get all the money?

53

As they headed out of town, Rachel was horrified by the number of women who were loitering along Main Street. It seemed that every lady in Stone Creek had turned out to see if the rumors of Seth and Rachel's picnic was true. Many people waved and calls of "Have a good time, Sheriff," followed them far down the road.

"I can't imagine how everyone found out about this," Rachel muttered.

"It doesn't matter. I'm used to it."

"Used to it?" she questioned.

"Yeah," he nodded. "When I first came to town, every time I took a girl anywhere, it seemed like we had an audience. Sort of died down after I started seeing only Etta, but I guess going on this picnic with you is something new to gossip about. I've never understood why anybody cares what I do. It's not like I'm the only man in town."

There was no question in Rachel's mind why the women of Stone Creek were interested in the romantic life of their sheriff. He might not be the only man in town, but he was by far the most attractive. "I hope you don't think I said anything," she remarked hurriedly.

Seth shrugged. "I wouldn't have cared if you had. I don't have anything to hide. I'm just glad I found this picnic place that nobody else seems to know about. I hate it when people gawk at me while I eat."

Rachel shook her head, suddenly feeling sorry for him. She was having difficulty getting used to the nosiness of a small town. When she lived in Boston, no one paid any attention to anything anyone else did and it was an adjustment being the object of the town's curiosity just because she was a doctor. But at least they didn't stare! She couldn't imagine living under the public scrutiny that Seth obviously had for the last three years. And all just because he was handsome, unmarried, and liked his privacy.

They rode on in silence until Seth turned the carriage into a wooded copse and stopped. Setting the picnic basket on the ground, he helped her down, then quickly dropped his hands from her waist. "Come on, the picnic spot is right down here."

They walked along the river's edge until they came to a bend where the bank widened out into a clearing fringed with trees. Rachel looked around in delight. "What a beautiful place!" she exclaimed.

Seth smiled. "I thought you'd like it. I was tracking one of Brady's men along the river one time and I came across it. It's secluded enough that no one else seems to have found it. I come here a lot when I want to be alone."

Rachel threw him a questioning look. "Why would you come here to be alone when you have that huge house?"

Seth looked uncomfortable for a moment, but then shrugged and said, "There's a difference between being alone and being lonely. It's never lonely here." Before Rachel could think of a reply, he shook off his reverie and said, "Let's spread out the blanket and eat. I'm starving."

When they were seated on the blanket with their plates in their laps, Rachel asked, "Did you build your house?"

Seth raised his eyes from his plate and nodded, his mouth full of chicken.

The next question was so obvious that she couldn't stop herself from asking. "Why?"

He chewed a long time, swallowed and looked out over the sluggish river. "You gonna ask me questions all afternoon?"

"No," she said, ducking her head in embarrassment. "I'm sorry. I didn't mean to pry."

Annoyed with himself for snapping at her, he muttered, "I built the house for several reasons but, well, they're personal."

"I understand," Rachel responded. "Please forgive me."

Abruptly, he pushed his empty plate away, leaned back on one elbow and said, "Tell me about yourself. Why did you decide to go to medical school?"

Rachel smiled wistfully, idly plucking a blade of grass and rolling it between her fingers. "I don't think I ever wanted to do anything else. My father is a doctor and I spent my childhood trailing around after him when he went on his rounds. By the time I was fifteen, I was assisting him with minor procedures and keeping his appointment calendar. I guess it was then that I really knew I wanted to be a doctor."

"And did your father agree with your decision?"

"Well, not entirely," she admitted, tossing the grass away and cutting into the chocolate cake she had brought along. "He thought I should become a nurse instead, but once he realized how serious I was, he supported me all the way."

"What about your mother?"

"Oh, her," Rachel said, her voice hard.

"What's that supposed to mean?" he asked, sitting up and looking at her intently.

"Well, my mother was so busy being a society matron that she never had time to think about what I was doing, much less care."

"But, didn't you tell me that nice desk set you have was a gift from your parents?"

"Yes, but Papa picked it out. In fact, Mother was in Europe at the time I graduated."

"And she didn't come home?"

"No."

"You grow up in Boston?" he asked, taking a bite of the cake she handed him.

"No, New York. My father trained at a hospital there and then set up his own practice. I moved to Boston because the university there accepted women in the medical school."

"Was your family always wealthy?"

Rachel shrugged. "My mother was born to it. I guess

that's why she's such a snob. Papa wasn't. He's from a big family in Albany and he worked his way through school."

Seth threw her a bewildered look. "But, if she was rich and he was poor, how did they meet?"

"Mother was ill when she was eighteen and her parents put her in the hospital where my father was training. I guess they fell in love then."

"That's a nice story," he smiled. "Maybe that'll happen to you, Doc. Maybe you'll have a patient who will fall madly in love with you and you'll get married."

"Only if I want to marry a woman," she retorted wryly.

Seth threw his head back and laughed. "Oh, I don't think you have to worry about that. I bet there's a man or two out there who might be interested."

Rachel blushed, not knowing what to say. Finally she asked, "What about you? What kind of family do you come from?"

"Big," he said promptly. "I have six brothers and a sister."

Rachel's jaw dropped. "Eight children? I can't imagine! Tell me about them."

With a faraway look, Seth brushed cake crumbs off his hands and lay back in the grass, lacing his fingers behind his head. "Well, we were all raised in Colorado, although almost none of us live there anymore. Pa and Ma are dead and only my one younger brother and my sister still live in Durango."

"How come everyone moved?"

"I don't know," he shrugged. "Lots of reasons. Wanderlust, mostly. It's pretty confining living up in the mountains. Miles, my oldest brother, went to college in England and just never came back. He married an English girl and they have a horse farm south of London."

"Really?" Rachel exclaimed, her eyes lighting with interest. "Do all your brothers live in England?"

"No. Just Miles. Stuart, who's next in line, lives north

of Boston and works in a shipyard. He wanted to be a sailor but always got so seasick that he had to give it up. I guess he figures building ships is the next best thing. Then there's Nathan. He's in Texas. He was a ranger for a while, but now he's married so he ranches."

"What's a ranger?" Rachel asked.

"A Texas Ranger," Seth answered, surprised that she didn't know about the famous troop. "They're federal lawmen. But it's a dangerous profession and once Nate got married, he decided he better settle down so that his new wife didn't become a widow before she became a mother."

"So, who's left?" Rachel prodded.

"Eric. He's a farmer. Lives up in Minnesota. None of us know why. He was always the different one. Lived on a little homestead up there all by himself for years. Then, he met Kirsten—now, there's a story—and now they have a farm. Geoffrey's out in Oregon. He left home when he was just a kid. He, Eric, Nathan and I didn't want to go to college. Pa was a real stickler for education and when we wouldn't go on to school, he just gave us a little money and told us to make our own way. It almost broke Ma's heart to see all of us boys leave, but that's the way Pa was. British, you know. Education was everything. Anyway, Geoff went north to be a lumberjack. I haven't seen him in years—he doesn't write much, but I've heard he's married and has a whole passel of kids."

"So, is that everyone?" she asked, her eyes wide with delight at his recounting.

"Almost," he nodded, "There's my sister. She still lives in Durango. She married a blacksmith and she's gonna have a baby in a few months. It's their first and she's real excited about it."

"So, everyone is married?"

"Everyone except Adam. He's the youngest and is at Harvard studying law. Remember? I mentioned him to you the day you arrived."

Rachel nodded. "And you, of course."

"What do you mean, 'and me'?"

"I mean, everyone's married except Adam and you."

"Yeah, right," Seth said, averting his eyes.

Rachel suddenly felt a prickle of fear at his obvious evasion. Drawing a deep breath, she plunged on. "You aren't, are you?"

"What?"

"Married?"

Seth shot her a quick look and Rachel was amazed by the anguish she saw cloud his eyes. "You don't see a wife in my house, do you?"

"Well, no, but . . ."

"But what?"

"Well, you just looked so funny when I asked."

"I'm not married," he said flatly.

Rachel's brows drew together in perplexity, but realizing the subject was closed, she sought out safer ground. "I can't imagine being the only girl with seven older brothers."

"She was spoiled rotten," Seth smiled, relaxing again. "My Pa always said he wanted a pretty little girl to dandle on his knee and I guess he and Ma just kept trying until they got one. I don't think they ever intended to have such a big family. Just took that many tries before Pa got his daughter."

Rachel could feel her cheeks getting pink at his casual reference to begetting children. He noticed her embarrassment and said in a teasing voice, "You know, there's something that always puzzles me about you, Doc."

She looked at him questioningly.

"You've been through medical school. You know all about men and women and childbirth and all that stuff, but if anybody mentions anything about making babies, you always blush. It just seems funny to me."

Rachel turned an even brighter shade of red. "I don't know why it's funny. Just because I've studied human anatomy doesn't mean that I'm not a lady with a lady's sensibilities."

"Yeah," he agreed, "there's no doubt about that. You're a lady, all right. Maybe too much so."

"What do you mean by that?" she asked, feeling slightly offended.

Seth sat up, brushing grass off his shirt and wishing he'd never started this conversation. "Oh, I don't know. Somehow you just don't seem like the kind of woman who would want to get . . . messy."

"What?" she demanded.

"I shouldn't have said anything," he muttered.

"Well, now that you've started, you might as well finish."

"I didn't mean that the way it sounded. It's just that you always look so perfect and you're so well educated and everything, I just can't see you enjoying . . . well, getting messy."

Rachel's stiff back and thinned lips belied her next words. "I beg your pardon, Sheriff, but I can assure you that I can get as messy, as you call it, as the next woman."

Seth chuckled. "Well, for the sake of your potential suitors, I'm glad to hear that, Doc."

"I wish you wouldn't call me, 'Doc'. My name is Rachel."

"Okay," he smiled, leaning a little closer. "I'll call you Rachel if you'll quit calling me 'Sheriff' and call me Seth."

"All right," she nodded, smiling back at him.

They were suddenly both quiet and Seth knew that now was the perfect moment for him to broach the subject of their relationship. But, somehow, the words just wouldn't come. Instead, he leaned closer still and idly plucked the pins out of her hair until it tumbled down her back. "Would you get mad if I kissed you?"

"You kissed me last week," she whispered, her heart racing. "Why do you want to kiss me again?"

"I don't know," he replied honestly, his lips hovering above hers. "Maybe I just like to kiss pretty girls out in the sunshine."

Rachel wanted him to kiss her more than she could ever remember wanting anything in her life. But something stopped her. She suspected he was toying with her . . . testing her to see if she'd let him get her 'messy' and, for some unaccountable reason, it made her angry. Pulling her head back, she said in a prim voice, "Actually, Sheriff, I think if you want to kiss someone, you should go see Miss Lawrence. The way she looks at you, I'm sure she'd welcome your attentions and I can just about guarantee that the sun is shining over her house too." She scrambled to her feet and quickly started repacking the empty picnic basket.

Seth stood up at once and, catching her by the arm, pulled her so close that their lips were touching. "I don't want to kiss Miss Lawrence," he breathed. "I want to kiss you."

"I don't understand," she stammered, hating the way her voice was quavering. "Why?"

"Because you're beautiful and all I've wanted to do since the first day you stepped off that stage is kiss you."

Somewhere, in the back of his mind, a warning bell went off and he knew he should never have uttered those words. But at this moment, with this beautiful girl's soft, warm lips brushing against his, he didn't regret his rash statement.

Rachel closed her eyes against the intensity of his gaze and tried desperately to gather her thoughts. She knew she shouldn't let him take such liberties, but before she could think of a suitable set down, his lips were on hers—warm, firm, gentle. It was a kiss unlike anything she had ever experienced and as his mouth caressed hers, she felt giddy and lightheaded. His lips were soft and his skin smelled like sunshine, leather and horses. The moment was so intoxicating that she swayed on her feet and had to clutch his shoulders to steady herself. Feeling her lean into him, he buried his hand in her hair, gently stroking the back of her head as he tightened his other arm around her waist, drawing her closer.

It seemed like an eternity before he lifted his head, smiling down at her languidly. "Your hair's a mess," he murmured.

Rachel giggled nervously and stepped back, threading her fingers through her tangled hair.

"Don't fix it," he whispered. "I like it like that."

"Oh," she stammered, not knowing what to say. She pressed shaking fingers to her lips, gazing up at him with eyes bright with expectancy.

Realizing that things could quickly get out of control, Seth drew a long breath to steady himself. His heart was pounding and the blood was roaring in his ears, but he felt her vulnerability and was gentleman enough not to exploit it.

"I think we better go back," he whispered.

"I think you're right," she nodded.

Turning away to hide the evidence of his rampant desire, he quickly stooped and picked up the blanket, carrying it in front of him over to the buggy.

Neither of them knew what to say on the ride home and they were nearly back to town before Seth broke the silence. "I'm going to have to drop you off and leave right away," he said abruptly.

"Oh?" Rachel said, surprised. "Are you leaving town again? On a Sunday?"

"Not really," he hedged, "I just have an errand I have to do."

Rachel suspected there was more to this "errand" than he was letting on and hoping to draw him out, said, "Being a lawman seems so dangerous. Aren't you ever scared?"

"Sometimes," he answered shortly.

"But why do you do it?" she persisted. "Why did you

become a sheriff?"

Seth stared straight ahead. "Because somebody's got to."

"But, you could be killed!"

He shrugged. "Yeah, or you could be hit by a runaway wagon on Main Street. Just being alive is dangerous."

"Oh, come now," she protested, "certainly you have to admit that some people put themselves into more danger than others."

"Most of the time there's no danger at all," he insisted. "I lock up drunks so they don't bother the ladies, I get Diane Hagen's mean old Tom cat out of her elm tree, things like that. It's not nearly as exciting as most people think."

Sliding a look over at her, he frowned at her dubious expression. "And, as for the other," he continued quietly, "as long as I keep my wits about me and don't get distracted, I'm okay."

"But—"

"I don't want to talk about it, Rachel," he interrupted, his temper suddenly flaring, "maybe someday I'll quit, but for now, it's what I have to do."

"Have to do?" she questioned.

"*Want* to do," he corrected.

Rachel's curiosity was acute, but she didn't pry any further.

"Will you be back in time for supper? Do you want me to make you something?"

"No, don't count on me. I might be out late."

"That's okay," she assured him, "I don't mind waiting. I can fix something like stew that can just sit and simmer and then when you get home—"

"I said, don't count on me!" Seth interrupted angrily. He pulled the buggy over to the side of the road and stopped. "Look, we've got to get something straight here. I don't want you asking me questions like when I'm going to be home and do I want supper and should you wait up. I can't be pinned down to time schedules. Do you understand?"

Rachel flushed a deep red as her own anger ignited. "I understand perfectly. I'm sorry if you think I'm making demands on you. I certainly didn't mean to. I just thought that if you had to be out late, you would miss supper and you might be hungry when you got home."

Seth sighed. "I know what you meant and I appreciate it. But, I don't know when I'll be back. It might not be till morning and there's no reason for you to wait up. I don't want you worrying about me. I'm used to taking care of myself."

Rachel nodded and stared straight ahead as he clucked to the horses and they moved back out on to the road. They didn't speak the rest of the way home until they pulled into the yard and Seth stopped the buggy. Without waiting for his assistance, Rachel climbed down and slid the empty picnic basket from under the seat. Turning toward the house, she walked rapidly up to the back door. When she reached the step, she looked back at him and said, "Thank you very much for the pleasant afternoon, Sheriff." She started up the steps but before she reached the porch, Seth sprinted across the yard and caught up with her. He laid a gentle hand on her arm and turned her toward him, but she looked down, refusing to meet his gaze.

"Rachel, look at me," he commanded softly.

She didn't move, but continued to stare at his boots.

"Rachel, please."

Lifting her eyes, she looked into his handsome face, hoping desperately that her feelings didn't show. "I thought you were in a hurry, Sheriff. You better go before it gets too—"

"Kiss me," he whispered.

"What? No!"

"Please."

"No."

64

He hesitated a long moment, then dropped her arm and turned back toward the buggy.

Suddenly, the dam of emotion that had been welling up in her spilled over and she took a step forward. "Seth? I'm sorry. I don't understand—"

Before she could finish, he turned back to her, grabbing her to him and kissing her hard. All the pent-up desire they'd been fighting all afternoon was in that kiss and when they finally broke apart, they were both shaking.

Seth stepped back, acutely aware of her breathlessness and high color. "I don't understand either," he whispered. Quickly, he gathered up the horses' reins and led them into the barn.

Chapter Six

It was very late when Seth returned. He quietly let himself in the kitchen door, a small smile lighting his face as he spied the stew pot simmering on the stove. His smile widened as he glanced over at the table, seeing that it was set with a bowl and spoon, along with a small, wicker basket full of biscuits and the honey pot. A small piece of paper sat atop the bowl and he picked it up, walking over to the kerosene lamp so he could read it.

Stew is on stove and biscuits were made fresh tonight. I know you said not to bother, but I was sure you'd be hungry.

R.

Seth stared thoughtfully at the note. Ever since he'd dropped Rachel off that afternoon, he hadn't been able to stop thinking about her. Their picnic had been a jolt to his emotions, the kisses they had shared sending his senses reeling—a reaction he was totally unprepared for.

It had been a long time since a woman had affected him so deeply and, try as he might, he was unable to untangle the web of feelings Rachel was evoking within him.

But one thing was sure. There was no room in his life for her. Perhaps, if he'd met her at another time, things could have been different between them. But right now there was no future for them and he must, somehow, keep his head long enough to tell her that. And he needed to tell her right away before he lost his resolve. Even though it was late, he must talk to her tonight.

He headed down the hall toward her room, determined to set things straight between them. It was the only honorable thing to do and, above all, he was an honorable man. He wouldn't lead her on. Better that she know exactly how things were before those impetuous kisses led her to conclusions he didn't want her to draw.

When he reached her door, he paused a moment, his hand on the knob. What was he going to say to her? He couldn't just walk in, uninvited, and say, "I just want you to know that there will never be anything between us so if you're starting to care for me, don't." So, what excuse could he give her for this highly improper midnight visit?

He stood for a long moment, staring at the door and pondering. Then, suddenly, his face lit up with a relieved smile. The stew! He'd tell her he wanted to thank her for the stew. Hopefully, that would break the ice enough that he could apologize for his impulsive behavior and say what had to be said concerning their future—or lack of it.

With a nod of satisfaction, he quietly opened her bedroom door, pausing just inside the threshold to let his eyes become accustomed to the darkness.

"Rachel, are you awake?" he whispered.

Rachel's eyes fluttered open and she groggily focused on the man standing above her. "Seth? What are you doing in here?"

"I, ah, just wanted to thank you for making that stew for me." The excuse sounded lame even to his ears and he winced in embarrassment.

Rachel propped herself up on one elbow, unknowingly pulling down the neckline of her nightgown so that one alabaster breast was almost completely exposed. "The stew?"

"Yeah," he stammered, his breath catching in his throat as he focused on the provocative sight of her nearly bare breast. He swallowed hard, trying to keep his mind on his purpose. Forcing his eyes back up to her face, he slowly started backing away, suddenly realizing her bedroom was definitely not the place to have a serious talk.

Rachel sat up, shaking her head to cast away the last remnants of sleep. "Just a minute," she murmured. "I'll get up."

"No," Seth responded in a tight voice, moving back to the bed. "I'll leave. I just wanted to tell you how much I appreciated you making supper for me, especially after what I said this afternoon."

She looked up at him with dark, velvet eyes and, unable to resist, he leaned over her, pushing back a strand of hair that was tumbling over her face. The intimate brush of his fingers against her temple made Rachel sigh with a longing she wasn't even aware of.

"You're welcome," she breathed, her eyes closing.

With a groan, Seth gathered her in his arms and kissed her. His mouth was gentle, searching, and she responded with a shy longing. Feeling her tremble beneath him, he drew her closer into his embrace, his muscular arms supporting her. Finally, he raised his head and gazed at her, the moonlight streaming across her delicate features. "You're beautiful," he murmured "So beautiful . . ."

Rachel felt as if she might faint as he sank down on the bed and again lowered his mouth to hers, his lips seeking and his tongue brushing against her teeth. Her lips parted and she drew in her breath as his warm, velvety tongue invaded the silken recesses of her mouth, intimately caressing her honeyed sweetness.

Burying his hand in her hair, he lowered her to the pillows, bending close as his lips traveled from her mouth to her ear. He whispered something, punctuating his words with light kisses as his tongue sensuously outlined the shell of her ear and his teeth nibbled the sensitive lobe.

Rachel shivered with reaction, turning her face and inviting his tongue back into her mouth.

Seth's breath was coming harsh and fast, rasping in his chest as their tongues continued their erotic play. He knew he had to stop. He could feel his manhood straining against his levis and realized he was becoming dangerously aroused. But the exquisite woman lying beneath him and responding so passionately to his caresses made it nearly impossible for him to keep his head.

In a last, gallant attempt to rein in his burgeoning lust, he tore his mouth away from hers, burying his head in her neck as he struggled to calm himself. In her innocence, Rachel misunderstood his actions and threw her head back, offering him greater access to her throat. Twining her fingers in his thick hair, she unconsciously guided his head downward toward her throbbing breasts.

He opened his eyes briefly, noticing that her gown had now ridden down until both her breasts were completely exposed, the nipples hardened to rosy peaks. He moaned, giving up the battle and burying his face in the exquisite softness. His tongue sought a beckoning pebble, tracing slow, erotic circles around it.

The touch of his tongue courting her so intimately suddenly brought Rachel to her senses, and with a tortured little cry, she wrenched away from him.

"What are you doing?" she cried, her eyes wide in the darkness.

Seth leaped off the bed, guilt and remorse engulfing him. Unable to meet her stricken, accusatory gaze, he turned away, breathing hard and visibly shaking. You

69

damn fool, he chastised himself roughly, you damn, stupid fool!

Her face flaming with embarrassment, Rachel quickly pulled the sheet up to her chin, mortified by the fact that her breasts were still exposed to his view, the nipples hard and taut from his intimate attentions.

After a long, tense silence, he rasped, "Are you all right?"

She nodded, unable to look at him.

"Rachel . . ." he whispered, his voice hoarse.

She cast her gaze up to meet his and vehemently shook her head. "No. Don't say anything. Just leave."

When he didn't move, she repeated, "Please, Seth! Go. NOW!"

He hesitated a moment longer, then walked swiftly toward the door. Turning, he said, "Rachel, I'm sorry. I didn't mean to . . ."

"Just go!" she pleaded.

She squeezed her eyes shut as she heard the door close softly behind him. Collapsing against the pillows, she drew a long, shuddering breath, trying desperately to figure out what caused her to react to him so wantonly. Why did she always seem to lose control with him? And, what was it about the man that caused one small kiss to escalate so quickly into a storm of passion?

It wasn't as though she'd never been alone with a man before. While in medical school, she had spent many evenings with male classmates. In some cases, she had even allowed them a kiss or two. But, nothing like this! Never had she allowed a man to take such liberties! But, she admitted reluctantly, never had she met a man who made her feel like Seth did. She'd had an almost tolerant affection toward the men she'd known in Boston, but none of them had ever unleashed the flood of carnal longing that this tall westerner did. What made him so different? True, he was handsome and charming, but so were any number of men she had known in the past. There must be something else that made her react so strangely to his touch, but try as she might, she could not pinpoint what it was.

All she knew was that the man was dangerously attractive and every time he touched her, she reacted like some strumpet from a saloon. Thank God that, at least tonight, she had regained a semblance of reason before she had made a tragic mistake. Someday she might want to get married and it was imperative that she save herself for her husband. Since Seth was obviously not the marrying kind, she must find the strength to resist him.

She turned on her side and stared out at the moonlit night. This must never happen again, she told herself firmly. You're a grown woman and you simply have to resist him.

Even as she made this vow, she hoped that she'd never again be in the position she'd been in tonight, for she had very little confidence that she would ever be able to resist Seth Wellesley.

It was almost dawn, but still Seth lay awake, furious with himself over the incident in Rachel's bedroom.

Well, you sure did one hell of a job of cooling things off, Wellesley, he thought angrily. Just went right in there and told her that you don't want to get involved in an intimate relationship. Great job, man, great job!

Turning over, he pounded his pillow, irritably wondering, for the hundredth time, how things had gotten so out of hand so fast. Why did his lust erupt like a volcano every time he got near her? It was damn unnerving how fast he lost control around her. He'd never been a man whose passions ruled his brain — not even when he was a kid. So why now?

He had to put a stop to it. Tomorrow morning. First thing. Even if he had to shout at her from another room, he was going to keep his head and set things straight between them.

Kicking off the tangled covers, he clasped his hands behind his head and determinedly closed his eyes.

Tomorrow morning. First thing.

Rachel was pouring two cups of coffee when Seth walked into the kitchen.

"Good morning," she said in what she hoped was a breezy voice. When he didn't immediately answer, she turned away from the stove and looked at him expectantly. "Can I fix you something for breakfast?"

He shook his head and reached out to take the cup she offered. "Rachel," he began, "about last night—"

"I don't want to talk about it," she interrupted hurriedly. "Now, what can I get you to eat?"

"I don't want food. I want to talk about last night."

"Really?" she laughed nervously. "I don't. I think we should just pretend it never happened."

"It happened," he said flatly.

"All right," she snapped, gripping the edge of the counter, "it happened. But, it was just a mistake."

"Was it?"

"Yes! You got carried away . . . I got carried way. Things like that happen."

"They don't happen to me," he muttered.

"Oh, come now, Sheriff. Are you trying to tell me that you've never . . . kissed a woman before?"

"It was a hell of a lot more than a kiss and you know it!" he exploded. "What kind of game are you playing, Rachel?"

"I'm not playing a game," she responded flippantly. "I just think you're making mountains out of molehills."

Seth threw her a hard look, noticing, for the first time, her flaming cheeks and clenching hands. "Why are you denying it? You know what almost happened. Why are you pretending it didn't?"

"The important thing is that 'it' *didn't* happen," she answered firmly. "And it won't . . . will it?"

He looked at her for a long moment, aware that she was offering him exactly the opportunity he was looking for. But, instead of launching into the speech he'd been mentally preparing all morning, he said simply, "No, it won't."

Then, turning abruptly on his heel, he set his coffee on the counter and strode out the back door.

Chapter Seven

It was two weeks later when Rachel was startled awake by someone pounding at her door. Looking around her dark room, she pushed her hair out of her face and sat up groggily. The pounding came again, followed by a strange man's voice calling, "Dr. Hayes! Please open up!"

Leaping from her bed, she hurriedly pulled on her bathrobe and stumbled through her office to the back door. Flinging it open, she saw the man who ran the telegraph office standing on the other side. Without ceremony, he grabbed her by the arm and gasped, "You gotta come quick. There's been a shooting at the saloon!"

Rachel's heart leaped into her throat. Wrenching her arm from the man's panicked grasp, she said, "Wait a minute. I have to put some clothes on and get my bag."

Her soft voice seemed to calm him and he stepped back, whipping off his hat and saying, "I'm sorry, ma'am, but please, hurry!"

She tore back into her bedroom, ripping off her bathrobe and nightgown, and yanking on the first dress she found. It was a simple cotton day dress that she had bought at Ecklund's and it only took a moment to settle it into place and button it. Still shod in her bedroom slippers, she raced back into her office, grabbed her bag from beside her desk and ran out the door.

"Tell me what's happened," she panted as she sprinted down Main Street next to the distraught man.

"I'm not sure," he yelled, running along beside her. "The sheriff's been involved in a shooting. I was just walking by the saloon when it happened and somebody yelled to get you. I don't even know who's been shot."

"The sheriff!" Rachel gasped, the blood pounding in her ears. She had seen almost nothing of Seth since their fateful encounter in her bedroom, but he'd never been far from her thoughts. And, now, this man was saying he'd been involved in a shooting! With a small, distressed cry, she hoisted her skirts above her knees and took off like a shot, leaving the winded telegrapher well behind her. She got a stitch in her side and was almost doubled over in pain by the time she rounded the corner onto Hutchinson Avenue where the saloons were, but she kept running. It didn't take her long to determine at which saloon the incident had occurred. A large crowd was gathered outside of Rosie's and she was hard pressed to elbow her way through the milling throng of men.

"Move! Let me through. I'm a doctor. MOVE!" Somehow, above the chaos, the men heard her and parted the way. She burst through the saloon's bat wing doors and the sight that met her almost made her knees buckle with relief.

Seth was standing on the outside of a circle of men who were kneeling above a body which was lying motionless on the floor. As Rachel sped across the saloon, Seth turned and looked at her, a grim yet somehow satisfied expression on his face. She threw him a hasty glance, assuring herself that he wasn't hurt and then proceeded toward the downed man.

One look and Rachel knew he was dead. She pushed her way through the hovering men and knelt down next to the body.

"You're too late, Miss Hayes," one of the men said. "He's dead."

"I see that," Rachel responded. There was a large, gaping hole in the man's chest and his eyes stared up sightlessly. Straightening, she said in a louder voice, "Someone better get Mr. MacDougall and have this man removed. Does anyone know who he is?"

There was a general muttering among the men in the saloon and all heads turned toward Seth.

"It's Eli Jenkins," Seth announced, "one of Clint Brady's gang. Get him out of here. Just tell Mac to throw him in a hole." Turning on his heel, Seth walked out of the saloon.

At that moment, Martin Fulbright charged through the doors. "What happened here?" he demanded.

Dick Schmidt, the bartender, stepped out from behind the bar and said, "Well, Mayor, seems this dead weasel here is one of Brady's men. He came in here tonight and right away started causin' trouble. He was drinkin' real heavy and botherin' some of the girls." As if just remembering her presence, Dick shot a hasty, embarrassed glance in Rachel's direction but she stood riveted to the floor, not blinking an eye.

"Anyway, one of the boys called the sheriff and when he got here, he seemed to recognize him right away. They started havin' words, Seth pushed him toward the door, and the guy drew. It was self-defense on Seth's part, Mayor. This Jenkins guy drew first."

Martin Fulbright nodded grimly and said, "Has anyone called Mac?"

Dick nodded and walked back behind the bar.

"Okay, boys," Martin announced, "the saloon's closed for tonight. Pack up your gear and go on home. The show's over." Turning toward Rachel who was still staring at the body, he said quietly, "Could I escort you home, Dr. Hayes?"

Rachel nodded and allowed herself to be led out the door. As they walked down the street toward Seth's house, she asked, "Is the sheriff a good shot, Mayor?"

"The best," Martin confirmed. "I've never seen anybody with an aim like Seth's."

"So, if he killed that man it was because he meant to, right?"

"I don't know exactly what you're asking, Doctor."

"What I mean is, if Sheriff Wellesley's such a good shot, then he could have just wounded that outlaw if he'd wanted to, correct?"

"Well, now, I don't know about that," Martin hedged. "It's hard to aim true when you're returning fire on somebody. But, whether Seth meant to kill him or not, what's done is done and I'll not question his motives. He's the best sheriff in the whole state and we're lucky to have him. Maybe he only meant to shoot this outlaw in the arm and his aim was off, or maybe he aimed for his heart and hit it dead-eye accurate. I don't know and I don't care. If he really is one of that thieving, murdering bunch of Clint Brady's, then the world is better off without him, believe me."

They had reached the little side entrance to Rachel's office and as she unlocked the door, Martin looked at her and said, "Don't be too hard on Seth, Dr. Hayes. He's a good man."

Rachel nodded and softly closed her door. She flung her bag down next to her desk and passing through her bedroom, entered the kitchen. Seth was there, sitting at the table.

Ignoring him, she walked over to the sink and pumped some cold water, splashing it on her flaming face. Gripping the edge of the counter, she willed herself to be calm.

"You okay?" came his quiet voice from behind her.

Whirling around, she pinned him with a hard stare. "Sure, Sheriff. I'm fine. Eli Jenkins isn't, but I am."

"You don't know anything about it. You weren't there."

"I didn't have to be," Rachel spat, "I heard all about how he drew on you first and that it was self-defense,

77

and how you just happened to hit him straight in his heart when you returned fire. Why, Seth? Why didn't you aim at his leg or his arm or his foot, for God's sake? Why did you kill him?"

"Don't question me, Rachel. I don't have to answer to you," he growled.

"Oh, no! The mighty Seth Wellesley doesn't have to answer to anyone, does he? You can just walk into a saloon and kill a man and no one questions you because you're such a 'good man'! Even Mayor Fulbright believes that! Well, I'm questioning you, Sheriff."

"Stop it!" he demanded. "You don't know what you're talking about."

"Don't tell me to stop it," she raged. "And don't tell me I don't know what I'm talking about! You know you could have wounded that man and brought him to me. I could have healed him and he could have been brought to trial like this country's Constitution guarantees. But, I guess this frontier justice of yours doesn't pay any attention to the Constitution, does it? As far as you're concerned, there is no law of the land. There's just your law, isn't there?"

"God damn it, lady," Seth thundered, rising from his seat and slamming his fist on the table. "Who do you think you are to tell me how to do my job? I don't tell you how to do yours, so just back off!"

"Of course you don't tell me how to do my job," Rachel railed. "By the time you're done, there's nothing left for me to do. When you finish, the only thing left is to call MacDougall and have him build a pine box."

The two combatants glared angrily at each other for a long moment and then Seth sank into his chair. "Have you ever heard anything about Eli Jenkins?" he asked quietly. "Do you know what kind of man he was?"

"No, I've never heard of him," Rachel admitted, "but that's not the point."

"Yes, that *is* the point!" Seth shot back. "Let me tell you about the scum you're defending so righteously. Eli

Jenkins is wanted in at least four states. He's a thief, a murderer and a rapist."

At Rachel's startled look, Seth drove his point home. "Yes, madam, a rapist. Jenkins' idea of a fun day was to swoop down on some settler's home, rob them, rape the wife in front of her husband and then kill them both. If there was a pretty young daughter, he'd have her too and if the rape didn't kill her, he'd usually finish her with his knife. And, if there were little kids, he'd just leave them surrounded by their dead parents and ride off with everything he could carry or herd. And you're upset that he's dead?"

"But," Rachel stammered, "you killed him on purpose. No matter what the man did, he deserved a trial. If a jury of his peers decided he should hang, then so be it. But, you played judge, jury, and executioner all at one time and that's wrong."

"Maybe," Seth conceded, "but at least I know he's not going to rape and murder some thirteen year old girl tonight."

"Is that who you've been trailing all these weeks?" Rachel asked. "Was Jenkins your 'errand' the day we went on the picnic?"

"Yeah," he admitted. "For a while, he was part of Clint Brady's gang. A big part. Then I heard from a friend of mine in Denver that he and Brady had a falling out and Jenkins was headed east. I figured he was on his way to Kansas City and that he'd have to pass near here. I didn't expect to find him at Rosie's, but I guess he wanted to prove he wasn't scared of me."

"Had you ever seen him before? Was he here looking for you?"

Seth shrugged. "Maybe. I don't know. We'd never been formally introduced, but we weren't exactly strangers either."

Rachel leaned back against the sink and exhaled a long sigh. "I don't have any doubt that the man was the criminal you say he was, but it was wrong of you to kill him. There's nothing you can say that will convince me otherwise."

Seth's fist hit the table with a resounding crack. "Jesus Christ, woman, he was Clint Brady's right hand man! That in itself is enough reason for him to die!"

Pressing her lips together, Rachel shook her head and insisted, "That's up to a jury to decide. Not you."

"And just how are you so sure that I killed him on purpose?" Seth asked, his voice cold.

"Because all I've heard for the past two months is what a great shot Sheriff Wellesley is. A master at marksmanship. Can outshoot anybody. Wins every contest. For some reason that is totally beyond my understanding, the citizens of Stone Creek seem to think that being dead-eye accurate with your killing machine is something to be proud of."

"You might feel a lot different if my 'killing machine' was protecting your life, lady."

Rachel pushed away from the counter and walked over to where Seth stood on the other side of the room. Looking straight into his eyes, she said, "Did you kill Eli Jenkins on purpose, Sheriff? Did you aim to kill?"

It was one of the longest moments of her life as Seth stared back at her. Finally, in a quiet, steady voice, he said, "Yes."

Rachel sucked in her breath, horrified by his answer. "Then, Sheriff, all I can say is that you've lost your humanity. You're just big and cold and mean."

Turning on her heel, she walked down the hall to her room and closed the door behind her, snapping the lock into place for the first time in many weeks.

For a long while Seth stared after her as the full implication of her words washed over him. Big, cold, and mean . . . He gazed out the window into the blackness, appalled by what a terrible description that was. And most terrible of all was that maybe, just maybe, she was right.

Chapter Eight

Seth cupped his hand over his eyes to shield them from the piercing August sun. The glare on the dusty trail was so intense that it was almost impossible to see any tracks.

He had been on Deke Miller's trail for three days. Three hot, dirty, frustrating days — and still the desperado eluded him. Miller was an integral part of Brady's gang. In fact, they were cousins and had formed the gang together when they were still boys back in Nebraska. For years, Deke and Clint had avoided capture — always together, always escaping. But, this time, Seth knew he had him. They had pulled a bank job in Garden City, and from the telegram Seth had received from the sheriff there, had headed straight into Seth's jurisdiction. He had immediately taken off after them, but by the end of the first fruitless day of tracking it became obvious that the gang had split up.

Seth found the fork in the trail where they had separated and chose to follow a specific set of tracks. He knew it was Deke Miller he was tailing by the unique shape of his horse's right rear shoe. Every lawman west of the Mississippi knew that Miller rode a horse with a slight imperfection in his back right hoof, necessitating a specially constructed shoe. It was this set of tracks that Seth honed in on.

The tracks had led him along the banks of the Arkansas River, and despite the cool water and high bluffs flanking the path, it was hot and steamy. He pulled his horse to a halt and ran his arm across his forehead, wiping away the sweat and grime that had accumulated. Squinting, he swung around in the saddle, scanning the bluffs for signs of an ambush.

It was this quick perusal of the surrounding terrain that saved him. High above him, a gun barrel caught the sun, nearly blinding him for a moment, but giving him the warning he needed to dodge the bullet which zinged past his ear a split second later.

Leaping off his horse and ducking behind it, Seth whipped his Peacemaker out of its holster and took aim over the back of the saddle. The sun reflected off the outlaw's gun again and Seth fired. Miller realized he'd been discovered and started running along the top of the bluff, weaving and dodging in an attempt to gain the shelter of a clump of trees.

His wild race gave Seth the advantage he needed. Sighting down the long barrel of the Colt, he drew a bead on the fleeing outlaw and fired. Miller staggered and then pitched forward, falling over the edge of the bluff and landing nearly at Seth's feet.

Warily approaching him, Seth pointed his gun at Miller's head and nudged the prone man over with his foot, hoping he was still alive. There had been no time to aim carefully enough to ensure that he only wounded him and now, as he stared down at the prostrate body, he realized his aim had been off. He had tried to strike him in the upper leg, but a rapidly expanding pool of blood was spreading across his abdomen.

"Damn," Seth cursed aloud, "he'll never make it." As much as he'd like to see Miller dead, he knew he could be the key to Brady's whereabouts. But now, it didn't look like Miller would live long enough to supply him with the information he wanted.

He squatted down and put his ear to the outlaw's chest, hoping to hear a heartbeat. There it was, he thought with grim satisfaction. The bastard was still alive . . . for the moment, at least. Unfastening the man's pants, he pulled off his shirt and wadded it against the gaping wound, trying to stanch the river of blood. There was no chance to question him now. He was unconscious and likely to stay that way, considering the fall he had taken and the amount of blood he was losing. With his hands on his hips, Seth stared at him in frustration, not knowing what else he could do to prolong the man's life.

Then it came to him. Rachel. He'd take him to Rachel! He straightened and took a close look around, trying to gauge where he was and how long it would take to reach Stone Creek. Not long, he thought with satisfaction. He knew this area. For the past two days, he had been working his way eastward and now he wasn't more than five miles from town. If he could just get Miller up on his horse and back to Stone Creek, maybe, just maybe, Rachel could save him.

Regardless of the fact that she had hardly spoken to him since their argument over Eli Jenkins, she was a doctor and he knew she wouldn't deny his plea for medical help. He gathered up his horse's reins and cast a quick glance around to see if Miller's horse was anywhere in sight. It wasn't. Seth frowned, knowing he was going to have to carry the man across his lap on his own mount. He leaned over and hefted him over his shoulder. Mounting awkwardly, he lowered him from his shoulder to his lap as carefully as possible, then nudged the horse into a walk.

The ride seemed interminable. The horse moved slowly, tired from three days on the trail and carrying the heavy burden of two large, muscular men. But, finally, Stone Creek loomed in the distance. Giving the lagging animal an impatient kick, Seth spurred him into a slow trot until he finally rounded the corner on to Main Street.

Dick Schmidt was just coming out of Rosie's when he heard a shout. Looking down the street, he saw the sheriff and what appeared to be a dead man slung over his horse's back. Seth was wildly waving his hat and shouting Dick's name.

"What is it? What's wrong, Sheriff?" Dick yelled, picking up his pace and hurrying toward the oncoming horse.

"Go to Dr. Hayes' office and tell her to get ready for an emergency. She's probably gonna have to do surgery and I want her to be ready by the time I get there."

With a quick nod of understanding, Dick shot off down the street in the direction of Seth's house, wondering if pretty little Dr. Hayes was up to doing surgery on a half-dead gunshot victim.

Rachel patted eight year old Reed Johnson on the head and rebuttoned his shirt. "He's fine, Mrs. Johnson," she said confidently. "It's just a cold. There's no sign of lung infection. I'll give him some medicine for his cough and he should be good as new in a few days."

"Thank you, Doctor," Mary Johnson answered shyly. "I was so worried when his cough got so bad. I didn't want it to—"

Her sentence was never finished as the door to Rachel's office slammed open and Dick raced in. "Sheriff's comin', Doc, and he's got a man slung over his saddle. Said to tell you to get ready to operate. Looks like the guy's taken a slug."

Reed's eyes widened and he jumped off the table excitedly. "Wow, Ma, did ya hear that? Somebody's been shot! Can we stay and watch? Please?"

With a frown at her son, Mary took him firmly by the hand and said, "We'll be on our way, Doctor."

"Aw, come on, Ma!" Reed protested. "I wanta see! There's probably gonna be lot of blood and guts and stuff. Please? Can't we stay? Just for a minute?"

Mary threw her son a shaming look and dragged him toward the door. "I'll get that medicine to you later," Rachel called after her, her mind already on the upcoming ordeal.

Suddenly, she realized Dick was following Mrs. John-son out of the office. She hurried after him, catching him by his arm and saying, "Wait a minute, Mr. Schmidt. Don't go. I need you to help me get ready."

"Me?" Dick exclaimed, whirling to face her. "What do you want me to do?"

Before Rachel could tell Dick how he could assist her, the door to her office opened again and Seth staggered in, carrying an unconscious man over his shoulder.

All business now, Rachel gave Seth and the outlaw a cursory glance and then directed, "Put him on the table, Sheriff — gently — and tell me what happened."

As Seth rapped out a brief recounting of the shooting, Rachel sped around the room, gathering instruments and washing her hands.

"Take off his pants, Mr. Schmidt," she ordered tersely.

"What?" Dick gasped. "You want me to undress him in front of you?"

"Forget it, Dick," Seth said dryly, "I'll take care of it from here."

"Thanks, Sheriff," Dick nodded in profound relief. Slapping his hat on his head, he quickly backed out of the room, rushing through the door and away from the gory scene.

"Some men just can't take the sight of blood," Seth muttered in disgust, pulling Miller's heavy denim trou-sers off. "Okay, what next?"

Rachel leaned over the outlaw, gently probing the flesh around the wound and shaking her head. "It looks bad. From the amount of blood he's losing, he must have been hit in the aorta. I haven't got time to try to get the bullet out. The best I can do is try to stitch up everything that's been ripped."

"You've gotta save him," Seth said urgently. "I need him."

Rachel threw him an anxious look. "I'll do my best," she assured him, pulling a clean piece of linen off a stack of towels by the table and covering Miller's nudity. Seth shot her a curious look, but remained silent.

"Can I help?" he asked.

"Yes, hand me the things on that tray when I ask for them."

Without another word, Rachel bent over Miller and went to work.

Seth was amazed by the composure and self-assurance she displayed. With quiet, precise commands, she directed him as to what she needed from her tray of supplies, rarely looking up unless he hesitated or handed her the wrong instrument. In those cases, she merely pointed at what she needed, then immediately returned to her task.

They worked for almost two hours, saying little, but functioning together like a well-seasoned team. Finally, Rachel straightened, wiping her bloody hands on a towel and rubbing the small of her back.

"That's all I can do," she remarked quietly. "It's in God's hands now." Walking to the head of the table, she placed her fingers against Miller's neck, feeling for a pulse. It was weak and thready, but it was there. She gazed at his ashen face with concern, not liking the grayish color around his lips. Lifting his upper lip, she shook her head at his colorless gums and said, "He's in shock, Seth. If his blood pressure dips any lower, we're going to lose him."

"No!" he answered fiercely. "We can't lose him. He's got information that could crack Brady's gang wide open."

"Who is he?" Rachel questioned.

"Deke Miller, Brady's cousin. He and Brady formed the gang years ago. He knows everything there is to know about them and if you can get him back on his feet, he'll tell me."

"How do you know that?"

"Leave that part to me. Just get him well."

Rachel shook her head. "I'm not going to kid you. He's sustained a very serious wound and his chances of mak-

86

ing it are slim at best. I've done everything I can, but he's lost a lot of blood and his color is bad."

"I know," Seth nodded. "Shit, but I wish my aim had been better! I was going for his leg, but he was running and I missed."

Rachel eyed her patient grimly, wishing she felt more confident of his prospects. Turning toward the small sink, she started washing the bloody instruments, saying, "You can go file your reports or do whatever you need to do. I'll sit with him."

"Okay," he agreed. "I need to send a telegram and let the Garden City sheriff know that I've caught him. I'll be back a little later."

For the next several hours, Rachel sat by Miller's still body. Things were not going well and her apprehension grew as the evening aged. His breathing became more shallow; his face more gray. By nine o'clock, she knew that she was losing him. There was nothing to do but wait.

Seth arrived home shortly after ten and found her sitting at her desk, filling out an official-looking report.

"How is he?" he asked with trepidation.

"He's gone," she answered quietly. "There was nothing I could do."

Seth cursed under his breath, then, with a curt nod, turned on his heel and left the office. Rachel heard his heavy footsteps trudging tiredly up the stairs and, suddenly, the enormity of her failure hit her. Until that moment, she had viewed Miller professionally — remaining detached and calm, and applying her knowledge to the best of her ability. Even when he had breathed his last, she had remained composed, noting the time and dutifully filling out the death certificate.

But the expression on Seth's face when she told him Miller had died suddenly made it no longer just the inevitable death of a mortally wounded gunshot victim. She had failed him. For the first time, Seth had put aside his desire to kill anyone connected with Brady and had only

87

wounded Miller. Then, he'd put his faith in her to save the man — and she had failed. Guilt and remorse washed over her like a tidal wave. If only she'd worked faster . . . if only she'd been more experienced with gunshot wounds . . . if only . . .

Her pen dropped from shaking fingers and tears fell unheeded down her cheeks. Seth had needed her to save this man and she'd not had the skill to do it. Somewhere, in the back of her mind, she knew she was being unfair with herself. The man had sustained a mortal wound. Probably no doctor, no matter how experienced, could have saved him. But, in her agitated state, that realization didn't matter. What did matter was that Seth had entrusted her with the life of a man of vital importance to him and she had lost him.

Blindly, she left her office and walked into her bedroom, mechanically shrugging out of her dress and pulling on a light nightgown and her silk wrapper. She stared at her bed in despair, knowing that despite her exhaustion, she'd never be able to sleep. She walked back out to the kitchen and fixed a cup of tea. Then, slowly, she trudged into the sitting room and sank wearily into a plush, upholstered rocking chair. Leaning her head against the back of the chair, she allowed herself to give way to the sobs she had been holding back. Her whole body shook as she rocked back and forth, sobbing out loud, lost in her misery.

Seth lay in his big bed staring blankly at the ceiling. If only he hadn't missed his shot! Why did this have to be the one time, the one man, who he would unintentionally kill? Furious with himself, he turned over and punched his pillow in frustration. If only Miller had lived, he might have been the key to ferret out Brady once and for all. But no. He'd had to miss and kill the bastard. Why? *Why?* He'd needed him so badly!

There was no doubt in Seth's mind that Miller would have eventually swung and he would have been glad to see it happen — but not before he was done with him.

88

Forcing him to divulge information would not have been pleasant, and Seth was not one to revel in punishing another man, no matter what his crimes, but, in this case, he would have done whatever necessary to make Miller tell all he knew. Now, he'd never get the information he so desperately sought.

His thoughts drifted to Rachel. She'd done a hell of a job today. He really hadn't known what to expect from her when he'd arrived at her office, but she had risen to the challenge and proven herself to be as competent as any man. He'd been impressed by her cool professionalism and awed by her skill. No one in Stone Creek need ever doubt that they had a "real" doctor in residence. Rachel was as fine a physician as he had ever seen and he intended to let every man in town know it.

He closed his eyes and vowed not to let this most recent setback prey on him. Although he hadn't gotten what he wanted from Miller, at least he would no longer be a threat to anyone. And if he was as integral a part of Brady's gang as rumor had it, then perhaps his death would be a chink in their armor, as well as a warning that the lawmen in the region meant business.

He was just starting to drift off to sleep when he heard a noise. Opening his eyes, he listened closer. What was it? It sounded like someone moaning. Throwing back the sheet, he hurriedly pulled on his levis and walked out of his room. The sound was louder now that he was in the hall. He could clearly hear someone crying . . . and the sound was coming from downstairs.

As he padded barefoot down the staircase, he realized the noise was coming from the sitting room. Walking silently through the doorway, he saw Rachel's shadowy figure in the rocking chair.

"Rachel?" he called softly. "What's the matter? Why are you crying?"

Startled by his unexpected appearance, Rachel jumped in fright, but, wallowing in the depths of self-condemnation, she didn't answer him.

Puzzled by her silence, he walked over to the chair and squatted down next to her. "Rachel! For God's sake, what's wrong?"

"Oh, Seth . . ." she stammered, "I'm so sorry . . ."

The tortured expression on her face made him draw in his breath in alarm. Almost without realizing it, he picked her up from the chair and sat down with her on his lap, snuggling her head against his shoulder and soothing her as if she were a small child. "Shh, baby, don't cry. What's wrong that you're so unhappy?"

Rachel gulped and hiccoughed, barely able to believe that the man whom she was sure would despise her was actually comforting her. The effect of his concern, however, was merely to make her cry harder. "I . . . I failed you!" she sobbed.

"What?" he questioned, leaning back to get a better look at her. "What in hell are you talking about?"

"Mil — Miller . . ."

"What about him?"

"You needed him!"

"Yeah?"

"He died and it's . . . it's my fault!"

"No it isn't!"

"Yes . . . yes, it is! I tried, I re — really did, but he jus — just died and it's my fault!"

Seth was shocked by the depth of her despair and took her chin between his thumb and index finger, gently tilting her head back until she was looking at him. "It wasn't your fault," he said firmly. "I knew he probably wouldn't make it. I've seen enough men shot in the belly to know they usually don't. What you did was incredible. No one could have done any better."

Rachel gazed at him through tear-glazed eyes, and seeing the sincerity in his gaze, sighed tremulously and leaned her head back against his shoulder. "You mean . . . you're not mad at me?"

His smile was soft as he pressed her head to his chest and rocked back in the chair. "Of course I'm not mad at you. Poor little doctor," he crooned, "did you think the big, mean sheriff would be mad at you if you didn't save the outlaw he shot?"

Rachel's tired, troubled mind eased a bit at his gentle, teasing words. Nestling her face against his neck, she whispered, "Thank you for understanding. I really did try my best but . . . it was just too late."

Tipping her head back again, Seth gazed into her eyes, his expression tender and sympathetic. "I know, my brave, beautiful doctor," he murmured, "I know you did." His lips covered hers.

His kiss was infinitely gentle; a soft, whispering caress that made her sigh and thread her fingers through his thick tawny hair.

He moved his arm down her back, stroking her as he drew her tighter against him. She was sitting sideways on his lap and as his big, calloused hand slid along the light silk of her robe, she could feel his warmth against her hip.

She parted her lips and they kissed endlessly, both of them reluctant to end the intimate moment. Rachel bent her knee slightly in an effort to not slide off his lap and Seth's hand dipped lower, softly rubbing her thigh. His breathing became ragged as his starved passions ignited. He buried his hand deep in her hair, pressing her closer to his seeking mouth.

Waves of sensation washed over her as his tongue plunged and retreated with increasing fervor. She moaned and pulled her mouth away from his, gasping for breath and rolling her head against his shoulder.

Spreading her robe open, he trailed his mouth down the sensitive cords of her throat, burying his face in the valley between her breasts and breathing deeply of her unique, spicy scent. His fingers kneaded the outside of her thigh as his thumb rubbed along the inside, moving ever closer to the center of her. He drew a hard, aroused nipple into his mouth, groaning as he licked and teased the tiny bud.

Rachel arched her back and bent backward over the

arm of the chair, parting her thighs slightly as she unconsciously extended the ultimate invitation.

"Oh God, Rachel, I want you so much . . . so much!" Beside himself with need, Seth stretched his fingers up and touched her. She was hot and wet where he stroked her and a low moan escaped from deep in her throat as she reacted to his intimate caress.

He opened his eyes and gazed at her; head thrown back, lips parted, her hair flowing to the floor like an ebony river. Moving his hand to the back of her head, he pulled her up against him until she was sitting straddled across his lap, facing him. Startled by the intimacy of her position, her eyes flew open, but they quickly closed again as he branded her with another searing kiss.

Rachel was lost. Breathlessly, she unbuttoned his shirt, exposing his massive, furred chest. Entwining her arms around his neck, she boldly pressed her naked breasts against him and succumbed to the sensuous magic of skin on skin.

It was Seth who stopped it. The exquisite eroticism of Rachel's breasts pressing against him made him suddenly, acutely aware of what they were about to do, and he knew he couldn't let it happen. Abruptly, he lifted her off his lap and leaped to his feet, steadying her with his hands on her shoulders while she struggled to catch her balance. The two of them stood staring at each other for a long moment as they both tried desperately to calm their frenzied breathing and wobbly legs.

"We can't do this," he rasped, releasing her and taking a shaky step backward.

Rachel stared dumbly at him, the expression in her dark eyes passing from languid, sexual intoxication to confusion to embarrassment. Finally, she nodded in mute agreement.

Another long moment ensued with neither of them knowing what to say. Seth exhaled a long, shuddering breath, trying hard to keep himself from grabbing her again. His passions were flaming so high that it took every bit of will power he could muster not to cast convention to the wind and take her right there on the sitting room rug.

"Go to bed, Rachel. Right now."

But she didn't move. Rather, she continued to look at him, confused and angry by the accusing tone in his voice.

He knew that if she didn't get out of his sight in the next few seconds, he was going to do something they would both regret. Her tousled hair, kiss-swollen lips and flushed cheeks were more temptation than he had ever faced in his life and his resolve was quickly slipping.

"Rachel, don't do this to me. Get out of here!"

With a last hurt and bewildered look, Rachel turned and fled from the room. He heard her receding footsteps as she tore down the little hall and slammed her bedroom door.

Taking a deep, calming breath, Seth stood where he was, trying to calm his rampaging lust enough to negotiate the staircase. Finally, he took a step forward, then winced in pain as he glanced down to where his huge erection still strained against his denims.

"Jesus Christ," he groaned, throwing back his head and taking several more deep gulps of air, "this has got to stop!"

Unbuttoning his fly, he reached inside and gingerly rubbed the throbbing organ, trying to adjust it to a more comfortable position before he attempted to climb the endless flight of stairs.

Standing there in his luxurious sitting room, staring in disgust and frustration at the enormous bulge in his pants and wondering how he would ever make it back up to his bedroom, he resolved that whether Rachel wanted to or not, they were going to talk. He had to make her understand how things were before the fire that ignited every time they touched blazed totally out of control.

Chapter Nine

Reaching warily under an irate hen, Rachel pulled out a fresh, warm egg and added it to the small basket on her arm.

"That's all for today, girls," she said cheerfully. Turning toward the chicken coop door, she almost ran into Seth who was leaning against the doorjamb, a tense, troubled look on his face.

"If you're finished in here, I want to talk to you," he said quietly.

With a curt nod, she brushed past him and walked back toward the house, dreading the confrontation she knew was coming.

Hearing him enter the kitchen behind her, she softly closed the door and turned to face him. "What do you want to talk about?" she asked in what she hoped was an unconcerned voice.

"Last night," he said flatly, "and, don't tell me you don't want to discuss it, because we're going to."

"All right," she agreed, nodding. She walked over to the counter, poured herself a cup of coffee and sat down at the small table. "Just what do you want to discuss?"

"Us."

"What about us?"

"It's got to stop between us."

"And just what is your definition of 'it', Sheriff?"

"Don't play dumb with me, Rachel, it doesn't suit you."

"Why don't you just say what you're here to say?" she demanded, a slight quaver in her voice.

"Okay." He hesitated, gripping the edge of the sink behind him. His throat worked reflexively and his voice sounded strained and unnatural, even to himself.

"You've got to stay away from me. You're a beautiful woman and I'm a — well, I'm a grown man. It . . . affects me when I find you sitting around half dressed . . . like last night. I just want to make sure you understand that and keep it in mind when you're . . . relaxing. I'm only human, Rachel, and I don't want to be tempted to do something we might both regret."

Rachel was speechless. For a moment, she just stared at him, unable to believe what he was insinuating. When she finally found her voice, she rose out of her chair and said icily, "I beg your pardon, Sheriff, but I think you're a little confused as to who has approached whom here. Have you forgotten that on the two occasions you've been "tempted," you came to me? Once, I was in *my* room, asleep in *my* bed, and you came in — uninvited. And, last night, I was innocently sitting in a chair in the parlor when you practically leaped on me. Please remember, also, that you invited me to make use of the common rooms in this house. I have never, *ever*, trespassed into your private domain — which is more than I can say for you. So, if anyone needs to mend their ways as far as "tempting" the other, it is you, not I!"

Seth was silent for a moment, then nodded in grudging agreement. "You're right. I have a hell of a time keeping my hands off you. That's why it's so important you stay away from me."

"I don't see why your lack of control should be my problem," she returned tartly, throwing herself back into her chair.

"God damn it, Rachel!" he exploded. "Quit baiting me. I'm trying to do the honorable thing here and warn you that you're too tempting by half and, unless you want to find yourself in my bed, you better keep your distance!"

"The last place I want to find myself is in your bed," she lied, "so I thank you for the warning. From now on, maybe I should just retire to my room the minute I see the sun setting."

For a moment, she thought she saw a hurt look in his eyes, but he quickly masked it. "You're being a bitch," he growled.

"And you're being an ass!" she returned, turning her back on him. "You're not sixteen years old, Sheriff. As you just pointed out, you're a grown man. You should be able to control your base instincts."

"Just goes to show how little you know about grown men," he snorted, circling the little table so that he again faced her.

"I beg your pardon," she retorted hotly, "I am not entirely without experience with men, I assure you."

"Well then," he sneered, "I guess it must be that those over-educated dandies you knew in Boston spent so much time with their heads in books that they didn't know what real living is all about."

"Oh!" she gasped, again jumping to her feet as his insult hit its target. "And you think that 'real living', as you call it, includes forcing your attentions on disinterested women?"

"Disinterested!" he shouted. "I'd hardly call your reactions to my attentions 'disinterested'."

She had no response to this last barb and felt an embarrassed flush creep up her cheeks, knowing that what he said was true. She had lain in bed for many hours last night, berating herself for her wanton behavior. Her very proper upbringing and innate maidenly modesty seemed to completely desert her whenever she was exposed to a full onslaught of his overwhelming masculinity. The silence lengthened as they stood glaring at each other over the kitchen table. It was Rachel who finally dropped her eyes. "All right," she conceded, "I'll admit that you caught me at a vulnerable moment and I might have overreacted to your primitive advances. But you needn't concern yourself. It won't happen again."

"You've said that before. This time, make sure it doesn't." He started toward the door, hitting it with his fist as he slammed through it. But, before it stopped swinging, he did an about face and came back through it.

"What the hell do you mean, 'primitive advances'?"

Rachel had all she could do not to laugh, so offended was the look on his face. "You heard me. Your kisses are, well, primitive."

"You don't know the meaning of the word, lady," he lashed out, furious at this last insult. "If I'd let myself get 'primitive' last night, you would have found yourself on your back in the middle of the sitting room rug, and that's a fact. So, don't talk to me about primitive."

Rachel stared at him incredulously, and with more bravado than she was feeling, said, "You wouldn't do that."

In a voice that brooked no argument, he snapped, *"Don't tempt me!"* Then he wheeled around and stomped out of the kitchen.

Rachel sank back into her chair and raised shaking fingers to her lips. She stared off into the distance for a moment, trying to gather her scattered emotions. So, Seth was having trouble resisting her . . . Heady nectar, that, considering she hadn't even *tried* to tempt him! She knew she should be incensed by his high-handed attitude, but, despite herself, a thrill of excitement skittered down her spine. There was something intoxicating in knowing that her mere presence could tempt the implacable Sheriff Wellesley, and she couldn't help but be pleased by the knowledge that he wasn't immune to her feminine charms.

She exhaled a long sigh, suddenly yearning for things she was afraid would never be. If only he felt more than just lust for her! She knew, deep down, that she was slowly, inexorably falling in love with the enigmatic sheriff, but she was totally at a loss as to how to encourage a like feeling in him.

But, she smiled wryly, at least lust was a start! Just knowing he'd thought about making love to her on the parlor rug made her shiver deliciously. Although she'd sooner die than admit it to him, she knew the images that thought conjured up were going to keep her awake nights.

Chapter Ten

Rachel peeked curiously out her window at the young woman walking up the path to her office. She had been in Stone Creek for three months now and knew that this well-dressed, stylish lady was not a resident. Nor was the child with her familiar. They were a striking pair, this pretty girl and her daughter. The resemblance between them was obvious—blond, blue eyed and delicate. Although the woman was obviously pregnant, she was still slim and her piquant face was vibrant. By the time they reached the door, Rachel's curiosity was acute.

As the woman raised her hand to knock, Rachel opened the door. "May I help you?" she asked, smiling.

The woman's eyes swept over her with a slightly appraising look and in a soft, husky voice, she replied, "I hope so. I'm looking for Seth Wellesley. I was given this address but no one answered the front door. I wonder if you know where I might find him?"

The fact that this gorgeous blond creature was looking for Seth made Rachel's heart contract painfully. Still, she opened the door wider and said, "I'm sorry, I don't know where the sheriff is, but you're welcome to step inside to wait, if you wish."

"Thank you," the woman smiled. "It's rather warm out here and I'd appreciate being able to sit down."

"By all means," Rachel agreed. "Do come in."

Leading the little girl by the hand, the woman walked into the waiting room and sank gratefully onto the sofa.

A flicker of concern crossed Rachel's face. "Are you feeling all right? Can I get you anything?"

"No, thank you," she smiled. "It just feels good to sit down. It was a long walk from the train depot and I'm afraid I don't have as much energy as usual right now."

"I understand," Rachel smiled. "Why don't I get us some lemonade?"

"If you're sure it's no trouble, that would be wonderful," the girl replied.

"No trouble at all," Rachel assured her and hastened back into the main house.

When she returned and they were all seated, the woman extended her hand and said, "I'm Paula O'Neill and this is Amelia. You must be Dr. Hayes."

Rachel looked at her in surprise. "Why, yes, I am. You must forgive me, Mrs. O'Neill, but I seem to be at a loss. Do we know each other?"

"No, but, they told me at the depot that Seth had the town's new doctor living in his spare room and I assume that must be you. I must confess I was expecting a man."

"Everyone was," Rachel laughed, liking the vivacious woman despite herself. "Are you a friend of the sheriff's?"

"Well, yes, you might say that. I'm his sister."

A wave of relief washed over Rachel and she smiled broadly. "How wonderful! I'm sure he'll be delighted to see you. He told me he had a sister and he speaks so fondly of you."

"Really?" Paula chuckled. "I've always thought most of my brothers considered me more of a nuisance than anything else. I'm glad to hear that at least Seth harbors a little affection for me."

Rachel leaned back into the sofa cushions, relaxing

100

and thoroughly enjoying the girl's company. "Your daughter is lovely, Mrs. O'Neill. How old is she?"

Paula's brows lifted in surprise, but she smiled and answered, "Amelia is four, but she's not my daughter."

Now, it was Rachel's turn to look surprised. "No?"

"No," she replied with a shake of her golden curls. Her voice dropped so that the child couldn't hear her. "Lia is Seth's little girl."

Rachel felt as though she'd been punched in the stomach. "Seth's?" she whispered.

"Yes," Paula nodded, "you didn't know he has a child?"

"No," Rachel stammered, "he's never said anything about it." She quickly turned her face away, but not before Paula saw the shock and hurt registered on it. Staring blankly at Amelia, Rachel willed herself to be calm. She didn't want Seth's sister, of all people, to see how upset she was.

A child . . . he has a *child,* she thought miserably. And, what about a wife? Does he have one of those too?

This thought made her stomach lurch sickeningly. Dear God, would he have almost made love to her if he had a wife somewhere? And, if he did, why wasn't she here with him?

A sudden feeling of desolation engulfed her — one so devastating that she wasn't sure she'd be able to voice the question she knew she had to ask. Clearing her throat, she rasped, "Is . . . is Seth married?"

"No," Paula said quickly, concerned by Rachel's stricken expression. "He's a widower. You didn't know that either?"

"He's never said a word!" Rachel responded, her voice louder as anger asserted itself. "I even asked him once if all his brothers and sisters were married and he told me that everyone but he and his youngest brother were."

101

"Well, that *is* the truth," Paula defended. "He's not married . . . now."

"Has his wife been dead long?"

Paula looked at Rachel speculatively for a moment, then nodded. "Childbirth?" Rachel prodded.

"No . . ." Paula hedged, unsure of how much Seth would want her to divulge. "He's never said anything at all about his family?"

"Well, he told me all about his brothers and you, but nothing about a wife or a child."

"Oh, Seth," Paula sighed. "That's just like him. He never did talk much. He's always so private about everything. He's almost as quiet as our brother Eric and *he* hardly says anything from one month to the next."

Rachel didn't reply. She just sat on the couch and stared at Amelia. "A child," she murmured unconsciously.

Paula remained silent, sipping her lemonade and eyeing Rachel pensively.

Finally, Rachel broke the awkward silence. "How did you happen to pick this time to bring Amelia visiting? Wouldn't you be more comfortable in your own home?"

"She's not here for a visit," Paula said quietly, moving closer to Rachel so as not to be overheard. "I'm leaving her here. My husband, Luke, and I are going East for a while."

"You're leaving her?" Rachel gasped. "Does Seth know?"

Paula shook her head. "No. That's why I need to see him before I leave."

Rachel stared distractedly at Amelia, wondering how Seth would react to this sudden, momentous change in his life.

Forcing her eyes away from the beautiful child, she smiled politely and asked, "Why are you making this trip now?"

"The doctor in Durango is concerned that I might have a hard time delivering my baby," she explained. "He advised me to go east to seek medical attention there. The doctors and facilities in the big cities are so much more advanced than out here and I don't want anything to go wrong."

Rachel swept her with a professional gaze. "I think your doctor is right. You're narrow in the hips and if your husband is a large man and your baby is large also, you might have a difficult time."

"My husband is even bigger than Seth," Paula chuckled. "We're going to Boston to stay with my brother, Stuart. I don't feel right taking Amelia with me, so I thought it would be best to bring her here. Seth has only seen her a few times since she was born and I think it's time he started raising her. She's at the age now where she should know her real father."

Rachel nodded shakily, feeling overwhelmed by all she had heard. "How do you think he's going to react to having Amelia?"

"I don't know," Paula admitted. "But, I hope he'll be happy about it."

Both women jumped as they heard the front door slam. Seth was home.

"Do you want to go into the kitchen to talk to him?" Rachel asked. "I don't want to interfere."

"Yes," Paula nodded. "That might be best."

"Rachel?" Seth's voice boomed down the hallway. "Where are you?"

"In my office," she called back.

"Has anybody been here looking for me? I heard that some woman with a little kid was asking . . ."

He stopped in mid-sentence as he walked into the room and saw his sister. His face broke into a smile of sheer delight as he pulled Paula off the couch and enveloped her in a hug. "Well, look what the wind blew in!" he exclaimed, taking a step back to get a better look at her. Then, noticing her girth, he grinned and said, "Look at you, little girl. You're big as a cow!"

"I am not!" Paula protested indignantly. "I've hardly gained any weight at all, Seth Wellesley, so don't you *dare* say I look like a cow!"

Seth continued to guffaw as he pulled her back into his arms. "It's good to see you, darlin'," he crooned. "Is that blacksmith of yours treating you good?"

"Obviously," Paula chuckled with a meaningful look at her stomach.

Suddenly, Seth noticed the child sitting quietly on the floor. His arms dropped away from around Paula's waist and he took a tentative step forward, his face pale. "Lia?" he whispered.

The little girl looked up and smiled engagingly. "Hi," she chirped.

His eyes slid back to Paula. "What is she doing here?"

With a quick glance in the child's direction, Paula said, "Come on, Seth, let's go in the kitchen for a minute. I need to talk to you."

His eyes never leaving his daughter, he said quietly, "Does she know who I am?"

"No," Paula answered shortly. "Now, come on. I don't have much time."

Seth still made no move to leave. Instead, he squatted down in front of Amelia and said, "Hello, sweetheart."

Amelia looked at him with interest for a moment, then returned to combing her doll's hair.

He straightened up, glancing over at Rachel as if noticing her for the first time. "Has Paula told you?"

She nodded.

He again turned to his sister, pinning her with an accusatory glare. Paula, however, was unconcerned, accustomed to dealing with seven older brothers.

"Don't glare at me, Seth," she chuckled. "Just come

in the kitchen and we'll discuss this. And quit dallying! My train leaves in less than an hour."

"Train? What train? You leaving already? Where are you going? What are you doing here, anyway?"

"Seth," she sighed, "if you'll just come with me, I'll explain everything."

With a curt nod, Seth followed his sister down the hall. Amelia got up to follow Paula, but Rachel waylaid her. Sitting down next to her on the floor, she said, "Would you show me how you braid your dolly's hair?"

The little girl nodded, sufficiently distracted to remain in the office.

Rachel slid backward until she was sitting near the door, knowing she shouldn't eavesdrop, but unable to control her curiosity. By positioning herself so, she could hear everything Seth and Paula said but, as the conversation progressed, she became more and more confused.

Paula's voice floated down the hall as she finished explaining the reason for her brief visit. ". . . so you see, you're going to have to take her now."

There was a long silence, then she heard Seth say, "You know I can't do that, honey."

"You have no choice," Paula said briskly. "She's your daughter and it's time you both realized that."

"Paula, be reasonable. I have no one to take care of her and, God knows, with my schedule, I can't."

"Well, then, you're just going to have to change your schedule," she answered. "There must be some woman in town who can help you."

"No one in town even knows I have a child."

"They will now."

"Paula, you know there's more to it than that. If Brady finds out . . ."

Paula hesitated for a moment. "I know that's a concern, but there's nothing that can be done about it, Seth. You'll just have to think of something."

Seth's voice rose in annoyance as he realized Paula wasn't going to be swayed. "I'll just have to think of something *else,* you mean," he muttered. "Maybe I can send her up to Eric and Kirsten."

Paula shook her head. "Kirsten's pregnant again and they already have three. You can't burden them with another."

"Damn it, Paula, you're putting me in a hell of a spot here."

"I'm sorry, Seth, I know this is all pretty sudden. But, it's time for you to give up this nonsense about Brady and start living again. I think having Lia is just what you need to do that."

Seth rose from the table, his voice tense and angry. "You, of all people, should understand why I can't do that."

"I do understand," Paula soothed, "but, it's time to put it behind you. It was a long time ago and your daughter is more important than your vendetta."

Rachel peeked out the door and saw Seth pacing across the kitchen, raking his hands through his hair in agitation. Paula rose from the table and walked over to him, putting her arms around him and drawing him close.

"I have to go, Seth. Please understand, there's no other way."

Seth looked down at her and, finally, smiled in resignation. "I know, Paula, and you've done more for me than any sister ought to."

"You'll thank me for this, Seth," she said positively. "Now, will you drive me back to the station?"

"Yeah. It'll just take me a minute to hitch up the team."

As he went out the back door, Paula walked back to Rachel's office. After speaking quietly to Amelia for a few minutes, she turned to Rachel and said, "I need to ask a favor of you, Dr. Hayes."

106

Rachel nodded, bewildered by what she had just overheard and hoping that maybe Paula would offer some explanation.

"It's obvious you don't know anything about Seth's past and it's not my place to tell you. But, it's also obvious that there's more between you two than you want to admit. So, if you feel that you have any influence at all over my brother, please help him with this. Don't let him send Lia away again. He needs her more than you could ever know."

"I'll do anything I can to help," Rachel promised, "but, I really don't think—"

Paula held up her hand. "Just do your best . . . that's all I'm asking. I know Seth is a hard man, but he's been through a lot. He needs Lia and he needs you."

"Me?"

"Yes, you. I saw the way he looked at you when he walked in here."

"Oh, Mrs. O'Neill, I'm afraid you're wrong . . ."

Paula gave her a level look and then said, "Do you care for Seth, Dr. Hayes?"

After a long moment, Rachel nodded.

Paula smiled. "I thought so. And since you've admitted that, I have another favor to ask. Will you do one more thing for me?"

At Rachel's nod, Paula gave her a quick hug and whispered, "Marry my big brother. Give him about ten kids and love him for the rest of his life."

Rachel stepped back, gaping at Paula in stunned silence, but before she could utter a response, Paula turned and, with a last wave, disappeared down the hall.

Chapter Eleven

Seth leaned against the porch pillar, smoking a cigarette and staring into the deep blackness of the moonless prairie. The quiet squeak of the screen door told him that Rachel had joined him, but he didn't turn around.

"Is she asleep?" he asked quietly.

"Yes," she sighed, "finally."

It had been a terrible evening. Scared, confused, and lonely for Paula, Amelia had cried for hours after they put her to bed in one of the huge guest rooms upstairs. Rachel had sung to her and told her every bedtime story she had ever known, but nothing worked. Finally, in desperation, she lay down and rocked her until the exhausted child finally fell into a fitful sleep.

"I appreciate you tending her," Seth said. "I don't know anything about little girls."

"Well, I'm afraid you're going to have to learn," she returned wryly.

A long silence ensued and Rachel was just turning to go back in the house when Seth spoke again, his voice strained. "I know I should have told you. I just didn't know how."

"You don't owe me any explanations, Sheriff," she said stiffly, her hand on the door.

He turned, annoyed that she had again reverted to

using his title instead of his name. "Please try to understand. Some things are hard for me to talk about."

Rachel nodded curtly and pulled the door open.

"You're mad, aren't you?" It was a statement rather than a question.

She paused. "Of course, I'm not mad," she lied. "I just said, you don't owe me any explanations. Your personal life is your own and I respect that, Sheriff."

"For Christ's sake, quit calling me 'Sheriff'! I hate it when you act like this."

"Act like what?" Rachel exploded, whirling around to face him. "Act like I'm not involved in your life? Well, obviously, I'm not. If I was, I think you would have told me something as important as the fact that you've been married and have a daughter."

"I just told you, some things are hard for me to talk about."

"I understand that, but some things are important enough to make the effort. Don't you think this is something I deserved to know with what . . . what's passed between us? Did you think I'd never find out?"

"No. I just hoped the time would come that I could tell you."

"You mean, when you felt you could trust me?" she asked, her voice bitter.

"No, I trust you now."

"Then, what?"

Seth took a deep breath, knowing the time had come to break his long silence about the past. Taking Rachel's hand where it still rested on the doorknob, he said, "Come out in the yard with me. I don't want to wake her."

He didn't drop her hand and Rachel felt a surge of longing just having him touch her. They walked out into the yard and Seth sat down cross legged, pulling her down in the grass next to him.

"I've never told anyone outside of my family what I'm going to tell you and you have to promise to keep it absolutely secret. It could mean Amelia's life."

"Her life!" Rachel gasped. "What in the world are you talking about?"

"My wife, Anna, didn't just die, Rachel. She was murdered, along with my son, James. Amelia's all I have left and the only reason she's still alive is that the murderer didn't know she existed."

"Oh, my God," Rachel cried, her hand flying to her mouth in horror. "Who? Why? Do you have any idea who did it?"

"Yeah," Seth answered, staring off into the distance. "I know."

"Well, who?"

"Clint Brady."

Rachel's eyes widened in sudden understanding, realizing how many things had just been explained. "Seth, please tell me," she whispered shakily.

He looked at her for a long moment, then nodded. Lying back in the grass, he pulled her down with him, curving his arm around her shoulder and nestling her head against his chest. His voice was tense and strained and Rachel knew what an effort it took for him to confide in her.

"Six years ago, I took a job as sheriff of a little town about thirty miles from Durango where I grew up. I met a girl and we got married. We had a son the first year and then Lia followed the next."

"Everything was fine for the first year. We were happy, my job was going well, we had a son and another baby on the way . . . Then, the trouble with Brady started. He and his gang were robbing banks, trains, ranches. They killed anybody who got in their way, especially lawmen. I went after them and caught

110

several of his boys, but I could never get to Brady. I had him scared though. He killed my deputy, Tom Bolt, and sent his body back to me thrown over a horse with a message pinned to it that if I didn't back off, I'd be sorry."

"Oh, Seth, how awful!"

"Yeah," he nodded. "But I couldn't give up. Tom was my best friend and I vowed I'd get Brady if it was the last thing I ever did. And I finally caught him."

"Yóu caught him?" Rachel asked, perplexed. "Then, why isn't he in jail?"

"Because his gang busted him out . . . the same night I brought him in. Brady left another note on my desk at the jail telling me that I should have killed him while I had the chance because now it was personal between us and I was going to pay."

Seth gently removed his arm from around her shoulders, sat up and stared across the prairie. Rachel sat up next to him, lightly placing her hand over his. When he finally continued, his voice was shaking. "I should have killed him."

"Seth," she said with a shiver, "you don't have to tell me anymore. I can guess the rest."

"No," he rasped. "I need to tell you. That way, maybe you'll see why I feel the way I do about having Lia here."

Rachel nodded hesitantly and waited for him to continue. He threw back his head and closed his eyes.

"He went to my house one day while I was at the office. He . . . he tied Anna and James up. Then . . . then, he set fire to my house and burned them alive!"

"Oh my God, Seth!" Reaching toward the trembling man, Rachel pulled him into her embrace,

111

stroking his hair and crooning to him as if he was a small child.

"So, you see," he continued, his voice muffled against her neck, "that's why I've had to hide Lia. If Brady ever found out about her, he'd kill her for sure."

"How did she escape him when he came to your house?"

"She wasn't home. Anna was recovering from a bout of birth fever and I'd taken the baby over to a friend's for the day so Anna could rest. Brady must not have known that I had another child because he bragged to all his cronies that he'd wiped out my entire family."

"I don't know what to say," Rachel whispered. "It's monstrous. I don't know how you survived with your sanity."

"I almost didn't," he admitted. "And I'll never rest until I catch him. Maybe now you'll see why I have to send Amelia away. I can't take the chance that somebody will find out she's my child. If even one person knows, it could get back to Brady and it might mean her life."

Rachel stared at him for a long moment, hating to break the intimacy his confession had created between them, but knowing she must.

"I can't agree with that, Seth. You can't keep shuttling Amelia off. She's your daughter, not a ball to be bounced from one of your brothers to the next. Her place is here with you."

Seth's lips thinned. "You make it sound like I don't want her," he said defensively.

"I don't think that. I just think you're being selfish."

"Selfish? What the hell do you mean, selfish? Damn it, Rachel, I've just explained this whole situation to you and you still don't understand. It's not safe for her to be here and I won't risk her life just to have her with me. What's selfish about that? If anything, I'm being *un*selfish. As soon as I get Brady, then she can live with me."

"Seth," Rachel said, her voice conciliatory, "Amelia is already four years old. You've been after Brady all that time. What if it takes you the next ten years to get him? She could be all grown up before that happens."

"You don't have much faith in me, do you?" he asked, his voice hurt.

"That isn't the point! Your daughter is growing up not even knowing she *has* a father and you're the only one who can remedy that."

"And, what if Brady finds out?"

"He won't if we can come up with a plan to deceive everyone about who she is."

"*We?*" he said meaningfully, slanting a sideways look at her.

"Yes, *we*," she answered, looking straight back at him. "I think I can help you with this."

"How?" he asked, his expression rapt.

"Let me think a minute. Subterfuge . . . what we need is to make people accept Lia's presence in Stone Creek without guessing who she really is."

"Yeah," Seth nodded, "but how?"

Rachel closed her eyes a moment, leaning back on her arms and thinking. Suddenly, she sat up straight, a broad smile wreathing her face. "I've got it! We'll tell everyone she's related to me—my niece or something."

As Seth started to shake his head, she grabbed his hand and continued, "Oh, don't say 'no'! It could work, Seth! We'll just say that—that Lia is my niece—my sister's child, maybe—and that my sister

113

was recently killed in an accident or something and that I have been appointed her guardian."

"No," he said, shaking his head, "absolutely not."

"But, why?" Rachel protested, feeling deflated.

"Lots of reasons. Mostly because you pretending to be her aunt will just confuse her more than she already is. I won't raise her with lies and deceptions. If she's living with me, then I want her to know that I'm her pa, not just some stranger who sits down to supper every night."

Rachel frowned, understanding his logic but stubborn in her belief that Amelia should live with him, regardless of who she might think he is.

"It's only temporary," she placated. "As soon as you catch Brady, you can tell her the truth. She's young enough that a temporary deception isn't going to have any lasting effects on her."

"How do you know that?"

"Well, I don't for sure," she admitted. "But, I'm sure that as she gets older and understands why it was necessary to deceive her, she'll understand. And, I think if she was old enough to voice an opinion, she'd tell you she wanted to be with you, no matter what."

Seth pulled his hand away and ran his fingers through his hair. "If even one person found out who she really is, it could mean her life."

"No one is going to find out!"

Seth stared out into the darkness for such a long time that Rachel feared the conversation was over. Finally, he turned toward her, a haunted look in his eyes. "Do you have any idea what she means to me? Can you possibly imagine what it was like to ride up to my house and find it burned to the ground? To know that my wife and my son were dead?"

"No. I can't imagine," Rachel replied quietly. "No

one should ever have to know what that's like. But, it's in the past, Seth. Life is for the living and all of us must face that. We can't bring back the dead and we can't undo what's been done. All we can do is try to go on with what's been left to us. And Amelia is what God left you. It's as simple as that."

"Nothing's simple," he argued. "I can't take care of her."

"I just told you I'd help you," she repeated, her heart in her throat.

"No." He shook his head.

"Why?"

"It's out of the question," he insisted, rising. "I'll write my brothers tomorrow and see who can take her." Turning, he started walking back toward the house.

Rachel also jumped to her feet, incensed by Seth's stubbornness. Racing after him, she grabbed him by the arm, spinning him around to face her. "You're pathetic, do you know that?" she raged. "You've built such a wall around yourself that you won't let anybody help you. They might get too close and you might be forced to feel something again. That's why you won't accept my help, isn't it?"

Seth looked away, unable to meet her blazing eyes. "Yes, that's exactly why," he answered softly. "Because if you get involved with Lia, then you get involved with me and I'm not ready to get involved with anyone—especially you."

"Oh . . ." Rachel breathed, devastated by his flat rejection.

Seth had never felt so awful in his life. He turned back toward her, his expression filled with pain and remorse. "Rachel, I'd like for us to be friends, but don't try to get close to me. I don't want to hurt you, but you have to understand that I'm just not capable

115

of ever loving a woman again. Enforcing the law is my life now and it's all I want."

Rachel stared at him for a long moment, feeling a hollow emptiness in the pit of her stomach. "I understand," she said quietly, "and I promise you, I won't interfere again. I thought I could help you through a difficult time. But, it's obvious you don't want my help. Well, Sheriff, you can rest easy. You've made your feelings perfectly clear and I can assure you that I won't impose myself on you again."

With great dignity, she lifted the hem of her skirt and walked up the steps, closing the kitchen door softly behind her.

Abruptly, Seth moved toward her, but then checked himself, leaning against the porch pillar and swearing softly under his breath. What the hell was wrong with him? Why did he treat this beautiful, caring woman so shabbily? He knew he was being unfair, but, damn it, she evoked feelings in him that he just wasn't ready to face.

For four long years, he had isolated himself from emotional entanglements of any kind. And, despite his self-imposed loneliness, there was a comforting sense of security about his life. When you had no one to lose, you had nothing to fear.

Then Rachel had entered his life and, despite himself, he was again suffering the exquisite tortures of passion and longing—emotions he'd thought long dead and ones he had no desire to resurrect. But, every time he looked at her piquant face or heard her melodic laughter, his long-repressed desires to love and be loved rose like a phoenix, demanding that he admit he was still capable of feeling a man's yearnings.

And, with gentle persuasion and irrefutable logic, she was forcing him to face other truths, as well. He *did* want to keep Amelia with him. His life had been empty for so long. And Rachel, with her generous heart, was offering to help him obtain what he wanted most in the world. So, why had he thrown that offer back in her face?

He lit a cigarette, drawing on it deeply. He knew the answer to that question. He was falling in love with her and he couldn't allow that to happen. Moodily, he continued smoking, considering his options.

He probably could convince one of his brothers to take Lia, but was that really fair to anybody? Miles was out of the question way off in England, and Stuart had Paula and Luke on his hands. Paula had said that Kirsten was pregnant again and she and Eric already had three kids and a huge farm to run. Nathan might be a possibility—or Geoff—but it had been so long since he had corresponded with either of them that he had no idea what their current situations were. That left only Adam and he was just a kid in college, so there was no help there.

What other choice did he really have except to try Rachel's plan? And maybe, just maybe, it *could* work. If she was willing to live with the ruse that Amelia was her niece, couldn't he? In all likelihood, no one *would* find out the truth unless one of them told it. And, when he finally caught Brady, then he could shout it to the world that Amelia was his daughter.

Rachel was right. Lia was his responsibility. And, somehow, the thought of having the little tow-headed sprite cavorting around the big house he'd built for her filled him with a sense of joy he had not felt in a long, long time. Smiling into the darkness, he flicked his cigarette away, knowing that he had made his decision.

With a light step, he hurried back into the house

and proceeded down the short hall to Rachel's room. He knocked on her door, hoping that she was not already asleep. His smile broadened when the door opened and she peered sleepily out at him.

Without a word, he clapped his hands on the sides of her face, and gave her a resounding kiss on the lips. Stepping back, he grinned hugely and said, "Thank you, you wonderful woman." Then, he pivoted on his heel and disappeared into the darkness, leaving her to stare after him in wonder.

Chapter Twelve

Seth walked into the kitchen just as Rachel set a bowl of oatmeal in front of Amelia.

"Good morning," she said cheerfully. "Can I fix you something for breakfast? Would you like some oatmeal?"

"No thanks," he answered, walking over to the counter and pouring a cup of coffee.

"Auntie Rachel and me are going to have ice cream," Amelia announced from the table.

"You are?" Seth chuckled, sitting down next to his daughter.

"Yes," she affirmed. "Chocolate ice cream."

"Everyone meets at the Icy Treat on Sunday afternoons so I thought it would be a perfect opportunity to introduce Amelia to Stone Creek," Rachel explained.

"Sounds like a good idea," Seth nodded. "Do you want me to go along?"

"I don't think so," she answered quietly. "I don't want anyone to get the idea that the three of us are somehow involved, so I think it would be better if I took her alone."

Seth nodded again, then turned his attention back to Amelia. "Do you like that stuff, honey?" he asked.

Amelia looked up, surprised that the big man was talking to her. "Yes," she nodded. "It's sweet."

"Sweet?" Seth looked over at Rachel questioningly.

"Brown sugar," she smiled.

He grinned knowingly. "That's what my ma used to put on it to get us to eat it too." Draining his coffee cup, he said, "I'm going to feed the horses, then I've got to go to the office for a while. Will you two be all right here alone till I get back?"

Rachel nodded. "We'll be just fine. You go and do what you need to do and don't worry about us."

Seth rose, ruffling Amelia's hair affectionately as he passed behind her. Pausing, he said, "Do you know what my name is, Lia?"

The child nodded confidently.

"What?"

"Lawman," she said without hesitation.

"Lawman?" he snorted. "Who told you my name is Lawman?"

"Uncle Luke said the man I was going to see was a lawman."

Unable to help herself, Rachel burst out laughing. "Let's see you refute that one, 'Lawman.' "

"Damn it," Seth growled, turning toward her, "I don't want her calling me that!"

"What do you want her to call you?"

"Well," he hesitated, "what is she calling you?"

"Auntie Rachel."

"No help there," he muttered. "But, she's not going to call me, 'Lawman,' damn it!"

"Quit swearing!" Rachel ordered.

"Sorry," he said sheepishly, casting a furtive glance in Amelia's direction.

"What do you want her to call you?" Rachel asked again.

"You know what I'd like her to call me."

"That's impossible. She might slip and call you that in front of someone."

"I know," he admitted bitterly. "God, I hate this already."

"Just be patient," she advised. "It will all work out."

Seth sighed heavily. "Can't come soon enough for me."

"In the meantime, what should she call you?"

He thought a moment and then said, "Seth, I guess. I sure as hell don't want her to call me Mr. Wellesley and, I suppose 'Uncle' Seth is out of the question."

Rachel nodded. "Absolutely." Turning toward Amelia, she said, "This man's name isn't 'Lawman', honey. Why don't you call him Seth like I do."

"Okay," Amelia nodded agreeably, returning to her cereal. "Who is he?"

Seth bit down hard on his lip.

Rachel shot him a quick glance and seeing how close he was to revealing the secret, quickly interjected, "He's the nice man who owns this house and lets us live here."

Amelia looked at Seth assessingly and said, "His hair's the same color as mine."

"I know," Rachel responded, throwing a worried glance in Seth's direction.

Seth, too, was frowning at his daughter's astute observation, but when he saw Rachel looking at him, he shrugged and said, "Can't be helped." With a last affectionate caress to Amelia's hair, he started toward the door. "See you later."

Rachel watched him out the window as he headed toward the barn, her thoughts drifting back to the previous night's kiss. "Put it out of your mind, girl," she told herself firmly. But still, a wistful smile hovered at the corner of her mouth as her mind's eye envisioned his lips descending—soft, warm, and delicious.

Dressed in their very best, Rachel and Amelia pushed open the door of the Icy Treat Ice Cream Parlor. The small establishment was full of people and Ra-

121

chel drew a deep breath, hoping that her yet untried acting talents would carry her through the coming performance.

The first person she saw was Betsy Fulbright sitting at a small table with her grandson, Sam. Sam, as usual, was behaving badly and Mrs. Fulbright was discreetly trying to prevent the unruly child from climbing on top of the table.

Betsy's struggles with her grandson were instantly abandoned, however, when she saw the small child holding Rachel's hand.

"Come on, honey," Rachel encouraged, propelling Amelia toward Betsy's table. "Let's beard the lion in her own den."

"Hello, Mrs. Fulbright," she said brightly, a dazzling smile on her face.

"Hello, Dr. Hayes," Betsy answered, grabbing the back of Sam's jacket as he took off toward the soda fountain. Pushing him into a chair without ever breaking eye contact with Rachel, she asked, "And who do we have here? Why don't you and your little friend join us?"

Rachel sat down, helping Amelia into the chair next to hers. "This is my niece, Amelia."

"Your niece?" Betsy repeated, her eyebrows disappearing into her hair.

"Yes," Rachel said smoothly. "My sister's daughter."

"Was that your sister who got off the train with her yesterday?"

Rachel cringed, wondering how their luck could be so bad that Betsy Fulbright, of all people, would have seen Paula.

"Well, no," she stammered, trying to think of a plausible explanation for who had accompanied Amelia. "You see, my sister and her husband were recently killed."

"Oh?" Betsy responded, looking hard at Amelia.

"Yes, and since I'm Amelia's only living relative, I've been appointed her guardian. She's going to be living with me now, so I thought I'd bring her to have some ice cream and get acquainted." Rachel held her breath, hoping that Amelia wouldn't innocently refute her lies.

"I'm so sorry to hear of your loss, dear," Mrs. Fulbright gushed, not sounding sorry at all. "How is it that you haven't mentioned your niece coming before this? I just saw you last week and you didn't say a word about it."

"Well," Rachel hedged, "actually, I didn't know. I mean, I got word that my sister had been killed several weeks ago, but I didn't know that Amelia was coming yesterday until she arrived."

"You mean you didn't know that you'd been appointed her guardian?" Betsy questioned, her eyebrows rising to new heights. "How strange that your sister's attorneys wouldn't notify you before just sending the child on."

"Oh, I knew," Rachel said hurriedly. "I just didn't expect her so soon."

"So, who *was* the woman who brought her on the train. A friend of yours?"

"No," Rachel answered, casting another look at Amelia to see if she was paying any attention to the conversation. Thankfully, the little girl was too engrossed with trying to prevent Sam from stealing the cherry off the top of her sundae to pay any attention to the adults. "She was a court-appointed temporary guardian."

"I see," answered Betsy slowly. "Well, this is certainly going to make a change in your life, isn't it?"

"I imagine so, Rachel nodded. "But, Amelia is the age to start school in the fall so I don't think her being here will cause any problems with my practice. I'll just have to find someone to watch her for a short while after school every day."

"It's gratifying that you take your responsibility toward the health of Stone Creek's citizens so seriously," Betsy said, delicately sipping her phosphate. "And what does the sheriff think about having a child under his roof?"

"I . . . I really don't know. We haven't talked about it."

"You mean Seth doesn't know about this new development?"

"Well, yes, he knows. I mean, he was there when Amelia arrived yesterday, but he didn't seem to have any problem with her moving into my room with me."

"Seth certainly has an understanding nature," Betsy remarked.

Hearing her father's name, Amelia gave up the battle for the cherry and said, "Seth's a lawman."

Betsy's head whipped around and she stared at the child for a long moment. "How do you know that, Amelia?" she asked, her voice sharp.

"Auntie Paula told me."

Rachel's heart dropped into her stomach. Dear God, she thought desperately, was the game going to be up so soon?

"And who is Auntie Paula?" Betsy prodded, leaning forward in eager anticipation.

Amelia shrugged and looked at Rachel. "Auntie Paula."

"The woman who accompanied her on the train was named Paula, Rachel replied hurriedly. "Maybe she told Amelia to call her 'Auntie Paula'."

"And this court-appointed guardian told Amelia about Sheriff Wellesley?" Betsy questioned.

"Must have," Rachel laughed a trifle nervously.

"But how would this woman even know about Seth?"

"I don't really know. Maybe the court did some investigating into my situation before naming me Amelia's guardian."

"I suppose that's possible," Betsy said doubtfully, again looking at Amelia. "Well, Dr. Hayes, your niece is lovely. It's interesting that she's so fair when your hair is so dark."

"My sister was blond," Rachel answered. "She looked like our mother while I favored Father's side of the family."

"Interesting how that happens sometimes," Betsy noted, finishing her soda and pulling on her gloves. "One would think that children in the same family would all have similar looks and coloring, but, I guess, that isn't always the case."

"No," Rachel answered, "not always."

Betsy rose from the table and smiled benignly down at Amelia. "Come on, Sam, time to go home." Turning toward Rachel, she said, "It was a pleasure to see you, my dear. If there's anything Mayor Fulbright or I can do to help you make this sudden transition into motherhood, please don't hesitate to ask."

Taking Sam by the hand, she exited the ice cream parlor, nodding and smiling to the other patrons as she went.

Rachel exhaled a long sigh and stared down at her suddenly shaking hands. Had the old biddy believed her story? It was hard to tell but, even if she didn't, she had no way to prove that Rachel was lying. At least the interview was over, and for that she was extremely grateful.

"Are you finished with your ice cream, Amelia?" she asked.

"I want a cherry!" Amelia responded, her little rosebud mouth screwed up into a pout.

"Did that naughty Sam take your cherry?"

"Yes," Amelia nodded. "He's nasty."

"He certainly is!" Rachel agreed. "Well, you just come with me. I bet that man behind the counter over there has another one that he might give you if you ask nicely."

Betsy Fulbright sailed through the front doors of her house and headed directly for her bedroom, never slowing her pace even when Martin called out a greeting.

"Wait a moment, dear," she called over her shoulder as she passed the parlor where he was reading the newspaper. "I have an incredible story to tell you, but I have to get something from the bedroom first."

Betsy disappeared through the door, reappearing a moment later with a worn letter in her hand. Hurrying into the parlor, she perched on the edge of a velvet settee and said, "I just had the most extraordinary time at the Icy Treat. I could hardly wait to get home to tell you about it."

Knowing his quiet interlude was over, Martin regretfully folded the newspaper, set it in his lap and turned his attention to his flushed and excited wife. "I'm all ears," he smiled.

"Well," Betsy confided, leaning forward in her most conspiratorial manner, "Rachel Hayes came into the ice cream parlor with a small girl in tow and told me that the child is her niece, Amelia, who has come to Stone Creek to live with her. According to Rachel, this Amelia is her sister's child and her sister and her husband were recently killed, leaving Rachel with the guardianship of their daughter."

A long silence ensued as Martin waited for more, but when Betsy remained silent, leaning back in her chair and waiting for his reaction, he said blankly, "So?"

"What do you mean, 'So'?" she asked in annoyance. "Rachel Hayes has no sister. I have the letter she wrote us before she came to town in which she says, and I quote, 'Because I am an only child and my parents do not live in Boston, I have nothing to keep me here and am, therefore, most willing to relocate to Kansas.' Now, what do you think of that?"

"Well, uh," Martin stammered, "I don't know exactly what to think. What do you think?"

"I'll tell you what I think. I think that child is Dr. Hayes' daughter, not her niece!"

"But, she's never been married, has she?" he asked.

"My point exactly," Betsy retorted with a smug smile.

"Now, Betsy, whatever might be in Dr. Hayes' past is none of our business. She's doing a fine job—even you said that—and if she has secrets that she doesn't care to share with us, then that's her right."

"Oh, I knew you'd say that!" Betsy snapped, "but I haven't told you everything yet."

Martin sighed. "Then, perhaps you should."

Betsy nodded and with great pretense, announced, "The child is the spitting image of Seth Wellesley!"

"What?" Martin cried. "Oh, now, Betsy, *really!*"

Betsy bolted to her feet and turned an angry glare on her laughing husband. "Don't you dare laugh at me, Martin Fulbright. That child is Seth Wellesley's daughter. Why, she looks exactly like him—even her mannerisms are his."

"So, what you are saying, my dear," Martin wheezed, struggling mightily to stop laughing, "is that Rachel Hayes and Seth Wellesley have a child between them and that they just now decided to let the world know about it? Betsy, I'm sorry, but that's preposterous."

"Oh, Martin, you're infuriating! You haven't even seen the girl. How can you be so sure she's not Seth's child?"

"Now, Betsy, think how illogical this all is," he chuckled. "If what you're saying is true, then we must assume that Seth and Rachel knew each other years ago, had a child together, didn't marry, and didn't see each other for several years. Then, we just *happened* to hire Rachel to be Stone Creek's doctor and she just *happened* to move into Seth's house and now they have decided to bring their child out here, but lie about who she is. Really, dear, does that make sense?"

"Oh, Martin, don't be a fool. Of course that's not the way it happened. Will you at least admit the possibility that before Seth came to Stone Creek he might have known Rachel?"

"Where would he have met her?" he asked. "Seth's from Colorado."

"But," Betsy countered, raising a finger meaningfully, "he has family in Boston. Remember? He told us once when he was here for dinner that he has a whole passel of brothers and I know he said that at least one of them lives in Boston. So, maybe he was in Boston at some time and he met Rachel and, well, you know . . ."

Martin shook his head stubbornly. "Seth's an honorable man. If he got a girl in the family way, he'd darn well marry her. *That* I know."

"Maybe she didn't want to marry him," Betsy suggested.

"What girl who's single and in trouble wouldn't want to marry the man responsible?" Martin snorted.

"Well, of course, any *normal* girl would want to get married immediately," Betsy agreed, "but Rachel's a strange one. She's a doctor, for heaven's sake. That in itself is odd enough. Maybe she's peculiar about other things, as well."

"But, why would she come here now?" he persisted, shaking his head stubbornly.

"I don't know! I haven't had time to think all this through, but we both know how hard Seth worked to bring a doctor to Stone Creek. And, when the town council was trying to find a place for the doctor to live,

128

he was the first one to offer his house. And then, the day Rachel arrived, when they were both here and we were trying to figure out what to do with her, Seth agreed *very* quickly that she could live in his spare room. Maybe he and she planned all along that she would join him here. Coming as the town's doctor would certainly be an easy way for her to move in with him with no one suspecting anything."

Martin rose to his feet, taking off his spectacles and laying the paper aside. "I'm sorry, Betsy, but I think your imagination has run amuck this time. If the child is Rachel's daughter, then why didn't she arrive with her last spring? And, why hasn't Seth married her and claimed the child?"

"Maybe he's embarrassed," Betsy offered. "After all, it would be terribly embarrassing for them to admit that they had . . . that they were . . . well, you know!"

"Nonsense!" Martin protested. "Everyone would understand. The whole town loves Seth. And eventually they would all have accepted Rachel even if her morals were a little lacking—just out of respect for her position as the sheriff's wife. Now, in light of that, why wouldn't they admit their liaison?"

"Well, I don't . . . uh . . ." Betsy faltered.

"And," Martin continued, warming to his subject, "the whole town knows that Seth's been sparking Etta Lawrence for more than two years and he's still seeing her even now that Rachel's here. Do you think he'd be doing that if he and Rachel were involved enough to have begat a child between them?"

"No, you're wrong there," Betsy announced gleefully. "Seth hardly ever sees Etta anymore. Cynthia told me that Etta told her that Seth never comes over to her place anymore and that she heard he took Rachel on a picnic—a deux!"

"Well, my dear," Martin chuckled, passing Betsy's chair and dropping a chaste kiss on her forehead, "this is all very titillating, but I think we should take Rachel's word at face value until there is a great deal more evidence to the contrary."

"Well, I don't," Betsy huffed. "I aim to get to the bottom of this and I think I know how."

"Don't do anything we're all going to regret," Martin warned.

"Oh, I'm not going to," she said defensively, "but, Cynthia has become friendly with Rachel and I'm just going to drop a bug in her ear to see if she can find out anything the next time she sees her. After all," she added self-righteously, "Rachel is being sponsored by the community and we have every right to know if she is, indeed, what she says she is."

"Let it go, Betsy," Martin ordered with more firmness than he'd shown in years. "All Rachel has told us is that she's a doctor and we all know that's true. That's the only thing that matters. I want you to promise me that you'll stay out of this and not do anything to embarrass either Rachel or Seth."

"But, Martin!" Betsy protested.

"Promise me, Betsy."

Betsy blinked in surprise at her husband's vehemence. "Oh, all right," she pouted. "I promise I won't question Seth or Rachel."

"Good," he nodded. "I'm glad that's settled."

As he exited the room, Betsy smiled smugly. She'd never broken a promise to her husband and she wouldn't now. She wouldn't question Seth or Rachel — but that didn't mean that someone else couldn't!

Chapter Thirteen

Rachel finished applying a bandage and smiled at the woman whose foot she held. "There, Miss Hagen, that should feel much better now. I really think you should take my advice, though. You're never going to stop having trouble with ingrown toenails until you start buying bigger shoes."

Diane Hagen threw Rachel a haughty look. "I'll have you know, Dr. Hayes, that I have worn a size four shoe since I was thirteen years old and I doubt very much that my feet are growing now that I've reached my twenties. It must be something else that is causing this problem."

Rachel threw her patient a wry look, knowing the woman was thirty if she was a day. "Whatever you say," she smiled. "It's just a suggestion. I know how much an ingrown toenail can hurt and I don't want to see you suffer needlessly."

Diane rose awkwardly from her chair and limped toward the door. "I'm sure it will be fine now. Thank you for seeing me."

"Anytime," Rachel nodded, holding the door open for the hobbling woman. As Diane took her leave, Rachel saw Cynthia Fulbright and her mother, Jeanette Ecklund, walk around the corner of the house. Opening the door again, she smiled in genuine pleasure. Cynthia, who was now six months pregnant, had been

131

one of her first patients and the two young women had developed a close friendship in the months since Rachel's arrival.

"Hello, Cynthia, Mrs. Ecklund," she beamed. "How wonderful to see you. No one's sick, I hope."

"No, nothing like that," Jeanette assured her, taking Cynthia's arm and guiding her through the door. "We just thought we'd stop to see if you had time for a visit."

"I certainly do!" Rachel enthused. "Come in and I'll make some tea."

The three women sat down at Seth's kitchen table and exchanged small talk while Rachel poured the tea. Finally, as the conversation waned, Jeanette looked over at Cynthia who nodded encouragingly. Drawing a deep breath, Jeanette launched into the real reason for their visit. "Dr. Hayes, there are some disturbing rumors floating around town that Cynthia and I think you should know about."

"Rumors?" Rachel asked, her heart leaping into her throat. "Rumors about what?"

"Rumors about your niece," Cynthia answered, confirming Rachel's worst fears. "By the way, where is she?"

"Upstairs taking a nap. She should be up any minute, though. It's too bad you didn't bring Sam. They could have played together."

"Please!" Cynthia laughed. "This is my afternoon out. Let me enjoy a few minutes of peace, will you?"

"Sorry," Rachel chuckled. "Okay, so tell me the latest scandal. I assume it somehow involves me."

Cynthia nodded. "My beloved mother-in-law came to see me the other day," she said, an unmistakable thread of dislike in her voice, "to tell me that she had seen you and Amelia at the Icy Treat."

"That's right," Rachel confirmed. "We ran into each other last Sunday."

"Yes, well, she has taken it into her head that Amelia isn't who you say she is."

Rachel felt herself flush, but managed to stay calm. "How odd. Who does she think Amelia is?"

Cynthia looked at her friend for a long moment and, in a quiet voice, said, "She thinks Amelia is your daughter."

"My daughter?" Rachel blurted in genuine amazement. "Whatever would make her think that?"

"That's not all, dear," Jeanette interjected. "She thinks Amelia is Seth's daughter too."

Rachel was dumbstruck. This was much worse than anything she could have imagined. Picking up her teacup with shaking hands, she asked, "Where did she come up with such a preposterous idea?"

Jeanette chuckled. "I've known Betsy Fulbright all my life, Rachel, and preposterous ideas are her specialty. She's never been any different—even when we were girls."

"Actually," Cynthia said, "we were hoping you might be able to tell us why she thinks this."

"I have absolutely no idea," Rachel responded honestly, placing her cup back on its saucer with a slight clatter. "Does she think Sheriff Wellesley and I are married?"

"No," Cynthia murmured in embarrassment, "she doesn't think that."

What was left unspoken made Rachel suck in her breath in horror. "Oh, this is outrageous!"

"Please, dear, don't be upset," Jeanette said, leaning forward and patting Rachel's hand. "We just thought you ought to know that Betsy thinks she's got her claws into a juicy tidbit and when she gets hold of something, she never lets go."

"I can't believe this," Rachel moaned. "Do you suppose she's told anyone else about her suspicions, Cynthia? Has she said anything to Ben?"

"No," Cynthia assured her. "Ben might be her son, but she knows he has no time for idle gossip. She wouldn't tell him because she knows he would just tell her to mind her own business."

"Well, the whole thing is crazy," Rachel said emphatically. "Sheriff Wellesley and I have never been involved in any way. I never laid eyes on the man before I arrived in Stone Creek."

Both women noticed that Rachel was adroitly skirting the issue of Amelia's true parentage, but neither of them pressed her.

"You know," Rachel added thoughtfully, "I've always had the feeling that Mrs. Fulbright didn't like me. Ever since the day I arrived and she discovered I wasn't a man, I think she hasn't trusted me. It's a shame, because I've never tried to deceive anyone about anything." A sudden needle of guilt pricked her as she voiced this lie and she cast a quick plea heavenward, begging forgiveness for the small sin.

"Rachel," Jeanette said quietly, toying with a cookie on her saucer, "there's something I want you to know. No one, and I mean *no one*, in town cares about your past. You are a wonderful doctor and we all feel very lucky that you decided to stay with us. Our family has to deal with the Fulbrights since Cynthia and Ben are married, but, as Cynthia knows, I don't like Betsy and I never have. She's the worst busybody in town and except for her few close friends, nobody pays any attention to anything she says. Cynthia and I didn't come here to confront you, dear. We just thought you should know what Betsy's saying because it's bound to become a matter of speculation among her cronies."

"Well, it's ridiculous speculation," Rachel insisted.

"You're right," Cynthia agreed. "But my mother-in-law is a ridiculous woman, so what can you expect?"

Rachel chuckled despite herself, breaking the tension that had been hanging over the little table. "Thank you for telling me. I can't think of anything I can do or say to quell the rumors, but I'm glad I know about them."

"Honey, you don't have to say or do anything,"

Jeanette comforted. "Just consider the source."

Rising from the table, Jeanette helped Cynthia to her feet and they moved toward the front door.

"I'm going to take Sam on a picnic tomorrow," Cynthia said. "Would you and Amelia like to join us?"

"Oh, I don't want to intrude on a family outing," Rachel demurred.

"Nonsense, Ben is going to be haying and he wants Sam out of the way. It's just going to be the two of us. Please come."

"All right then," Rachel agreed. "We'd love to. Amelia will be thrilled."

Hearing her name, Amelia suddenly appeared at the top of the stairs.

"Auntie Rachel? Can I get up now?"

"Of course, sweetie," Rachel answered, walking toward the staircase. "Come on down and say hello."

Jeanette looked up the stairs at the beautiful blond child, and one eyebrow rose almost imperceptibly. She cast a covert glance at Cynthia, but her daughter's expression was carefully blank.

Introductions were made, plans firmed up for the following day's outing, and Jeanette and Cynthia took their leave. Walking down the dusty street toward the Ecklund home, Cynthia said casually, "Pretty little girl, isn't she?"

"Yes," her mother smiled, "looks exactly like her daddy."

"Mother!" Cynthia said in shocked voice. "Are you saying what I think you are?"

Jeanette chuckled. "Don't you find it a little odd that Rachel lives in that little room off the kitchen, but Amelia sleeps upstairs?"

"I hadn't really thought about it," Cynthia mused, "but, now that you mention it, I suppose it is."

"This really gets my goat," Jeanette complained.

"What does?"

With a long sigh, Jeanette answered, "I just *hate* it

when Betsy Fulbright is right!"

Rachel threw a steak into the frying pan and set it on the stove.

"The old bitch," she muttered vehemently. "Everything has been going along so well and now that damn Betsy Fulbright has to stick her nose into something that is absolutely none of her business."

What had ever led the old harridan to think that Amelia was her daughter? She could understand her thinking the child was related to Seth. Lia looked exactly like him . . . there was just no denying it. But where had she come up with the assumption that she was her mother? It made no sense at all. Betsy, of all people, should know that Rachel had applied for the position in Stone Creek with no knowledge whatsoever of the town or its inhabitants. Plus, she was only one of about twenty doctors who had applied. It was just pure luck that she had been the candidate chosen. Had Betsy thought that Rachel coming to Stone Creek as a physician was merely a ploy to be near Seth? The whole idea was ludicrous. If she had wanted to be near Seth, there would have been a thousand easier ways to accomplish it than struggling through four years of medical school and hoping that she might *happen* to be hired by the town in which he resided.

Rachel shook her head as she dropped a handful of sliced onions on top of the steak. The woman was absolutely crazy!

But, crazy or not, Betsy was a force to be reckoned with and Rachel's next step was to decide whether to tell Seth what she had heard. All afternoon, she had mulled over the possible pros and cons of confiding in him and, even now, she still hadn't decided if she should.

The timing's just so blasted bad, she thought in annoyance, furiously mixing up a bowl of biscuit batter.

Everything is finally getting back on an even keel between us, and now this.

A whole week had gone by since Seth had kissed her so impulsively outside her bedroom door. Neither of them had mentioned it but several times during the week, she had caught him staring at her with an enigmatic expression on his face. She hoped he'd continue to keep his distance. It made living under his roof so much easier when she wasn't being tempted by him. Although she feared that she was falling seriously in love with Seth, he made it so obvious that he wanted nothing more from her than friendship that she knew it was best to resign herself to that fact. She felt confident that she could keep her true feelings from him as long as he didn't touch her. But, she also knew that she'd never be able to resist his advances if he approached her again.

So, to bring up the subject of Betsy Fulbright's assumption that they were involved in a clandestine love affair would be like opening a door she very much wanted to keep closed.

On the other hand, Seth deserved to know what was being said about them. He was a powerful enough figure in town that, perhaps, he could stop the rumors before they spread any further. After all, his reputation was at stake as well as hers, not to mention the matter of keeping Amelia's identity a secret for safety's sake.

She was so lost in her thoughts that she didn't hear Seth come in the front door and she nearly jumped out of her skin when she heard his low timbred voice next to her ear. "Something sure smells good. Are we having steak . . . I hope?"

Whirling around, she almost bounced off his chest, he was standing so close. "Yes," she said, a trifle breathlessly, "and it's all ready, so sit down."

"Yes, ma'am," he grinned, seating himself at the table and snapping open a napkin. "Where's Lia?"

"In bed," Rachel answered. "It's nearly nine o'clock."

"I know," Seth nodded. "I got tied up at the office. I wish she was still up, though. I hate it when I don't get to see her in the evening."

"As cross as she was when she finally went to bed, you wouldn't have wanted to see her."

Seth chuckled, having become intimately acquainted with his daughter's obstinate streak during the past week. "Have you eaten already?" he asked, noticing that she held only one plate in her hand.

"Yes, with Lia."

"You don't have to fix me supper, you know. I mean, I really appreciate it, but I don't want you to feel like my housekeeper. You're doing more than enough already."

Rachel shrugged and sat down, unwilling to admit how much she enjoyed cooking these late suppers and sitting with him while he ate. "It's okay. I only had one patient today, so I've been pretty lazy. I don't mind cooking when I've nothing else to do."

"Well, thanks, it tastes great." His gaze swept over her, noting the little furrow of worry between her brows.

Swallowing, he reached out and took her hand. "What's the matter?"

She pulled her hand out of his warm grasp and giggled nervously. "Matter? Nothing's the matter. Why would you say that?"

Seth casually buttered a biscuit. "Something's bothering you. I can tell. You always get that funny little wrinkle in your forehead when you're worried about something."

"I do not," she protested, rubbing furiously at her forehead with her index finger.

"Yes, you do," he chuckled. "But, never mind. I just thought maybe you were upset about something . . . like what Betsy Fulbright is saying about you and me."

Rachel gasped. "You know?"

"Sure," he said casually. "I hear everything."

"Well, you certainly seem calm about it!"

Seth shrugged. "What can we do? Anyway, she's nuts and nobody believes a word she says."

"But what about Clint Brady? What if he hears the rumor? Aren't you concerned about that?"

"Yeah, I *am* concerned about that. But there's nothing I can do about it and I figure the more nonchalant the two of us appear, the better. Anyway, I heard he's back in Colorado and I'm hoping that by the time he gets back to Kansas, this will have blown over and he won't hear about it. In the meantime, it's important that you and I act like there's nothing to it."

"Well, that won't be hard," Rachel remarked, "there *is* nothing to it. It's just too bad that Lia looks so much like you."

"Yeah. But there's no help for that." Suddenly, he snapped his fingers and abruptly stood up. "Wait a minute! Maybe there is. I'll be right back."

He walked out of the kitchen and up the stairs. Returning a few minutes later, he handed her a framed picture.

"Who's this?" Rachel asked, astounded by the similarity between Seth and the man in the picture.

"My brother, Miles, and his wife, Alicia. Your sister."

"My sister? What are you talking about?"

"Come on, think about it. Miles and I look so much alike that he certainly could have sired a child with Lia's looks. All we have to do is make sure that all the busybodies in town see this picture and then tell them that Alicia is your sister, instead of Miles being my brother."

"That's inspired, Seth!" Rachel exclaimed. "Everyone will think you're not her father, that you just happen to look like the man who is."

"Exactly," he grinned. "Not a bad plan, eh? Now, we just have to figure out where to put the picture so people will see it."

"In my office," Rachel said promptly. "On the desk. Every woman in town who comes to me will see it and it certainly won't be long before Betsy and her friends find a reason to visit so they can take a look too. It'll work, Seth. I know it will!"

Sitting back down in his chair and smiling in smug satisfaction, Seth pulled out a cigarette and held it up for Rachel's approval.

She nodded and beamed happily at the picture she still held. "Oh, but, wait a minute. Has anyone in town ever seen this picture?"

"No," he answered, "it was in my bedroom on the dresser so no . . . uh . . . no one has ever seen it."

Raising a knowing eyebrow at his lie, Rachel said tartly, "You needn't worry. Miss Lawrence doesn't use my services."

"It's not what you're thinking, Rachel," he said quietly.

"It wouldn't matter if it was," she retorted glibly. "What you do with your private life is your business, not mine." She stared out the window for a moment, the thought of Etta Lawrence being in Seth's bedroom making her heart wrench with pain.

"Rachel?" he said quietly.

She looked up, surprised at the sudden intensity in his voice. "Yes?"

"I just want to thank you for all you're doing for Amelia and me. I realize how embarrassing this gossip must be for you and I want you to know that if there's any way I can stop it, I will."

"Thank you, Seth. I appreciate your concern."

"You know," he chuckled, "part of this is your fault."

"*My* fault! What do you mean?"

"Well, you're so damn good with Lia that it's easy for people to think that you're her mother."

Rachel blushed, unable to think of a response.

Seth inhaled deeply on his cigarette and continued,

"You should think about getting married and having a few little ones of your own someday."

"Me?" Rachel laughed. "I don't have time for children in my life."

"Really? You seem to find time for Lia."

"Well, that's different. I know this is a temporary situation."

"Tell me something," he prodded. "Is it children you don't have time for, or their fathers?"

Rachel rose from the table and began clearing away his dirty dishes. "I really don't think my feelings about love or marriage are any of your concern, Sheriff. But, since you're so insistent, I'll tell you that my feelings are much the same as yours. You said that upholding the law was all you wanted out of life. That's the way I feel about medicine. It's all I need." Wiping her hands on a dish towel, she said, "Now, if you'll excuse me, I'll say good night."

With a slight inclination of his head, Seth bid her good night and watched her disappear down the little hall to her room.

Staring at her closed door, he leaned back in his chair and took a final drag on his cigarette. "You're not kidding me any more than I'm kidding you, sweetheart," he murmured. "Work isn't enough for either one of us, and if we weren't so damn scared of each other, we'd both admit it and do something about the way we feel."

Stubbing out his cigarette, he blew out the lamp and climbed up the stairs to his lonely bed.

Chapter Fourteen

The weather was perfect — warm, sunny and breezy. The creek rolled by lazily and insects droned monotonously in the background. Rachel and Cynthia reclined on a blanket, feeling drowsy and relaxed. Rachel gazed over at the children and saw they were also nodding off, satiated with food, fresh air, and sunshine. She closed her eyes and dozed peacefully. When she opened them again, she was surprised to see the sun was far down on the horizon. Sitting up, she gently shook Cynthia's shoulder. "Wake up, sleepyhead," she chuckled. "We've slept the afternoon away."

Cynthia got awkwardly to her feet and began to clear away the dishes and leftover food.

When everything was packed up, Rachel looked around to make sure that they had everything they had come with. They didn't. Sam was missing. A prickle of apprehension made the hair on the back of her neck stand up, but she strove to keep her voice even. "Have you seen Sam?" she asked casually.

"No," Cynthia answered in surprise, turning in a circle to seek out her wayward son.

Her heart beating faster with every passing second, Rachel turned toward Amelia. "How about you, Lia. Did you see where Sam went?"

Amelia nodded and pointed to a nearby oak tree.

"You mean he's up in that tree?" Cynthia asked in relief.

Again, the child nodded.

Hurrying over to the tree, the women shaded their eyes and looked up. There, high in the branches, sat Sam. "What are you doing up there?" his mother called.

No response.

"Sam, can you hear me?"

No response.

Rachel looked at Cynthia curiously. "What do you think is wrong with him? Why doesn't he answer?"

Cynthia shrugged and again looked up into the branches. "Sam! Come on down now. It's time to go home."

Sam didn't move.

"Oooh, this child," Cynthia muttered in annoyance. "Sam! Stop playing games and come down immediately!"

Rachel and Amelia remained standing beneath the tree, staring up at Sam seated in his lofty bower. Finally a quaking voice called, "I can't get down."

"What?" Cynthia yelled. "Did you say you *can't* get down?"

"Yes," came the small answer.

"Cynthia," Rachel said, her voice anxious, "I think maybe he's stuck."

"Nonsense!" Cynthia protested. "He can't be stuck." Throwing her head back again, she shouted, "Sam, you aren't stuck, are you?"

"Yes."

Cynthia paled. "He can't be stuck. He got up there, he must be able to get down!"

Rachel shrugged and bit her lip warily.

"The thing to do here is stay calm," Cynthia murmured. "You're okay, honey," she yelled into the leaves. "Just come down one branch at a time. You're a big boy and big boys who can climb up trees can climb back down them."

"I can't."

"Has he ever done this before?" Rachel asked.

"No," Cynthia shook her head. "He's climbed trees before but I've never seen him go so high. I think he was showing off for Lia."

Rachel groaned. "How in the world are we going to get him down?"

"I guess somebody will have to go up after him," Cynthia answered, her voice anxious.

"Who?" Rachel gasped. "You certainly can't climb up there in your condition, and I can't either. I have this long skirt on and, anyway, I'm scared of heights."

"Well, someone has to go!" Cynthia cried. "One of us better go get Seth."

"No!" Rachel said hastily. "He's at the office and I don't want to bother him." The last thing she wanted was for Seth to think she couldn't handle anything as simple as taking two children on a picnic. Somehow, they had to talk Sam down.

"Sam," she called. "There's nothing to be afraid of. Just don't look down. Step from one branch to the next, and before you know it, you'll be back down here. Your mother and I will be right here under you, so you don't need to worry about falling. If anything happens, we'll catch you. Now, come on. Be a good boy and try moving down one branch."

"I can't."

"He's not coming down," Cynthia announced with finality. "He's too scared."

"You're right," Rachel agreed. "I'll just have to climb up and get him."

"Better take your clothes off first," Cynthia advised. "Your skirt might get tangled in the branches and your shoes will probably make you slip."

"Take my clothes off? I can't take my clothes off!"

"Why not? Who's going to see you, except me?"

From high above them, Sam started to whimper. "I want to get down. Ma, get me down!"

"Just a minute, Sam," she yelled. "Dr. Hayes is coming."

Hoisting herself up onto the first branch, Rachel willed herself to think of this moment as one that she might laugh about later. Never an athlete, she hadn't climbed a tree since childhood and never one of this height. But she tenaciously grabbed the branch above her and reached tentatively for a toe hold along the trunk. As Cynthia had predicted, her long, lacy petticoat became hooked on a twig and she found herself caught on the branch from which she was trying to ascend.

"You're caught, Rachel," Cynthia called from below her. "You're going to have to take your skirt off."

Rachel gave her skirt a ferocious tug, but it was caught fast and refused to budge. Cursing under her breath, she slowly moved back down to the offending branch and attempted to dislodge the stubborn twig.

The next thing she knew, she was lying on her back on the ground. Sitting up groggily, she found Cynthia looming over her with a look of horror on her face while Amelia stood nearby, clapping her hands in glee. "Funny, funny Auntie Rachel," she giggled.

"Are you all right?" Cynthia asked, leaning over to help her to her feet.

"Yes, I'm fine," Rachel snapped, brushing leaves off the back of her skirt.

"I better get Seth," Cynthia asserted.

"No, please don't! I can handle this. I'll just take my skirt off like you said."

Cynthia looked at her doubtfully, wondering why she was so opposed to getting help.

Meanwhile, high above them, Sam was now crying in earnest. "I want to go home," he wailed. "Help me . . . MA!"

"Hush!" Cynthia yelled. "You're perfectly all right.

145

Just stay where you are and quit crying. Dr. Hayes will be up to get you in a minute."

Rachel tugged her dirty skirt and ripped petticoat off and, clad only in her camisole and pantalettes, again pulled herself up to the first branch. Kicking off her shoes, she cast a determined look above her. "I *will* do this," she told herself. "It isn't so frightening. After all, I've cut people open and stitched them back together again. If I can do that and not be scared, I can certainly climb this tree!"

Doggedly, she continued to hoist herself from branch to branch until she was standing just beneath the terrified child. "Well, Sam," she said brightly, "here I am. It's very pretty up here, isn't it? Now, just step down here on this branch beside me and we'll climb down together."

"I can't."

Rachel took a firm grip on her temper. "Yes, you can. It's easy and I'll be right here next to you."

"Come up and help me, please," he begged.

She exhaled a long sigh. "Okay, but you'll have to move over so I can sit next to you on your branch."

Grasping the limb where it joined the oak's trunk, she climbed up to the next branch and sat down. "Well, here we are," she smiled. "Now, let's get down. We'll just step down to the next branch and keep moving down. Okay?"

Sam nodded happily, all smiles now that he had an adult on the branch next to him.

Rachel looked down, trying to gauge the best place to put her foot but, suddenly, her stomach took a nauseated roll and she felt as if she might faint. She was at least a hundred miles up in the air. Climbing up through the branches, she hadn't realized just how high she was going. Now, as she looked down, a sickening sense of dread washed over her. She was going to fall. She just knew it. She was going to fall and break her neck.

"Are we getting down now?" Sam demanded.

"Just a minute, honey," Rachel croaked, placing both arms around the tree's massive trunk.

"What's the matter?" Cynthia's voice coming from the ground below sounded like it was a million miles away. "Why aren't you coming down?"

"I think Dr. Hayes is sick," Sam called.

"What?" Cynthia gasped. "I'm going to get Seth! Just stay there. I'll be right back."

"No, don't," Rachel called weakly.

Cynthia ignored the entreaty and took off as fast as her girth would allow.

Rachel leaned her head against the tree trunk, tears rolling down her cheeks.

"Ah, don't worry, Dr. Hayes," Sam comforted, patting her on the shoulder. "The sheriff will get us down."

Rachel nodded and gazed off across the prairie, sure that her feet would never touch solid ground again.

Seth was in his office, going over a new batch of Wanted Posters. Hearing the door open behind him, he turned to see Cynthia Fulbright rushing into the office, breathless and flushed. "Seth! Come quick!" she panted.

He immediately sprang into action, bolting out of his chair and instinctively grabbing for his gun. "What is it, Cynthia? Is somebody hurt?"

"No, not yet," gasped the winded woman. "And you don't need your gun. Sam and Rachel are up in a tree and they can't get down. You have to hurry, though. I'm afraid someone is going to fall." Grabbing his hand, she began pulling him out the door.

"What in the hell is Dr. Hayes doing up in a tree with Sam?" Seth demanded.

"We were having a picnic down by the creek and Sam climbed that big oak and couldn't get down, so Rachel went up after him and now she can't get down either. They're really high, Seth. Please hurry!"

"Okay, I'll meet you there." Pulling his hand out of her grasp, he leaped on his horse and tore off down Main Street at a dead gallop. When he reached the creek, he dismounted, clambering down a slight incline and scanning the shoreline. He spotted Amelia standing beneath a large tree and raced toward her, finally coming to a skidding, panting halt next to his daughter. Squinting against the sun, he looked up into the tree and spied Sam and Rachel sitting on a branch at least thirty feet off the ground.

"Hi, Sheriff!" Sam called happily. "Dr. Hayes and me are up here in this tree and we can't get down. Will you come up and get us? The doc's awful scared. I think she's gonna throw up."

Seth glanced up at Rachel, his eyes widening as he noticed that she was clad only in her pantalettes and camisole. "Are you all right, Rachel?" he called.

She nodded weakly.

Pulling off his boots, Seth swung himself onto the first branch and worked his way upward. When he reached the branch below them, he stood up and extended one arm toward Sam. "Come on, boy, let's get you down."

Sam eagerly lowered himself into the protection of Seth's muscular arms, saying, "What about her?"

"Let's get you down first. Then, I'll come back and get Dr. Hayes." Glancing up at the pale, trembling woman clinging to the tree above him, he asked quietly, "Are you really all right?"

Unable to form a reply, Rachel nodded and closed her eyes.

In what seemed like only seconds, Seth had Sam safely on the ground and was on his way back up to retrieve Rachel. Again reaching the branch beneath her, he said, "Can you let go of the tree and take my hand?"

"I don't think so," she whispered.

"Okay. You don't have to let go completely. Just give

me one hand. If I can lower you enough to get an arm around your waist, we're home free. Trust me, Rachel. I'm not going to let you fall."

The promise in his voice somehow gave her the courage to release the tree and hold a shaking hand out toward him.

"Good . . . good," he praised in a soothing voice. He grasped her small hand in his big, warm one and softly directed, "Now, slip off that branch until your feet touch the one I'm on. Come on, honey, you can do it. Just let yourself slide off. I'm right here and you're fine."

Rachel did as he bade. For a split second she was suspended in mid-air, but then she felt his arm grip her tightly around the waist and her feet touched the branch next to his.

"That's my girl. You did it, sweetheart. Now, come on, we're going to do the same thing down to the next branch. I'll go first and you just lower yourself against me. That's right. You're doing fine."

Little by little the couple descended the awesome distance until finally, standing on a branch eight feet from the ground, Seth said, "Now, just sit down on this one."

Rachel obediently lowered herself to a sitting position and, once there, he let go of her hand. Somersaulting around the branch like an acrobat, he dropped lightly to the ground. "Lean forward and I'll lift you down."

She placed her hands on his shoulders and he grasped her around her slender waist, lifting her from the branch and letting her slide against him to the ground. He didn't immediately remove his hands, but stood there quietly holding her against the solid security of his chest.

"I've never been so scared in my life," she murmured. "I'm sorry for all the bother."

Seth chuckled. "You're no bother. If I can risk my life to rescue Diane Hagen's nasty cat, I guess I can rescue you." He still hadn't released her from his embrace and it was a long moment before she became aware of the intimacy of their pose and the fact that she was very scantily clothed. Gasping, she stiffened and hastily stepped back.

"Please turn your back, Sheriff, so I can put my clothes back on," she said in a clipped voice.

Seth frowned at her sudden turn of mood, but complied with her request. Standing with his back to her, he said, "I've been staring at you for the past ten minutes and I haven't attacked you yet. What makes you think I'm going to now?"

"Seth, *please*," Rachel exclaimed. "You're embarrassing me."

He grinned in unrepentant delight. "Tell me, Dr. Hayes, why didn't you take your clothes off when you and I went picnicking, or is this a recently acquired habit? And, if so, would you like to go on a picnic with me tomorrow?"

"Sheriff! I'll thank you to watch your tongue!"

He turned to face her, his grin fading. "Oh, don't be such a prude. I'm just teasing you. And, anyway, this isn't the first time I've seen you undressed and you know it."

"Seth, that's enough," she warned.

He flashed her another wicked grin and handed her her skirt. "You might want this," he said blandly.

Glaring at him, Rachel stepped into her skirt and with a haughty toss of her head, marched off to gather up the picnic supplies.

Seth ambled after her, saying, "Doctor Hayes? You didn't say 'thank you, Sheriff.' "

Relenting, Rachel turned toward him and said, "I'm sorry. Thank you very much. I don't know what came over me. I was just suddenly so frightened that I felt paralyzed. I thought I could handle getting Sam down, but I guess I'm just not cut out for tree climbing."

"Don't be so hard on yourself," he admonished gently. "Lots of people are scared of heights."

"You don't seem to have any problems with it," she observed.

"I had five older brothers and if I wanted to go anywhere with them, I had to learn to act fearless. It was purely self defense. Their favorite pastime was terrorizing me. I *had* to be tough."

Rachel looked doubtful. "I think it's more than that. Everyone out here is the same way. Self reliant, unafraid . . . I think it has something to do with growing up in the wilds."

Without commenting, he reached out and took the picnic basket from her hand, placing a reassuring arm around her shoulder. The small contact prompted a quick shrug of her shoulders and he dropped his arm, looking at her in confusion.

"Now, where's Sam?" she asked, ignoring the question in his eyes.

"We're right here," Cynthia answered, stepping out from behind a tree where she had been sitting with her son on her lap.

Rachel jumped at the sight of her friend. How long had she been there—and how much had she heard? Blushing to the roots of her hair, she said brightly, "Are we all ready?"

"Yes," Cynthia nodded, noticing Rachel's heightening color. "By all means, let's go home!"

Later that evening, Cynthia sat in her mother's parlor and filled her in on the afternoon's events. "I don't think there was anything between them in the past," she confided. "Rachel's too standoffish with him to have ever been intimate. But, there's definitely something between them now."

"What makes you think that?" Jeanette asked, sipping her lemonade.

151

"I got back just as Seth was lifting her out of the tree. I know I should have said something right away, but, they just seemed so . . . involved that I didn't want to interrupt. I know I shouldn't have eavesdropped, Ma, but I just couldn't help myself."

Jeanette chuckled. "So, what did you see?"

"Seth's in love with her. That's for sure. My heavens, just the way he looked at her made me blush. Never, ever, has Ben looked at me like that!"

"Ben's a good man, Cynthia," Jeanette reminded her.

"I know, and I love him dearly, but if he ever looked at me the way Seth was looking at Rachel, I think I'd faint!"

"Just how *was* he looking at her?"

"Like he wanted to eat her!"

"Oh, my!" Jeanette laughed. "That bad, huh?"

Cynthia nodded. "But, the strange thing is, Rachel was fighting it. I can't understand her. There isn't an unattached woman in Stone Creek who wouldn't lie down and die to have Seth look at her the way he was looking at Rachel, but she just pulled away and told him to mind his manners."

"Maybe she knew you were there and you didn't realize it," Jeanette suggested.

"No," Cynthia answered with assurance. "She didn't, because when I finally made my presence known, she got red as a beet."

"Hmm . . ." Jeanette mused. "This is all very puzzling. Maybe she just isn't interested."

"I can't believe that," Cynthia protested. "There isn't a healthy, red-blooded woman in the world who wouldn't be interested in a man like Seth. Maybe she's just playing hard to get but, mark my words, Ma, he's going to get her. The lucky thing . . ."

"Cynthia!" Jeanette admonished. "You sound like you're jealous!"

Cynthia blushed. "Of course I'm not jealous. But, if

you could have seen them, why, it would make even *your* hair curl!"

Jeanette frowned at her daughter's teasing reference to her straight, unruly hair. "Well, if what you say is true, then poor Etta better give up and find herself a new man."

"She might as well," Cynthia nodded. "She's lost Seth for sure—if she ever had him."

"Ah, romance!" Jeanette sighed. "Imagine! Seth Wellesley being in love . . ."

Cynthia sighed too, her eyes dreamy. "Imagine being the girl Seth Wellesley's in love with . . ."

Chapter Fifteen

It was the night of the Stone Creek Summer Jamboree Dance and Rachel was all smiles as she and Seth walked into Ecklund's large barn. She had been thrilled when Seth asked her if she'd like to attend the dance with him and she'd eagerly looked forward to this evening all week.

"One of the things I like best about Stone Creek is all the celebrations we have," she commented as they entered the cavernous building.

"Yeah, it's fun," Seth agreed. "And it's pretty common all over this part of the country. We had lots of dances and socials and picnics when I was growing up in Colorado too."

Rachel looked at him in surprise. It was seldom that he mentioned anything about his family or childhood. "Really?" she asked. "I know you said you were raised in Colorado, but you never said what business your father was in. Did he farm or ranch or did you live in town?"

"Oh, he did a lot of things," Seth said vaguely. "Mostly ranching."

"Cattle or horses?"

"A little of both."

"Was it a big ranch?"

He shrugged. "Fair size."

154

"Does your family still own it?"

"Yeah."

Rachel sighed in exasperation at his non-committal responses. "Seth, if you don't want to talk about this, just tell me."

For the first time since they'd entered the barn, he looked at her, a slightly tense expression on his face. "There's nothing to tell, Rachel. My folks had a ranch outside of Durango and my family still owns it. Paula and her husband live there now and when Adam finishes school, I imagine he'll go back to it too. He loves cows."

"And you don't?" she persisted.

"Not much. If I did, I'd probably still be there. Let's dance."

Rachel looked at him quizzically, wondering why he always avoided talking about himself, but before she could ponder the question any further, she found herself squaring up for the first dance. She had never square danced in her life and the lightning-fast calls and whirling, dipping movements took all of her concentration to follow.

When the dance finally ended, she was winded and panting. "I've got to sit down," she laughed. "I'm used to waltzing!"

Seth led her over to one of several benches which had been set around the perimeter of the barn. "Too strenuous for you?" he chuckled as she slumped wearily on to the bench's hard surface.

"I'm afraid so, and much harder than I thought it would be!"

"You just have to do it more often," he advised, sitting down next to her and leaning back against the wall. "Then you learn the calls and it gets a lot easier."

"I have a feeling that if I stay in Stone Creek, I'll have plenty of chances to learn."

"What do you mean *if* you stay in Stone Creek?" he

155

asked suddenly, his voice losing its teasing note. "You thinking about leaving?"

"Well, no, of course not," she stammered. "After all, I have a year's contract."

"Are you thinking about leaving at the end of the year?" he persisted.

"No! It was just a figure of speech. Right now I have no plans to do anything except what I'm doing. But, come April, when it's time to renew my contract, well, we'll see. A lot of things can happen between now and then."

"Like what?"

"Who knows? The people in town may decide not to hire me for another year."

"That won't happen," he answered shortly.

"It could," Rachel argued. "I still have not had one single male patient—except Deke Miller, of course, and he probably wouldn't have allowed me to touch him if he'd had a choice."

"It won't happen," he repeated positively.

"I appreciate your faith," she said wryly, "but, then too, there's always the possibility that I may decide to leave."

She jumped as Seth lurched forward, his hand clapping down over hers. "Why would you do that?"

Rachel shrugged, knowing she was being perverse, but taking great delight in the fact that Seth actually seemed concerned that she might leave. "Oh, I don't know," she said breezily, "I might get a better offer."

"What kind of offer?"

She was having a hard time controlling her delight at his increasingly tense voice "Any kind of offer. You know, a better situation somewhere . . . maybe a different job or a different living situation."

"Are you unhappy with your room at my house?"

"Not at all," she assured him, "but, naturally, someday I'd like to have my own home."

156

"Usually women have to get married to get that," he pointed out.

"Yes, I know that's the usual way. Come on, the music's starting again."

Seth tightened his grip on her hand. "Are you toying with me, Rachel?"

She looked at him, her eyes shining with mischief. "Of course not! I'm merely speculating on how many things can change in a person's life in just a short time. Oh! There's Charlie Stimson. Excuse me for a minute. I want to go over and say hello."

Before Seth could protest, she sprang up from the bench and swept across the barn floor toward a young man who stood near the door. Charlie Stimson was a handsome, friendly man in his mid-twenties who ran the stage depot. Although Rachel didn't know him well, they had spoken on several occasions when they'd run into each other in town. He was sometimes at Ecklund's General Store when she was shopping and one time he had walked her home from the Icy Treat. She smiled as she approached him and his brown eyes sparkled with pleasure.

Seth, however, wasn't smiling as his eyes followed Rachel's every move. Damn, but she looked gorgeous tonight. She was dressed in a green lawn dress, dotted with tiny white flowers. The neckline was slightly scooped and the puffy sleeves that came just to the edge of her shoulders allowed for a tantalizing view of her neck and the upper swell of her breasts. The full skirt floated softly around her, giving the impression that she was gliding rather than walking. He had noticed many of the town's women eying the gauzy creation with a mixture of envy and awe. Some of the older matrons had frowned in blatant disapproval at its slightly daring décolletage, but Seth thought she looked exquisite. She outshone every woman in the room and he was proud to be her escort.

His warm, appreciative gaze suddenly narrowed, however, when he saw her lean toward Stimson, laughing and placing her hand on the man's arm. Charlie's laughter could be heard all the way across the room and did nothing to erase Seth's scowl. Angrily, he rose from the bench and strode over to the refreshment table.

Every unattached young woman at the dance had seen the little drama which had just passed and they now clustered around Seth, offering him a glass of punch and hoping that he might single out one of them with an invitation to dance.

Rachel, who was still pretending to be entranced by Charlie, did not miss the way the girls swooped down on Seth. Despite the fact that she had been playing her own little game with him, a surge of jealousy coursed through her as she saw him smiling at the bevy of hopefuls around him.

"Would you like to dance, Dr. Hayes?" Charlie asked politely, not quite sure what he had said that had suddenly lost her attention.

"Not right now, Mr. Stimson," she replied with a smile, "perhaps later, though."

Charlie nodded, extracting a promise that she wouldn't forget him. Rachel assured him she wouldn't and waving gaily, headed back over to where Seth stood. By now, there were at least a dozen women fawning over him and the closer Rachel got to the giggling throng, the more annoyed she became.

Reaching the table, she stood on the outskirts of the group, trying her best to look unconcerned and detached. Seth had watched her return out of the corner of his eye, and with his usual charm, made his way through the crowd of eager girls and back to her side, pleased by the possessive way she immediately took his arm.

"Did I tell you that you look wonderful tonight?" he

whispered, inclining his head so only she could hear.

"Thank you," she replied, blushing at his compliment. "I'm afraid I'm overdressed, though. I'm still not used to how casual people are out here. All my clothes seem so inappropriate."

"You're never inappropriate," Seth assured her, stroking her hand where it rested on his arm. "The dress is beautiful and so are you."

Rachel was thrilled by his unaccustomed effusiveness and smiled shyly. "Let's dance again," she suggested. "Everyone's staring at us."

"Everyone's always staring at us. Aren't you used to it yet?"

"No," Rachel corrected, "everyone's always staring at *you*."

"Only the women," Seth chuckled. "The men don't even know I'm in the room tonight."

Rachel blushed again as he swept her into his arms for a rousing dance which she suspected was some kind of polka. When the music came to a sawing, crashing crescendo, she put her hands to her flaming cheeks and laughed, "Doesn't the orchestra know *any* slow tunes?"

Seth chuckled and led her back to the bench, seating her and saying, "Stay here. I'll get you some punch."

Rachel sat fanning herself and looking at the large, boisterous crowd with interest. The barn was a huge structure and yet it was full of people. She suspected everyone in town must be present to fill it so completely.

Seth returned, carrying a small glass of punch which he handed her. She gulped the cool liquid gratefully. "Let's go outside for a minute," he suggested. "It's cooler out there."

She nodded eagerly and the two of them wove their way through the crowd toward the entrance. As the cool evening air assailed them, Rachel took a grateful breath and looked up at the huge, late-summer moon.

"Look at how beautiful the moon is tonight," she said, pointing.

Seth looked up and nodded. "A lover's moon."

"What?" she asked, turning toward him, astonished by his provocative description.

"A lover's moon," he repeated, smiling. "You know, the kind of moon that people make love under."

"Sheriff!" she admonished, aghast at his boldness.

"My name's Seth," he reminded her, his voice full of laughter. Before she could say anything more, he turned her toward him and kissed her.

As his mouth touched hers, a warning bell clanged somewhere in her mind, but she ignored it, wrapping her arms around his neck and parting her lips. He deepened the kiss, pulling her more firmly against him and teasing her lips with his tongue. His hands moved up to cup her face, his thumbs gently massaging her temples. Drawing away just enough so that their mouths barely touched, he murmured, "You have the softest lips of anyone I've ever known."

Rachel sighed, her breath warm against his lips and, again, his mouth descended on hers. She was pliant and responsive to his caresses and he felt as if he could spend the rest of his life standing in that spot, kissing her.

As always, the passion between them built quickly until Seth felt like he was going to explode. He was just starting to pull her down in the deep grass when, suddenly, the sound of voices nearby wrenched him back to his senses. Breaking apart, they stared at each other in shock, both of them realizing how close they had come to losing control. Rachel took two hasty steps backward, reaching up and frantically patting her hair. Seth turned away for a moment, breathing in great gulps of the chilly night air as he tried desperately to cool his overheated body and calm his raging lust. More than a minute passed before he turned back toward her, finally confident that he could walk back into the barn without disgracing himself in front of half the town.

"You ready?" he rasped.

"I . . . I think so," she stammered.

Without touching, they quickly returned to the barn. Rachel was so anxious to escape Seth's overwhelming sensuality that she practically ran to join a group of women who stood chatting on the far side of the room.

Seated on a bench against the back wall, Cynthia Fulbright had seen Seth and Rachel go outside. Such a long time had passed since they'd left, however, that she'd thought they must have decided to go home. Her eyebrows lifted in surprise when she saw them re-enter the barn looking flushed and embarrassed. She was further astonished when Rachel bolted away from Seth as though he had the plague. Her flaming cheeks and slightly mussed hair spoke volumes and Cynthia glanced quickly over at Seth, noticing, for the first time, the tension around his mouth and the rapid rise and fall of his chest. His breathing was so labored that he looked like he'd just run a long race. Cynthia smiled to herself. There was no doubt in her mind that the couple was fighting a war they were destined to lose. She felt a jolt of envy shoot through her, imagining what Rachel had in store for her when she finally conceded defeat.

Strolling over to where Rachel stood at the edge of the crowd of gossiping matrons, Cynthia put a hand on her arm and whispered, "Are you okay?"

Rachel turned startled, overly bright eyes on her friend and said, "Of course. Why do you ask?"

Cynthia shrugged. "You just look kind of . . . flushed."

"Do I?" Rachel asked nervously. "Well, it is rather warm in here, isn't it? How are *you* feeling?"

Realizing by her quick change of subject that Rachel wasn't ready to confide in her, Cynthia prudently did not pursue her interrogation. "I feel fine. Fat, but fine."

"It won't be long now before it's over," Rachel comforted, her voice sounding more normal now that they were on safer conversational ground. "Would you like to go over and sit down? I haven't talked to you in days."

"Sure," Cynthia agreed, relieved to see her friend's high color receding. As the two of them walked toward a bench, Rachel's eyes darted about the huge room, seeking out Seth.

"He's over there by the orchestra," Cynthia murmured.

"What?"

"Seth. He's over talking to Matt, the fiddle player."

Rachel's gaze flicked over in that direction and then immediately fled as she saw Seth talking to the band leader, but looking at her.

As her gaze again lit on Cynthia, her friend smiled sympathetically and gave her hand an affectionate pat. "It's all right, you know."

"I beg your pardon?" Rachel hedged. "What's all right?"

"You know very well what I'm talking about. You can't take your eyes off him."

Rachel sighed. "Is it that obvious?"

"Only if you're really watching," Cynthia assured her. "Do you think he's equally infatuated?"

"I honestly don't know." Rachel shook her head. "He's a hard man to understand."

Cynthia nodded. "That's part of his charm. But from what I've seen, you have nothing to worry about. He's just as much in love with you as you are with him."

"I'm not in love with him!" Rachel protested vehemently.

"Rachel . . ." Cynthia smiled, "why are you denying

it? It's written all over your face every time you look at him."

"Is it?" Rachel asked, horrified. "Oh, Cynthia, I'm so embarrassed."

"Don't be. There's not an unmarried woman in this barn who wouldn't like to trade places with you. Every female in Stone Creek is a little in love with Seth Wellesley. The only difference is that you're the only one he feels the same way about."

"No, you're wrong about that," Rachel protested. "Seth is definitely not in love with me!"

Cynthia shook her head in exasperation. "Suit yourself, Doctor." She sat quietly for a moment, then leaned toward Rachel, whispering in her ear. "You're a good friend and I don't want to see you get hurt, so I'm going to give you a piece of advice."

Rachel looked at her curiously, then nodded her head.

Cupping her hand around Rachel's ear, Cynthia whispered, "Don't let him make you a mother before he makes you a wife."

Rachel jerked her head back, gasping in astonishment.

"Listen to what I'm saying, Rachel," Cynthia chuckled. "I've seen the way the man looks at you and I know what I'd be doing with him if he looked at me that way."

"Cynthia Fulbright! I don't believe you said that!" Rachel's expression was so shocked that Cynthia threw back her head and laughed delightedly.

"Oh, there's Ben," she said suddenly. "I've got to go." Getting awkwardly to her feet, she paused a moment, then leaned down and again whispered in Rachel's ear. "I envy you, you know. If Seth makes love as well as he looks like he would, you're probably the luckiest woman on earth. Just remember what I said, and be careful."

Rachel's scandalized expression was so comical that

Cynthia chuckled all the way across the barn as she went to join her husband.

For a long time, Rachel just sat and stared straight ahead. Could Cynthia be right? Was it possible that Seth was in love with her? Lord, what she wouldn't give for that to be true. But, somehow, she just couldn't quite believe it. He had pushed her away too many times and had never been anything but brutally honest in admitting that although he was attracted to her physically, he had no interest in a serious relationship with her.

No, unfortunately, Cynthia was wrong and Rachel knew she would be wise not to start believing her own fantasies. To try to make her secret yearnings into reality was just inviting heartbreak.

Deep down, she knew she was in love with Seth—and had been for a long time. But it was difficult for her to admit it, even to herself, when she was so sure of Seth didn't return that love. Better that she keep her council and never let him know how she felt. As she sat on the bench, oblivious to the dancers twirling and dipping in front of her, she resolved not to let her guard down again. Not with Seth . . . not with Cynthia . . . not with anyone.

Feeling better now that she'd made that promise to herself, she looked up to see him walking toward her, a bland smile on his face. Sitting down next to her, he said casually, "Want to dance?"

She nodded, not trusting her voice. As she started to rise, though, he put his hand on her arm and gently halted her. "Let's wait till the next dance starts. It'll be the last one of the evening."

With a slightly quizzical look, she sank back down on the bench and leaned against the wall. Seth sat quietly watching the dancers as the orchestra finished a loud, energetic piece.

Matt, the fiddler, stepped up to the front of the platform and said loudly, "This here next one is the last one of the evening, folks, so make it count!" Then, much to everyone's surprise, the small band struck up a waltz.

A murmur of delight ran through the female members of the crowd as the men looked at each other in horrified surprise. Rachel glanced over at Seth with a look of sheer delight on her face. Her smile widened as he grinned back at her. Rising, he held out his hand. "Guess you got your waltz, Doctor."

"You did this, didn't you?" she questioned as he led her out on to the floor, placing one arm around her waist and taking her hand in his.

He shrugged, his expression slightly sheepish. "Oh, I might have said something about how much ladies seem to like to waltz. Guess Matt just took it from there."

Rachel threw him a knowing look and was astonished when his cheeks turned red and he dropped his gaze like an embarrassed boy.

Smiling at his discomfiture, she moved closer to him and let herself flow with the music. Seth was surprisingly accomplished at waltzing and the two of them flew across the dance floor, swooping and dipping as Rachel's gauzy dress floated out in great swirls of color.

She wished the dance would last forever, but much too soon, the music came to its sweeping conclusion. For a moment, there was complete silence in the echoing barn as everyone listened to the final, dying strains from Matt's haunting violin. Then, suddenly, the entire room resounded with enthusiastic applause and calls of appreciative congratulations for a job well done.

It was the perfect end to the dance and as the hundreds of people filed happily out of the barn, climbing into creaking wagons and heading for home, the camaraderie between them was almost tangible.

Seth and Rachel were quiet as his luxurious buckboard made its way down Main Street. Rachel again stared at the moon, realizing this was a night she would remember the rest of her life.

Seth also seemed to be moonstruck as they passed through the silent streets and pulled up next to his house. Without a word, he jumped down and circled around behind the conveyance to help her down. Placing his arms around her tiny waist, he slowly lifted her from the seat and lowered her until her feet touched the ground. Without removing his hands, he gazed down into her velvety eyes, their dark beauty reflected in the moonlight.

He lowered his lips to hers and gave her a long, tender kiss. Then, raising his head, he ran his knuckles along her temple and whispered, "Goodnight, sweetheart."

Rachel stared speechlessly back at him and it was a long moment before she collected her thoughts enough to return his farewell. "Goodnight," she whispered. Quickly turning away, she unlocked the side door of the house and disappeared through it.

Seth stood motionless for a long time, riveted to the spot as he stared after her. Finally, with a long sigh, he turned and led the horses toward the barn, somehow knowing that this night had been a turning point in his life.

Chapter Sixteen

"Where's Lia?" Seth asked as he walked into the kitchen the next morning.

Rachel, who was peeling carrots at the sink, didn't turn around. All morning she'd been nervous about seeing him after the previous evening's romantic interlude and although she was relieved that he sounded completely normal, she still wasn't ready to face him. "She's gone over to the Johnson's," she answered, her knife continuing its rhythmic scraping over the carrot. "Mary stopped by and asked if Lia could spend the day with Julie and Laura. I didn't think you'd mind."

"Damn!" Seth cursed. "I wish I'd known."

Rachel turned, surprised at the displeasure in his voice. As her eyes swept over him, however, she forgot all about his curse, so astonished was she by his appearance. He was almost naked. Barefoot and bare chested, he wore nothing but a pair of old levis which had been hacked off well above the knee. His blatant masculinity was boldly in evidence in the brief attire and she quickly turned back to her carrots, her eyes wide and her pulse racing.

Seth glanced at her quizzically, then, venturing a look downward at his near nudity, he grinned. "Thought I'd teach Lia to swim today," he said to her rigid back. "It's too hot and muggy to do any real

167

chores, but it's a great day to spend in the water."

"I'm sorry, Seth," she said, still scraping the same carrot, which was now about the size of a toothpick. "I never dreamed you'd mind. I suppose I should have asked you first, but you were still asleep and I didn't want to bother you."

"It's okay. I can teach her next weekend. What time is she gonna be home?"

"Well, actually, Mary asked if Hank could bring her back tomorrow morning after church since it's such a long drive out to their farm. I told her it would be okay." Throwing a brief glance at him from over her shoulder, she added, "I'm really sorry. I should have awakened you. I honestly didn't know you had plans, and Lia was so excited about going . . ."

"Forget it," he said. "And, for God's sake, take a new carrot before you end up without a finger!"

The knife Rachel was holding clattered into the sink and she whirled to face him. "You're making me very nervous."

Seth grinned, delighted by the effect his state of undress was having on her. When he'd decided to give Lia a swimming lesson, he'd never dreamed what a sexy turn this morning was going to take. "I don't know why," he said innocently. "I went swimming one morning when you first came and it didn't seem to bother you then to see me like this."

"That was different," she muttered.

Dropping his towel, he sauntered purposely toward her, a wicked smile on his face. "Was it now? How come?"

"Seth, stop it!" She was standing with her back against the counter and he loomed over her so that she had to bend backward to escape his blatant seduction.

He continued to lean over her until she couldn't bend back any further. As his lips touched hers, he leered, "Want to go swimming, lady?"

"I . . . I don't know how to swim," she stammered.

"Want to learn?"

"Seth, will you please stop this? I have work to do."

"Don't work today," he drawled. "Come play with me instead."

"Seth!"

Planting a quick kiss on her lips, he grinned like a naughty boy and backed up a step. "You really don't know how to swim?"

"No."

"Well then, come on and I'll teach you."

"Don't be silly," she protested. "I can't go swimming with you!"·

"Why not? Are you scared?"

Rachel knew that in his current mood, her answer to that should be an unequivocal 'yes,' but instead she said, "I don't have anything to swim in."

Seth cocked his head, frowning. "That *is* a problem. Can't you just take off a couple layers of whatever you have on now and swim in what's left?"

"Seth!"

"No, I mean it!" he laughed. "Tell you what. I know a swimming hole where no one ever goes so no one will see you. We'll walk down there and I'll get in the water and turn my back. That way, you can take off most of your stuff and then get in the water with me and I promise I won't look until you're neck deep. How's that?"

"I should be offended that you'd even suggest such a thing!" she admonished primly.

"But you aren't, are you?" he laughed. "Come on, Rachel, you know you're safe with me. I'll just teach you to swim and I promise I won't do anything you don't want me to do."

Rachel knew that was the very crux of her dilemma. Standing there, half nude, with his tawny hair falling over his forehead and his bare chest and bulging muscles exposed, she felt like she might want him to do *everything* . . . and that thought scared her to death.

"Say you'll go," he persisted, taking another step toward her until she was again bent backward over the sink. "Say you'll go or I'll spend the rest of the day chasing you around this house. Come on, say it!"

Rachel gazed up into his dancing blue eyes, realizing that she'd never seen him so happy and playful. Unable to deny him, she nodded reluctantly. "Well, all right, but only if you promise to behave."

With a wide grin, he stepped back. "Promise." As he leaned over to retrieve his towel, the thought shot through his mind that he'd behave . . . he didn't know if he'd behave *well*, but he'd behave!

A half hour later, they arrived at the swimming hole. Due to the lateness of the season, the water was a bit murky near the shore, but farther out, it was still clear and blue. To Rachel's profound relief, Seth had been right. There wasn't a soul around, and the only sound to be heard was the loud buzzing of late summer cicadas in the bushes.

True to his word, Seth marched into the water, wading out until it swirled around his chest. Turning, he called, "Okay, I'll turn my back now so you can get undressed."

Rachel hesitated, remembering Cynthia's warning the night before, and feeling like she could be making a serious mistake in agreeing to this madness. But, knowing it was too late to change her mind, she peeled off her hot dress and petticoat. Leaning over, she removed her shoes and stockings so that she was clad only in her camisole and drawers. She hurried into the water, her eyes never leaving Seth's broad back as she prayed he wouldn't turn around. He didn't, and she continued to wade through the cool, refreshing water until, by the time she reached his side, it was closing over her shoulders.

170

"Here I am," she announced.

"I know," he chuckled. "I heard you coming." Turning to face her, he was careful not to look down, knowing he would be able to see her breasts just under the surface of the clear water.

"The first thing you need to learn is how to float. Now, I'm going to put my arms like this and you just lie down in them. I'll hold you up." He stretched his arms out in front of him on the surface of the water, demonstrating how he would support her.

"Okay," she nodded. "Do I lie down on my back or my stomach?"

Seth frowned, realizing that he had just set himself a nearly impossible task. If she lay facedown, her lovely breasts were going to be rubbing against his arm. But, if she lay on her back, he was going to see them as well as if she were lying naked in bed with him. Already fighting the beginnings of his arousal, he was in a complete quandary as to what to tell her.

"I guess it's best to learn to float on your back first. Just lie down and put your arms at your sides."

Rachel nodded and without a qualm, dropped back into his arms. Despite himself, his gaze swept over her, noting her tight, hard little nipples pushing against the transparent camisole and the hazy triangle enticingly visible beneath her drawers at the juncture of her thighs. He felt his manhood spring to life and swallowed hard, willing himself to look only at her face. He mustn't allow his gaze to dip below her neck or he was going to take her right there in broad daylight in the middle of the pond. That thought, in itself, was so erotic that he shivered in reaction.

"Are you all right?" Rachel asked from her prone position. "Am I too heavy to hold up?"

"No," he answered quickly. "No one's heavy in the water. I'm not really holding you up at all—the water is. Now, I'm going to take my arms away and you just stay exactly as you are and you'll see what I mean. Even without me supporting you, you'll still float."

Slowly dropping his arms away from her, he took a step backward. "See?" he smiled. "You're floating."

As soon as Rachel realized that his arms were no longer supporting her, she jackknifed. With a small shriek of fear, she disappeared under the water for a moment, only to surface gasping and sputtering as she pushed her hair out of her face and wiped water from her eyes.

"It doesn't work if you're not holding me. I sink!"

"No, you don't," Seth explained patiently. "You just panicked when you realized I wasn't supporting you and you let your bottom go down. You have to keep your back arched. Come on, now, let's try it again."

He held his arms out and again Rachel lay back in them. This time, she wrapped one arm around his neck and threw the other one over her head as she reclined in the water. Her posture caused her camisole to stretch even more tightly across her bosom and Seth knew he was lost. Totally against his will, his gaze dropped, drinking in the beauty of her straining breasts, flat stomach and the slight mound of her womanhood. Her legs were long and shapely as they floated on the water's surface and a little pool was forming where her thighs came together. His erection was throbbing out of control under the water and he knew that if he didn't get away from her immediately, he was going to disgrace himself in front of her.

"Lesson's over, Rachel," he said suddenly, dropping his arms and rushing off toward shore.

Again, Rachel felt her derriere touch bottom as she plummeted to the floor of the pond. Struggling to her feet, she called, "What's the matter? What do you mean the lesson's over? I haven't learned how to swim yet!"

"I can't teach you," he yelled over his shoulder. "Not

today, anyway. Maybe some other time . . . in about fifty years."

Rachel stood in the water, completely confused by his sudden change of mood. She waded toward shore until the water was at waist level. Glancing down at herself, she gasped, and in a lightning flash of understanding realized what Seth's problem was. Horrified by her naked display, she clapped her arms over her breasts and called, "Seth, I'm sorry! I didn't realize!"

He was just stepping up on shore and craning his head around, he called over his shoulder, "I know. I'm sorry too. I didn't know how . . . impossible it would be. I'll get dressed and leave and then you can get out."

Rachel nodded miserably from where she stood in the water and watched as he gathered up his clothes and fled toward the road like all the furies of hell were chasing him.

Trudging slowly out of the pond, she looked down at herself in shamed mortification. Every curve, every contour showed. How could she have been so stupid as to not realize that the opaque camisole would be transparent when wet. She felt like the worst kind of tease and prayed that Seth would not think that. Pulling her dry dress over her cold, wet underwear, she pushed her sopping hair back over her shoulder and began the long walk back to the house.

Supper had been ready for over an hour, but still there was no sign of Seth. Rachel had agonized all afternoon over their ill-fated swimming lesson. She couldn't decide whether she should apologize to him for unwittingly seducing him, or just let the matter drop. She had finally come to the conclusion that her decision would have to wait until she saw what his mood was when he got home . . . if he ever did.

She was sitting at the kitchen table, drumming her

nails and idly straightening the cutlery when she finally heard the front door open and his footsteps come down the hall. He walked into the kitchen and looked at her in surprise. "Haven't you eaten yet? It's after eight."

"No," she shook her head. "I was waiting for you."

"You shouldn't have."

"Why? Did you already eat?" She had a sudden terrible vision of him sharing an intimate dinner with Etta Lawrence.

"No," he responded, allaying her fears.

"Then, do you want some supper?"

He stood and looked at her for a moment as if debating what to answer. Finally giving in to his most basic needs, he nodded and sank into a chair. "Guess I should," he mumbled. "I haven't had anything all day."

Rachel quickly got the plates out of the warming oven and set one in front of him. "It's roast beef," she said hopefully. "I know you like it."

"Yeah, I do."

The meal progressed in strained silence with neither of them knowing how to bring up the subject they both knew had to be discussed. When Seth had eaten every scrap of the huge portion she'd given him, Rachel rose and removed the plates from the table.

"Don't do the dishes tonight," he said softly, "it's too damn hot. Let's go sit in the front room. The sun's over on this side of the house now and it's a lot cooler in there."

Rachel nodded her agreement and followed him down the hall to the sitting room. He sank down onto a brocade-covered settee and moved over to make room for her. Cautiously, she sat down, folding her hands in her lap and looking at him expectantly. Suddenly, they were both talking at once.

"I'm sorry, Rachel."

"No, I'm sorry. It was my fault."

"No, I should have known better."

"Well, I should have too!"

Simultaneously, they began laughing, breaking the unbearable tension between them. Grabbing her to him, Seth buried his head in her fragrant hair and whispered, "I wasn't trying to take advantage, I really wasn't."

"I know that," Rachel answered, pulling away slightly. "And, I wasn't trying to tease you. I didn't know I'd look so . . . so naked with my camisole wet!"

Seth sat back and took a deep breath, looking at her closely. "I don't know what it is about you. I can't seem to keep my hands off you and there's never been a woman I couldn't walk away from when I knew I should."

"Not even your wife?" Rachel whispered.

He stared off into the distance for a moment. "It was good between us, he admitted softly. "Always good. But never . . . crazy. With you, I'm crazy."

"Seth—"

Whatever Rachel had been about to say was lost forever as, suddenly, he was all over her. His kisses were almost desperate in their intensity and his fevered words nearly unintelligible against her ear. "Tried to stay away . . . nothing works . . . want you so bad . . . I love you."

The last three words registered. Scrambling to sit up, Rachel pushed him away and stared at him in disbelief. "What did you say?"

Seth closed his eyes, knowing he'd said it . . . knowing he'd meant it. "I love you," he repeated softly. "More than I've ever loved anyone in my life. I want to marry you . . . be with you forever. Have kids with you. Get old with you." He was staring down at his hands and when his voice finally trailed off and he looked up, he was appalled to see she was crying. "I shouldn't have said it, should I? I'm sorry, Rachel. I didn't mean to say it. It just came out!" Burying his head in his hands, she heard him mutter, "Jesus Christ, what a mess!"

She nearly knocked him over in her haste to kiss him. "What do you mean, you shouldn't have said it? I've waited forever to hear you say it! Oh, God, Seth, I love you so much!" Nearly throwing him onto his back, she buried her fingers in his thick hair and kissed him with all the passion and longing she'd felt for so many months. He loved her! He wanted to marry her! And he thought he shouldn't have said it!

Seth was so astonished by her frenzied reaction to his confession that he was speechless. All he knew was that proper little Dr. Hayes was crawling all over him like a barroom whore. It was the best feeling he'd ever experienced! Loosening her death grip on his hair, he pulled her under him and whispered, "Go slow, baby. This is important."

She looked up at him with fathomless eyes, then whispered shyly, "Show me."

He looked at her hard. "Don't invite me to start unless you want to finish."

Her gaze was serious as she looked back at him. "You wanted me in the water today, didn't you?"

At his nod, she smiled, feeling for the first time the power a woman could wield over a man. "And if I walk up those stairs, take off all my clothes and get into your bed, you'll want me again, won't you?"

Seth's mouth dropped open, then immediately snapped shut. "You better mean this, Rachel, because if you're teasing me, by God, I'm going to horsewhip you!"

She stared boldly up at him. "I'm not teasing, Seth."

It was all the encouragement he needed. Leaping off the settee, he scooped her up in his arms and headed for the staircase. He took the steps two at a time, entering his room where a small kerosene lamp threw a soft, mellow light over the sumptuous furnishings. Laying

Rachel on his huge bed, he braced his arms on either side of her as he bent to kiss her. His breathing was harsh and ragged, but whether from the exertion of his headlong flight up the stairs or his rapidly mounting sexual excitement, he didn't know.

Lowering himself next to her, he propped up on one elbow and began to slowly, sensuously unbutton the front of her light cotton dress.

Flushed, excited and embarrassed by his passionate assault, Rachel lightly stroked his hair and closed her eyes. Seth paused, looking at her closely to see if he was pushing her too fast. As she felt his hand still on its journey down the front of her dress, she opened her eyes. Seeing his concerned expression, she asked, "Is something wrong?"

He gazed at her flushed face and smiled. "Are you okay?"

"Wonderful," she sighed, closing her eyes again, "but I wish you'd kiss me."

His response was immediate as he covered her parted lips with his own and seductively invaded her mouth's silky recesses. At her groan of pleasure, his progress down the front of her dress accelerated as, in a frenzy to touch her skin, he ripped button after button from its hole. Finally, he lifted her up on to her knees and pushed her dress and chemise off her shoulders, baring her to the waist as he continued to kiss her.

Suddenly, her eyes dark with passion's awakening, Rachel wrenched her mouth away from his, pulling his shirt free of his pants and unbuttoning it. But Seth was not to be denied even for a moment and, as her fingers traveled down his chest, he leaned forward and buried his head in the exquisite softness of her bare bosom, groaning softly as he kissed and sucked at her tight, aroused nipples. His hands stroked the sides of her breasts, pushing them together as he lifted them and rubbed his open mouth across them.

His intimate attentions made Rachel's hands shake as she fumbled with the never-ending row of buttons. Finally reaching the last one, she gave it a hard tug, hearing the material rip and silently vowing that she'd mend it in the morning.

Seth shrugged the shirt off and pulled her hard against him, causing her eyes to widen in wonder as his crisp chest hair caressed her breasts. She stroked the muscles covering his ribs and rubbed her taut nipples against his hard, flat ones until he thought he just might die from sheer bliss.

Without warning, he bolted off the bed, his breathing labored and his eyes aflame with lust. Backing up a few steps, he said in a hoarse voice, "We've gotta slow down, little girl, or I'm going to ruin it for you."

Rachel threw him a perplexed look. "Am I doing something wrong?"

"God, no!" he laughed shakily, running his hands through his hair, "you're doing it too right!"

Then, turning away from her, he peeled off his levis and underclothes. He paused a moment to get himself under control before turning back toward her, revealing his perfectly honed masculinity in all its naked splendor.

Rachel's eyes flew to the center of him and she gasped at her first sight of the bold, jutting proof of his desire. She raised shaking fingers to her lips and her eyes widened even further as he walked deliberately toward her, a sensuous chuckle rumbling in his chest.

"What's the matter, Doctor?" he teased, his voice low and beguiling. "Haven't you ever seen one interested before?"

Rachel's eyes lifted to his face. "Interested?" she smiled. "Is that what you call it?"

He nodded. "That, and other things."

"What other things?"

"Needy," he whispered, pulling her to her feet. "So needy . . ."

He was looking her directly in the eyes now as he moved close enough for his impassioned manhood to brush against her. Her eyes closed and her hand came up to stroke his chest as he covered her mouth with his. He didn't touch her, but stood with his hands at his sides, his tongue toying with hers and his throbbing erection pressing against her stomach. She could feel the heat of him through her light skirt and with a sharp intake of breath, took a small step backward to break the erotic contact.

"Am I scaring you?" he asked softly.

"No," she stammered, "it's just sort of . . . overwhelming."

"I won't hurt you, sweetheart," he promised, his breath feather light on her lips.

"I know you won't," she whispered and retraced her step until she was again pressed against him.

Covering her hands with his own, he guided her palms lightly over his naked body, gently familiarizing her with his masculine swells and contours. At the same time, he kissed her until she was swaying on her feet. Then, he sank slowly to his knees in front of her, hooking his thumbs into the waistband of her dress and pulling it and her petticoats down until they lay in a forgotten heap.

Throwing her head back in an agony of sensation, Rachel twined her hands in his hair to steady herself as he lifted one foot, pulling off her shoe and rolling a stocking down her long, shapely leg. His lips followed the trail of the stocking as he kissed the inside of her calf down to her ankle. She stood perfectly still as he removed her other shoe and stocking, his lips continuing their erotic play with her other leg — only this time they moved up from her ankle and continued past her knee.

Rachel gasped at his intimate touch, almost losing her balance as she fought to untangle her feet from the pool of clothing in which she still stood.

Shaking and breathless, Seth got to his feet and yanked the bedclothes off, then turned to gather her in his arms and pull her down with him. She fell against him, her body molding to his . . . softness against hardness, white flesh against bronze. He rolled until she was stretched out full length on top of him. Placing his hands on either side of her face, he whispered, "Open your eyes and look at me."

She did, staring into the deep pools of blue.

"I love you, Rachel, and I want to marry you. I want to spend every night of my life doing this with you, but I need to be sure you want to do it now."

"Yes," she answered, a catch in her throat. "Oh, Seth, yes!"

"Good," he smiled, exhaling a long, relieved breath.

Turning her in his arms, he kissed her again, angling himself above her so that she could feel his throbbing arousal pressed against her thigh. His hand swept provocatively down her stomach, coming to rest in the fleecy down. He left it there, hovering . . . asking the ultimate question.

And Rachel answered. Subtly, she opened herself to him, pressing upward against his hand until his fingers slipped into her satiny sheath. She moaned, rolling her head against the pillow as his fingers skillfully played with her womanhood, driving her inexorably toward something she didn't even know existed.

"Oh, Seth," she moaned, "what you're doing to me! May I touch you too?"

His breath was hot and his voice hoarse against her ear as he answered, "God, yes, sweetheart, you can do anything you want to."

She didn't hesitate at all. Moving her hand between them, she wrapped soft, tentative fingers around him, marveling at the silky texture of his skin and the heat which filled her palm.

He groaned, a sound which reminded her of a male animal calling its mate and she reacted with inborn instinct, rubbing her hand up and down his pulsating shaft, guiding him toward her.

He entered her slowly, carefully, but still she gasped, seized with the first searing pain of invasion.

A surge of primal male exultation coursed through him at this undeniable proof that he was her first. But, sensitive to her innocence, he clamped down hard on his fiery need. With amazing control, he paused, giving her a moment to accustom herself to him. He kissed her soothingly, murmuring soft words of encouragement and apology for her pain. As his hands stroked her, she relaxed, allowing him to complete their union.

Again, he stilled so she could rest a moment, nuzzling her ear and kissing the soft hair at her temple. "You like this?"

"Oh, yes," she breathed, "but I want . . . I want . . ."

"I know what you want," he murmured, "and if you're ready, I'll give it to you."

"Oh, please . . ."

He needed no further encouragement. Slowly, exquisitely, he began the timeless rhythm of love, subtly increasing his pace as he felt her respond. Despite his flaming lust, he held himself in check until he felt her near fulfillment. Then, as a scream of ecstasy tore from her throat, he finally allowed himself to seek his own heaven, groaning and shuddering as he poured himself into her.

In the quiet moments that followed, as their hearts slowed and their breathing returned to normal, he nestled her head against his shoulder and lightly kissed her, whispering words of love and praise. "I love you,

Rachel," he breathed. "I'm going to wrap you up in diamonds."

"Mmmm," she sighed contentedly, "that's nice. I love you too, Seth. You're even more beautiful than all the ladies in town think you are."

"What?" he gasped, suddenly sitting up and gaping at her in disbelief. "What did you say about the women in town?"

"Never mind," she smiled, her eyes closing in sated exhaustion, "I'll tell you in the morning."

"You bet you will, lady," he chuckled, lying back down and pulling her back against him. "If you weren't so sleepy, I'd make you tell me now. In fact, tired or not, I want to know now. What are the good 'ladies' of Stone Creek saying about me?"

When she didn't answer, he propped himself on an elbow and looked down at her, but she was sound asleep.

"Sweet little virgin," he smiled, tenderly pushing a strand of hair out of her face, "did the big sheriff wear you out?"

Then, lying back with a happy, contented smile, he closed his eyes and fell into the most peaceful sleep he'd known in four long years.

Chapter Seventeen

Rachel's eyelids fluttered open and she shivered deliciously. Casting a vague, sleepy gaze downward, she tried to identify the source of the tingling pleasure she was experiencing.

The source was kneeling above her in the shadowy dawn light, his tongue tracing erotic little swirls around her right nipple. He lifted his head, and seeing that she was awake, smiled languidly and drawled, "Want to go swimming, lady?"

She blushed, embarrassed to be caught watching his intimate ministrations in the light of day.

Seeing her discomfiture, Seth again lowered his head and returned to his sensuous play. "Want to go swimming, lady?" he repeated.

With a small smile, she reached down and stroked his tousled hair, sighing, "No, not now . . ."

Pleased with her shy but provocative answer, he looked up and said, "Want to get up and make me some breakfast, lady?"

Catching on to the game, she giggled lazily and returned, "No, not now . . ."

A shudder of expectation ran through him as he again drew a nipple into his mouth and toyed with it till he heard her catch her breath and squirm beneath him. Lifting his head again, he whispered, "Want to make love, lady?"

Rachel shivered with delight and whispered back, "Yes, right now . . ."

With a triumphant laugh, Seth rose out of his crouched position, sitting back and pulling her up against him until she was seated high on his thighs, her legs wrapped around his hips. His hard, hot shaft pressed against her as he nearly devoured her with his mouth.

"You mean like this?" she gasped.

"Yes," he muttered, sucking her lower lip into his mouth and biting down gently on it. "and about a hundred other ways I'm gonna teach you."

"All this morning?" she giggled.

"It's only five . . . we've got hours . . ."

But his playful mood changed abruptly as Rachel pushed herself a little higher up his thighs so the tip of his manhood teased at her most intimate spot. She was wet and ready for him and all thoughts of playfulness disappeared as he growled, "Lean back a little and brace yourself on your arms."

She did as he instructed, then promptly let out a small scream of surprise as he pushed himself forward and slid into her. Supporting her back, he locked his ankles behind her and began lazily circling his hips, filling her full of himself and causing her to gasp and cry out in reaction.

"Am I hurting you?" he asked, instantly starting to withdraw.

"No, not really. You're just . . . so big!"

"I know." He shook his head regretfully. "And, you're tiny. Lie back, sweetheart . . . you're not ready for this lesson yet."

Gratefully, she sank back into the pillows and, without breaking their intimate embrace, he followed her.

"I'm sorry," she murmured. "I guess your hundred ways will have to wait a bit . . ."

He smiled and tenderly brushed a lock of hair off her

184

forehead, kissing her jaw and the soft skin behind her ear.

"We've got the rest of our lives, baby . . . it doesn't really have to all happen this morning."

"I know, but I feel bad that . . ."

"Shh," he crooned, sensuously rotating his hips against her to remind her that he was still with her. "You'll get used to me soon enough. In fact, I plan to make love to you so often that you'll probably get bored with it."

"Oh, I don't think so," she sighed, wrapping her legs around his waist. "I have a lot to learn."

Seth gasped as his manhood slipped all the way up her sheath. "You're learning real fast, darlin' . . ."

And then, words were forgotten as together they sought and found their paradise . . .

They lay quietly for a long time afterward, watching the sun come up and wishing they never had to leave their intimate nest. But Rachel knew that Amelia would be home soon and it certainly would not do for her to meet Mary Johnson at the door looking like a woman who'd just been made love to all night. However, the thought that that was exactly what she was, was so titillating that she again rolled toward Seth, toying with the hair on his chest and kissing a sensitive nipple.

"Oh, no, you little pistol," he laughed, sitting up and giving her a last, quick kiss. "Not again. I've got chores to do and you've gotta feed me if you expect me to keep this up every night."

Rachel giggled and threw her arms around his neck, kissing him and laughing. "Every night, Sheriff? Surely, you don't expect me to share your bed again until after we're married. Lia might say something to someone and both our reputations would be ruined."

She felt him stiffen and sat back on her heels, feeling suddenly wary. "What's wrong, Seth? I'm only talking about a few days. I just want a small ceremony with a few friends as witnesses and I don't think that should take more than a week to plan."

Seth looked at her for a long moment, then got up from the bed, paced the length of the room, and turned back to look at her again.

His silence was deafening and the apprehension Rachel was feeling doubled and redoubled as he continued to stare at her from across the room. "What's wrong?" she asked again.

"Nothing's wrong, exactly," he answered quietly, "but you know very well you can't make definite plans to get married yet . . . not next week, maybe not next month."

"Why?" she asked, biting her lip anxiously, already knowing the answer.

"Why?" he asked incredulously. "Because we can't get married until I catch Clint Brady, that's why!"

Rachel closed her eyes, fighting the surge of panic that coursed through her. Rising from the bed, she walked very slowly over to him, willing herself to remain calm. "Please tell me you don't mean that, Seth," she pleaded.

"Of course I mean it," he said, throwing his arms wide. "Did you think I would marry you and take the chance that he'd come after you? I'm sure he'd enjoy killing my second wife as much as he enjoyed the first."

Tears stung the backs of Rachel's eyes as she saw her dreams crumbling around her. "I understand your concern, Seth, but I don't want to wait. It could be a . . . a long time before you catch him and—"

"Don't start that again," he warned, his voice rising angrily. "You've got to have faith in me."

"But, Seth!"

"This discussion is over, Rachel. I will *not* jeopardize

you and Amelia. My God, think about it. Brady would kill you both in a minute if he knew you were married to me and that she was my daughter, or your niece, or in any way connected with me. I won't take that chance just so you and I can sleep together next week."

"It's not just sleeping with you, Seth, and you know it," Rachel cried, her lower lip quivering as she valiantly tried to fight back the threatening tears.

Closing his eyes in anguish at the pain he was causing her, Seth groaned, pulling her cold, naked body into his embrace. "Please don't cry, sweetheart. It won't be long, I promise you. I'm close . . . really close. In fact, that's where I was yesterday afternoon . . . tracking him. I got word that he's set up a new camp near here. It'll be over soon, but you're just going to have to put wedding plans on hold until it is."

Rachel looked up at him and then, stepping out of his embrace, said very calmly, "No."

His eyes widened in amazement. "What do you mean, 'no'?"

"I mean 'no'!" she repeated. Averting her eyes from his, she looked down as if suddenly aware that they were both still nude. Grabbing the quilt off the end of the bed, she wrapped it around herself. "Please get dressed."

"Get dressed?" Seth shouted, "we're in the middle of the most important discussion of our lives and you're worried about whether or not I'm dressed? Jesus Christ, Rachel! What the hell is wrong with you?"

"Nothing's wrong with me," she answered, "except that I'm not going to stop living while you pursue your revenge. Killing Clint Brady may be your life, but it's not mine."

"Are you saying you won't wait for me?" he asked, aghast. "I don't believe this! Maybe I was wrong about how you feel about me. Maybe you don't love me at all. Maybe you just want to get married *now* and it doesn't matter who it is as long as it's next week!"

"How dare you?" Rachel raged. "After what we shared last night . . . how dare you accuse me of not loving you!"

"After what we shared last night," Seth shouted back, striding toward her until she was backed up against the bed, "I figured we loved one another enough to weather just about anything together. But, the first time you don't get your way, you want to pack it in."

"That's not true," Rachel stormed. "But I won't be Etta Lawrence and sit by patiently for years while you chase your outlaw. I don't want your spare time, Seth. I want a whole lot more than that from you."

"Spare time? Is that what you think I'm offering you? My *spare time?*"

"What I think," she blazed, looking up at him with flashing eyes, "is that you'll give me as much as you can of yourself, as long as it doesn't take you away from your real love, which is chasing Clint Brady."

Seth was dumbfounded by her vehement words and stood staring down at her, at a loss to respond. Finally, he turned away and tiredly pulled on his levis and torn shirt.

"If that's really the way you feel, Rachel, then there's nothing more to be said. I offer my deepest apologies for last night. Let's just pretend it didn't happen and go back to the way things used to be."

"Oh?" she asked, her voice quavering as her resolve slipped a notch, "and what way was that? You go back to Etta Lawrence and pretend I don't exist?"

"Yeah," Seth said coldly, "exactly. I'll go back to patient, undemanding Etta and you go back to adoring, dull Charlie Stimson. I'm sure he'd be more than happy to abandon his job at the depot to devote *all* his time to you, since that's what you really seem to want from a man."

"You bastard!" Rachel gasped, tears springing to her

eyes. "You probably never had any intention of marrying me. You just wanted a quick roll in the hay and I was the easiest way to get it."

At this last accusation, Seth's hands clenched at his sides and the veins stood out in his neck as he struggled to hold on to his quickly disintegrating control. Taking a deep, steadying breath, he looked down at the woman facing him and said, "Do you really think that, Rachel?"

The tears she had held back for so long rolled unheeded down her cheeks. "Yes," she sobbed, hating herself for the lie even as she said it. "Yes!"

Seth sighed and shook his head. "Okay," he whispered, "then, we're done."

Without another word, he turned and walked out of the room and down the stairs.

"I'd love to go with you, Seth." Etta Lawrence smiled in pleased surprise. Seth hadn't come calling in weeks and she'd been delighted when he'd stepped onto her veranda that evening and sat down on the swing next to her as if nothing had changed between them. Although she hadn't lost hope that he would get over his fascination with Dr. Hayes, enough time had passed that she was beginning to think she'd lost him for good. But, here he was, asking her to go to the Harvest Picnic. Etta couldn't remember when she had been more thrilled.

"Gotta go, Etta," he said suddenly, giving her hand a slight squeeze and standing up. "I'll call for you about noon on Sunday."

"Fine," she answered with a happy smile. "I'll be ready."

As Seth sauntered off down the boardwalk, Etta shook her head in wonder. She'd never figure him out. One minute he seemed to really care about her, and the next he acted like they were nothing more than casual acquaintances. But Etta was patient and determined. She was willing to wait, hoping he'd realize that she was the best possible woman with whom to build his future. If only he'd show a little bit more interest in her romantically. She had considered trying to entice him into her bed, confident that once he realized she was willing to give up her virginity to him, he'd know how serious she was. But, even if she could find the courage to seduce him, he'd never given her the opportunity. He'd held her hand, danced with her, and occasionally kissed her in the darkness of the late evening. Once she'd even been in his bedroom when he'd given her a quick tour of his beautiful house. But, he'd never surpassed the bounds of proper behavior or given her any encouragement to do so. There was no real passion in his touch and she was at a loss as to how to ignite it.

Oh well, she thought as she rocked slowly back and forth, at least he asked me to the picnic, and not Rachel Hayes. She rose from the swing and walked thoughtfully into the house, wondering how to make the most of Sunday afternoon.

"Can I go help with the ice cream, Auntie Rachel?"

"Sure, honey," Rachel smiled, "just don't get your new dress dirty."

"Okay," Lia nodded, scampering off to join a large crowd of children who were taking turns sitting on ice cream freezers while several of the town's men turned the cranks.

Rachel sat down on a bench and looked around with interest. The Harvest Picnic was in full swing and it was hard to believe that just that morning, the area where she sat had been nothing more than a freshly cut wheat field. Now, thanks to the efforts of most of the town's citizens, there were gaily decorated tables and chairs sitting everywhere. Brightly colored streamers waved in the late summer breeze, and the air was filled with the sounds of boisterous laughter and children's shouts of glee. A corner of the field had been roped off for games and a portion of Main Street was being blocked off for horse races which were to be held after lunch.

There was a large grove of trees at the south end of the field and it was there that the town's women were busily laying out food. Everyone had donated a dish to the picnic and the tables fairly groaned with fried chicken, casseroles, salads and dozens of pies and cakes. The women had their hands full trying to keep unruly children away from the tempting desserts, but even the sternest mothers' warnings were laced with good humor.

Rising from her seat, Rachel walked toward the tables, intending to offer her assistance in setting out the food. She stopped short, however, when she heard her name being called. Turning in the direction of the sound, she saw Etta Lawrence coming toward her, her arm linked securely through Seth's and a triumphant smile on her face. Forcing herself to smile back, Rachel waved and walked toward the couple, determined that Seth would not see her dismay.

"Good afternoon, Miss Lawrence, Sheriff," she said pleasantly. "Lovely afternoon, isn't it?"

"It certainly is," Etta trilled. "An absolutely perfect day!"

"I didn't know you were coming to the picnic," Seth said quietly, his eyes boring into hers.

"Well, why wouldn't she come?" Etta asked. "Dr. Hayes is part of our community and everyone would think it strange if she didn't attend at least a few of our functions."

Seth ignored Etta's remark and continued to stare at Rachel. "Where is Amelia?"

"She's over there with the other children," Rachel

pointed. "They're taking turns sitting on the ice cream freezers."

"Better keep your eye on her," Seth advised, causing Etta to throw him a perplexed look. Knowing he was arousing her curiosity, he quickly covered his faux pas by saying, "She's a little dickens. You turn away for a second and she's gone."

"She's perfectly all right, Sheriff," Rachel said coolly. "I appreciate your concern, but you need not worry about *my* niece."

Etta was aware of the charged atmosphere between Seth and Rachel and wished she hadn't drawn Rachel's attention to them. With a feigned squeal of distress, she cried, "Oh, Seth! They're already starting the men's foot races. You were going to run in those, weren't you? We better get over there!"

Seth tore his gaze away from Rachel long enough to glance over to where Etta was pointing. "Yeah, I guess we better."

"Good luck, Sheriff," Rachel said, and hurriedly headed off in the opposite direction. Thank God that little encounter was over, she thought with relief. One more minute of watching Etta Lawrence hang on Seth and smile at her with that superior smirk and she just might have slapped it off her face!

As Seth let Etta steer him toward the races, he realized he didn't feel at all like competing. What he felt like doing was shrugging off Etta's clinging arm, grabbing Rachel and kissing her till she admitted she still loved him. He hadn't seen her at all in the last few days and the sight of her with the sun shining on her face and her cheeks pink with excitement and fresh air made his heart wrench. He loved her, and no matter how much they disagreed about Clint Brady, nothing could change that.

Rachel was suffering from the same affliction. She had told herself that it was better to make a clean break

192

TO GET YOUR 4 FREE BOOKS WORTH $18.00 — MAIL IN THE FREE BOOK CERTIFICATE T O D A Y

Fill in the Free Book Certificate below, and we'll send your FREE BOOKS to you as soon as we receive it.

If the certificate is missing below, write to: Zebra Home Subscription Service, Inc., P.O. Box 5214, 120 Brighton Road, Clifton, New Jersey 07015-5214.

4 FREE BOOKS

FREE BOOK CERTIFICATE

ZEBRA HOME SUBSCRIPTION SERVICE, INC.

YES! Please start my subscription to Zebra Historical Romances and send me my first 4 books absolutely FREE. I understand that each month I may preview four new Zebra Historical Romances free for 10 days. If I'm not satisfied with them, I may return the four books within 10 days and owe nothing. Otherwise, I will pay the low preferred subscriber's price of just $3.75 each; a total of $15.00, *a savings off the publisher's price of $3.00.* I may return any shipment and I may cancel this subscription at any time. There is no obligation to buy any shipment and there are no shipping, handling or other hidden charges. Regardless of what I decide, the four free books are mine to keep.

NAME

ADDRESS _____ APT _____

CITY _____ STATE ____ ZIP _____

TELEPHONE
(   )

SIGNATURE _____
(if under 18, parent or guardian must sign)

Terms, offer and prices subject to change without notice. Subscription subject to acceptance by Zebra Books. Zebra Books reserves the right to reject any order or cancel any subscription.

GET
FOUR
FREE
BOOKS
(AN $18.00 VALUE)

ZEBRA HOME SUBSCRIPTION
SERVICE, INC.
P.O. Box 5214
120 BRIGHTON ROAD
CLIFTON, NEW JERSEY 07015-5214

and had, by sheer dint of will and careful planning, managed to avoid Seth all week. After all, there was obviously no future for them, so why prolong the agony by seeing him? For the first few days after their argument, she had sat in her lonely room at night, hoping that he might come to her. But, he didn't and after a week, she finally had to admit to herself that he had meant it when he said they were through. She even thought she had convinced herself that it was better that way, but one look into his blue eyes had made her heart slam painfully against her ribs, and the sight of Etta Lawrence with her arm entwined in his made a veritable volcano of jealousy erupt within her. Rachel sighed, knowing deep down that she would never get over Seth Wellesley.

She reached the heavily-laden food tables and forced herself to smile brightly in response to the greetings being extended to her. People were starting to gather as delicious aromas wafted on the breeze, reminding them it was time for lunch.

Rachel busied herself pouring huge glasses of lemonade for those who were already seated, chatting as she moved between the tables. It was a pleasant diversion and her tightly strung emotions finally started to unwind, allowing her to relax and smile in earnest at the friendly celebrants. She was walking back toward the tub where the lemonade was being cooled when she again heard her name being called, but this time, by an unfamiliar male voice.

She turned around to see Charlie Stimson walking toward her.

"I was hoping you'd be here today," he said by way of greeting. "Have you eaten yet?"

Rachel shook her head, gesturing to her empty pitcher. "I haven't had time," she laughed. "I've been too busy serving lemonade."

Charlie's face brightened and he flashed her a grin.

193

"Good! Then maybe you'd have lunch with me. Afterward we could watch the horse races together."

"Are you competing?" she asked.

"Naw," he chuckled. "There's hardly any point. Sheriff Wellesley wins every year with that black devil of his."

"Oh, I see," she responded lamely, wishing that just once, she could have a conversation that didn't ultimately work itself around to Seth. "Well, Mr. Stimson, I'd be delighted to have lunch with you, but I have to find Amelia and fix her a plate first. Perhaps I can meet you somewhere."

"Fine," Charlie nodded eagerly. "I'll wait for you at that table right over there." He pointed to an unoccupied table under the trees.

Rachel nodded and turned away to find Amelia. It was no small feat to induce the child to leave her place atop the ice cream freezer, but Rachel finally managed to get her seated at the table with a plate in front of her. With a stern reminder to stay where she was and eat her lunch, she and Charlie moved off to fix their own plates. Returning to their table, they seated themselves and dug into their meals. Rachel was surprised at how hungry she was and felt almost embarrassed at how quickly the mound of food on her plate disappeared. The next several minutes passed quickly as she and Charlie chatted amicably, devouring huge quantities of chicken and potato salad. Rachel found herself enjoying his easy company. A simple, straightforward man, there was no guile or mystery about him and for the first time in a week, she really relaxed. But, her peace of mind was short lived when she heard Amelia calling to someone and looked up to see Seth walking toward them carrying two plates, a smiling Etta close behind him.

"Do you have room for two more?" he asked nonchalantly, coming to a halt in front of them.

"Sure thing, Sheriff," Charlie nodded and slid closer to Rachel. "There's plenty of room."

Seth waited for Etta to catch up and then, seating himself next to her, turned to Amelia. "Are you having fun, sweetheart?"

The little girl nodded happily and launched into a verbose recounting of her experiences on the ice cream freezer. As usual, Seth was completely captivated by his daughter and didn't notice the slight elevation of Etta's brows when she heard his casual endearment.

But, Rachel had seen it and now bit her lip in vexation. Realizing the best way to defuse Etta's suspicions was to get Amelia away from Seth, she stood abruptly and said, "Well, I think we're finished. Let's go and see if the ice cream's ready, shall we? Excuse us, please," she added, nodding at Seth and Etta.

Charlie Stimson rose, a slightly bewildered expression on his face at Rachel's sudden desire for ice cream. Casting an embarrassed glance at Seth and Etta, he said, "See you later, folks. Good luck in the races, Sheriff. My money's on you, so don't let me down."

"I'll try not to," Seth murmured, never taking his eyes off Rachel. His expression, which only she could see, was angry and jealous. But Rachel didn't think that his scowling countenance was caused by her being with another man. Rather, she attributed his cold glare to be a reaction to her removing Amelia so abruptly.

He turned his attention back to Etta, who was shocked by the animosity she saw in his eyes. "Seth, what's wrong?" she asked anxiously.

"Nothing," he muttered, clenching his jaw in a valiant attempt to tamp down his flaring temper. "Better eat quick, Etta. I've got to get ready for the race."

Etta looked at him for a moment, wondering whether she dare press him, but decided not to risk antagonizing him with more questions. She silently returned to her food, but her appetite had disappeared.

There was no doubt in her mind that there was something between Seth and Dr. Hayes—something that she was powerless to stop. She watched Rachel's retreating back, a defeated expression on her face and a painful ache in her heart. Why, oh *why* hadn't the blasted woman stayed in Boston where she belonged?

Chapter Eighteen

The entire town was lined up along Main Street, anxiously awaiting the starting gun. The horse race was always the finale of the picnic and this year was no exception. Betting among the men had been heavy all week, although most agreed that as long as Sheriff Wellesley was riding Demon, no one else had much of a chance. But, despite the overwhelming odds in Seth's favor, six other men were competing against him and everyone hoped for a good contest.

Rachel stood near the finish line with Charlie and Amelia, nervously watching the seven snorting, skittish horses line up at the far end of the street. She nearly jumped out of her skin when the gun went off, and then gasped in amazement at the speed of the horses as they pounded down the street toward them. Grabbing Amelia and taking a hasty step backward, she didn't see Seth until he flew by, a full length ahead of his nearest competitor. Her nose and mouth filled with dust as she joined in the cheers that followed him across the finish line. Despite herself, a rush of pride raced through her as she watched him circle Demon around, waving his hat and grinning at the clapping, stamping crowd. The mob swelled forward, cheering Seth and jeering the losers good-naturedly. Rachel found herself being swept along with the tide of well wishers and looked around anxiously for Amelia. She was relieved to see that Charlie had swung the little girl up into his arms and was working his way through the crowd toward her. They had almost reached the area where Seth was standing when Rachel saw Etta push her way through the throng and throw herself into Seth's arms, kissing him soundly on the mouth. Throwing his head back with an exultant laugh, Seth picked Etta up and swung her around, setting her on the ground and putting a possessive arm around her shoulders. The crowd cheered its approval at his impulsive act and Etta beamed happily.

Rachel stopped dead in her tracks, causing Charlie to run smack into her back and almost knocking the breath from poor Amelia who was wedged between their bodies. Whirling around, she tugged on Charlie's arm and said sharply, "I want to take Lia home now. There's too many people here. She might get hurt."

Charlie looked at her in surprise, but nodded and placed his hand on the small of her back, guiding her toward the boardwalk. As they detached themselves from the crush of people, Rachel looked back over her shoulder and saw Seth scanning the crowd. When his eyes lit on her, he raised his hand in greeting, but abruptly dropped it. The wide grin on his face disappeared and even from this distance, she could see his eyes narrow. She saw his gaze shift from her to Charlie who was standing close to her, still holding Amelia. With a self-satisfied smile, Rachel turned her back on Seth and sauntered off down the boardwalk, inclining her head toward Charlie as if hanging on his every word.

"I hope you don't mind me wanting to leave," she said apologetically as Charlie set Amelia on her feet. "I don't like large crowds and I really was concerned that Amelia might get hurt."

"It's all right," Charlie said graciously. "It was pretty

jammed up back there and I can congratulate the sheriff later."

They walked along in comfortable silence, watching the sun make a fiery descent. When they reached Rachel's door, she turned toward him and said, "Thank you so much for a very pleasant afternoon. Amelia and I really enjoyed ourselves."

Charlie swept his hat from his head and answered shyly, "You're welcome. I had a wonderful time too. Maybe we could go on a picnic next weekend. The leaves are starting to turn and it'll be real pretty down by the river."

His mention of the river made Rachel think of Seth and a fleeting look of pain crossed her face. Recovering herself, she answered, "Perhaps. I'll let you know later in the week."

"Well, okay, then," Charlie said, a trace of disappointment in his voice. "Goodbye Dr. Hayes. Bye, Amelia."

Rachel summoned an encouraging smile. "Goodbye, Mr. Stimson. Thanks again."

Closing the door, she turned toward Amelia and said, "Come on, honey, I think you and I could both use a bath."

She was just finishing tucking Lia into bed when she heard Seth come in downstairs. Quickly closing the bedroom door behind her, she hurried down the stairs, hoping to reach the privacy of her room before he saw her.

She sped through the sitting room and headed for the kitchen, praying that he'd gone into his study. Luck was not with her. As she pushed through the kitchen door, he was there, hands on his hips and a black scowl on his face.

Never slowing her pace, she swept by him, saying brightly, "Congratulations on the horse race, Sheriff. That was quite an impressive victory."

She started down the hall, hoping that he wouldn't stop her, but even as she thought it, his voice lashed her like a whip.

"Where are you going?"

"To my room," she called over her shoulder. "Good night."

"Rachel? Rachel!"

She stopped. "What do you want?"

"Come back here . . . please. I want to talk to you."

She walked back into the kitchen, furious that her heart was pounding just because she was in the same room with him. When he didn't immediately say anything, she looked at him expectantly and said, "Well?"

"What the hell were you doing today?"

All her feelings of longing disappeared at his rude words. "What are you talking about?" she asked, her voice frosty.

"Look," he frowned, "you made it perfectly clear last week that you don't care about me, and I can live with that. And, ordinarily, I couldn't care less what men you keep company with. That's your business. But, I want to make one thing perfectly clear too. *You will keep company with nobody but me when you have my daughter with you!*"

At first, Rachel was aghast at his callous words. Then she became very, very angry. "How dare you speak to me like I'm some trollop from a saloon?" she raged. "I didn't hear you offering to accompany Amelia and me to the picnic today. In fact, you didn't seem to have any interest in us at all, you were so wrapped up in showing Miss Lawrence a good time."

"I would have taken Lia with me if I'd known you were going to take up with a man while you were there," Seth growled.

"Take up with a man!" she cried. "Why, you boorish jackass! I'll have you know that Charlie Stimson has

200

more gentlemanly qualities in his little finger than you have in your entire body!"

"Yeah, Charlie's a nice guy," Seth agreed. "Like I told you last week, if you want him to court you, that's fine with me. Just don't do it with my daughter in tow."

"He's not courting me!" Rachel insisted through clenched teeth. "We just happened to see each other at the picnic and he asked if I wanted to have lunch and watch the race with him. That's all there was to it."

"So when he walked you home, he didn't ask to see you again?" Seth asked, eyeing her closely.

She flushed. "It's none of your business what he asked me."

"Oh, yes it is, when he's walking down Main Street carrying my baby like she's his own!"

"Seth, you're being an ass! Charlie picked Lia up to keep her out of harm's way when you and those other madmen came tearing down the street on those wild animals you all prize so highly! Maybe if you cared a little more about your daughter's welfare, you'd be standing in the crowd holding her instead of galloping around like some sixteen year old!"

Seth's face suffused with color and he took an angry step forward, clenching his fists at his sides. "I'm not going to argue with you about how good a father you think I am. But let's get one thing straight. If you want to go out with a man, you let me know and I'll see to Lia."

Rachel's eyes were blazing as she stepped up to face him. "Just who *did* you think was going to take her to the picnic, Sheriff? Everyone in town finally believes she's *my* niece. That picture of your brother and his wife we put on my desk has done wonders to stop the gossip about her being your daughter, but even you must realize that it would all start up again if I went to the picnic alone and you arrived with Etta Lawrence and Lia. And nothing, I repeat, *nothing* happened this afternoon that was inappropriate for a child to witness. Can you say the same? The last time I saw you, you were trying to peel Etta Lawrence off of you!"

Seth opened his mouth to protest this latest accusation, then suddenly snapped it shut. "Did that bother you, Rachel?" he asked meaningfully. "Why do you care what I do with Etta?"

He was eyeing her so closely that Rachel averted her face so he wouldn't see her true feelings reflected in her eyes. "I . . . I don't care!" she stammered. "It's just unseemly."

"Unseemly?" he snorted. "You dare preach to me about unseemly? I'll tell you what's unseemly. Unseemly is me looking over and seeing my daughter being carried around by some man who's also rubbing his hands all over your back. That's unseemly!"

"Oh!" Rachel gasped, speechless with anger. "I beg your pardon! Mr. Stimson was not rubbing his hands all over my back! He was merely guiding me through the crowd as any gentleman would."

"He had his hands all over you!" Seth shouted, his tightly held control finally snapping. "I could see it perfectly from where I was standing!"

"I don't know how you could see anything with Etta Lawrence crawling all over you."

Seth's eyes narrowed, then an almost triumphant smile lit his face. "That *did* bother you, didn't it? By God, you're jealous!"

"Jealous," Rachel blustered, *"jealous!* You flatter yourself, Sheriff. Of course, I'm not jealous. I told you before, I couldn't care less . . ."

"Did he kiss you?" Seth interrupted.

"What?" she asked, momentarily confused. "Did who kiss me?"

"Charlie Stimson! Who the hell do you think I mean?"

"It's none of your business!"

"Did he kiss you?" he repeated, taking her by the shoulders.

"Let go of me!" she warned.

"Not until you tell me."

"No!"

"Tell me!"

"I am telling you. No!"

Instantly loosening his grip, Seth stepped back in surprise.

"He didn't kiss you?"

"No!" Rachel cried, tears welling. "He didn't kiss me."

"Good," he nodded, exhaling a long, tense breath.

"Why do you care? Are *you* jealous?"

Seth looked at her for a long moment, then sighed tiredly. "Let's quit playing games, okay? You know why."

"Because of Lia?" Rachel persisted. "You should know that I would never—"

"Lia has nothing to do with it," Seth interrupted quietly. "I admit I was jealous when I saw Charlie carrying her around, but she really isn't a part of this." He dropped his gaze and looked at the floor.

"Oh, Seth . . ." Rachel groaned miserably, then turned toward her room before he saw the tears spill down her cheeks.

"Rachel," he whispered, halting her progress.

She didn't turn around. "What?"

"God, Rachel . . ." he repeated, taking a halting step toward her.

She heard the anguished plea in his voice and whirled to face him.

Then he was there, pulling her against him and folding her into a crushing embrace. His voice was hoarse; strangled as the words spilled out. "*Why* don't you love me?"

Rachel drew in her breath, tears wetting his neck where her face was buried.

"I do love you!"

He pushed her away almost roughly, searching her eyes for the truth. When he saw it, his voice dropped so low that she had to lean closer to hear him.

"Then, why won't you marry me? Why won't you wait?"

Looking up at him, she whispered, "I will."

For an endless moment, Seth just stared down at her as if he wasn't sure he'd heard her right. "Don't say it if you don't mean it," he warned.

"I do mean it," Rachel smiled. "More than I've ever meant anything in my life."

An answering smile lit his face and without a word, he swept her up in his arms and carried her down the hall to her room, booting open the door and laying her gently on the bed. Sitting down next to her, he kissed her with a tender passion that made her head reel.

Just when Rachel was positive she was going to faint, Seth raised his head and stroked her temple with the back of his hand. She struggled to open her eyes, tangled in an erotic web of languorous sensations. With a supreme effort, she lifted her eyelids and focused on his handsome face. His expression was so gentle that she again felt tears welling.

"I wonder if you might consent to marry me, Dr. Hayes," he murmured, giving her a light kiss, "that is, unless you've already promised Charlie Stimson."

Rachel smiled and cocked a brow, as if giving this alternative her utmost consideration. "No, I think I'd rather marry you, Sheriff Wellesley. That is, unless you've already promised Etta Lawrence."

Seth's smile widened into a grin and his eyes sparkled with mischief. "I don't think Etta's interested. When I mentioned it to her, she didn't seem too keen on the idea."

Rachel's dreamy smile disappeared. "What?" she demanded, raising herself on one elbow. "You mean you asked Etta Lawrence first and when she said 'no,' you decided to ask me?"

Seth threw back his head with a great, gusty laugh, pressing Rachel's rigid body against his. "Yeah. I ask two or three women a day to marry me. But, you're the first one who's been foolish enough to say 'yes.'"

"Seth!"

"Ah, baby," he chuckled, rubbing his nose against hers, "I'm just teasing you." Then sobering, he added, "You're the second woman I've ever asked to marry me . . . and you'll be the last."

"Oh, Seth," she sighed. "I love you so."

"And I'm mad in love with you, girl, but you gotta quit sighing like that or I'll end up doing something that will make you accuse me of being primitive again. I know how fussy you are about Lia not finding us and you not taking chances with your reputation and all that stuff . . . so, I better get out of here."

As he started to stand up, Rachel took him by the hand, halting him. "But, Sheriff," she crooned, leaning back in the pillows, "Lia's asleep."

Seth's brow arched and his smile widened and widened and widened. Without ever taking his eyes off her, he sat back down on the edge of the bed and pulled his boots off. They hit the floor with two loud "thunks" that were soon followed by the sound of his belt being whipped through its loops.

Yanking his shirt off, he reached for the top button of his denims, but, before he could unfasten it, Rachel stretched across the bed and brushed his hands away. With a seductive smile, she rose to her knees, languidly pulling off her robe and slipping her nightgown over her head. When she was completely nude, she ran her hands slowly up her body, lifting her breasts and pressing them together with a little sigh. Then, very slowly, she gazed up at the breathless, aroused man standing above her.

"Tell me, Sheriff," she said in a deep, throaty voice, unbuttoning the top button of his levis and lightly caressing his straining erection, "is this swelling . . . painful?"

Her hands meandered down the placard of his jeans, releasing the buttons until she freed his hard, pulsing shaft. Stroking him up and down the velvety length, she looked up at him with wide, innocent eyes.

"Yeah," Seth groaned, "it's painful. But, what you're doing makes it feel a whole lot better."

"I'm so glad," she cooed, continuing to stroke him. "After all, I *am* a doctor . . . relieving pain is my job."

Her caresses became more intimate and Seth threw his head back, a moan of ecstasy coming from deep within him. With a smile of satisfaction, Rachel stretched upward, kissing him lightly on the lips and whispering, "So, Sheriff, what else can I do that would help relieve your pain?"

And the sheriff showed her . . .

Chapter Nineteen

"Do you really have to go? I wish you wouldn't."

Seth gave the girth on his horse's saddle one final tug and turned toward Rachel, an impatient expression on his face. "Don't do this to me," he frowned. "You know I have to go."

Rachel nodded miserably. "I know, but it's so dangerous. Can't you at least take a posse with you?"

"No," he answered shortly. Then, seeing the anguished look on her face, he gently grasped her shoulders and said, "We've been all through this, Rachel. You know I have to do this—and I have to do it alone. It's the only way I can catch him unawares."

As tears welled in Rachel's eyes, Seth's expression softened and he drew her against the solid wall of his chest. "Don't cry, sweetheart. I'll be okay, I promise you. I have the whole thing planned. I know where they are and how I'll infiltrate. As long as I keep my wits about me, I'll be fine. But," he admonished gently, "if I ride away and my last memory is of you in tears, it's just going to be that much harder to concentrate. So, come on, give me a smile and a kiss I can remember."

Biting her lip, Rachel made a valiant attempt to smile. With trembling lips and eyes bright with unshed tears, she murmured, "I love you so much, Seth. Please be careful."

A relieved smile spread across his face as he lowered his head to kiss her. "I will," he whispered, his mouth hovering above hers. "I'll be back by Wednesday at the very latest. Then this whole thing will be over and we'll start making wedding plans. How about a month from today?"

Knowing she would start to cry if she answered, Rachel merely nodded.

Seth grinned. "Good. October 20th it is, then. Now, I've gotta go, so give me a kiss that will last me till Wednesday."

Rising on her toes, Rachel threw her arms around his neck and kissed him with a desperate yearning. Seth returned the kiss and hugged her so tightly she was afraid her back would break, but she didn't care. She was sending her knight off to battle and she wanted him to remember her while he was gone.

Finally breaking her viselike grip around his neck, Seth stepped back and chortled, "Yup, that should keep me. See you Wednesday, baby. Take care of Lia and make some of that stew I like. I'll be hungry when I get back."

Stepping into the stirrup, he swung himself up on his horse and clapped his hat on his head. With a last wave, he reined Demon around and trotted away. Rachel watched him until he turned the corner onto Main street. Then, gazing heavenward, she cast up a fervent prayer for his safety and, blinking back her tears, walked slowly back to the house.

It was Thursday. Thursday afternoon. And Seth wasn't back. Rachel couldn't work, she couldn't eat, she couldn't think. She had spent the last 24 hours standing by the window, staring down the street, hoping against hope that she would see him turn the corner off of Main and ride into the yard. But he hadn't and now, as she heard the clock strike three times, she was on the verge of panic. Something had happened to him. She knew it. Something terrible had happened.

When he didn't arrive home on Wednesday afternoon, she told herself that he'd be back that evening and set about making the stew he'd asked for. When midnight came and he still hadn't arrived, she took the stew off the stove and went to bed, trying desperately to convince herself that he was just delayed and that by morning he would certainly be back. But, when she got up that morning and he still hadn't returned, her fears began to grow and as the day had passed, they escalated into full blown panic. He'd been gone too long and all the excuses she made to herself to explain the delay no longer seemed plausible. Something had happened to him and she had to take some action or she'd surely go mad.

Putting on her hat and picking up her reticule, she rushed out of the house and headed toward Main Street. She walked directly to Seth's office and pushed open the door. His deputy, Jim Lambert, was seated behind the desk, absently shuffling through a pile of papers.

Rachel wasted no time with pleasantries, but marched straight up to the desk and said, "Mr. Lambert, I'm afraid something has happened to Sheriff Wellesley."

Jim stood up, looking at her in surprise. "What makes you say that, Dr. Hayes?"

Rachel looked at the deputy, knowing that Seth had not told anyone except Jim and herself about his plans. "I know where he went . . . and why," she said quietly. "He assured me he'd be back by Wednesday and since it's now Thursday afternoon, I'm convinced that something has happened to him."

Jim answered her level gaze with one of his own. "He told me the same thing . . . and I'm afraid you're right."

"Then why haven't you done anything?" she demanded.

"I was just sitting here thinking the same thing," he admitted. "Let's go see the mayor. I have to have his permission to raise a posse."

"Do you think you can convince the men in town to join you once they know who you're tracking?"

"That's the least of my worries," he assured her. "The way the people in town feel about Seth, I'll probably have to turn them away."

Buckling on his gun, Jim took Rachel's arm and together, they hurried out of the office and strode down the street toward City Hall.

Martin Fulbright was sitting at his desk reading a journal from Washington when Rachel and Jim walked through his door. His smile of greeting quickly faded as he looked at their grim faces. "What's wrong?" he asked, rising from his chair.

In a quiet voice, Jim explained where Seth had gone and what he intended to do, ending his story with their concern that Seth hadn't returned on schedule.

Martin sank back into his chair, his face troubled. "Damn fool," he muttered, then threw a chagrined look at Rachel. "Sorry, Doctor," he apologized hastily, "but, why does Seth *always* insist on going alone?" Looking at the tight, worried faces of the couple across his desk, he shook his head and said, "Well, Seth is Seth and I guess nothing's going to change him. But, I agree. Something's wrong or he'd be back. Form a posse immediately, Jim. There's still a few hours of daylight left and we should be able to at least get a start yet this afternoon. Do you have any idea which direction he was heading?" At Jim's affirmative nod, Martin responded, "Good, then let's not waste any more time."

As the three of them walked back out into the sunlight, Martin put his hand on Rachel's arm. "Don't worry, Dr. Hayes," he said, giving her a comforting pat. "Jim's nearly as good a tracker as Seth is. As long as he knows the general direction Seth was heading, he'll find him. You just be ready at your office in case . . . in case we need you."

Doing her best to remain composed, Rachel nodded and assured Martin that she would be prepared for any eventuality.

In less than an hour, Jim Lambert and a dozen other men rode out of town, heading due west. Although the sun was already low on the horizon, Jim assured Martin that they could track Seth for at least a couple of hours and he hoped to catch up with him by then.

Rachel stood on the boardwalk outside Seth's office and watched the posse gallop out of town, knowing that the next time she saw any of those men, she'd also know the future of the rest of her life. She slowly walked home, stopping at Cynthia Fulbright's to collect Amelia. Cynthia had given birth several weeks before and since delivering the baby, Rachel had gone to visit her newest patient several times. In glowing good health, Cynthia was again up and around, and had invited Lia to spend the afternoon with Sam. Rachel stopped for only a minute, anxious to return home and prepare her surgery for an emergency, all the while praying that her preparations would be unnecessary.

They weren't. About ten o'clock, she heard the sound of horses' hooves outside, and leaped up from the chair where she had been dozing. Flinging the door open, she was met with a disheveled and distraught Jim Lambert who nearly fell into the room when the door was jerked open. "We've got him," he panted. "They're bringing him in a wagon. He's hurt bad, Doc. I don't think he's gonna make it."

Rachel's hand flew to her throat as she attempted to quell the panic which immediately gripped her. For a moment, she thought she was going to faint until she heard Martin Fulbright's voice commanding her attention from behind Jim's shoulder.

"Don't you *dare* fall apart," Martin warned her. "I know how you feel about Seth, but you've got to remain professional. You can have a fit of the vapors later, but right now, he needs a doctor, so pull yourself together!"

Gulping, Rachel nodded and stepped out the door just as a wagon lumbered around the corner. Racing over to it, she caught a glimpse of Seth's ashen face where he lay in the wagon bed. Suddenly, her years of training and discipline asserted themselves. "Don't touch him until I look at him," she ordered the men clustered around her. "I want to see if he has any broken bones before we move him."

Without a word, the men moved back and waited for her instructions. Hiking her skirts up above her knees, she stepped onto the wagon wheel and leaned over the bed, quickly pulling off the blanket that covered him. Her head swam for a moment as she stared at his blood-soaked shirtfront. Darting a look at the men crowded behind her, she demanded, "What happened here? Does anyone know?"

"He's been shot in the chest, Doc," one man offered. "We found him layin' out on the trail goin' to Nickerson. We don't know how long he'd been there, though."

Rachel nodded, running her hands expertly down Seth's legs and arms. "There doesn't seem to be anything broken," she advised the men. "All right. I need six of you to get up here in the wagon and lift him out."

As several men surged forward, she held up a hand and in a voice that would have done credit to a drill sergeant, commanded, "Slowly and carefully. Two at his shoulders, two at his hips, and two at his feet. *Slowly*, I said. And support his neck and head. BE CAREFUL!"

The men not attending Seth looked at each other in

212

amazement, astounded by the way the little woman had taken control of the situation. The men in the wagon simply did as she bade, accepting her authority and following her terse instructions exactly.

As they lay Seth on the operating table in Rachel's office, she turned to the group and said, "I'm going to need help here. Do any of you have any experience with surgery?"

A middle-aged man whom she didn't know stepped forward and said, "I was a medic in the war. I can help you."

"Good," she nodded. "What's your name?"

"Hamilton Foster, ma'am."

"All right, Mr. Foster, go scrub your hands in the sink. The rest of you must leave. I need to have it quiet in here. Mr. Lambert, will you wait outside, please? I want to talk to you after I'm finished here."

Jim nodded and walked out to the waiting room, sinking tiredly down on the couch next to Martin Fulbright who had also decided to stay until Seth's fate was known.

"She's something, ain't she?" Jim said, turning to Martin.

"Yes," Martin nodded. "If anyone can save him, she can."

"I hope you're right, Mayor . . ."

"Do you need any chloroform, ma'am?" Ham asked.

"No," Rachel shook her head. "He's unconscious and unless he starts coming to, I don't think we'll need it."

She closed her eyes for a moment, praying for the strength to see this ordeal through. Then, she ripped open Seth's bloody shirt. Her heart again surged into her throat as she stared at the gaping wound in his chest. Hurrying over to the sink, she quickly scrubbed her hands, then returned to the table carrying a sponge which she used to wash away the dried blood. The wound was directly above the heart and Rachel knew that if it had been an inch lower, he wouldn't be alive.

"He's lost an awful lot of blood," Ham noted, lifting Seth's upper lip and looking at his gums. "God knows how long he laid out there before we found him. Are you gonna take the shell out?"

"I have to," Rachel said grimly, prodding around the wound to see if she could feel the bullet. "If I don't, it will infect and that will kill him."

"I just hope he can take it," Ham said worriedly, shaking his head. "He's gonna lose more blood when you cut him."

"I know, but I have no choice," Rachel reiterated. "Hand me that probe and let's get started."

As the surgery progressed, Rachel found that the bullet was not as deeply imbedded as she'd first thought. The greatest danger was the amount of blood that Seth had already lost and the fact that the bullet had stayed in him long enough that an infection was almost inevitable. When she finally dislodged it, she held it up and said triumphantly, "There! I got it!"

Dropping it into a pan sitting next to her, she washed away the fresh flow of blood that followed, nodding in satisfaction. "Let's sew him up, Mr. Foster. Draw this skin together so I can start stitching."

Ham Foster had heard all the jokes and snickers about Dr. Hayes ever since she had arrived the previous spring. But as he stood across the table from her, his admiration knew no bounds. A veteran of hundreds of operations during the Civil War, Ham knew he'd never seen a more accomplished surgeon. As Rachel carefully sewed Seth's wound with neat, precise stitches, he picked up a piece of gauze and leaned across the table, patting her perspiring brow. When she looked up in grateful surprise, he said shyly, "Hell . . . I mean, heck of a job, Doc. I think he's gonna make it."

214

Cutting the silk thread, Rachel shook her head and laid the back of her hand against Seth's icy cheek. "I appreciate the vote of confidence, but it's much too soon to tell."

"He ain't gonna die," Ham assured her positively. "I've seen hundreds of shot-up men. Seth's strong as a bull and if it didn't kill him to lay out there on that road, he ain't gonna die now with you takin' care of him."

A small, tired smile curved the corners of Rachel's mouth. "Thank you, Mr. Foster," she said quietly. "Let's pray you're right."

After cleaning up her surgery, Rachel walked out into the waiting room and sank down next to Martin.

"How is he?" the mayor asked anxiously.

"I've done all I can," she responded, "but he's not out of the woods yet. Where did Jim go?"

"Over to the office to look something up."

Rachel threw him a puzzled glance, but before she could question him further, Ham Foster walked into the room and threw Martin a satisfied look. "He's gonna be fine, Mayor. The doc did some job!" Slapping his hat on his head, he turned to Rachel and said, "You need anything, you just come fetch me."

"Thank you, Mr. Foster, you were a great help."

"Seth's gonna be fine," he repeated, "just fine."

Rachel watched Ham take his leave, then turned to Martin. "Please tell me exactly what you found out there.

"It was bad," Martin admitted. "We were about ten miles west of here when we found him. Looked to us like he was ambushed. But he got whoever did it."

"Oh?" Rachel asked, surprised to hear this startling news.

"Oh, yes, Martin affirmed. "Directly across the road from where Seth was lying was another man's body. I'm

215

not sure who. Jim thinks it was one of Clint Brady's men so he's looking through his Wanted Posters to see if he can identify him. He'd been dead for at least a day, I'd guess. We won't know for sure until Mac looks him over. But, it's obvious that he tried to ambush Seth and Seth killed him. Too bad the other guy got a shot off first."

"A day," Rachel moaned, shaking her head. "You mean, Seth has been lying out on that road for a whole day?"

"Could be," Martin said grimly. "That was our guess, anyway."

Rachel raised a shaking hand to her forehead, trying to ease away the exhaustion and shock. "My God, he was out there suffering for a whole day. If only I'd known . . ."

Martin laid a comforting arm across her shoulders. "It's not your fault. You couldn't have known. None of us could."

"I'll never forgive myself if he dies," she moaned.

"Come, come, my dear," Martin soothed, "he's not going to die. You heard Ham. Seth will be fine."

Rachel threw him a grateful look and rose from the settee. "I'd better get back to him. Do you suppose you could help me transfer him to my bed? I think that would be the easiest place to care for him."

Martin nodded and went to the door where most of the members of the posse were still loitering in the yard. "Come on, boys, we need to move the sheriff into the doctor's bedroom."

Although several of the men's eyebrows lifted at this startling statement, no one said a word.

When Seth had been moved and two of the men had changed him out of his dirty clothes and into a clean pair of longjohns, the members of the posse took their leave, promising to return in the morning to see if there was anything Rachel needed.

"You need some rest, dear," Martin advised. "Why don't you go sleep awhile and I'll sit with him."

"No, thank you," she demurred. "He needs a doctor's care tonight. It's a critical time. I'll sit with him till morning."

"All right," Martin agreed, not arguing after seeing the determined set of Rachel's jaw. "I'll send Mrs. Fulbright over in the morning with some food for you. Perhaps we can take your niece for a few days and relieve you of the burden of her care."

Rachel nodded her thanks and quickly ushered the mayor out the door, anxious to return to Seth. Turning down the lamp next to her bed, she pulled up a chair and sat down to begin her vigil. Seth hadn't moved and his grayish pallor still worried her. Leaning forward, she ran her hand tenderly over his cold cheek, brushing his dusty hair back from his temple. "You're not going to die, my love," she whispered fiercely, "because I won't have it. You promised to make an honest woman of me and, by God, I'm going to hold you to it!"

Chapter Twenty

Three days later the fever started. For a time, Rachel thought Seth was going to escape it, but on the morning of the third day, she woke from where she was dozing in a chair by his bed to find him tossing in delirium, his skin mottled and dry.

For the next two days, she fought a merciless battle for his life. There was little she could do to ease his misery except to sponge off his hot body and try to spoon broth through his parched lips. But, despite her efforts, by the evening of the fifth day after the shooting, Seth's fever was still raging and Rachel was exhausted.

She had just dozed off when she heard the doorbell. Tiredly, she heaved herself out of her chair and trudged down the hall, absently patting her disheveled hair into place.

Opening the door, she was astonished to find Etta Lawrence standing on the porch, a small valise in her hand.

"Good evening, Dr. Hayes," Etta said, her lips pursing slightly at Rachel's appearance.

Rachel's mouth tightened with annoyance at the damning perusal, but she merely smoothed her wrinkled dress and answered politely, "Good evening, Miss Lawrence. May I help you?"

Without waiting for an invitation, Etta stepped

through the door and set her valise down. "Actually, I've come to help you."

"I beg your pardon?"

"I heard from the menfolk in town that you've been caring for the sheriff night and day since he was shot."

"Well, yes," Rachel nodded. "I'm a doctor. Caring for people is what I do."

Etta smiled knowingly. "I understand your commitment to your patient, Doctor, but even angels have to sleep. So, I've come to relieve you."

"What?"

"It's obvious just looking at you that you're badly in need of rest. I know you've told everyone in town that you prefer to care for the sheriff yourself, but that's just plain nonsense. Now, tell me what you're doing for him and then scoot off to bed."

"Miss Lawrence—"

"Doctor Hayes, let's not beat about the bush. Seth means as much to me as he does to you. He's not your private property. I would think that would have been obvious to you after the town picnic. I have just as much right to be with him as you do."

Rachel longed with every fiber of her being to tell the presumptuous woman that Seth had proposed to her but, knowing that she'd sworn to keep their betrothal a secret, she remained silent.

Assessing Etta's determined expression, she briefly contemplated how to get rid of her, then decided she was just too tired to try.

"All right, Miss Lawrence, come with me."

With a triumphant nod, Etta started up the stairs.

"Not that way," Rachel halted her, "the sheriff is in my room."

"Your room!" Etta exclaimed, her tone speaking volumes.

"Yes," Rachel affirmed. "We had no way to get him upstairs so we put him in my bed."

"Then where are you sleeping?" Etta demanded.

"In a chair, Miss Lawrence," Rachel responded, throwing her a shaming look. "I can assure you that Sheriff Wellesley is in no shape to be a threat to anyone's virtue, regardless of whose bed he's in."

Unable to think of a suitable response to this setdown, Etta simply nodded and followed Rachel down the hall.

Entering the small bedchamber, Etta set her valise down and hurried over to the bed. Gazing in horror at Seth's drawn face, she whispered, "He's dying, isn't he?"

"Absolutely not!" Rachel blazed. "He most certainly is *not* dying."

Etta whirled around to face her. "Dr. Hayes, this is the man I love. Tell me the truth."

Jealousy surged through Rachel at the other woman's declaration, but she said evenly, "He's a strong, healthy man. If I can just get the fever down, he stands a good chance."

"All right," Etta nodded, looking somewhat mollified, "what can I do?"

Rachel spent the next few minutes explaining the procedure for sponging Seth and feeding him broth. After finishing her instructions, she added, "If you'd like, I will show you how to do it."

"No," Etta declined. "I understand. Just go and sleep. I'll take care of him and if he takes a turn for the worse, I'll come get you."

With a reluctant nod, Rachel walked out of the room. She wouldn't actually go to sleep, she thought as she climbed slowly up the stairs. She'd just lie down for an hour or so and then return to Seth. That way, she would give Etta the satisfaction of sitting with him and then, hopefully, the woman would leave.

Rachel walked through the first door she came to, not even thinking about the fact that it was Seth's

220

room. All she saw was the bed looming in front of her. With a weariness so acute that she could hardly focus her eyes, she climbed up on to the large bed and was instantly asleep.

The night waned and the first gray light of dawn crept under the window shades. Although the constant stooping and sponging made Etta's back feel like it was going to break, she remained steadfast in her duties. Her tenacious efforts seemed to be of no avail, though, as Seth tossed and fretted, raving with delirium. All through the long, hellish night he uttered only one word that could be understood: Rachel. Over and over he called her name and no matter what solace Etta offered, he was only aware that the hands soothing him were not the hands he wanted. And so, his plaintive cry continued—as Etta slowly felt her heart break.

Finally, as the mid-morning sun beamed through the windows, he calmed, lying so still that Etta pressed her ear to his chest to make sure he was still breathing. Assuring herself that he was, she sat down on the edge of the bed. Tears welled in her eyes as she stared down at the man she loved. He was lost to her. And, somewhere, deep inside, a voice told her what she had long known but refused to admit. She had never really had him. For two years, she had tried to convince herself that he cared—that, with time, she could make him love her. But hearing his anguished calls for Rachel had dispelled that fantasy as no amount of time spent in his halfhearted company could. Tears of resignation rolled down her cheeks as she longingly brushed a lock of his hair off his forehead.

It was at that moment that Rachel walked back into the room. She took one look at the still man and the weeping woman and clapped her hand over her mouth in horror. He was dead!

With a strangled cry, she flew over to the bed and dropped to her knees. Startled, Etta jumped up and backed away, gaping at the doctor in alarm. Rachel brushed her hand over Seth's brow, expecting it to be icy with death. For a moment, her brows knit with surprise, but then relaxed as an elated smile lit her face. Seth's skin was cool and moist — and he was very much alive. It was over. The fever had broken.

Heedless of Etta's intense scrutiny, Rachel leaned over and kissed his cheek, rousing him so that he opened his eyes.

"Where've you been?" he croaked.

A happy sigh escaped as she sat down next to him. "Where have *you* been?" she responded.

Seth frowned. "What're you talkin' 'bout? You're the one who's been gone."

"Shh," she soothed. "I'm teasing you. I'm right here and I promise I won't leave."

"Good. Don't." He closed his eyes and immediately lapsed back into a peaceful sleep.

With a last caress to his cheek, Rachel stood up and adjusted the covers. Turning, she was surprised and embarrassed to find Etta still standing there.

"Oh, Miss Lawrence!" she exclaimed, her cheeks flushing with embarrassment.

"I'm leaving," Etta said quickly. "I can see that Sheriff Wellesley is out of danger. I guess there is no reason for me to be here any longer."

Knowing full well the import of her words, Rachel nodded solemnly. "I truly appreciate your help."

"Yes, well," Etta replied curtly, pulling on her gloves and struggling to remain poised, "if there's anything else I can do, just send a message over to the school."

Rachel followed her out to the foyer, placing her hand on Etta's arm as she opened the front door. "Thank you," she said quietly.

With a quick nod, Etta turned away and strode briskly down the walk.

Seth's recovery was remarkable. With the infection behind him, he healed with incredible speed, gaining strength every day. Within three days, he was able to get out of bed and less than two weeks after the fever had abated, Rachel came downstairs one morning to find him dressed and sitting in the kitchen.

"What are you doing up?" she demanded, placing her hand on his forehead to assure herself that his fever had not returned.

"Quit babying me," he chuckled, pushing her hand away. "I'm fine and it's time I quit layin' around in that bed like an invalid."

"But, do you really think you're ready to be up and dressed?" she persisted. "I don't want you overdoing and pulling out your stitches."

"Don't worry about me," he said, hooking his arm around her waist and pulling her down for a long, lingering kiss.

When he finally released her, Rachel straightened up, her cheeks pink and her eyes bright. "Now, I know you're okay," she giggled.

"Yup, you've cured me, Doc," he affirmed, standing up with just the slightest wince of pain.

Rachel didn't miss the fleeting grimace. "Seth, I mean it," she warned. "Don't overdo."

"I won't," he promised. "But, I just figured when a fella is going to ask a girl to marry him, he should be dressed in more than his longjohns."

Rachel looked at him in confusion. "You've already asked me to marry you. Did the fever affect your memory?"

"No," he smiled, "it didn't affect my memory."

Reaching across the table and taking her hand, he said quietly, "Rachel, would you do me the honor of becoming my wife?"

Rachel was becoming more alarmed every moment.

Maybe he really *didn't* remember that he'd already asked her this. "Seth . . ."

"A week from Saturday?" he finished.

Dead silence.

"Rachel?"

"Yes?"

"Well?"

"A week from Saturday, Seth?"

"Its October 20th. I thought we'd settled on October 20th."

"Yes, but that was before . . ."

"I know," he interrupted, "and all the time I was laying in that bed, I was thinking about how God damned mad I'd be at myself if Brady's man had killed me and I hadn't married you first."

"Seth, don't say that!" Rachel cried, a look of horror on her face. "Don't even think it."

Seeing her stricken look, Seth's expression turned serious. "Rachel, we've got to think about it. It's my job. Coming so close to dying made me realize that I don't want to wait to marry you. I want to do it right now so that whatever time I have left in this life — whether it's five days or fifty years — is spent with you."

"Oh, Seth . . ." she whispered, biting her lip.

"I've got it all figured out, sweetheart. We'll go to Wichita on the train and get married there. I have a friend who is an Episcopal minister and I'm sure that if I explain our situation, he'll marry us right away."

Rachel stared at him for a long moment, her heart near to bursting. "I'll go anywhere you want to and marry you any day you say," she smiled, "but, I honestly don't understand why we need to go to Wichita. Why can't we get married here in Stone Creek so our friends can come? And, what you mean by 'our situation'?"

Seth frowned at her seeming lack of understanding. "Brady, Rachel; Brady."

Rachel shook her head uncomprehendingly. "What about him?"

"Rachel, for God's sake, think! He can't know. If we get married, we have to keep it secret until I catch him. *No one can know!*"

Rachel struggled mightily to summon a smile, but she couldn't hide her disappointment. "I don't know what to say," she murmured. "I want to get married too, but, at the same time, I want a church ceremony with our friends there to share our day and a dinner and a dance and all those . . . those wedding things."

"We can have that," Seth assured her. "I want a celebration too, and as soon as I catch Brady, we'll get married again here and invite the whole damn town."

Rachel's eyes were bright with unshed tears. "You'd marry me twice?"

"Sweetheart, I'll marry you a hundred times if it makes you happy. But, most important, I want to marry you the first time — and I want to do it now."

Rachel's tears spilled over and, embarrassed by her emotional display, she rose from her chair and came around the table. Sinking down on Seth's lap, she put her arms around his neck and whispered, "So, you're going to keep your promise, huh?"

Nuzzling her neck, he muttered, "What promise is that?"

"To make an honest woman of me," she giggled shakily, shivering in reaction to his caresses.

"Yeah, I thought I better," he murmured, kissing her behind her ear. "I wouldn't want you to be a mother before you're a wife, and now that I'm feeling so much better . . ."

With a small cry of dismay, Rachel pushed him away and leaped to her feet. "Seth Wellesley, don't even think about it! You're not well yet!"

"Oh, yes I am!" he laughed. "Well enough, anyway."

"No, you're not! You're going to have a relapse!"

"What? You don't believe me?" Rising from his chair, he started toward her. "Guess I'll just have to prove it to you, then. I swear," he sighed, unbuckling his belt, "folks would think you were from Missouri the way you have to have everything proved to you before you'll believe it."

"Seth, don't you dare!" Rachel shrieked, spinning on her heel and taking off down the hall. "So help me, if you pull out those stitches with this nonsense, I'm going to let you bleed to death!"

Undaunted, Seth strode down the hall after her but, as he reached the doorway, he suddenly paled and grabbed the wall for support.

Rachel's laughter evaporated. "What's wrong?" she gasped, racing over to where he was leaning against the wall. "Seth! What is it?"

"Nothing," he said, forcing a wan smile. "I guess I'm just not quite as ready as I thought I was. I feel a little dizzy."

"Oh, you great horny fool!" she chastised, putting her arm around his waist to help him over to the bed.

"Horny!" he exploded. "Doctor, I'm shocked! Where did you learn a word like that?"

"Oh, hush up!" she said crossly. "I learned it from going to school with great horny fools just like you."

"Oh, really?" he questioned in genuine surprise. "I think we better discuss this."

"We're not 'discussing' anything right now," Rachel assured him, "except getting these clothes off you and getting you back into bed where you belong."

"Now, *there's* an offer," he laughed, looking at her meaningfully. "Will you get in with me?"

"That's enough, Sheriff," she admonished primly. "Just sit down and let me get you undressed."

Ten minutes later, Rachel had her patient cozily tucked up in bed. With a tired sigh, Seth closed his eyes. "I have to admit, it feels good to lie down. Guess I'll take a little nap."

"Yes, you do that," Rachel nodded, turning to leave.

His voice stopped her. "Rachel . . ."

"Yes?" she responded, looking back at him.

His eyes appeared to be closed, but she knew when he smiled that he could see her from under his lids. "Will you sleep here with me tonight?"

"Seth—"

"Aw, don't say 'no.' I promise I'll behave. But, it sure would be nice to have you here."

A little thrill of anticipation coursed through her but, in her best physician's voice, she answered, "We'll see, Sheriff. Now, go to sleep."

"But, you'll think about it?" he persisted.

"Yes," she promised, trying hard not to smile. "I'll think about it."

Turning back toward the door, she got as far as putting her hand on the knob.

"Dr. Hayes?"

"Yes?"

"I love you."

Slipping out the door, she closed it softly behind her and leaned against it. With a smile of sublime contentment, she closed her eyes and whispered, "Oh, Sheriff Wellesley, I love you too."

Chapter Twenty-one

Rachel sat on a bench in the early morning sunlight and anxiously peered down the tracks, looking for the eastbound morning train.

Twisting the gloves she held, she closed her eyes, ordering herself to be calm. If she didn't get on the train soon, she just knew that someone was going to notice how strangely she was acting. After all, here she was, on her way to Wichita to marry the most handsome, most eligible man in six counties — and she couldn't even tell anyone!

A little smile played at the corners of her mouth as she glanced down at the valise sitting at her feet. Wouldn't Betsy Fulbright be shocked if she knew that in addition to tomorrow's day dress, the bag also held a gossamer, sheer white silk nightgown? Rachel blushed just thinking about the plunging neckline and transparent lace insets. It was a bride's nightgown — provocative, yet innocent — and a little shiver of anticipation raced through her as she thought about wearing it tonight.

So far, their plans had come off without a hitch. Seth had left the previous day, telling Jim Lambert that he had to meet with a federal marshal and that he'd be back Tuesday. He offered no further explanation and Jim, accustomed to his boss's penchant for privacy, didn't ask.

Rachel had told her patients that she was going to a medical meeting and would be gone for several days. She had asked Cynthia to keep Lia for her, feeling terrible that she had to lie to her friend and wishing that she could share her happiness with her. Even though she was convinced that she could trust Cynthia with their secret, she had kept her counsel, knowing how important it was to Seth that no one know.

Now, however, her excitement had grown to the point that she was afraid she might just jump off this bench and run down Main Street, screaming to anyone who would listen that by this time tomorrow, she would be Mrs. Seth Wellesley.

Chewing on the finger of one of her much-abused gloves, Rachel leaned forward again, casting a hopeful look down the tracks. This time she was rewarded. The huge belching monster was slowly approaching. She leaped to her feet and grabbed the valise, grinning as the train's deafening whistle rent the air.

The train pulled to a stop and people seemed to appear from nowhere, some gathering in small groups to meet arriving passengers and others sidling up to the edge of the platform to board. Rachel cast a quick glance around, hoping that none of the boarding passengers were friends. She knew that in her present mood, she'd never be able to carry off two hours of small talk. If anyone so much as mentioned Seth Wellesley's name — which *always* seemed to happen — she would probably blurt out the truth and the secret would be out. She was greatly relieved when she found that she didn't know any of her fellow passengers.

She settled herself in a seat, wishing that the journey was behind her. This was her wedding day and she wanted to spend every minute with her groom. It seemed like an eternity since Seth had left the previous morning. He hadn't said much, had merely given her a lingering kiss and promised to meet her at the station in Wichita. She had clung to him for a moment, knowing that it was two hours until his train and wishing that he would take her by the hand, lead her upstairs to his big bed and make love to her before he left. But he didn't.

In fact, he hadn't touched her since the night she had so blatantly seduced him after he'd proposed. She didn't know why he'd suddenly left her to herself. For a while, of course, he'd been recuperating from the shooting, but even since he'd recovered, he still hadn't approached her. From the hot looks he constantly gave her, she didn't think he'd lost interest in her, but she was still a little concerned that he suddenly seemed so immune to her feminine charms.

As the train picked up speed, she gazed idly out the window. The fields were well past their harvest and now lay fallow and brown, lending a poignant loneliness to the already stark, flat landscape. But there was a beauty to the plains that Rachel had come to appreciate during her months in Kansas and she smiled with a sense of contentment, knowing that she would be happy living here the rest of her life.

The only blot on that happiness was the ever-present threat of Clint Brady. Rachel desperately wished that Seth would abandon his pursuit of the outlaw, but she also knew that no amount of cajoling on her part would make that happen. She had finally resigned herself to the fact that Seth would never forego his vengeance and that until Brady was caught, they must both live with the day-to-day danger the man posed.

Firmly pushing all thoughts of Clint Brady from her mind, she leaned back in her seat, closing her eyes and dreaming about the night to come. Seth *would* make love to her tonight — she was sure of that. But, would it be different after they were married? Less exciting now that everything was legal? She smiled at that thought, seriously doubting that she would ever feel indifferent toward Seth—married or not. With his blond, good looks and big, muscular body, she was sure that he would always have the power to take her breath away. Even on their fiftieth wedding anniversary, he would undoubtedly still make her shiver with delight. Just thinking about him made her heart pound a little faster and with each turn of the train's wheels, her excitement grew.

Seth's thoughts were much the same that morning. Everything was arranged. He had convinced his friend, Father Whitman, to marry them immediately, explaining their situation and the necessity of the marriage being kept a secret. John Whitman was an old college friend of Seth's father and had known all the Wellesley brothers since they'd been boys. Regardless of the irregularity of Seth's request, Father Whitman knew him well enough to know that there must be no legal reason for the marriage not to take place, and so had agreed.

Seth had then rented rooms at Wichita's finest hotel, The Carey. Although it had taken a sizable stack of bills to convince the desk clerk to break a standing reservation and give him the best suite in the house, it had been worth it. As he'd entered the sumptuous rooms, he'd smiled in satisfaction, pleased that he could offer Rachel the elegance she deserved on their wedding night.

Their wedding night—how he was looking forward to the evening ahead. It had been pure hell keeping his hands off her for the past couple of weeks, but he was glad he'd done it. And, tonight he would make up for all the times he'd wanted to make love to her and hadn't let himself. Even though he knew they had to be circumspect after their return to Stone Creek, tonight was theirs. He could take his new wife to dinner at a fine restaurant, court her, touch her, even seduce her in the moonlight if he wished. Tonight they didn't have to pretend as they did at home—feigning disinterest when they were actually dying for want of each other. Most of all, tonight there would be no parting. Tonight they could love each other with no concern for anything but each other's pleasure. And their lovemaking could continue all morning since he would not be returning to Stone Creek until tomorrow afternoon and Rachel not till the next day.

With a last glance at the huge, beckoning bed, Seth clapped his hat on his head and with an eager grin, headed for the train station to meet his bride.

Rachel saw him before he saw her. Although she was sure he'd be waiting for her, she sighed in happy relief when she saw him standing on the platform. He looked more handsome than she'd ever seen him, wearing a dark, well-tailored suit and a snowy white shirt. His grooming was so impeccable that she self-consciously smoothed the skirt of her pink travelling suit, hoping that she didn't look wrinkled and travel worn.

As the train pulled to a halt, Seth saw her through the window and raised a hand in greeting. With an answering wave, she rose from her seat and hurried to the back of the car. He was waiting by the steps and she smiled almost shyly as he extended his hand and helped her descend.

"Good morning, Dr. Hayes," he smiled, removing his hat, "I trust you had a pleasant trip."

"Very pleasant, Mr. Wellesley, thank you," she answered as he tucked her arm through his.

As they strolled down the platform toward the baggage car, he suddenly turned serious, casting her a long look and saying quietly, "I wonder if you might be interested in marrying me today?"

232

With a slight inclination of her head, Rachel returned his sober gaze with one of her own. "By all means. I'd be delighted."

Then he laughed and kissed her. Right there in front of everyone at the Wichita train station, he whirled her around into his arms and kissed her full on the mouth. Several older ladies who had witnessed the unseemly display looked disapprovingly at the laughing couple, but Seth quickly dispelled their frowns by announcing, "We're getting married today! If you're not busy this afternoon, come over to St. John's Episcopal Church and share our happiness."

His enthusiastic invitation, coupled with his handsome looks and laughing charm made even the most severe of the matrons blush like a school girl.

Then, with a last sweeping bow to the tittering ladies, he whisked Rachel on down the platform and out the station's door.

Rachel was speechless. Never, in all the time she had known the enigmatic Seth Wellesley had she seen the man he was showing her today. He was like a boy—laughing, teasing, happy and carefree. She couldn't help but wonder if this was the man his first wife had fallen in love with—if this was how he had been before Clint Brady had killed his happiness. Could she dare hope that this might be the man he would again become when Clint Brady had been brought to justice and could finally be relegated to the past?

She couldn't stop smiling as Seth laced his fingers through hers and escorted her down the street toward the Carey Hotel.

"I thought you might like to freshen up before lunch," he told her as they swept through the opulent lobby, "so I rented a room."

Walking up to the desk clerk, Seth nodded a greeting and said, "I made a reservation for Dr. Hayes earlier this morning. Could I have the key, please?"

The desk clerk looked with interest at the couple and responded, "I'm sorry, Mr. Wellesley, but Dr. Hayes must sign the register himself before I can release the key. Is he here?"

"I am Dr. Hayes," Rachel smiled, "and if you will allow me to use your pen, I will be happy to sign your book."

The desk clerk turned crimson, then, coughing loudly to cover his embarrassment, swiveled the register around and presented the pen with a flourish. "Please sign line 48, madam," he croaked and quickly turned away, making a great pretense of finding the correct key.

Seth threw Rachel a smug grin and, taking the proffered key from the desk clerk, said, "No need to call the bell captain. I have the doctor's bag here and I will personally see her to her room."

"As you wish, sir," the desk clerk answered, his eyebrows lifting knowingly.

As Seth and Rachel walked away, he smiled. Obviously, Mrs. Wellesley, for whom the suite must have been rented, hadn't arrived yet and Mr. Wellesley was taking advantage of his wife's absence to dally with this Dr. Hayes. A most interesting situation, the clerk decided, and one that could become even more interesting when Mrs. Wellesley arrived. He'd have to keep his eyes open for that.

Ascending the sweeping staircase, Rachel threw Seth a shaming look. "Imagine what that man must think," she hissed.

"Yeah, imagine!" Seth laughed, unrepentant. "Come on, let's hurry so we'll have time to eat before the service."

"By the way, what time *are* we getting married?" she asked.

"One o'clock," he answered sheepishly. "Sorry. Guess I just forgot to tell you. One o'clock is okay, isn't it?"

Rachel assured him it was and they continued up the stairs, arm in arm. When they reached the door of her room, Seth unlocked it and swung it open. Ushering her into the small chamber, he set her bag down and said, "I'll be waiting in the lobby. Come down when you're ready." Then, after giving her a kiss that contained enough promises to set her hair on fire, he disappeared out the door.

Rachel looked around the room, frowning slightly at the narrow, single bed. Oh well, she sighed, it would just have to do. She was sure this small room was probably all Seth could afford and she certainly wasn't going to complain that they would be too cramped in the bed. She didn't think it was possible that they could be too close tonight.

She poured cool water into the basin sitting on the bureau and paused a moment, gazing at her reflection in a small mirror as the realization hit her that she was actually preparing for her wedding. She smiled a bit wistfully, wishing again that she could share this day with friends and family, but knowing also that she'd never regret her decision to marry Seth, no matter what the circumstances.

They shared a light lunch in the hotel's lavish dining room and, although Rachel was sure the food was delicious, she didn't taste a thing. Seth checked his watch a dozen times as they silently sipped their coffee, finally standing and saying, "Come on, sweetheart, it's quarter to one."

Rising, Rachel accompanied him out of the hotel and into the sunshine. "We certainly have a beautiful day," he remarked as they headed down the boardwalk.

"The most beautiful day of my life," she agreed.

Seth stopped, turning to look at her. "Do you really mean that?" he asked earnestly. "You're not sorry that it has to be this way? I know it's not exactly a young girl's dream to get married in a strange place with only strangers as witnesses."

Rachel's answering smile said it all. "I'll never be sorry, Seth. Now, come on! I don't want to be late for my own wedding and if you don't quit stalling, I'll think you've changed your mind."

Seth threw back his head and laughed in sheer delight, lifting her hand and exuberantly kissing it. "By all means, madam," he agreed. "We mustn't dally here talking. We have a wedding to attend!"

As they entered St. John's, they were astonished to find that the little band of matrons whom Seth had so casually invited to their wedding had all turned up — and two of them were even holding small gifts!

Seeing the women, Rachel smiled in delight and hurried down the aisle to greet their unexpected guests.

Father Whitman came out of a side door near the altar and motioned to Seth. As he moved off to join the priest, Rachel chatted with the ladies, thanking them for coming and accepting their small tokens and glad wishes.

When Seth returned, he was carrying a bouquet of roses which he offered to his bride.

Rachel's gaze was soft as she took the flowers from him. "Roses," she murmured, "my favorite."

Seth gave her hand a quick squeeze and they turned toward the priest, listening as he intoned the ancient words of the marriage ceremony. When he asked Seth for the ring, Rachel had a moment of anxiety, fearing that Seth had none to give her. But, to her utter amazement, he reached into his vest pocket and pulled out a narrow gold band set with the most stunning diamond she had ever seen. As he placed the magnificent ring on her finger, he leaned forward and whispered, "Close your mouth, sweetheart. I didn't steal it."

Rachel looked at him in astonishment, wondering where in the world he would have gotten a gem of this quality and worth. She didn't have long to ponder it, though, before the priest was asking her to repeat her vows. Then, suddenly, the brief ceremony was over.

Father Whitman told Seth he could kiss his bride, and as he placed his lips gently on Rachel's, he whispered, "I promise you we'll do this again in front of everybody you ever knew. Even Betsy Fulbright."

And, at that moment, Rachel knew it didn't matter if they did or not. The man standing next to her was all she'd ever need. Closing her eyes, she kissed her new husband and thanked God for the gift of Seth Wellesley's love.

Chapter Twenty-two

They shook hands with Father Whitman and left the church in a hail of rice. The ladies had forgotten nothing.

Seth paused long enough to kiss every one of them on the hand, causing the little contingent to nearly swoon with delight. Then, with a last sweep of his hat, he ushered Rachel into a large carriage which was parked at the curb.

They had barely pulled away when he grabbed her, pulling her into his arms and kissing her until she gasped for breath.

"Seth! My hat!" she protested, clutching at the lacy little confection she had so artfully pinned into her curls.

"To hell with your hat," he laughed. "I'll buy you ten new ones tomorrow. Now, kiss me, wife."

With a little shriek of laughter, she allowed him to bend her back over his lap and kiss her again. Her hat fell off, her hairpins fell out, and before she even realized what was happening, he had her bodice open and was fondling her breasts. It was completely outrageous behavior for two o'clock in the afternoon on a busy thoroughfare in Wichita—and Rachel loved it.

"Seth!" she giggled, squirming under him as he fastened his mouth over her bare breast, "what if someone sees us?"

Without raising his head, he reached over and yanked the shades down over the windows. He grunted something that sounded suspiciously like, "Who cares?", and then proceeded to slide his free hand under her skirt and up the inside of her leg.

As titillating as her husband's advances were and as loathe as she was to discourage him from his amorous play, Rachel realized that the moment was fast getting out of hand. Reluctantly, she pushed him away and struggled to sit up. Her color was high and her voice shaky as she clutched her gaping bodice together and gasped, "Do you mean to take me right here in the carriage?"

Seth was breathing so hard that it was a moment before he could speak, but when he finally got control of himself, he grinned like a naughty school boy. "I didn't really mean for that to happen," he confessed, "I just sort of got carried away when I realized that we're finally alone — and married — and we can play as much as we want."

Rachel smiled, relieved that her worries that he had lost interest in her were obviously unfounded. "Well, you certainly are playful today."

He grinned, glad she wasn't angry. "Yeah," he said meaningfully, "and that's not all I am."

"Oh? And what else are you, Sheriff?"

"Horny, lady," he growled, caressing her breast with a teasing finger. "So horny that I may never walk again if I don't have you in the next five minutes."

Slapping at his hand, Rachel threw him a shaming look and primly buttoned up her bodice. "Shouldn't we be back at the hotel by now?"

Seth groaned. "I hate to say this, but we're not going back to the hotel yet."

"Oh?"

"I thought you'd like a little party after the wedding,

so I planned a private celebration at a restaurant I know."

"Will there be cake and champagne?"

"Well, no. Actually, the cake and champagne are waiting in our room."

Smoothing her skirts and pinning her hat securely back into her hair, Rachel said nonchalantly, "You know, Seth, I'm not the least bit hungry, but a little champagne would be wonderful."

Seth looked at her for a moment, then with a slow smile he tapped his walking stick on the roof of the carriage. They immediately drew to a halt and at the driver's call of "Yes, sir?", Seth said, "We've changed our minds. Drive us directly to the Carey Hotel, please."

"Yes, sir. Right away, sir."

"And, hurry!" Seth added and again drew the shade.

"Newlyweds!" the driver laughed to himself, shaking his head and turning the team around.

By the time they arrived back at the hotel, Rachel had repaired most of the damage that Seth's passionate onslaught had wrought. "Do I look presentable?" she asked hopefully.

"You're gorgeous," he assured her.

"That's not what I asked. I asked if I'm presentable."

"More than I am, I'm afraid," he answered, glancing ruefully down to where the bulge in his trousers was still obvious.

Rachel blushed to the roots of her hair and as they pulled to a stop in front of the hotel, she whispered, "Are you all right?"

"Yeah, I'll be okay. Just stay in front of me and get up those stairs as fast as you can."

Throwing him an arch look, she stepped down from the carriage and waited for him to alight. She could tell by the way he winced as he descended that he was truly uncomfortable, but she couldn't help but feel a little thrill that she could rouse such passion in him.

They walked quickly through the lobby, past the smirking desk clerk and up the stairs. As they reached the fourth floor landing, Rachel started down the hall to her small room, but Seth halted her. "Up another flight, sweetheart," he said, pointing.

"But, the room is down there," she argued.

"That's not the room we're staying in. Our room is on the fifth floor."

"But, Seth—"

"For God's sake, Rachel," he pleaded, "don't argue. Just get up the stairs!"

"All right," she nodded, picking up her skirts and continuing up the next flight. When they reached the fifth floor, she stopped and waited for him. He seemed to be walking a little more easily now.

"Are you feeling better?" she asked quietly.

"Yeah. Climbing stairs and thinking about funerals always helps."

"Funerals?"

"Never mind. I'm okay." Putting his hand on her waist, he guided her down to the end of a long hall where they were met by a set of massive double doors. Pulling a key out of his pocket, he opened the huge portals, then turned and swung Rachel up in his arms.

"Oh, Seth, no!" she protested. "You're going to hurt yourself!"

"I couldn't hurt any more than I do already," he answered wryly, "so just hush up and enjoy the ride."

Sighing happily, Rachel put her head on his shoulder and he carried her over the threshold into the luxurious suite.

As they entered the room, she looked around, stunned by the rich appointments. "Oh, Seth," she breathed as he set her on her feet. "I've never seen such a beautiful room . . . but, can we afford this?"

"Quit worrying about money," he admonished, chucking her under the chin. "If you have to worry

241

about something, worry about getting out of that dress before I rip it off you."

With a giggle, she whirled around and looked down to where his erection again bulged. "It's back?"

He shrugged sheepishly. "Shouldn't have picked you up."

"Is there anything I can do?"

Rolling his eyes, he answered, "Just help me get these damn pants off. I'll be okay when I get out of them."

"Sit down on the divan," she suggested, then disappeared into a large dressing room.

When she returned a moment later, he was gingerly lowering himself onto a beautiful blue velvet chaise lounge. He leaned back with a groan that was somewhere between misery and ecstasy.

Rachel removed his shoes and socks, then bent over him, releasing his belt and tugging at his trousers. "Lift your hips," she instructed throatily.

Seth complied, and with a gentle tug, she pulled his trousers and underclothes off, freeing him from the painful restraint.

"Better?" she asked, gazing hungrily at his hard, jutting shaft.

Without opening his eyes, he nodded. "A little."

"Maybe this will help," she murmured, and lifting her skirts, she stepped over the divan and sat down on him.

Seth's eyes flew open as he sank easily into her satiny warmth. Rachel's answering look was so blatantly sexual that he let out a hoarse shout of sheer exultation. It was the most erotic moment he'd ever experienced and he wasn't sure he could live through the storm of ecstasy that was coursing through his body.

Then Rachel started moving and he was lost. Throwing back his head with a groan of surrender, he gave himself over to her, captivated by her unexpected, passionate assault. When it was over, she collapsed against his heaving chest and he ran his hand gently over her hair, his eyes still closed and a huge, satisfied smile on his face.

They remained that way for several minutes until Seth finally lifted her head from his shoulder and softly kissed her. "Time to cut the cake, Mrs. Wellesley?"

With a small laugh, Rachel moved off him and stood up on trembling legs. "I think I need a little rest first."

Rising from the couch, he gathered her into his arms and carried her over to the huge, soft bed. Gently laying her down, he whispered, "Now it's my turn to make you comfortable."

"Oh, Seth, no, not yet!"

He put a finger over her lips, laughing. "Hush, you silly girl. I didn't mean *that*. Good God, you must think I'm some stud if you believe I'm ready again this soon!"

Rachel blushed. "Well, I didn't know," she stammered, "I just thought—"

"I know what you thought," he chuckled, sitting down next to her, "and I appreciate the compliment. But, right now, we both need some rest."

He helped her disrobe, handling her as carefully as he would a small, precious child. By the time she was naked, she could hardly hold her eyes open. Lying back in the pillows, she patted the sheet next to her and said, "Come sleep with me."

With a nod, Seth pulled off his shirt and slipped into the bed beside her, drawing her close.

"I have a nightgown with me that I want to wear," she yawned.

"You will," he whispered. "Just sleep for a little while and then we'll get up and eat cake and drink champagne and you can wear your nightgown for me and we'll make love some more."

"Mmmm . . ." Rachel murmured, "sounds wonderful." And nestling against her husband, she instantly fell asleep.

It was dark when Rachel awoke. It took her a minute to realize where she was, but when she did, she sat up with a start, looking around the luxurious room for Seth.

He was standing by a small table, dressed in a light blue silk wrapper. He had lit candles and Rachel watched him open a bottle of champagne by their soft glow.

Without gaining his notice, she slipped out of bed and stole into the dressing room. Her valise had been delivered from the other room and she quickly donned her white gown. After checking to make sure he was still occupied, she dashed across the room and slipped back into bed.

Seth poured two glasses of champagne, then looked over at the bed, noticing that Rachel was awake. With a smile, he silently walked over and handed her a glass. Sitting down on the edge of the bed, he smoothed back her tousled hair and softly kissed her. "You're beautiful and I love you."

Rachel pushed herself up against the pillows. "You're beautiful too," she returned, and clinked her glass against his in a toast. "In fact," she added, her eyes sparkling with mischief, "you're even more beautiful than all the ladies in Stone Creek think you are."

Seth instantly set down his glass and turned on her with a frown. "Okay," he said, "enough is enough. You're going to tell me *now* what the town ladies are saying about me."

Rachel giggled in delight. "Oh, Sheriff, you wouldn't *believe* how the ladies speculate about you."

His expression became incredulous. "What do you mean, 'speculate'?"

"Oh, you know — about how you might kiss or what it would be like to kiss you or what you must look like without your shirt or without . . . your other clothes. You know, things like that."

"You're making this up," he accused, shaking his head in disbelief.

"I am not!" she protested. "You should hear them!"

"Well, then it's disgraceful."

"What's disgraceful?"

"Good Christian women gossiping about what a man looks like with his pants off."

"I think it's fun," Rachel laughed, sipping her champagne innocently.

"Fun?" Seth was aghast. "What's fun about it? It's damn embarrassing."

Leaning close, she whispered conspiratorially, "What's fun about it, Sheriff, is that *I* know the answers to all their questions. And, what's more, everything they'd like to see belongs to me. I get to see it . . . and touch it . . . and kiss it anytime I want to."

Seth's look of embarrassed annoyance suddenly dissolved into an open leer. Plucking the half empty champagne glass out of her hand, he pulled her up against him and growled, "You're right, lady. Everything I have is all yours and you can look at it and touch it and kiss it anytime you want to."

The look in his eyes was so hot that Rachel was suddenly embarrassed by her own boldness. Groping for a new topic of conversation that would cool things off, she asked abruptly, "Do you like my gown?"

"Yes, it's beautiful," he whispered, running a finger down the inside of the daring décolletage until he freed a soft, round breast. Twirling her hard little nipple between his fingers, he added, "I especially like the neckline."

"Thank you," she stammered, her voice shaky. "I bought it in Boston."

He nodded, dipping a finger into his champagne and tracing little wet champagne swirls over her nipple. "I thought so. Doesn't look like anything you'd get in Stone Creek."

Rachel swallowed hard and a strangled little giggle erupted from her throat. "I . . . never really thought . . . I'd wear it . . ." she stammered, unable to speak coherently because now he was leaning forward and licking off the champagne.

"I'm glad you did, but, you know what?"

"What?" she gulped as his mouth moved to her other breast which had somehow also escaped her bodice.

"I want to take it off."

Rachel shivered as she felt his hands sweep the gown's skirt up toward her waist. Raising her arms, she helped him lift it over her head. Then, as he sat drinking in her naked beauty, she reached out and boldly untied the sash of his robe, spreading it open. Running her hands over his massive chest, she whispered, "You really are the most beautiful man in the world."

She let her hands drift down over his muscular chest and tightly ribbed abdomen until her fingers encircled him. After their provocative play he was again fully aroused and the sensation of his hard, velvety shaft in her hand made her shiver in anticipation.

With a groan, he lay back, pulling her over on top of him and kissing her until she was nearly swooning.

"Do I kiss as good as they think I do?" he whispered.

"Better," she gasped against his lips.

"And am I as big as they all hope?"

"Bigger," she murmured, caressing him so intimately he was afraid he might explode.

"And is it as nice to kiss as they all think it would be?"

"I don't know," she answered breathlessly. "I've never kissed it."

There was a long pause and then, in a voice so low

he almost didn't hear him, he breathed, "Well . . ."

Without a word, Rachel moved off him, picking up her champagne glass and trickling a bit of its effervescent contents over his throbbing shaft. The amber liquid splashed lightly against him, sparkling in the thick blond hair. Leaning forward, she licked at the shimmering wetness, rubbing her face lightly against him and kissing him up and down his turgid length. The raw sensuality of her mouth on him quickly pushed Seth past the limit of his control and with a groan, he pulled her up and gave her a fiery kiss.

"You're making me crazy," he panted. "I can't play anymore. Please . . ."

With a come hither look that set him ablaze, Rachel rolled on to her back, pulling him over on top of her and wrapping her legs around his hips. Reaching down, she guided him into her, lifting her hips and offering herself fully.

Seth forced himself to set a slow rhythm, knowing that despite her lusty eagerness, Rachel was still fragile and new to the games of love. But she held him tightly and encouraged him, and, together, they exploded in a blinding climax.

When it was over, they lay drowsing in the candlelight, replete and happy. Lazily, Seth stroked the hair back from Rachel's temple and leaned over to kiss her gently on her eyelids. "You look like you've just spent the last twelve hours making love," he teased her softly. "You better get some sleep tomorrow after I leave because if you get off that train looking like you do now, there's going to be a hell of a lot of speculation by the good Christian ladies in Stone Creek about just what doctors do at medical meetings."

Rachel smiled sleepily. "Do you really have to go back tomorrow? Couldn't you stay here with me and we'll go back together on Wednesday?"

"I can't stay, baby," he said, kissing her lightly, brush-

247

ing his thumb across her cheek. "I told Jim I'd be back Tuesday and I don't want anyone to suspect anything. You know they would if we got off the train together."

"You're right," she sighed, "but I don't want to be away from you . . . even for a day."

"Shh," he whispered, "we've got the rest of the night and all morning. I don't leave till three."

Rachel opened her eyes and rolled over on top of him. "Then let's not waste time sleeping . . ."

In spite of her fatigue, Seth's answering grin set her pulses racing. Gently biting her earlobe, he whispered, "I love you, Rachel, my beautiful wife . . ."

And, at that moment, Rachel didn't care if she ever slept again.

But she did sleep, and when she woke again, the night had waned and the sky was lightening to the deep violet of early dawn.

At first she wasn't sure what had awakened her, but then she felt something tickle and she opened her eyes, gazing down toward her feet.

Seth was sitting cross legged at the end of the bed, slowly threading something between her toes. Confused, she lifted herself up on an elbow and squinted down at him, trying to focus on what it was. Her perplexed expression soon turned to disbelief as she realized that what he was so casually weaving was the most magnificent diamond necklace she had ever seen. As she stared at him in stunned silence, he looked up and smiled. Then, he again bent over her jewel-encrusted foot and slowly drew her big toe into his mouth. Rachel nearly came off the bed, letting out a little shriek of delight as he sucked on her toe. Well satisfied with her reaction, Seth chuckled and redoubled his efforts.

After sucking all five toes and running his tongue along her arch until she screamed, he finally relented, taking the necklace in his teeth and pulling it between her toes until he freed it. Rachel shuddered in relief, sure that she could not have stood another moment of his amorous torture.

But Seth was far from finished with her. He moved up the bed next to her, drawing the necklace along her body as he came. She gasped and let out a small whimper, knowing her moment of respite was over as goose bumps rose all over her body. He paused when he reached her breast, releasing the diamonds until they lay like a coronet around her nipple. Then, kneeling above her, he idly played with the necklace, slowly drawing it back and forth across both breasts until her nipples stood up like hard little pebbles.

"Good morning, Mrs. Wellesley," he whispered. "I forgot to give you your wedding present last night."

Rachel lay staring at the dazzling jewel being swept so provocatively across her breasts. It was a long moment before she collected herself enough to speak and when she finally did, her response was not what her husband was hoping to hear. "It's not real, is it, Seth?" she asked softly. "It's paste, isn't it?"

"Paste!" he cried, sitting upright in startled offense. "Do you seriously think I'd give you fake jewels for a wedding present?"

"But," Rachel stammered, instantly regretting her insulting words, "where did you get it? I've never seen such a magnificent piece. Surely you didn't buy it here in Wichita!"

"Hardly," Seth muttered. "I ordered it from New York at the same time as I ordered your ring."

"Oh, Seth," she fretted, taking the necklace from him and running the cold, glistening stones between her fingers. "You shouldn't have done this."

"Why not?" he asked, his voice laced with disappointment, "don't you like it?"

"Like it? Of course, I like it! But, the expense! How

can you possibly afford such an extravagance?"

"Is that what you're worried about?" he laughed in relief, reclaiming the necklace and casually running it over her stomach. "I keep trying to tell you, sweetheart, money is the least of my concerns."

"But, Seth—"

"Rachel, don't," he interrupted, all traces of humor fading from his eyes. "I wouldn't have bought it if I couldn't afford it. You should know by now that I'm not an irresponsible man."

"I'm sorry," she said contritely. "It's beautiful, Seth. Thank you."

But her hurt and bewildered expression remained and seeing it, his voice softened, again becoming deep and sensuous as he traced circles lower and lower across her abdomen with the sparkling gem. "I have plenty of money, my love, and I'm going to use it to give you the world. Then I'm going to give you about a dozen babies to fill it up with. So quit worrying. I can think of far better things to concentrate on right now—like making those babies."

With a dreamy smile, Rachel succumbed to the erotic web her husband was weaving. The combination of his low-timbred voice and the icy hot diamonds being run across the inside of her thighs was so heady that she couldn't even think, much less worry.

Seth's tense features relaxed as he watched her react to his seduction. Moving back down to her feet, he kissed and licked his way up the inside of her legs. Rachel held her breath as he reached her thighs, hoping that he'd give her the release she craved. But he was not ready to grant her surcease. He paused for a moment, gazing up at her flushed face and passion-glazed eyes. When he lowered his head again, she tensed, waiting for him to touch her. But she didn't expect that it would be his tongue she would feel and at his first intimate stroke, she nearly crawled up the headboard.

"Seth, stop!" she shrieked, squirming to get away from the sheer eroticism of this new game.

"Shh . . ." he murmured, lifting his head. "Let me, Rachel . . ."

And with a moan of surrender, she lay back again, writhing and shuddering beneath him as the raw, carnal pleasure he was bestowing flowed over her.

Finally, he moved up next to her, weaving the diamonds through her ebony hair. "Like ice on black velvet," he whispered, pulling her close and kissing her.

"Oh, Seth," she moaned, not even realizing she was begging, "Please . . ."

With a low, throaty laugh, he sat up, straddling her as he rested lightly against her thighs, his jutting erection intimately pressed against her. "What do you want, Rachel?"

"I don't . . . I . . ."

"You don't know?" he murmured. "Well, maybe you'll like this." And weaving the diamonds around his fingers, he began to massage her where she was moist and glistening from his intimate attentions.

Rachel was totally undone, knowing she could not bear the ecstasy of his soft fingers and the hard diamonds being pressed against her hot flesh at the same time. With a primitive cry, she begged him for release from this newest torture.

Then, suddenly, he was in her, his seductive games finally having inflamed him past his ability to endure. In a frenzy of need, they came together, then immediately fell apart, hot, sticky, and sated.

Seth lay back, spent and exhausted. Never had he experienced anything like the last twenty-four hours with this woman, and as he closed his eyes, he smiled, convinced that he now knew what heaven must be like.

Rachel's thoughts as she drifted into slumber were much the same. Despite her inexperience, she somehow knew that the sexual chemistry between them was

251

unique and rare. She sighed with contentment, sure that she had married the most perfect man in the world. Forcing her eyes open for one last look at him, her gaze was caught by the diamonds which still lay glittering next to her on the sheet. Despite her happiness, she felt a twinge of unease. Where had he gotten the money to buy that necklace?

Chapter Twenty-three

Rachel stepped off the train and quickly scanned the long platform. Although she knew that Seth probably wouldn't be there to meet her, she still held out the hope that he might have found some excuse to come to the station this morning.

But he wasn't there, and with a small sigh of resignation, she picked up her valise and hailed Stone Creek's only cab, requesting that she be driven to Cynthia Fulbright's.

Amelia's shriek of delight when she saw her "aunt" coming up the walk more than compensated Rachel for her brief disappointment. After all, she told herself sternly, she had a husband to go home to and Amelia was now truly hers to love and nurture. She certainly had nothing to feel sorry for herself about, even if Seth couldn't meet her at the train and she wasn't free to tell anyone about their marriage.

Cynthia came to the door, carrying the baby on one hip and wiping her hands on a dishtowel. "Train was right on time, I see," she beamed, pushing open the screen door. "Come in and warm up. We'll have some tea and you can tell me all about your trip."

"Wonderful," Rachel smiled, hoping her voice didn't betray her sudden trepidation. She had absolutely no idea what she could tell Cynthia about Wichita since she had seen almost nothing of the town and hadn't really met anyone.

Following her hostess into the kitchen, she sank down wearily at the table and accepted the cup of tea she was offered.

Cynthia gave Sam and Amelia a cookie and sent them back to his room to play. Then, plunking the baby down on Rachel's lap, she sat down across from her, eyeing her closely. "Tell me," she said, "are you as tired as you look?"

"Tired?" Rachel asked, a trifle too brightly. "Do I look tired?"

Cynthia nodded.

"Well, yes, as a matter of fact I am," she admitted. "We had a very late session the first night and I didn't sleep well last night."

She could feel her face flame at the thought of what had really been involved in that first night's "session", but Cynthia seemed not to notice.

"Where did you stay?" she asked casually.

"At the Carey Hotel."

"Oh, that's a nice place, isn't it? Ben and I stayed there on our honeymoon."

Rachel nearly choked on her tea.

"So, was it a nice ceremony?" Cynthia asked nonchalantly.

"I beg your pardon?" Rachel hedged, swallowing hard. "What ceremony?"

Cynthia laughed out loud and reaching over, she plucked the baby off Rachel's lap. "I better take her before you drop her. You don't seem up to managing a baby today."

"Oh, I'm sorry," Rachel stammered. "I guess I *am* tired."

"Brides usually are," Cynthia observed wryly.

Rachel's eyes widened. Setting her cup down carefully, she whispered, "How did you know?"

With a squeal of delight, Cynthia plopped the baby on the floor and raced around the table to envelop her friend in a hearty hug. "I didn't for sure, but I've been a bride too, and there's only one time in a woman's life when she can look as tired as you do and still be radiant. Ma always calls it the 'honeymoon look'."

Rachel pressed her hands to her cheeks, blushing. "Is it really that obvious?"

"Probably not to a man or a young girl, but let me warn you, honey. When you leave here, you better go straight home and get some sleep because every married woman in Stone Creek is going to know what you've been doing the minute they see you."

Rachel's face flamed with embarrassment, but she laughed and said, "Oh, Cynthia, I so wanted to tell you, but Seth made me promise to keep our plans secret."

"Why?" Cynthia asked, sinking back into her chair and scooping up the baby.

"I . . . I can't tell you," Rachel answered.

"Okay," Cynthia nodded agreeably. "I'm not going to pump you. As long as it isn't that you or Seth has another husband or wife somewhere, I guess it really doesn't matter."

"Oh, it's nothing like that!" Rachel gasped. "It's . . . it's Clint Brady."

"Uh huh!" Cynthia nodded knowingly. "I knew there was something going on between Seth and that outlaw. Seth just turns into a different person whenever Brady's name is even mentioned."

"Oh, Cynthia," Rachel pleaded, "even though I can't tell you why it's so important, you have to promise me that you won't tell anyone about Seth and me being married. And no one can know that Seth is related, in any way—even by marriage, to Amelia. It could mean her life."

"Her life!" Cynthia gasped. "My lord, Rachel, of

course I won't tell anyone! You should know me well enough to know that I can keep a secret. But, if you ever need anything, you know you can count on me."

"Thank you," Rachel smiled, rising from her chair and embracing her friend. "I don't know what I'd do without you."

"So," Cynthia said, wiggling her eyebrows meaningfully. "Do you want me to keep Amelia another night?"

"No," Rachel blushed. "I better take her with me. You were right when you said I needed sleep. I have a full schedule of patients tomorrow and if I go home without Amelia, I just know I won't get any rest!"

Cynthia laughed, and together they moved toward the front door, their arms around each other's waists. But, before they reached the foyer, Cynthia paused, her expression intense. "Rachel, there's something I simply have to know. Is Amelia *really* your niece?"

Rachel hesitated for a moment and then shook her head. "No. She's Seth's daughter."

Cynthia's eyebrows rose imperceptively. "Does she know that?"

"No, and we don't feel we can tell her yet. She might let it slip."

Cynthia nodded and called the children as Rachel pulled on her coat. When Amelia appeared, Rachel bundled her into her heavy outer clothes and after saying their goodbyes, they started to take their leave.

But as Rachel stepped through the door, Cynthia caught her by the arm and said, "Can I ask you one more thing? Something, well, personal?"

Rachel looked a bit startled, but nodded.

Taking a deep breath, Cynthia screwed up her courage and whispered, "Is Seth as good as he looks?"

Rachel put her hands over her mouth and giggled like a school girl, her eyes bright. Leaning toward her friend, she whispered back, "I don't have any basis of comparison, of course, but, I'd say he's better!" Then, with a gay wave, she took Amelia by the hand and hurried off down the walk.

They were just turning the corner on to Main Street when they ran into Cynthia's mother, Jeanette. After exchanging a brief greeting, they hurried off toward home and Jeanette continued on to her daughter's house.

Cynthia met her mother at the door and helped her out of her coat and scarf. As they walked back toward the warmth of the kitchen, Jeanette said casually, "Well, I see Rachel is back from her medical meeting."

"Yes," Cynthia answered noncommittally, "she arrived on the morning train."

"I saw Seth this morning too, so he must have gotten back from his trip too," Jeannette continued, nodding her thanks as Cynthia set a cup of hot tea in front of her.

"Oh?"

"Yes," she smiled, "and they both look like they've been ridden hard and put up wet."

"Ma!" Cynthia gasped. "What a thing to say!"

"Well, people usually do look like that after the wedding night."

Cynthia whirled around toward the stove so that her face wouldn't betray her. "I don't know what you're talking about."

Jeanette laughed delightedly "Yes, you do. They went to Wichita and got married, didn't they?"

"How would I know?"

"You never could lie to me, Cindy. Well, if they didn't get married, then they're having an affair—but I'd have thought better of Seth."

With a sigh, Cynthia turned back to face her mother. "It's not an affair, Ma. They're married. But, you can't tell anyone. Not even Pa."

"Why the secret?" Jeanette asked. "Is there something wrong?"

"Yes. But I promised Rachel I wouldn't say a word, so I can't even tell you what little I know."

Jeannette nodded solemnly. "I'll not ask you to break a confidence, dear. And you have my word that no one will hear about this from me."

Cynthia patted her mother's hand gratefully. "I know I can trust you, Ma. But you're right about Rachel having the 'honeymoon look'. I just hope she has enough sense to tell that big hunk of a man to leave her alone tonight so she can get some sleep, or every woman who walks into her office tomorrow is going to know the truth."

Jeannette shook her head. "Cynthia, if you had married Seth Wellesley two days ago, would you tell him he had to leave you alone so that you could look fresh for your appointments?"

"Lord, no!" Cynthia laughed. "I'd just break the appointments."

Rachel walked into the house, smiling to herself as she realized that it wasn't just Seth's home anymore, it was hers, too. Pulling off her gloves and looking around at the beautiful furnishings with a new sense of pride, she called, "Is anyone home?"

The kitchen door banged open so hard that it bounced off the wall as Seth came down the hall at a near gallop, holding something behind his back. Skidding to a halt, he grinned at his wife and daughter. "I thought you two were never going to get here!"

Kneeling down in front of Amelia, he helped her off with her coat and said, "Did you miss me, Lia?"

At her smiling nod, he continued, "Well, I missed you too. In fact, I was so lonesome for you while I was gone that I decided to go shopping. And, you know what?"

She shook her head.

"I saw this in a store window and it said, 'Take me home to Amelia!' So I did." Reaching behind him, he held out an exquisite doll with a painted porcelain face and real hair, dressed in a beaded black dress with a matching coat, hat and reticule.

"Oh . . ." Amelia breathed, so awed by the doll's beauty that she didn't even reach out to take it.

"Do you like it, honey?" he asked hopefully.

Finally tearing her eyes away, Amelia looked at him and nodded.

"Then, take her," he chuckled. "She's yours."

Her tiny hands trembling with excitement, Lia took the doll, holding it close and rocking it back and forth. "Thank you," she said happily, her eyes shining.

"You're welcome, darling," he murmured, his voice sounding strangely gruff. He straightened for a moment and looked at his daughter, then squatted down again.

"Lia?"

She turned back toward him, looking at him expectantly.

"Could I have a kiss?" His voice was hesitant, almost shy.

With a blinding smile, Lia handed her doll to Rachel and threw her arms around her father's neck, placing an exuberant kiss on his cheek.

For just a moment, Seth buried his face in her neck, giving her a squeeze. But at her grunt of surprise, he quickly released her, laughing and saying, "Lia, do you suppose your Auntie Rachel would give me a kiss?"

"Do you have a present for her too?" she asked.

Rachel's cheeks flamed as Seth guffawed, "Oh, you bet I do!"

"Then you can kiss her," Lia pronounced.

Armed with his daughter's permission, Seth walked over to Rachel and whispered hoarsely, "Come here, you."

Rachel stepped eagerly into his arms, tilting her head back as his lips swooped down on hers with a hunger that took her breath away.

"This has been the longest damn day of my life," he muttered against her ear, sliding his hands down her back to cup her buttocks and pull her hard against him.

"Seth!" she protested, looking over his shoulder at where Amelia stood watching with interest. "Not now!"

With a groan of disappointment, he kissed her again before finally releasing her and turning back toward Amelia.

"You really like to kiss a lot, don't you?" Lia asked, giggling.

"Yeah, I sure do," Seth agreed, a shudder coursing through him.

"Come on, Lia," Rachel said quickly. "Let's get unpacked and make some supper."

Ushering the little girl down the hall, she looked back over her shoulder at her husband and hissed, "And you better go take a dip in the river!"

"The river!" he exclaimed. "For God's sake, Doctor, it's October!"

"Exactly!" she answered tartly, then disappeared through the kitchen door.

It was very late before Amelia finally got settled in bed and Rachel and Seth had a moment alone.

He was sitting in the parlor, staring out the front window into the darkness when Rachel walked in carrying two cups of tea.

"What are you doing in here?" she asked as she set the cups on a small table.

"Thinking about how happy I am," he smiled, pulling her down next to him and taking her in his arms. "And thinking about how I'll be even happier when I can shout to the world that I'm married to you."

"I know," she sighed, snuggling up against his big, warm body. "I can't wait either. I want to tell every woman in Stone Creek that you're mine!"

Seth pulled away just enough to see her face clearly and said, "But, that's all you're going to tell them, right? I mean, you wouldn't give them any details about how I kiss or what I look like naked or anything, would you?"

"Of course not," she giggled, feeling a moment of guilt for what she had already told Cynthia about his sexual prowess.

"Good," he nodded. Leaning his head against the back of the settee, he sat quietly for a moment, then shifted his weight and pulled something out of his hip pocket.

"Rachel?" he whispered.

"Yes?"

"I *do* have a present for you."

"Oh, Seth," she said almost fearfully, "another present?"

"Yeah. Just a little one. I know you can't wear the wedding ring I gave you yet, so I bought you this. I don't think anyone will even notice it, but I'll know you have it on."

Picking up her left hand, he slipped a delicately wrought gold band, hardly wider than a coarse thread, onto her finger. "You're my wife," he murmured, "and I want you to wear my ring so you don't forget."

Rachel leaned toward the dim glow of the single lamp Seth had lit and gazed at the fragile ring. "I love it, Seth," she smiled, "and even though you never need to worry about me forgetting I'm your wife, it's nice to have a little reminder for when we're not together."

"You really like it?" he asked, his voice relieved and pleased. "It's not much, but I promise you it won't be long till you can wear the real one."

Leaning toward him and kissing him lightly on the lips Rachel said, "I couldn't love any ring more than I love this and even when I can wear my diamond, I'll still wear this one too. I don't know how to thank you."

Seth grinned, elated with her reaction. "Well, why don't you crawl up here on my lap and wiggle around a little bit? That'll do."

"No," she said firmly. "I know what will happen if I sit on your lap and I'm just too tired. I have patients all day tomorrow, Seth. I *have* to get some sleep."

"Didn't you sleep last night at the hotel?" he asked, his voice tinged with disappointment.

"Not really. Somehow, that bed wasn't the same without you in it."

With a low chuckle, he pulled her across his lap and cradled her in his arms. "Come on. Let's go up and see how mine feels."

"I shouldn't," she sighed, her will power quickly waning. "I should sleep down here since I have to get up so early."

"No," he whispered, tugging at her lower lip with his teeth and gently brushing his knuckles across her breast. "We won't do anything but sleep if you don't want to, but you're not going to sleep down here unless I'm in that little bed with you. And I think we'd both be a whole lot more comfortable upstairs."

"Oh, Seth, you know what will happen."

"No, it won't," he assured her. "I promise I'll be good. We'll just sleep."

"Sure we will," she chuckled, slipping her hand between them to where an erection already strained against his denims.

"Well, we'll work something out," he promised, and picking her up, he started up the staircase. Striding into his bedroom, he plunked her down on the bed and said, "I have to go lock up. I'll be back in a minute."

"I have to comeback down too," Rachel sighed,

crawling reluctantly off the soft mattress. "I don't even have a nightgown up here."

Seth threw her a look that made her blush to the roots of her hair. "Think you need one?"

"Guess not."

"Good," he nodded and disappeared out the door.

It wasn't more than ten minutes before he was back and it only took him a minute to peel off his clothes, but when he climbed into bed and turned toward his wife, she was sound asleep.

Gazing down at his half-stiff manhood, he said ruefully, "Not tonight, Sheriff. The doctor needs her sleep and you've got the rest of your life to make love to her. One night without isn't going to kill you."

But just knowing that she was there in his bed took its toll and he quickly turned away from her, adjusting his now fully aroused manhood and willing himself to think of anything but the enticing little woman lying naked next to him.

Chapter Twenty-four

Seth sat at his desk at the jail and stared moodily out the window. There was never any time to make love. Never.

When they'd first returned from Wichita, Rachel's schedule had been completely jammed with appointments. Next, Amelia had caught a cold and Rachel had slept with her in the little room off her office for three nights. Then, some damn cattle rustler started causing trouble southeast of town and he'd had to leave for four days to track him. When he'd gotten home, Rachel (to his extreme disappointment) was having her woman's time and needed to be left to herself for a few days. Then, last night, when everything finally looked perfect, she'd been called out to deliver a baby.

His scowl got even blacker as he thought about the unfairness of it all. Obviously, some men got to make love to their wives or *his* wife wouldn't have to spend her nights delivering babies!

Rising from his chair, he paced irritably back and forth across his office. So much for the pleasures of the marriage bed. Their romantic life had been better *before* they'd gotten married! It had been more than three weeks since they'd come back from Wichita and, by Seth's count, they'd only made love four times — and two of those had been during the same night. Why, people who'd been married thirty years probably made love more than that!

Planting his hands on his hips, he glanced down at himself, frowning in disgust as he felt the first stirrings of an erection. For Christ's sake, he thought angrily, here he went again. All he had to do was *think* about his sexy little wife and his manhood sprang to life like some seventeen-year-old kid's. If he didn't get some relief soon, *he* was going to be the one who needed a doctor!

He stopped pacing. Need a doctor . . . need a doctor. That was *exactly* what he needed. A long appointment with the town doctor. A complete examination! Alone . . . in the privacy of her office with no interruptions . . . *Yes!*

He slammed his hat on his head and started for the door, but stopped short as he felt his manhood straining against his pants. His anticipation of a lusty hour with his wife had done nothing to cool his burgeoning desire and he sure as hell didn't want the entire town to know his intentions.

"Calm down!" he commanded himself. "The sooner you get it under control, the sooner you can go to her."

He took several deep breaths and thought hard about how he needed to whitewash the walls of the jail cells. Finally, he felt he could walk out the door without disgracing himself and clapping his hat back on his head, he strode purposefully out on to the boardwalk. All he had to do was make it down Main Street and over to Rachel's office without being waylaid. Then, if luck was with him and he caught her alone, he'd tell her he needed an emergency appointment. He grinned to himself as he headed off toward his house. Nothing like having a doctor in the family to cure what ailed you!

* * *

Rachel was sitting at the desk in her office, looking through a catalogue of medical supplies and daydreaming about her husband.

It seemed like they hadn't had ten minutes alone since they'd returned from Wichita. First, Lia was sick, then Seth had to go chase some cattle rustler and when he finally returned home, she (to her extreme relief) was having her woman's time. And in the week since, it seemed like every night something conspired to prevent them from having any privacy.

Well, tonight was going to be different, she promised herself. She didn't have any more appointments this afternoon and there wasn't a single woman in town who had a baby due this week. She would take a warm, relaxing bath, put Lia to bed early, cook Seth a big steak and let the evening progress as it might. Just the thought of a long, leisurely night of lovemaking with her handsome, virile husband made chills run up her spine.

She was so engrossed in her lusty ruminations that she jumped in surprise when her office door opened a crack and a hoarse voice rasped, "Dr. Hayes?"

"Yes?" she answered, rising.

"Are you alone?"

Rachel felt a moment of apprehension at the unfamiliar voice and wished that she weren't in the office alone. "Who's there, please?"

"Are you alone?" the voice repeated.

"Who's there?" she demanded, her voice rising nervously.

When she still received no answer, she walked over to the door and cautiously pulled it open, her mouth dropping in surprise when she saw Seth standing on the other side, holding his hat in front of him.

"Seth, for heaven's sake! You scared me to death. What are you doing here?"

"Are you alone?" he whispered.

"Well, yes," she nodded, stepping aside so he could enter. "Why?"

"Because I need you."

"Need me?" she asked, her eyes widening with concern. "What's the matter? Are you all right?"

"No. I'm in terrible pain."

"Pain!" she gasped. "Where?"

"Here," he said, gesturing toward his abdomen which was still covered with his hat.

"Oh, dear, I hope it's not your appendix," she said worriedly. "Is the pain on the right side?"

"No, more in the middle."

"The middle?" she shook her head in bewilderment. "It's probably not your appendix, then."

"No, I don't think it's my appendix," he choked.

"Well, come in and let's have a look."

He nodded, biting the inside of his cheek to keep from laughing, and followed her into her office.

Rachel walked briskly over to her examining table and said, "Can you climb up here so I can examine you?"

"I don't think so."

She whirled around to face him, her alarm increasing. "Is the pain really that bad?"

"Yeah," he nodded. "Look."

Pulling his hat away, he watched as her eyes took in the enormous bulge in his pants, then slowly rose to his face.

"Is that what's causing the pain?" she asked.

"Seems to be," he nodded. "Do you know anything that might help it?"

"Yes, it's definitely curable," she said, then walked over to her office door, closed it and snapped the lock into place. Then, very slowly, she removed her skirt, petticoat, shoes, stockings and pantalettes, leaving them in a pile on the floor. Now naked from the waist down, she walked back toward her husband, saying, "I

267

actually know several remedies for your problem, Sheriff, but there is one which is most effective, so I think I'll try it first."

Seth, by now, was so aroused that he could hardly stand still, and as Rachel reached for his belt buckle, he pulled her hard against him, kissing her with a passion that made her head swim.

"I want you so bad, I'm almost crazy just thinking about you," he growled against her lips. "I couldn't wait another minute. I *had* to see you."

Gently, Rachel pushed away from him and unbuttoned his shirt, pulling it off his shoulders and running her tongue across the massive muscles of his bronze chest. Then, with deft hands, she unbuttoned his denims and released him from his clothing, dropping to her knees in front of him as she removed his socks, shoes and underwear.

Seth stood above her, his legs planted wide, his eyes closed and his mouth slightly parted. Rachel glanced up at him and, as always, was awed by the stunning beauty of his nakedness. He looked like some ancient Greek god and she still couldn't quite believe that he was hers.

Gently, she took him in her hands, fondling him until he swayed on his feet. Every fiber in him cried out for consummation, but, as he reached for her, she brushed his hands away and, with a boldness that shocked and thrilled him, took him into her mouth.

A bolt of ecstasy shot through him, nearly knocking him off his feet. After weeks of wanting her, her tongue's sensual teasing was almost more than he could stand, and with a groan of agonized pleasure, he lifted her up until they were face to face and her legs were wrapped around his waist.

Carrying her over to her desk, he laid her on it and followed her down, entering her with one smooth thrust. But, the top of the highly polished desk was slippery and with each lunge, Rachel slid further along its surface until her head bumped into the wall.

Lifting herself onto her elbows, she found herself being pushed up into a sitting position until, finally, Seth was kneeling beneath her and she was seated high on his thighs with her back against the wall. As his lovemaking became more frenzied, he wrapped his arms protectively around her to prevent her back from being injured.

Seth's hot, sweaty chest rubbing against her front and the rough wooden wall rubbing against her back was the most erotic sensation Rachel had ever experienced and she shrieked with delight, reveling in the sheer lustiness of their wild coupling. Then, with one last powerful thrust, Seth collapsed against her in a blinding climax, slamming her against the wall as she joined him in his ecstasy. Sliding back down to the desk top, the two of them lay entwined on the hard surface, too spent to move.

"You don't have any more patients this afternoon, do you, Doctor?"

"No, thank God," she sighed.

"Where's Lia?"

"Over at Mrs. Dobbs' house. I have to pick her up at five o'clock."

"Good. It's only two." Smiling, Seth kissed her tenderly and smoothed her hair back where it was stuck to her temple.

Rachel smiled back at him, running her hands lightly down his back and over his buttocks. "Do you have some more entertainments in mind, Sheriff?"

With a suggestive leer, he slipped out of her and hefted himself off the desk, picking her up in his arms and carrying her out of the office and upstairs to his bedroom.

Laying her on the bed, he bent over her, removing her blouse and camisole and saying, "The way I figure it, we've got about three hours of complete privacy. Let's not waste it."

And, laying down next to her, he gathered her in his arms and started kissing her again.

Diane Hagen limped down the sidewalk toward Rachel's office, cursing her throbbing feet and the dictates of style which demanded that women of fashion force their feet into shoes three sizes too small.

She didn't have an appointment, but Dr. Hayes simply had to do something to relieve the pain she was suffering from the corn on her little toe. Rachel could surely fit her into her schedule long enough to fix her a plaster. She just couldn't be seen limping at Sunday's Ice Cream Social at the First Methodist Church! The doctor would just have to understand the immediacy of her problem and make time for her.

As she came around the corner of Seth's house, she heard a noise that sounded almost like a scream. She stopped and listened closely, thinking that if Dr. Hayes was performing some disgusting surgery on someone, she'd come back later. She didn't want to sit in that little waiting room and hear someone yelling in agony. The very thought made her stomach roll.

As she stood there, she heard another noise, but this time it sounded more like a low pitched moan than a cry of pain. Stepping up to the window, she peeked in warily, wondering if she could see enough to determine if she should go into the office or just leave. To her relief, there was no one on the examining table, but her attention was caught by a groan coming from the vicinity of Rachel's desk.

The desk was against the far wall and with her poor eyesight, Diane couldn't see it clearly. She moved closer to the window, cupping her hands around her eyes to shield them from the light but she still couldn't figure

270

out what was going on. It looked almost like Dr. Hayes was on top of her desk with someone. Knowing that was ridiculous, Diane finally gave up and pulled her hated spectacles out of her reticule. Hurriedly putting them on, she again peered through the dusty window. This time, her vision was clear and what she saw made her gasp in stunned amazement.

Dr. Hayes *was* lying on her desk and, what's more, she was clasped in an intimate embrace with . . . who was that? Impatiently, Diane rubbed at the dirty window, cleaning a small round spot.

Good Lord, it was Sheriff Wellesley—and he was NAKED! Why, it looked like they were—like they were—my God, THEY WERE!!

Diane clapped her hand over her pounding heart, knowing she should run, but unable to move. It was wrong to stay here and watch this. After all, Dr. Hayes and the sheriff were . . . fornicating! But, try as she might, she couldn't seem to take her eyes off the provocative scene unfolding on the other side of the window.

She stood as if transfixed, her eyes wide with awe as she watched Seth Wellesley make love to Rachel Hayes. Good Lord, she sighed, his body *was* as gorgeous as all the girls thought—and she, Diane Hagen, was seeing it with her very own eyes!

Oh, she thought irreverently, if only she'd arrived a few minutes earlier, she might have seen him standing up! Her face flamed with embarrassment at the thought, but, still, what she wouldn't give for just one little look at him from the front . . .

She stepped back, pressing her hands to her cheeks. She should leave right now. Right now! But she didn't. Instead, she moved back to the window. Seth and Rachel were now sitting up on the desk and, dear God, they were still doing it! Sitting up! Was that even possible?

Diane heard Rachel's back hitting the wall and wondered for a moment if she was being hurt. But, Rachel's face didn't look like she was hurting. Her face looked like—well, Diane wasn't really sure what her expression showed, but it definitely wasn't pain.

Then, suddenly, there erupted from both of them a triumphant shout and the sheriff seemed to collapse against Rachel. After that, they both just sort of oozed down the wall till they were lying on the desk. But, even then, they remained wrapped around each other.

Diane felt goose bumps rise all over her body as she watched Seth kiss Rachel, smoothing her hair back and murmuring something she couldn't hear. She saw Rachel smile up at him, stroking his back and running her hands intimately over his buttocks. Then, Seth withdrew from her (was it possible they had been joined *all* that time?) and got up, turning so that Diane was suddenly presented with a full view of his breathtaking physical endowments.

She knew she was going to faint. My GOD, what a man . . . even now, after all that! Taking great gulps of air, she watched him scoop the doctor off the desk and carry her out of the office.

As Seth passed the window, Diane leaped backward out of his line of vision, her hand clasped to her chest, her breath coming fast.

"Please, please don't let him catch me standing here," she prayed. But, he never even glanced her way and when she heard the office door close, she sank down into a heap on the ground, putting her head between her knees and praying that she wouldn't pass out here in Seth Wellesley's yard.

She sat there for a long time, unable to believe what she had witnessed. At thirty-two, she had never known a man intimately, but she had listened to enough matrons gossiping about the marital bed that she had a pretty good idea of what went on there.

But, what she had just seen bore little resemblance to what her married friends told her their husbands did to them. She had always thought that men's carnal demands sounded humiliating and horribly unpleasant. But, Rachel Hayes certainly hadn't acted as though what Seth Wellesley was doing to her was unpleasant.

Diane sat pondering this, replaying over and over in her mind the way Rachel and Seth had looked as they lay on the desk, reveling in their passion. Maybe, she mused, the reason why Rachel seemed to enjoy it so much was because she and Seth weren't married. Maybe sex was more fun for a woman when it was illicit. Diane didn't know why that would make any difference but what else could it be?

Unless, of course, the difference was Seth Wellesley. Despite her lack of personal experience, Diane was sure that very few men had the physical attributes Seth had been blessed with. It made her heart start pounding again just thinking about what he'd looked like when he'd turned toward her.

But, regardless of what had caused Dr. Hayes to succumb to Sheriff Wellesley, what she was doing was wrong and Diane should go tell someone what she had seen. After all, she thought piously, they weren't married and what they were doing was an affront to all the good, God-fearing citizens of Stone Creek. Their shocking behavior needed to be made public so that the townsfolk could decide whether they wanted to retain Dr. Hayes as their physician or replace her with someone of higher moral standards, although it never occurred to her to wonder if Seth's moral standards should be brought to account.

Diane rose to her feet, brushing off her skirt and thinking that, obviously, she had been right in not liking Dr. Hayes. Rachel always acted so superior and condescending with her pretty face, slender figure and cool poise. And here, all the time, she was just a common strumpet.

Her sore toe forgotten, Diane hurried off in the direction of Betsy Fulbright's, smiling in anticipation. It was her Christian duty to expose Rachel for the loose woman she was and everyone in Stone Creek knew that Diane never shirked her Christian duties.

Besides, she couldn't *wait* to see Cynthia Fulbright's face when she told her. Cynthia thought Rachel was so perfect — just wait till she heard about this!

And there was one more aspect of the afternoon's events that pleased her. She now understood why Sheriff Wellesley had not found himself a good woman and settled down. Why should he when he had his very own fancy woman living right in his house?

No wonder he'd never paid any attention to Diane . . .

No wonder . . .

even possibly tell Bo—all that seemed very distant from them suddenly.

He—but his story—he saw it weighing on the corner . . . . though something that information with the

Chapter Twenty-five

"They were *what?*"

"On her desk?"

"Against a wall?"

"Oh, my dear, are you sure?"

Diane looked around Betsy Fulbright's cluttered parlor and nodded in satisfaction. She couldn't have timed her appearance better if she'd planned it, for when she arrived at the Fulbright's she found Betsy serving tea to Cynthia and Jeanette while the three of them discussed the family's plans for Christmas.

"I saw them with my own eyes," she affirmed. "And in broad daylight too!" Fluttering her hands in a show of maidenly agitation, she added, "It was very upsetting."

Cynthia sat back in one of Betsy's uncomfortable little chairs and eyed Diane closely. "What I'd like to know," she said dryly, "is how you happened to see them."

"I *happened* to see them," Diane retorted haughtily, "because they were being so indiscreet! I was on my way over to Dr. Hayes' office with a little emergency and, as I passed her office window, I heard a strange noise coming from inside. Naturally, I didn't want to interrupt her if she was busy with another patient, so I just peeked in. And that's when I saw her and Sheriff

Wellesley engaging in . . . well, I won't offend everyone again by repeating what I saw."

"So," Cynthia said slowly, her anger escalating by the minute, "you peeked in the window. And was what you saw enlightening, Diane? Did it give you a thrill?"

"Cynthia!" Betsy exclaimed, horrified by her insinuation.

"Oh, come on, Mother Fulbright," Cynthia snapped. "Diane peeked through Rachel Hayes' window and watched something she had no business seeing. It's not as if Rachel and the sheriff were out in public. She just admitted they were in Rachel's office with the doors and windows closed! Who's really guilty of an indiscretion here?"

"Now, wait a minute," Diane interjected in a wounded voice, "you're twisting my words! You make it sound like *I* did something wrong. Well, I can assure you, Cynthia, that I did not get a thrill from what I saw," Diane desperately hoped her flaming face didn't give away the lie. "It was disgraceful — immoral — and I felt it was my Christian duty to report it. Something has to be done to put a stop to such obscene behavior."

"Christian duty, bah!" Cynthia flared. "And there's nothing obscene about it. Only a woman who's never known a man would feel that way. Why don't you just admit it, Diane, you're jealous! Everyone knows you've thrown yourself at the sheriff ever since he came to town and he's never given you so much as a look."

Diane and Betsy both gasped at Cynthia's insulting words and even Jeanette's eyebrows rose. She threw her daughter a quelling look, concerned that she would betray Rachel's secret in her effort to salvage her friend's reputation.

Cynthia caught her mother's warning glance but she still couldn't resist throwing one last barb. Looking pointedly at Diane, she said tartly, "It's my opinion that there isn't a healthy, red-blooded woman in Stone

Creek who wouldn't give half of all she owned to spend ten minutes against a wall with Seth Wellesley!"

Cynthia's veiled accusation hit home and Diane turned crimson while Betsy looked as though she might faint.

"Cynthia, that's enough," her mother said, trying hard not to laugh, "you're behaving shamefully."

"No, Ma, it's not my behavior that's shameful," Cynthia retorted angrily as she rose and pulled on her coat. "What's shameful is Diane spying on Seth and Rachel during a very private moment, and then running around town telling about it."

Glaring at Diane, Cynthia added, "There's a name for people who engage in your little entertainment, Diane. They're called Peeping Toms!"

And with that, she whirled around and marched out of her mother-in-law's home, calling back over her shoulder, "Count us out for Christmas dinner, Mother Fulbright. I think we'll spend the day with Rachel and Seth."

Utter silence echoed through the house after the front door slammed. A speechless Diane sank into one of Betsy's hard little chairs; Jeanette looked like she was about to choke on something, and Betsy just sat staring after Cynthia's departed figure, her mouth opening and closing like a fish out of water.

"Well, I never!" Betsy blustered when she was finally able to speak again. "Jeanette Ecklund, you need to do something about your daughter's tongue!"

"Way too late for that, Betsy," Jeanette laughed. "Cynthia's tongue is her own business."

"Well, her rudeness is deplorable," Betsy sniffed.

"Yes, well," Jeanette nodded, rising and reaching for her coat, "perhaps you're right. But, I'll take her honesty and loyalty any day over that of most of the 'good Christian women' in this town. Now, if you'll excuse me, I need to catch up with her and see whether Ty and

277

I are invited for Christmas dinner along with Rachel and Seth, or if it is going to be a private party."

Jeanette shot a last, reproving look at the gaping Diane as she walked out of Betsy's parlor. "Close your mouth, dear," she advised quietly. "You're going to steam up someone's window."

Rachel looked down at the brief message she held and shook her head. It was the third such missive she'd received this morning and she was baffled by the coincidence. Three patients cancelling appointments on the same day? It was very odd.

Oh well, she shrugged, at least now she'd have time to really peruse the medical supply catalogue she'd started looking at the previous afternoon. She blushed just thinking about how she'd been distracted from it yesterday. But, as she walked over to her desk to fetch it, there was a soft rap at her office door. Opening it, she smiled with pleasure to see Cynthia standing on the stoop.

"Got a minute?" Cynthia asked, trying hard to keep her voice light. She dreaded the task she'd set for herself, but she did not want Rachel to hear the gossip Diane and Betsy were so gleefully spreading from a stranger.

"Sure," Rachel smiled, ushering her through the office and out to the kitchen. "In fact, I have a lot more time today than I thought I would. I've had three cancellations this morning. Isn't that strange?"

Cynthia unwound her scarf from her neck and shrugged out of her coat. Dropping into a chair at the kitchen table she said slowly, "Rachel, I'm afraid it's not strange at all."

"What?" Rachel asked, smiling in bemusement. "What are you talking about?"

"Rachel . . ." Cynthia paused, wishing she could

think of some gentle way to break this news. "Rachel . . ."

"What?" Rachel asked again, her smile fading. "Cynthia, what's wrong?"

"There's no easy way to tell you this," Cynthia stammered, toying with her wedding ring, "but the reason people are breaking appointments is that there is a very nasty rumor circulating about you."

"What in the world are you talking about?" Rachel demanded. "What rumor?"

"Rachel, did you and Seth make love on top of the desk in your office yesterday afternoon?"

Rachel shot out of her chair, her face flaming. *"How do you know that?"*

"Because Diane Hagen told me."

"Diane Hagen! How does she know?"

"Because she saw you."

Rachel blanched and sank slowly back into her chair. "Saw us?" she whispered. "What do you mean, she *saw* us? How?"

"She watched you through your office window."

"She *what?*" Rachel cried, again bolting to her feet. "Do you mean that fat biddy watched us making love? And now she's telling people about it?"

Cynthia nodded miserably.

Beside herself with fury, Rachel paced up and down the kitchen, shaking her head in disbelief. "No one had the right to see that, Cynthia. It was private. We were . . . well, we hadn't had any time alone for days and Seth came to my office and we were so glad to be alone that . . . well, it just happened. But, it was private!"

Tears streamed down her face as she looked beseechingly at her friend. "Cynthia, he's my husband! What's between us is—well, you know, you're married—it's intimate! Oh, God, *wait* till I get my hands on that woman! Wait till Seth—"

Suddenly Rachel froze, staring at Cynthia in horror.

"My God! Seth! You know how he is about his personal life and how he made me promise to keep our marriage a secret. Now we're going to have to confess to it! Dear God, he's going to be furious!"

Burying her head in her hands, Rachel moaned, "She's ruined everything for us! *Why* would she do this?"

"I don't know, dear," Cynthia soothed, tears welling in her own eyes. She forced herself to remain calm for Rachel's sake, but, silently, she vowed she was going to strangle Diane Hagen the next time she saw her.

Finally, Rachel quieted and drew a deep, shuddering breath. "I have to go tell Seth. We need to decide how we're going to handle this."

Cynthia nodded silently and handed Rachel a linen cloth she had rinsed in cool water. "Here, put this over your face for a minute," she advised. "You don't want to walk down Main Street looking all red and puffy. The most important thing right now is to hold your head up and act like nothing is wrong. Just remember—Seth is your husband. You're not facing this alone and I'm sure he'll know what to do."

Rachel nodded and hurried down the hall to her office, putting on her coat and stepping out into the cold November morning. "You're right, Cynthia," she said with a brave smile as they headed toward the center of town, "Seth will know what to do."

Rachel walked down Main Street with as much dignity as she could muster, nodding cordially to people as she passed, but, by their very expressions, she could tell who had or had not heard Diane's tale.

The short walk seemed endless and she breathed a huge sigh of relief when she finally reached the jail. Opening the door, she found Seth seated at his desk, staring absently out the window. He glanced up as she walked in and, rising, said quietly, "I just heard it, sweetheart."

Seeing the tears that instantly sprang to her eyes, he hurried around his desk, slamming the heavy door which separated his office from the jail cells. "Two of last night's rowdies are still locked up back there, sleeping it off," he said by way of explanation.

Folding his wife into his embrace, he pressed his lips to her hair and said, "Don't cry, baby. She's not worth your tears."

"Seth, she—she *watched* us!" Rachel wailed against his shoulder.

"I know," he soothed, "but, look at it this way. We probably gave that fat old maid the biggest thrill of her life."

Angrily, Rachel pushed him away. "It's easy for you to joke! I'm sure every man in town is congratulating you on your sexual prowess. But, it's different for me. I've had three appointments cancelled so far this morning! No one trusts a doctor whom they think is a fallen woman."

Tilting Rachel's head back, Seth gently kissed her, first making sure that they were out of the line of vision of anyone looking through the jail's window. "I'm sorry, sweetheart. I wasn't trying to make light of it. I wish to hell there was something we could do."

Abruptly, Rachel backed out of his embrace. "What do you mean, you *wish* we could do something? What we can do—what we *must* do—is publicly admit that we're married."

"No."

Rachel gasped at the flat refusal. "Are you telling me that you won't admit we're married—even after this? Even to save my reputation?"

"We can't, Rachel. You know that."

"No, I don't know that! Not now . . . not anymore."

"Look," Seth said, running his hands through his

hair in a now-familiar gesture of frustration. "I'm not going to risk losing you and Amelia just to appease a bunch of dried up old prunes. I don't give a damn what they're saying about us. Probably none of them have had a tumble in twenty years and they're all just jealous. Hell, by the looks of that Hagen woman, I'm sure she *never* has!"

Rachel stood stock still, staring in disbelief at her husband. "I'm glad you find this all so amusing," she said quietly. "I wish I could share your attitude."

"Oh, come on, sweetheart," Seth cajoled, "it's the only way we *can* look at it. Anyway, it'll blow over. Just give it a little time."

"And, what if it doesn't 'blow over'?" Rachel demanded. "I spent years training to become a doctor and I'm not going to let some love-starved, jealous old maid destroy my career. No, Seth, we *have* to tell."

"We're not telling," he said flatly. "And as far as your career is concerned, what difference does it make now? You don't need to practice medicine anymore. I've got plenty of money. There's no reason for you to work."

Rachel stared at him in horror, aghast at his lack of understanding. Finally, in a very calm, very quiet voice, she said, "You know, Seth, maybe our marriage was a mistake. You obviously don't understand what's important to me, and suddenly I don't feel like I even know you." Turning on her heel, she headed toward the front door, determined to take her leave before she broke down in front of him.

"Oh, for Christ's sake," he growled, racing after her. Taking her by the arm, he spun her around and said angrily, "Now you listen to me, *Mrs.* Wellesley—"

"It's not 'Mrs.'," Rachel interrupted, "it's 'Dr.' Wellesley."

His mouth dropped open. "You mean, you're not '*Mrs.*' Wellesley?"

"Technically, no."

"You mean you and I are Mr. and 'Dr.' Wellesley?"

"Technically, yes."

His expression was so stricken that she almost laughed, despite herself. "Oh, I can use 'Mrs.' Wellesley if I want to," she relented. "Either title is proper."

"I'm very glad to hear that," he nodded in relief. "And that's just the point I'm trying to make. Whatever title you use, you're my *wife* and no amount of gossip can change that. *You* know we're married; *I* know we're married, and that's all that matters."

"No!" Rachel interrupted, her voice rising in frustration, "that's *not* all that matters. We don't live on a desert island and what people around us think matters very much—at least it does to me."

Seth frowned in exasperation. "Do you honestly think your goddamn reputation is more important than your safety—than Amelia's safety? How many times do I have to tell you that if Brady finds out we're married, he'll try to kill you! I don't care if the old bats in this town think you're the worst whore since Moll Flanders, I'm not going to risk losing you!"

"And what if I get pregnant?" Rachel asked suddenly.

"Are you?" Seth gulped, his eyes widening.

"Not that I know of," she admitted, "but we've only been married a few weeks, and if we spend many more afternoons like yesterday, it's bound to happen."

Seth nodded, unable to argue with her logic. "You're right, and it could be a big problem. But, I really don't think we need to worry about it because this whole thing with Brady is just about over."

"What do you mean?" she asked hopefully.

"I got word the other day that he's moving his headquarters into Kansas. It's exactly what I've been waiting for, sweetheart. It's only a matter of time before he comes into my jurisdiction, and then I'll get him."

"Right . . . just a matter of time." Rachel nodded

wearily, her voice heavy with disappointment. "Okay, Seth. You win. We won't tell anyone we're married. But we also won't take any more chances of being caught together or of me becoming pregnant."

"Now, Rachel—" he started.

She held up her hand to stay his argument. "No, don't interrupt. There's only one way to handle this thing. I'm moving out."

"What?" he barked. "No, you're not."

"Yes, I am. Once you've caught Brady and made a public announcement to everyone in town that you and I have been married since October, then we'll talk about our future. But, until then, I want nothing more to do with you. If I just ignore you from now on, maybe people will think Diane was dreaming, or lying . . . or something."

"What they'll think," Seth snorted, "is that Diane was absolutely correct in her dirty little accusations and that you're so guilty that you moved out to get away from further temptation."

"Well, then, they'd be right, wouldn't they," she snapped.

"Rachel, this is ridiculous!" Seth shouted, letting loose a full measure of his temper. "You're my wife and your place is with me. There's nothing for you to feel guilty about! We're married, for Christ's sake. Now, I'm sorry it has to be kept a secret, but that's just the way it is. If you want me to, once I have Brady, I'll climb up on the roof of this jail and shout the truth about us to everyone who will listen! Okay?"

Seth's outrageous promise was so sincere that Rachel almost agreed. But, steeling herself against him, she said quietly, "No, Seth, that's not good enough. I'm tired of your secrets and I'm tired of your promises. I think things would be a lot easier for both of us if we just stay away from each other until all the secrets can be told."

"Rachel," he said in a voice that brooked no further argument, "you're not moving out. As your husband, I forbid it."

"Watch me," she retorted, and turned angrily toward the door.

Seth instantly regretted his arrogant words and, in a last desperate attempt to sway her, pulled her back into his arms. "Sweetheart, don't do this to us," he whispered, his voice rough. "Please understand."

But she twisted out of his embrace and jerked open the office door. "I'm sorry, Seth, but I *don't* understand. And I don't want to hear any more of your secret promises. When the time comes that you're ready to tell the truth about us, let me know."

Heading out the door, she looked back one last time at his angry, incredulous face. "And, Sheriff," she added in an undertone, "the next time you have one of those 'pains' in your abdomen, ride over to Wichita to see the doctor. I don't treat that malady anymore."

Seth's jaw dropped in disbelief at this final rejection, but before he could utter a word, she was gone.

Chapter Twenty-six

"Merry Christmas, Mrs. Wellesley," Rachel muttered as she pulled her head out of the kitchen sink and reached for a towel to wipe off her face.

It was Christmas morning, and although she had no plans to exchange gifts with Seth today, he had given her quite a present at their last meeting.

She was pregnant.

With a sigh, she stumbled weakly over to a chair and dropped into it. It was amazing how many different ways she was being forced to pay for that moment of madness on top of her desk.

Whatever was she going to do? she wondered for the thousandth time. She could no longer deny the fact that she was going to have a baby. Everything pointed to it—she had missed her woman's time, she was sick every morning and everything, absolutely *everything*, made her cry. And mostly what she cried about was Seth.

It had been more than a month since she had moved out of his house and into this dreary little cottage, and although she had seen very little of her husband, he was never far from her thoughts.

Before she left, they had had a terrible row over Amelia. Seth had sworn that Rachel would not take his daughter out of his house but, in the end, common sense had won out and he had reluctantly agreed that Amelia must go with her for the sake of her safety.

Rachel knew how hard it was for him not to see Amelia every day and she made it a point to frequently take the little girl with her to her office so Seth could drop in unobtrusively and spend a few minutes with her. Rachel, however, always found other things to do while he was visiting so that she wouldn't see him.

But, avoiding Seth Wellesley wasn't easy to do, especially since he was doggedly pursuing her. He had made numerous attempts in the past month to reconcile, even going so far as to ride all the way to Wichita to buy her flowers. But, when she found the spectacular bouquet of roses laying on the desk in her office, she stubbornly marched down the little hall to his kitchen and placed them on the table.

Little gifts also arrived at her house; some for her, some for Amelia. The trinkets for Amelia she kept, giving them to her and telling her that the sheriff had sent them. But the gifts he sent to her were quietly returned, placed on his kitchen table, unopened.

After several weeks of these pointed rejections, the flowers and presents for her had finally stopped, as had the "chance" meetings when she was downtown shopping. Rachel didn't know whether she was relieved or disappointed.

Seth had been correct in his assessment of the town's reaction to her moving out, though. The gossip immediately became worse—with Betsy Fulbright and Diane Hagen seizing upon her abrupt departure as proof positive of her "guilt". Betsy and several of her cronies were even going so far as to try to get up a committee to evaluate Rachel's "fitness" for her position. Cynthia, however, assured Rachel that they were getting nowhere in their efforts and that most of the people in town were far more concerned with their Christmas plans than with where Dr. Hayes was living—or with whom.

As the weeks passed with no further fuel for the fire, the gossip ultimately died down. By the week before Christmas, things were back to normal and Rachel's appointment calendar was again full. It was with great relief that she realized that she could once more walk into Ecklund's General Store without having every eye in the place fall on her in speculation. But, even though she was grateful that the worst seemed to be behind her, she bitterly resented the staggering price she'd been forced to pay for her "respectability".

She missed her husband, more than she'd ever dreamed possible. She was confident she was successfully hiding her feelings, but her heart wrenched every time she saw him walking down the street, and the days when he came to her office to see Amelia were almost more than she could bear. Several times she'd had to abruptly leave the room before she threw caution to the wind and hurtled herself into his arms. The situation was made even more painful when she saw the hungry looks he threw her. It was obvious that if she offered him the slightest encouragement, their estrangement would be over.

But, somehow, she couldn't bring herself to do it. His seeming lack of concern over her reputation still rankled and she continued to feel that his refusal to publicly admit their marriage was unreasonable. And, now, to further complicate matters, they had a baby on the way. She could hide her condition for a few more weeks, but ultimately, she was going to have to tell him and they were going to have to make some decisions about their future.

Rachel dreaded the thought of another confrontation and decided she would keep this secret to herself until it was absolutely necessary to tell him. Maybe, just maybe, by the time her pregnancy was obvious, he would have apprehended Brady and everything would have worked itself out. Casting her eyes heavenward, she offered up a prayer that her predicament might be resolved in just that manner.

Rising wearily from the little table, she stoked the stove, determined, despite her depression, to give Amelia a happy Christmas. She decided to make her some hot chocolate to sip while she opened her presents. Amelia loved chocolate and a whole mug of the sweet drink would be a rare treat.

Although Rachel had initially been disappointed when Cynthia told her she'd made peace with her mother-in-law and felt she and Ben had to spend Christmas day with Martin and Betsy, she was now relieved. The way she was feeling lately, she didn't think she'd be up to a whole day of Sam Fulbright deviling Amelia. Rachel hadn't been able to afford to buy the little girl much, but the gifts she had purchased had been carefully chosen and she didn't relish Sam ruining them.

Idly stirring the pan of hot milk, Rachel thought how strange it was that Seth had not sent any presents to his daughter. She had fully expected to find a stack of them outside her door when she'd arrived home the night before, but there had been none. She was sure that Seth wouldn't forget Amelia on Christmas, but it seemed odd that she hadn't heard from him concerning his plans. Even as she stood pondering this mystery, the doorbell rang. She knew it was him. Who else would be calling at seven o'clock on Christmas morning?

She grimaced as she caught sight of her disheveled appearance in the kitchen window. Since she and

Seth were not living intimately, she could hide the physical changes her pregnancy was causing, but would he notice how pale she looked? And would he realize what was causing it? She fervently hoped not. She was just not ready to deal with him regarding this baby—especially not today. "Please God," she entreated as she hurried down the hall to the front door, "don't let him notice how wan I look!"

And he didn't. When she pulled the front door open, all Seth Wellesley saw was the woman he loved standing in her bathrobe with her ebony hair cascading down her back and her dark eyes wide and sparkling against her alabaster skin. "Wan" and "pale" were not the words that leaped to his mind as he stood on her little stoop and stared at her over the huge pile of packages he was holding.

He was so laden down that Rachel giggled, despite her discomfiture. "Merry Christmas, Seth," she said warmly, "are you making deliveries?"

Peering over the top of his mountain of gifts, he answered softly, "Only here, Rachel. Can I come in?"

Just hearing his rich, low voice gave Rachel goose bumps and she opened the door wider, saying, "Of course. Come in, Father Christmas."

Seth followed her down the narrow little hall, craning his neck as he looked around with interest.

"Put them here," she directed as she led him into the parlor. "Amelia isn't up yet, but I'm sure she'll want to say hello before you leave."

Seth deposited his huge load and slowly straightened, looking at his wife with a stricken expression. "Rachel," he said, his voice hoarse with emotion, "don't make me leave. Please, sweetheart, it's Christmas! I want to spend it with my wife and daughter! Is that so much to ask?"

"Oh, Seth," Rachel whispered, putting her hand

over her mouth and blinking back tears. "I want you to stay." She immediately regretted her impulsive words, knowing she had revealed too much. "And I know Amelia would too," she added quickly, trying to cover her slip. "But, what if someone saw you coming over here?"

"Oh, for Christ's sake, no one saw me!" he erupted. "It's not even light yet! Rachel, how long are you going to punish me? You're my wife, I love you, and I want to spend Christmas with you. Can't you at least give me that?"

Rachel stood and looked at him for a long moment, then, in a quiet voice, said, "Take your coat off. I'll go wake Lia."

With a grin that lit up the entire room, Seth nodded and eagerly began unbuttoning his heavy coat.

Flying up the stairs, Rachel sped into Amelia's little bedroom. The child's eyelids were just fluttering open when Rachel bent over her and, in a voice filled with joyful anticipation, said, "Merry Christmas, Lia. It's going to be a wonderful day, sweetie. Your father's here!"

Amelia's eyes slowly opened. "My daddy?" she asked in confusion.

Rachel clapped her hand over her mouth in horror as it dawned on her what she'd just said. "No, sleepyhead," she laughed nervously. "Not *your* father. I meant Father Christmas has been here and he's left some wonderful packages with your name on them."

Amelia promptly forgot Rachel's faux pas and flew out of bed, scrambling into her robe and slippers and dashing down the stairs. Rounding the corner into the parlor, she paused long enough to gasp at the huge stack of presents before launching herself into her father's arms. "Hi, Seth!" she trilled, kissing him exuberantly. "Look at all the presents Father Christmas left me!"

Seth kissed her back, his heart in his eyes, then reluctantly released her as she squirmed to get off his lap and dive into the mountain of packages.

"Now, wait a minute, Lia," he laughed, "not all of those are for you. Some of them are for Auntie Rachel."

Amelia looked at him in disappointment, but politely stepped back and said, "Which ones? Make everyone a pile, please."

"Well, I don't have any," Seth assured her, "so there will only be two piles."

"That's not true, Sheriff," Rachel commented, walking into the room with two packages in her hands. "I just happened to find a couple of things in the other room with your name on them."

Seth's eyes widened in pleased surprise and he threw her a smile that made her feel like she was melting. Thrusting the presents at him, Rachel backed quickly away and said, "Here. One is from Amelia and the other is from me."

"I made your present," Amelia announced proudly. "All by myself."

Seth looked lovingly at his daughter. "Then, that's the one I want to open first."

Sitting back on his haunches, he doled out the gifts he had brought — six for Amelia and two for Rachel. By the time all the other presents were also passed out, Amelia was nearly buried.

Giggling with delighted greed, the little girl dove in, ripping paper and tearing open box after box. Rachel and Seth sat back and watched, not wanting to miss a minute of the magic. It was the first Christmas either of them had shared with a child and they were both entranced by Amelia's squeals of excitement as she unearthed more and more booty.

When all her presents were finally opened and toys and dolls were strewn everywhere, she looked expectantly at the adults and said, "Aren't you going to open yours? Don't you want to see what you got too?"

"I sure do," Seth exclaimed and immediately began ripping open his gift from Amelia. Rachel couldn't help but smile at the look of rapture which crossed his face as he stared at the smeared little watercolor flowers his daughter had so painstakingly painted for him.

"Thank you, darling," he smiled, dropping to his knees and hugging her. "It's just exactly what I wanted."

"You did?" Amelia asked, beaming. "Auntie Rachel said you'd like it."

Seth stole a look at Rachel. "Well, your Auntie Rachel is a very smart lady, isn't she?" he said meaningfully. "She always seems to know exactly what I like."

Rachel blushed at the double entendre and hurriedly turned to her gifts. "Let's see what I have here," she suggested, picking up the larger of the two packages.

"Leave the big one till later," Seth said quietly.

Rachel nodded and obediently set it down, pulling the wrapping off the smaller package instead. She smiled with genuine pleasure as she held up a cookbook of recipes from France. "Oh, Seth," she sighed, carefully opening it and gazing down at the intricate drawings, "wherever did you get this?"

"I have a friend in New York who goes to Paris on business," he told her. "I asked him to pick it up when he was there last."

Rachel kept her head down, so touched by his thoughtfulness that she knew she'd start to cry if she looked at him.

"Thank you," she smiled tremulously. "I'll treasure it always."

Seth laughed, delighted that she was pleased. "Well, knowing how much you 'love to cook'," he teased, "I felt it was a fitting gift. Just make sure I'm on the guest list the first time you make something from it, okay?"

Rachel nodded, then quickly got to her feet. "I have to start dinner." She hesitated. "Will you stay?"

He closed his eyes for a moment, exhaling a small gust of air. "Yes, thank you. I'd love to."

With a nod, she hurried off toward the kitchen, trying hard to control the smile that threatened to erupt into a full-fledged shout of glee.

The day passed in a whirl of laughter and good cheer with both Rachel and Seth putting their differences aside, at least for the day. It was their first holiday as a family and although circumstances were strained, they were determined to enjoy each other and Amelia.

The only tense moment occurred while Rachel was in the kitchen peeling potatoes. Seth was standing next to the sink, idly chatting with her when he noticed she was wearing the tiny wedding band he had given her.

Impulsively, he picked up her hand and kissed her fingers. "You're wearing your wedding ring," he said, his voice soft and beseeching. "Does that mean you still think of us as married?"

"Yes, of course I do," Rachel stammered, nervously jerking her hand away.

"Does it also mean you still love me?" he pursued quietly.

Rachel stared at him for a moment, then turned

away. "I have to fix dinner, Seth. Why don't you go play with Amelia?"

She didn't see the shadow of disappointment that crossed his eyes, but before he left the kitchen, he muttered just loud enough for her to hear, "You wouldn't be wearing the ring I gave you if you didn't still love me."

And Rachel knew he was right.

When the ham, potatoes, green beans, rolls, cookies and pastries had all been devoured, they retired to the small front room, groaning in pleasurable misery. Seth and Rachel sat comfortably on the sofa, not quite touching, but close enough to be very aware of each other. Amelia sat at her father's feet, playing with her new toys in front of the fire.

The sun set and as the room gradually darkened, Rachel rose to light the lamps, noting that it was starting to snow.

With a sigh, Seth reluctantly got up and walked over to the window, pulling back the curtain to look outside. "It could get nasty out there," he predicted, "I better get going."

"Oh, do you *have* to leave?" Rachel blurted. The words were out before she could stop them and for a moment she just stood there, frozen, unable to believe what she had just voiced aloud.

Seth turned away from the window and looked at her steadily. "No, I don't have to leave," he said slowly, "and I don't want to. I have absolutely nothing to go home to except that big, empty tomb I live in. But, if I don't leave now, I won't be able to go until tomorrow morning."

Rachel looked at him, indecision warring on her face. Then she glanced over at Amelia who sat happily rocking the doll her father had brought her and quickly made up her mind.

"Don't go," she whispered.

Seth said nothing, just nodded and turned toward Amelia. "Isn't it about time for little girls to go to bed?"

"No," Amelia answered firmly.

"Yes," Rachel said just as firmly, and pulling the recalcitrant child to her feet, promised, "You can take all your new friends to bed with you, but you're going now. And, once you're in bed, you're going to stay there, aren't you?"

"I can take my dollies with me?"

"Yes."

"Okay," Amelia agreed readily, "I'll go."

Seth laughed and swept his daughter into his arms, twirling her around and kissing her soundly. "Good night, Amelia mine. Sleep tight."

Amelia giggled and hugged him, then staggered up the stairs, loaded down with her toys.

"I'll be right back," Rachel promised and hurried after the little girl.

It was almost an hour before Rachel came down again. Seth had built up the fire and despite the worsening weather, the parlor was warm and cozy. He had also set out two glasses and a bottle of expensive brandy.

"Where did you get that?" Rachel asked curiously, pointing to the bottle. "You didn't find it in the house somewhere, did you?"

"No, I brought it along," he said. "Just in case I was here long enough to share a Christmas toast."

Sitting down on the sofa next to him, she smiled. "What a nice thought. We haven't finished opening our gifts either. Maybe we could have some while we do."

"My thoughts exactly," he answered and poured them each a liberal draft.

Rachel lifted her glass. "What shall we toast to?"

"The future."

"The future?"

"Absolutely."

She nodded slowly. "All right. To the future."

They clinked glasses and without taking their eyes off each other, both took a sip of the brandy. Unnerved by the intensity of Seth's gaze, Rachel set her glass down and rose to retrieve the two gifts which still lay unopened on the table. "Open yours first," she suggested, handing him his gift and sitting back down.

With a nod, Seth tore off the paper and pulled out a beautiful, cream-colored shirt. It was made of the finest cambric, cut in the loose, flowing style popular for centuries with English men.

Holding it up against him to check the fit, he smoothed the delicate cloth with his big, work-hardened hand. "This is some of the most beautiful handwork I've ever seen, Rachel," he said sincerely. "My brother, Miles, the one who lives in England, wears shirts like this and I've always admired them. He's told me over and over that he'd have his shirtmaker make some up for me, but he's never gotten around to it. Now, I can tell him I have my own personal shirtmaker and I don't need his anymore."

Rachel smiled, flattered and a little embarrassed by Seth's effusive compliment. "I hope it fits," she said almost shyly.

"Only one way to find out," he chuckled, jumping to his feet and unbuttoning the heavy flannel shirt he was wearing. For a moment, his huge, bronze chest was reflected in the firelight and Rachel eagerly seized the moment to gaze at the perfection of his body.

Seth missed the naked longing in her brief inspection of him as he pulled the shirt over his head. Settling it over his chest, he looked at her and nodded. "Fits perfect." Sitting back down next to her, he added, "Thank you, sweetheart. I love it."

Rachel blushed and silently vowed to make him ten more. "May I open my gift now?" she asked, gesturing to the package she still held.

He nodded and watched her as she eagerly stripped the paper off the box. She pulled the cover off and with a small gasp of delight, pulled out a beautiful silk shawl. It was woven in shades of pinks, reds, and violets, which gave the impression of a summer sunset, and was made of the sheerest silk she had ever felt. The sheen of the cloth was such that the colors were highlighted differently, depending on how the material caught the light. It was the most exquisite shawl Rachel had ever seen and for a long time she just sat and stared at it.

When she finally raised her head and looked at her husband, she whispered, "Did this come from Paris too?"

Seth nodded. "Do you like it?" he asked hopefully.

"It's incredible, Seth," she said, running her hand gently over its surface. "The most beautiful thing I've ever owned. I don't know how to thank you."

Without a word, Seth rose and took her hand.

"Come over here," he whispered.

Puzzled, Rachel allowed him to lead her over to the doorway between the parlor and the dining room. When they were directly beneath the doorway, he stopped and glanced upward. "Look up there. Do you know what that is?"

Looking up to where he pointed, Rachel smiled. "Yes, I know what mistletoe is. But where did you get it? I haven't seen any since I left Boston."

"Every good Father Christmas finds mistletoe for

Christmas," he assured her. Then, turning her to face him, he added, "And every good Father Christmas who rides fifty miles to buy a damn weed deserves a kiss for his efforts, don't you think?"

Before Rachel could answer, he tipped her head back and placed a warm, gentle kiss on her lips. "I love you, Rachel," he whispered, "and I miss you so much I don't think I can stand another day without you."

"Oh, Seth," she moaned, burying her head in his shoulder, "what are we going to do?"

He picked up her left hand and softly kissed each knuckle. "Tell me you love me," he pleaded. "Please, Rachel, I need to hear it so much."

Throwing her arms around his neck, Rachel kissed him, laughing and crying at the same time. "Yes, I love you," she cried, raining kisses all over his face. "I love you. I love you. I love you!"

With a shout of sheer happiness, Seth wrapped his arms around her and returned her kisses until they were both reeling. Finally, Rachel pushed him away and taking his hand, led him toward the stairs.

"Are you planning to take advantage of me?" he asked hopefully.

"Absolutely," she nodded, starting up the staircase.

The next thing she knew, she was being swept up into her husband's arms. "Well, come on, then," he laughed, bounding up the stairs two at a time, "let's go make some spirits bright!"

Chapter Twenty-seven

There was nothing in the world better than being kissed awake by a handsome, naked man.

As this thought floated through Rachel's drowsy mind, she opened sleepy eyes and smiled up at her husband.

Seth gathered her close for one final caress. "It's late, baby. I have to go," he whispered against her lips. "You haven't changed your mind, have you?"

"No," she breathed, her lips brushing his, "I'll start packing this morning."

"Good," he grinned, and with a last squeeze, rose from the bed. "I have to meet somebody at the house this morning, but I'll be back this afternoon to help you. Even if we can't get all your things moved today, I want you and Amelia home tonight."

"All right," Rachel sighed, turning onto her side and closing her eyes again. They had made love all night long, sleeping only briefly toward dawn, and now, exhausted, sated, and completely besotted with her husband's masculine charms, the last thing she wanted to think about was getting up and packing boxes. All she wanted right now was several hours to languish and doze and dream about the previous night.

But Seth was not about to allow that. "Come on,

you lazy wench," he teased, bending a knee on the bed and tickling her in the ribs, "get out of that bed and get going."

When that got no response, he leaned close and whispered in her ear, "Look at it this way, sweetheart. If you get up and get your stuff ready, you can spend tonight in my bed. How's that?"

"Sounds wonderful," Rachel mumbled, pulling the pillow over her head.

Seth chuckled, understanding her reluctance to leave her warm little nest, but knowing that if he didn't get her up before he left, she'd probably still be asleep when he got back that afternoon.

"Rachel," he commanded, trying hard to sound stern, "get up *now!*"

"Oh, for heaven's sake!" she groaned, irritably throwing back the covers and sitting up. "All *right!*"

She looked so appealing, sitting on the edge of the bed and glaring at him that it took every bit of will power he possessed not to strip off his clothes and jump back in with her.

"Walk me to the door," he suggested.

She stood up slowly, immediately closing her eyes as she fought back her usual bout of morning nausea. It would certainly not do for him to see her get sick!

"Are you all right?" he asked, looking at her curiously.

"Yes, fine."

"You look kind of pale."

"It's just lack of sleep," she assured him, trying to smile. "My husband made demands on me all night long and I'm worn to a frazzle."

"The cad!" Seth joked, starting down the stairs. "Men like that should be horsewhipped!"

Rachel giggled weakly and followed him, struggling mightily against the vertigo which assailed her.

Thankfully, the blast of cold air from the open front door helped to clear her head and when Seth turned around to kiss her goodbye, she was able to hide her distress. Locking her arms around his neck, she kissed him back enthusiastically, following him out the door onto the cold stoop, still kissing him.

"Mmmm," he smiled when they finally broke the embrace, "kissing me right out the front door. Do I like that!"

"Goodbye, Sheriff," she waved gaily. "Stop by any time."

"You're a wicked one," he laughed, clapping his hat on his head, "and I love you." With a final wave, he bent his head to the wind and hurried off down the walk.

Rachel had no sooner closed the door than her smile disappeared and she bolted down the hall toward the kitchen, barely making it to the sink before retching miserably.

One thing's for sure, she thought as she washed her face, I'm going to have to tell him about the baby tonight because tomorrow morning he's going to know.

It was nearing eleven o'clock when she heard a knock at the front door. She set down a valise full of Amelia's clothes with a sigh, hoping her caller was not someone who wanted to visit. She still had a lot to do and Seth would probably be back within the hour. Pulling open the door, she was surprised to find a windblown Cynthia standing on the stoop.

"Hi, Rachel," she said, hurrying into the house. "I need to talk to you."

Cynthia was so obviously upset that a cold chill gripped Rachel as she followed her friend down the hall into the parlor. "Now, what's wrong?" Rachel asked.

"I always seem to be the bearer of bad news, don't I?" Cynthia commented. Before Rachel could answer, she rushed on. "Well, I'm afraid this time is no different. I hate to even tell you this, Rachel, but it's all started up again."

"What has?"

Cynthia turned on her with an exasperated frown. "What do you think? The gossip!"

At Rachel's look of bewilderment, she continued, "Rachel, you can't stand in the middle of the front yard in your nightgown and neck with Seth without somebody seeing you and remarking on it! For heaven's sake, girl, for a couple who's trying to keep a relationship secret, you two are hardly discreet! Don't you ever make love at night in the dark?"

"Every chance we get," Rachel snapped, her temper flaring. "And, for your information, we were *not* out in the middle of the front yard and we were *not* necking! But, even if we were, it's nobody's business!"

Cynthia's eyes widened at Rachel's defensive attitude. Sighing, she put her hand on her friend's arm and said, "I'm sorry, I didn't mean to snap your head off. But, old Joe Winslow saw you two kissing this morning and he just couldn't wait to hunker down in front of the cracker barrel at Ecklund's and tell everybody who cared to listen."

Rachel slumped into a chair, contrite and embarrassed. "I'm sorry too, Cynthia. I'm just so tired of having every move we make discussed and judged. I might as well tell you the truth. Seth and I have reconciled and, yes, he spent the night. And, yes, I kissed him out on the stoop when he left this morning. It was so early I never dreamed that anyone would be out spying on us."

"Oh, I don't think old man Winslow was spying, exactly," Cynthia said. "He prides himself on his morning constitutional and he just happened to be on your street at the wrong moment. But, you know how those old men down at Ecklund's love to gossip and I'm afraid you and Seth are once again everyone's favorite topic—including Betsy's."

"Oh, Lord, does she know already?" Rachel moaned.

"Not yet, I don't think, but she will by dinner time. You can count on it."

Rachel closed her eyes and shook her head in defeat.

"I'm just afraid," Cynthia continued slowly, "that this time the gossip won't die down and Betsy and her friends will demand your resignation. There's no way that what you and Seth were doing can be made to look innocent, honey. You two *have* to confess that you're married!"

Rachel stared blindly out the window for a long time. "All I did was spend Christmas with my husband," she mused. "Is that such a sin?"

"Absolutely not," Cynthia said reasonably, "except that nobody except me knows that he's your husband. Everybody else just thinks you're his fancy woman and, frankly, Rachel, you and he don't do much to alter that impression. Besides that, you and Seth are both paid by the people of this town and, right or wrong, they feel that entitles them to pass judgement on you."

At Rachel's downcast expression, Cynthia sat down and took her hand, giving it a comforting pat. "You've got to face facts, girl. Your behavior may be perfectly acceptable for a wife, although I'm sure there are some women in town who would even disagree with that, but it is certainly *not* acceptable for a single lady! And, that's what everyone thinks you are. I wish I could solve this for you, but I can't. You and Seth are the only two who can set the town straight."

Rachel nodded and rose, heading for the parlor door. "You're right," she said, "and I can't live with this any longer. We have to admit we're married and we have to do it today."

Cynthia followed her out of the parlor and down the hall toward the front door. "Where are you going?" she asked as she watched Rachel take her coat off the coat tree.

"To Seth's. We're going to settle this now. Could you stay a few minutes and watch Amelia for me?"

"Sure," Cynthia nodded. "My kids are at my mother's."

With a smile of gratitude, Rachel threw her muffler around her neck and strode purposely out the front door.

She entered Seth's house through her office and walked down the little hall toward the kitchen, pausing a moment when she heard voices. Then she remembered that Seth had said he was meeting with someone that morning. As she stood debating whether to interrupt him or wait until he finished his meeting, snatches of conversation wafted down the hall. What she heard made her heart pound and her stomach lurch sickeningly.

"What about your new wife? What are you going to tell her?"

Rachel didn't recognize the man's voice who asked this astonishing question.

"I'm not telling her anything and I don't want her to see you. She'd know something was up."

"Too bad," the other man chuckled, "I've heard that

she's gorgeous. I would've liked to meet her for myself."

Rachel gasped in offense at the stranger's familiarity concerning her. But she was even more outraged when she heard Seth's calm reply.

"Yeah, well, sometime you will," he said. "But, for now, let's get back to business so you can get out of here. I've set up the federal marshals and if we can just keep it quiet that I was involved, we're set."

"Shouldn't be a problem," the other man assured him. "All we need is one big job to score."

"Yeah," Seth agreed. "The biggest score of my life, buddy."

The other man chuckled. "It's a big one for both of us, partner. We've been in this for a long time."

"Too long," Seth responded. "But, if everybody does what they're supposed to, this should do it."

"Ah, don't worry, Sheriff. Everybody knows what to do. We can't miss on this one."

Rachel heard the men's chairs scrape as they pushed back from the table, but for a moment she just stood like a statue, unable to move. What she had just heard was so devastating, so totally shattering, that she didn't know if she'd ever be able to move again. By sheer dint of will, she forced her legs to function and flew down the hall and out her office door, never slowing her pace until she reached her little house.

Cynthia met her as she rushed through the front door. "Did you talk to Seth?" she asked.

"No."

"Why? Wasn't he home?"

"Oh, he was home," Rachel said bitterly, "but, he wasn't alone."

Cynthia looked at her friend's anguished expression

and gasped, "Oh my God, Rachel, was he with another woman?"

Rachel started to laugh, a sound verging on hysteria. "Heavens, no! I wish he had been!"

Cynthia was, by this time, completely confused. "Honey, what *happened?*" she asked.

"Nothing," Rachel answered flatly, starting up the stairs. "Nothing at all. I have some things I have to do now. Thanks so much for staying with Amelia."

"But, Rachel," Cynthia called after her, "wait a minute."

"I have to go now, Cynthia." Rachel's voice floated back down the staircase. "I'll talk to you later."

Cynthia stood at the bottom of the stairs, staring up after her friend. She couldn't imagine what had happened during the few minutes Rachel had been gone, but she knew it was something of catastrophic proportions. She considered following Rachel up to her room and demanding an explanation, but in Rachel's present state of mind, she decided not to pursue it. With a heavy sigh, she pulled on her coat and muffler and quietly left the house, hoping that, eventually, Rachel would tell her what had happened at Seth's.

"Rachel, where are you?" Seth called as he opened the front door and stamped snow off his boots. Receiving no answer, he pulled off his coat and started down the hall toward the kitchen. "Rachel? Are you back there?"

"She's up here."

He turned, looking up at Amelia who stood at the top of the stairs holding the doll he'd given her.

"She is, huh?" he smiled, bounding up the stairs. He paused briefly to give his daughter a hug. "Where? In her bedroom?"

At Amelia's nod, he continued down the hall, calling, "Rachel? I'm back." He walked through the door of her room, saying, "How are you doing with the packing, sweetheart?"

It was at that moment that something hard and sharp hit him in the face.

"Ouch!"

He looked down in confusion at the diamond necklace lying at his feet. As he stooped to pick it up, something else bounced off his shoulder. Rachel's diamond wedding ring clattered across the wooden floor. Straightening, he gaped at his wife in astonishment as she raised her hand to throw something else at him.

"What the hell are you doing?" he demanded, getting angry.

"I'm giving you back your blood-tainted gifts," she screamed.

Seth's jaw dropped. "Blood tainted—Rachel, what the hell is going on here?"

"I want you out!" she raged. "We're through. I don't want your presents, I don't want your passion, I don't want you! Now, get out and don't come back—ever!"

"Now wait just one goddamn minute!" Seth roared. "I'm not going anywhere until you tell me what's wrong!"

Rachel whirled on him. "All right, Sheriff. I'll tell you what's wrong. Cynthia Fulbright came to see me this morning to tell me that you and I had once again been caught in a compromising situation by one of the good citizens of Stone Creek, so I came over to your house to discuss how we should handle it this time. But, when I got there, you had company."

Seth blanched.

"Yes, Sheriff, and I heard everything."

308

"What do you mean, everything?" he asked quietly.

"I heard you two planning your 'big job.' I heard you tell him you'd set up the federal marshals and I heard him call you 'partner.' So, now I know."

"No, you don't. You don't know anything."

"Oh, don't I?" she shrieked, beginning to cry. "You know, I've always wondered where you got all the money you have. Your big house, your beautiful carriage, the expensive gifts you gave me . . . I've never understood how you could afford all those things on a sheriff's salary. Now I know."

Seth walked slowly toward her. "Just exactly what do you think you know?"

"I know that there's blood on everything you own. You're an outlaw, aren't you, Seth?"

This astonishing accusation nearly rendered Seth speechless. "Is that really what you think?" he finally asked.

"You bet it is!" Rachel retorted. "In fact, I think you might even *be* Clint Brady!"

"What?" he shouted, his face flushed with fury as he advanced on her. "For God's sake, Rachel, tell me you don't mean that!"

She immediately regretted her rash words. Taking a hasty step backward, she said, "All right, I admit, I don't really think that. But, I do think that maybe you're his main rival and maybe that's what's really behind this—this *thing* between you two."

A flicker of pain crossed Seth's eyes as he looked at her in disbelief. "Rachel, don't do this to us," he pleaded. "You're destroying everything we have."

"And what exactly do we have, Seth?" she pursued. "You desire me, that's obvious. Enough even to marry me, but not enough to protect my reputation—or yours, for that matter! My best friend practically called me a tart this morning and then asked if

309

you and I ever do anything besides make love in public!"

She was slightly gratified by Seth's startled, indrawn breath.

"And you know what?" she continued, warming to her subject. "When I started asking myself the same question, I didn't have an answer. You and I *don't* do much except make love. We don't have a marriage, Seth. We have an affair. And a cheap, tawdry one at that. I'm not your wife, not really. Husbands confide in their wives. They share their problems, their hopes, and, most of all, Seth, they *share their secrets!*"

"Rachel, please." Seth took a step toward her, his hands outstretched, his palms upward in supplication. "You have to trust me. I can't tell you what was going on this morning, but, sweetheart, I'm not an outlaw and you have to believe that!"

"Then what were you doing with an outlaw in your kitchen? Explain it to me, Seth, so I *can* believe you."

"He's not a . . ?" Seth blurted, then checked himself. He looked at Rachel for a long moment, desperately wanting to confide in her. But he couldn't. After an endless pause, he just shook his head and said quietly, "I can't tell you."

Tears of pain and frustration rolled down Rachel's cheeks as she turned away, presenting Seth with her back. "Go away," she said tiredly. "It's over between us."

"Rachel," he said, walking toward her and putting his hands on her shoulders. There was desperation in his voice but she steeled herself against it, shrugging his hands off.

"No, Seth. Please, for both our sakes, just go!"

There was a long hesitation and she could feel him still standing behind her, but, finally, he turned away and she heard him walk slowly down the stairs and out the front door.

Letting loose the flood of tears she had been fighting, Rachel threw herself down on the bed, crying out her sorrow and despair.

It was over. They were finished.

Chapter Twenty-eight

As the train pulled out of the Chicago station, Rachel leaned her head back against the worn upholstery of her seat and looked disinterestedly out the window. It was late March — gray, windy, and rain, rain, rain. It hadn't stopped in the two days since she'd left Kansas and staring up at the low hanging clouds, it didn't look like it ever would.

"Auntie Rachel, *when* are we going to be there?"

Rachel smiled sympathetically at Amelia who sat next to her in the crowded train car. "Not for awhile," she admitted to the restless child. "But, the next time we get off the train, we'll be there."

"How long is that?" Amelia persisted. "Today?"

"No," Rachel shook her head. "We have to sleep two more times and then we'll be there."

"Two more times?" Amelia whined. "I want to get off now!"

"I know, honey," Rachel sighed. "So do I."

As she gazed out at the bleak landscape, she wondered again at the wisdom of this trip. Was she doing the right thing taking Amelia back to Paula in Boston and then returning to her father in New York? Maybe not, but there hadn't seemed to be any other alternative.

She cringed just thinking of the nightmare the past two months had been. After the Christmas Indiscretion, as she had come to think of that debacle, her practice and her marriage had both fallen apart. Entire days would go by without a single patient seeking medical assistance and entire weeks would go by without a single word from her husband. He regularly sent notes, setting specific times to see Amelia, but Rachel made sure she was never present at those meetings.

She felt like a criminal in hiding, so mortified by what she knew the people in town thought of her and so disillusioned that Seth would not admit to their marriage that she rarely left her little rented house. The only person she saw regularly was Cynthia, and even those visits had become more and more infrequent. Now in her fourth month of pregnancy, Rachel knew her condition was becoming obvious and the easiest way to prevent anyone from finding out about it was just not to see them . . . even Cynthia.

As the months crawled by, she had become more and more lonely and miserable until it finally seemed that the only answer to her predicament was to leave Stone Creek once and for all.

Although she had made this decision in February, she had been unable to go until now. She knew Seth would never agree to her leaving, nor would he allow her to take Amelia away with her. Therefore, she had bided her time until she knew he was out of town, and then had made her escape.

Rachel glanced down at Amelia who was now dozing in the train seat and felt a familiar, sharp pang of guilt. She had no right to take Seth's daughter away from him, but she didn't know what else to do. Seth wouldn't even admit that Amelia *was* his daughter, so how could she leave her with him? And, even as angry and hurt as she was with her husband, something prevented her from betraying his confidence by leaving Amelia behind and allowing the town gossips to speculate why. Everyone now accepted, without question, that Amelia was her niece, and Rachel would not jeopardize the child or Seth by admitting that was not the case.

She sometimes wondered why she still cared if Seth's secrets remained safe. But deep down she knew why. She still loved him, still harbored the hope that all would be well between them, still hoped that he, Amelia, and the baby she carried might someday be a real family. Regardless of what had passed between them, Seth was her husband and the father of her child. No matter how hard she tried to deny it, she loved him and would continue to love him until the day she died.

But, until they reconciled and worked out their differences, if indeed they ever did, she had to do what she felt was best for everyone concerned. And, right now, that meant taking Amelia back to Paula, and then, seeking the solace and security of her father's house in New York.

Another wave of guilt assailed her as she thought about how she should have warned the Wellesleys she was coming. But, somehow, she hadn't been able to make herself send the wire she knew should be sent. How could she tell Paula in a telegram that she was married to her brother but abandoned by him, that they had been estranged for months but she was pregnant, that she was still officially employed, but dangerously low on funds because the people of Stone Creek thought she was beneath their contempt and refused to seek her services? How could she explain these problems in a telegram—or even a letter? She couldn't, so she hadn't even tried. Rather, she was taking her chances that she would find the right words when she and Paula were face to face. Lord, how she hoped that would be true!

She did intend to send Seth a letter as soon as she arrived in Boston, letting him know where Amelia was and why she had felt it necessary to leave and take the child with her. Then, the decision to bring Amelia back to Kansas and confess to the citizenry of Stone Creek that she was his daughter would be his. Rachel felt sure that if Seth ever caught Clint Brady, he would do just that. But, until that time, she felt she was right in seeking sanctuary for Amelia with Seth's family on the east coast. She knew Seth would probably be very angry with her, but he would have to concede that on this issue, at least, she had made a prudent decision.

And what about their future together? A little voice in the back of her mind kept prodding her with that question. But, at this point, Rachel wasn't even sure if they had a future. She knew that when Seth learned of his impending fatherhood, he was bound to feel a certain responsibility toward her, but would he feel more than that? She wished she knew.

With a deep sigh, Rachel closed her eyes, hoping the rhythmic clatter of the train's wheels would lull her to sleep, maybe even a peaceful sleep devoid of images of her handsome blond husband, as she always seemed to remember him now . . . as he had been the day after Christmas when she'd thrown his gifts in his face . . . his blue eyes full of pain as he turned and walked out of her house and out of her life.

"I don't want to ride anymore. You said we'd be there when we got off the train!"

Rachel took Amelia's hand firmly in her own and marched through the Boston train station. "I know I did, honey, but we have to take one more short ride."

"I don't want to ride anymore!" Amelia pouted.

"Lia, please! You want to see Auntie Paula today, don't you?"

Amelia nodded reluctantly.

"Well, then, we have to take one more little ride to get to her house." Pulling the recalcitrant, exhausted child along behind her, Rachel hoped with all her heart that this last short trip up the coast would pass quickly. Amelia was at her wit's end and, after five days on the train, Rachel was too. She had never been to the town of Marblehead where Seth's brother, Stuart, lived, but she knew it was only about twenty miles northeast of Boston and the train was the fastest way to get there.

Settling themselves into yet another train seat, Rachel smiled at Amelia and said, "Now, I promise you, the next time we get off the train, we really will be there!"

"Will Auntie Paula be there when we get off?"

"Well, no," Rachel admitted, "we'll have to rent a carriage and drive to her house."

"You said we'd be there when we got off!"

"Lia, that's enough!" Rachel's voice was sharper than she intended. "Just look out the window at the pretty scenery and stop complaining!"

The scenery *was* beautiful as the train wound its way up the Massachusetts coastline. Although the weather was chilly, the verdant foliage showed slight tinges of green and the sea to the south of them was blue and crystal clear in the cool, early spring morning.

They arrived in Marblehead, disembarked and hailed a cab. Rachel gave the driver the address Paula had left with her so many months before and was surprised at the man's raised eyebrows.

"Going to the mansion, eh, ma'am?"

Rachel frowned and repeated the address. Climbing into the coach, she sat back in the hard seat, wondering what the driver meant by 'mansion'.

They hadn't gone far before the carriage came to a halt and the driver jumped down, opening the door for Rachel and Amelia. "Here we are, ma'am."

Rachel stepped down from the cab and sucked in her breath in disbelief. Before her was the grandest, most imposing house she had ever seen. "There must be some mistake," she said to the driver, hoping that no one inside this palace would see her standing there and come to inquire why.

"This is the address you gave me, ma'am. The Wellesley mansion."

"The Wellesley mansion?" she repeated dumbly.

The driver looked at her curiously and nodded. "Ma'am, this house belongs to Mr. Stuart Wellesley, the owner of the Wellesley shipyard over in Essex. Is that who you've come to see or do you have your address wrong?"

Suddenly, the myriad of implications revealed by the magnificent house washed over Rachel like a giant wave from the nearby ocean. "Ye—yes," she stammered, "that's who I came to see."

"Well, this is it, then." With a bewildered look, the driver lifted their bags out of the cab and started up the walkway. Rachel didn't move. She just stood and stared, wondering how she ever could have been such a fool as to think that Seth was an outlaw.

The house in front of her was immense—three stories high with a cupola and a small portico—a perfectly crafted example of Georgian architecture. The lawn facing the street was bordered by a low fence which joined a stone wall. Although she was sure the house was more than a hundred years old, it was perfectly maintained; stately, gracious, understated in its beauty and elegance.

The man who owned this house was wealthy—probably beyond imagining—and he was Seth's brother. Rachel searched her mind, trying to remember what Seth had said about this particular brother. The day they'd had the picnic by the river, he'd given her a brief description of each of his brothers—where they lived and what they did for a living. She was sure he had said that Stuart worked at a shipyard near Boston. *Worked,* indeed!

The cab driver looked back from where he stood at the front door. "You coming, ma'am?"

Rachel jumped in surprise, so lost in her musings that she had almost forgotten where she was. "Yes!" she answered and hurried up the walk with Amelia in tow.

Raising her chin and her hand at the same time, she knocked softly on the front door, secretly hoping that no one would be home. But, luck was not with her. The door promptly opened, revealing an impeccably dressed butler who threw her a bland look and said, "Good afternoon, Miss. May I help you?"

Rachel forced a thin smile. "I'm here to see Mrs. O'Neill, please."

"And whom may I say is calling?"

"Dr. Rachel Hayes."

Suddenly there was a shriek from inside the house. "Rachel? Rachel, is that you?"

Glancing around the butler's shoulder, Rachel saw Paula flying down a magnificent staircase and, despite her anxiety, she smiled. "Paula!"

Brushing the startled butler aside, Paula grabbed Rachel, hugging her enthusiastically and saying, "How are you? What are you doing here? Where's Seth? Is Amelia with you?"

"I'm here, Auntie Paula," a little voice chirped from behind them.

Paula let out another ecstatic shriek, dropping to her knees and hugging Amelia until the child squealed in protest. "But this is wonderful, just wonderful!" she enthused, picking Amelia up and holding her close. "But why didn't you let us know you were coming?" she asked.

Then, seeing Rachel's downcast eyes, she quickly set Amelia on her feet. "Oh, oh . . ." she said under her breath and turned to the butler. "Edward, please ask Mr. and Mrs. Wellesley to join us in the library, and ask Emily to bring us some tea and cakes. Then, have

Mrs. Gardiner take Amelia up to the nursery and introduce her to the children."

As Paula rapped out orders like the mistress to the manor born, Rachel glanced surreptitiously around the huge foyer. The walls were paneled with mahogany halfway up to the twenty foot ceiling. Above the wainscoting was the most beautiful hand-painted wallpaper she had ever seen. One look at the richness and detail convinced her that it was imported from Europe.

Paula dismissed the butler and turned back toward her, smiling as she noted her awestruck expression. "Quite something, isn't it?" she chuckled.

Rachel nodded and in a quiet voice, said, "May I ask you something inexcusably personal?"

At Paula's curious nod, she drew a deep breath and plunged right in. "Is your brother, Stuart, self-made, or is all this from a family inheritance?"

"Well," Paula confided, drawing Rachel's arm through her own and strolling toward a massive set of double doors, "a little of both, actually. Papa was one of the wealthiest men in Colorado and he left an enormous estate which was split between the eight of us. But, Stuart has also been very successful in his shipbuilding business and has added to his portion. Not all of us are wealthy to the degree that he is, but Papa saw to it that none of us ever has to worry about money."

They walked through the huge doorway and entered a dark, quiet library. All four walls were covered with shelves from floor to ceiling and Rachel guessed there must be at least a thousand books contained in the large room. In the center of the floor stood two forest green leather sofas facing each other over a long, dark oak coffee table. It was here that Paula led her, sinking gracefully down on to one of the plush couches.

Rachel looked around, completely overwhelmed. When finally her eyes met Paula's questioning ones, she said simply, "I've been a fool."

Always the pragmatist, Paula sat back and said, "All right, Rachel, before Stuart and Claire get here, I want you to tell me why you're here and what is wrong. You know I'm delighted to see you and whatever is bothering you, I'll try to help, but you must tell me what's going on."

Rachel nodded, impressed by the other girl's frank and honest attitude. She had the same feeling toward Paula that she'd had the other time she'd met her — that here was a woman who would be a true friend. "I don't even know where to start," she said softly. "So much has happened and I've made such a mess of everything that it's hard to know where to begin."

"Well, let me see if I can help," Paula offered. "First of all, it's obvious Seth isn't with you, even though his daughter is. Second of all, I would guess you're running away from him, although I can't imagine why, and thirdly, I want to know if he knows that you're pregnant and, if he does, why isn't he here with you and why aren't you two married?"

Rachel threw Paula an astonished look, amazed at her astute assessment of the situation.

"You're right about most everything. I am running away from Seth, I am pregnant, Seth doesn't know it, and . . . we *are* married."

"What?" It was Paula's turn to look astonished. "You are? When? Why didn't you let us know? Rachel, tell me everything!"

In a halting voice, Rachel confided the entire story of their secret marriage and subsequent estrangement, telling Paula of her fall from grace with the people of Stone Creek, but leaving out the intimate details which had brought about that downfall. She didn't know how Seth's sister would react to her confession, but she certainly didn't expect the girl to break into peals of hearty laughter.

"So you thought Seth was an outlaw?" Paula giggled.

"Oh, Rachel, I know I shouldn't laugh, but that's rich! Imagine, anyone thinking Mr. Pure as Snow Lawman was an outlaw! It's just too funny!"

Then, seeing Rachel's embarrassed, humiliated expression, Paula forced herself to sober. "I'm sorry, dear, I know this situation isn't really funny at all, and we will figure out a way to set it to rights, but Seth an outlaw . . ." And, once again, the huge library rang with the sounds of her laughter.

She finally pulled herself together and took Rachel's icy hand in hers. "You have to go back, you know," she said earnestly. "It will kill Seth to lose Amelia again, not to mention the baby you're carrying. This whole situation sounds like nothing more than an enormous misunderstanding, and if the two of you love each other like I think you do, you'll work it out."

"No," Rachel shook her head sadly, "it's too late. Seth will never forgive me for not trusting him. But why didn't he tell me he was wealthy, Paula? So much of this could have been avoided if I'd just known."

"I have no idea," Paula shrugged, "but, I warned you that Seth was secretive. He and my brother Eric are both like that. I told you, Eric lives on a big farm up in Minnesota and I'm sure no one there knows he has a cent to his name. It's almost like they're embarrassed about the family fortune. My husband Luke is exactly the same way. We were in love for absolutely ages but he almost didn't marry me because he didn't want anyone to think he was marrying for money! Can you imagine?"

Rachel smiled tremulously.

"Who knows what goes on in men's minds when it comes to their masculinity?" Paula continued merrily. "It's one of the differences between men and women that keeps things interesting. And I say, thank God for the differences!"

321

Rachel laughed despite herself, unable to resist Paula's infectious good humor.

"But, as for you, Rachel Wellesley," Paula's voice was suddenly serious, "you're just going to have to accept Seth the way he is — if you love him and want to keep him."

"I love him . . . very much," Rachel whispered, "and I want to be his wife. But, I can't live outside of his thoughts. He always asks me to trust him, but, he needs to trust me too."

Their conversation was abruptly halted by the appearance of Seth's older brother Stuart and his wife, Claire. They were a magnificent looking couple. Stuart was tall with thick black hair that had a touch of silver at the temples. His gray eyes and wide mouth reminded Rachel of a picture of Seth's younger brother, Adam, that he had once shown her. Claire was tall and graceful with sparkling, sherry-colored eyes and burnished, copper-colored hair. Rachel guessed them to be in their early forties; still vital and handsome with a self-assured elegance that immediately put her at ease.

"So, this is Dr. Hayes," Stuart beamed as he reached down and took both of Rachel's hands in his own. "We've heard so much about you from Paula, my dear. Welcome to our home. We hope you'll stay with us for awhile so we can really get to know you."

"Thank you so much," Rachel smiled, touched by his warm welcome. "Please forgive me for arriving unannounced. It was horribly rude of me. And thank you for the invitation. But actually, I'm just here to leave Amelia with Paula. I'll be leaving tomorrow for New York."

"A visit to your family?" Stuart inquired politely.

"Well, no, not really. I'm returning to New York permanently."

"I see," he replied slowly. "Well, then, since you're not on a tight time schedule, we'll not hear of you leaving

322

tomorrow. We absolutely insist that you stay for at least a few days."

"Absolutely," echoed the soft, well modulated voice of his wife. Claire Wellesley stepped forward and gave Rachel a light kiss on her cheek. "We're delighted you're here and we'll hear no more about you leaving . . . at least for the time being."

Rachel looked at the beautiful couple welcoming her, a complete stranger, so graciously into their home, and a pain of longing shot through her. Somehow she had known that Seth's family would be just like this, and, with all her heart, she wanted to be a part of their warm, loving circle.

"You must be tired, my dear," Claire said. "Let me show you to your room so you can freshen up or rest, if you like."

"Oh, please, I don't want to be any bother," Rachel protested.

"Don't be silly," Claire laughed, taking Rachel's arm and guiding her toward the door. "We have more than enough room in this monstrosity my husband insisted on buying for me. There's a large guest suite which I'm sure you'll find most comfortable."

"Thank you so much," Rachel murmured and, nodding to Stuart, allowed the beautiful woman to guide her out the doorway.

A few minutes later, Claire rejoined her husband and sister-in-law in the library where they still sat sipping tea.

"So, Seth is going to be a father again," she said without preamble, seating herself next to Stuart and looking at Paula. "I hope you can tell me something, Paula, that will make me forget how angry I am with him right now."

"Be calm, Claire," Paula laughed. "I have every intention of setting your mind at ease."

323

Stuart looked at his wife and sister in astonishment. "When did Rachel tell you she's expecting?" he asked.

"She didn't," Claire responded calmly, "but, she is."

He looked toward his sister and at her confirming nod, shook his head in wonder. "You ladies are incredible. I swear, you two can spot a mother-to-be at a hundred paces."

"Experience, my love," chuckled Claire, squeezing her husband's hand affectionately. "When you've been in that condition as many times as I have, it's like a sixth sense."

Stuart looked at her dubiously, but conceded the point. "So, exactly what *is* going on?" he asked, turning toward his sister.

Paula recounted the story that Rachel had told her, finishing by saying, "And the first thing I'm going to do is wire Seth and tell him to put aside his damnable Wellesley pride and come get his wife."

"Sounds like an excellent idea to me," Stuart agreed. "Do you think he'll come?"

"He'd better," Claire warned, "or he'll answer to me."

"And me," Paula seconded.

"Poor Seth," Stuart laughed, shaking his head. "God help him if he tries to buck you two. I wouldn't be in his shoes for all the tea in China!"

Chapter Twenty-nine

"Hey boys, come quick! You ain't gonna believe this!"

The six old men paused in their whittling and chewing long enough to look up at their friend, Ezra Anderson. He was standing in the doorway of Ecklund's General Store, squinting against the bright May sun as he looked at something down the street.

"What is it, Ezra?" called Joe Winslow.

"Come here and see! It's the sheriff. He's finally back and he's bringin' somebody in."

"So?" came the disappointed reply. "Ain't like the sheriff never brought anybody in before."

"Yeah, but this one's in chains!"

There was a loud scraping as six chairs were hurriedly pushed back and the old men rushed to the door as fast as their ancient joints would carry them.

"Well, I'll be damned!" chortled Zeke Herbert, wheezing from exertion, "Seth does got somebody in chains! Wonder who in tarnation it is!"

The men pushed their way through the door, vying to be the first to identify the criminal.

"It's Buck Hunter!"

"No, it ain't, ya old fool. He's dead!"

"Since when?"

"Months ago! They caught him over to Dodge last fall and the marshal gunned him down cold. Where you been?"

"Well, pardon me! I ain't happened to hear that particular bit of news, okay?"

More shoving followed as the men jostled for position on the narrow boardwalk. As they peered down the street, they saw that they were not the only ones who had noticed Seth's arrival. A band of young boys was gathering along the edge of the road, gawking at the sheriff and his prisoner.

"Who is it?" one boy asked.

"I don't know, but must be somebody mighty bad. Looks like the sheriff's got him tied to his horse! And he's got an extra guard with him too."

"Yeah, who is that other guy?"

"I ain't never seen him before. But I'll bet he's a federal marshal or a bounty hunter or somebody like that. Funny, he looks just like the sheriff."

Seth passed by the group of boys, his mouth set in a grim line and his eyes trained straight ahead, seemingly oblivious to the many curious questions being hurled at him.

Hearing the commotion out on the street, Jim Lambert, Seth's deputy, rose from his desk and ambled out on to the boardwalk. His eyebrows rose and a small, satisfied smile lifted the corners of his mouth as he sighted his boss bringing in the famous outlaw.

"Who is that, Jim?" called one of the old men.

"Why, that's none other than Clint Brady!" Jim yelled back.

"Clint Brady! *Whooee!* Now, that *is* a prize!"

The general ballyhoo swept up and down the street as the word quickly spread that Sheriff Wellesley had Kansas's most notorious outlaw in custody. Hats were thrown in the air, feet stamped, and voices cheered. A celebratory atmosphere quickly filled the air as the citizens of Stone Creek welcomed home their conquering hero.

The man riding next to Seth chuckled. "I guess they're as glad to see you got Brady as you are."

"I doubt that," Seth answered dryly, but, for the first time in a long time, he smiled. "Couldn't have done it without you, Nate. I'll never be able to thank you for what you've done the last couple of months."

Nathan Wellesley, the former pride of the Texas Rangers, leaned over and punched his younger brother in the arm. "You know, Seth, it was kinda fun, being out on the hunt again. But, I gotta admit, I'm awful anxious to get home."

Seth grinned. "We must be gettin' old, because I feel exactly the same way. You want to get back to Texas so you can see your wife and I want to get Brady locked up tight so I can see mine!"

Nathan grinned back with a smile so similar to Seth's that it was almost like a reflection in a mirror. "Go on then, boy. Jim's standin' in front of the jail waitin' for us and I think he and I can manage to get our friend here tucked in for the night."

Seth nodded, looking back at Brady sitting on his horse with his arms chained behind him and his legs tied to his stirrups. "Just don't take the chains off until you've got him inside the cell and the door locked. And tell Jim we need two guards on twenty-four-hour watch. I'm not taking any chances this time."

"Quit worryin'," Nathan snorted. "I was bringin' in and holdin' desperados when you were still a kid."

"Like hell!" Seth laughed. "You're only a year older than I am."

"Why don't you stop arguin' with me, little brother, and go hop in bed with your bride?"

"Now, there's an idea," Seth laughed, silently praying that Rachel would be amenable to that very suggestion. Giving his mount a sharp slap with the reins, he cantered off in the direction of her rented house.

Turning into the yard, he reined his horse to a halt and jumped down, pausing at the pump to splash some cold water over his head and upper body. God, but he was dirty! He probably stunk too. After two months out on the trail with almost no chance to bathe, he knew he must be pretty ripe. Maybe he should have stopped at the public bath house downtown and cleaned up, but he just couldn't wait another minute to see his wife.

"Please," he beseeched the pump handle, "please don't let her be mad." He knew that was probably a lot to expect, especially when he had taken off after Brady without giving her any idea of where he was going or when he might be back. But, that was all behind them now. Brady was in custody and there was no further reason for subterfuge. They could shout it to the world that they were married.

He toweled himself off with his shirt and hurried toward the door, hoping that the dousing had washed away enough of the smell that Rachel would at least be willing to kiss him hello.

Later, after they'd had time to catch up on the last couple of months' events, he would take a real bath. He smiled to himself, thinking about what a pleasant diversion that might be!

He knocked five times before he finally accepted the fact that she wasn't going to answer. Walking down the veranda, he cupped his hands around his eyes and peered into the parlor window. He was astounded when he saw that all the furniture was covered with sheets. Taking a step backward, he frowned, noticing, for the first time, how grimy the glass was that he had been looking through. After looking through the dirty window one more time, he finally admitted the obvious—the house was vacant.

"Where in the hell is she?" he muttered to himself.

Then, suddenly, a smile lit his face as he realized where she must be.

Leaping on his tired horse, he gave him a hard kick, sending the startled animal flying down the street in the direction of his house.

The horse had hardly come to a stop before Seth jumped down. Tossing the reins over the hitching post, he bolted up the porch steps, pausing for a moment as he noticed that the tulips and daffodils Rachel had planted the previous fall looked wilted, and that the flower beds were overgrown with weeds. He looked at them curiously, wondering why she had neglected them. Flowers were usually so important to her.

Shrugging, he bounded up the back steps and eagerly turned the handle of the door, crashing into it when it didn't open.

"Why in hell is this locked?" Another surge of disappointment coursed through him as he realized that Rachel must not be here either.

"Damn, damn, damn!" he cursed, reaching high over his head for the key he'd always kept hidden on the top of the door sill. He stuck it in the lock and pushed open the door, slamming it irritably behind him as he stepped into the kitchen.

What he saw made a cold chill run down his spine. The room was blanketed with a thick coat of dust and an industrious spider had woven a huge, magnificent web between the stove and the sink. Something was very wrong.

"Don't panic!" he commanded himself aloud. "She has to be somewhere!" But, where? He whirled around, looking for any sign of Rachel's presence. Heading down the hall to her office, he strode through the little bedroom and pushed open the office door. Although this room was as dusty as the kitchen, everything was in its place — medicine bottles stacked neatly on the shelves, surgical instruments gleaming dully on a tray next to the operating table.

In a familiar gesture, Seth raked his fingers through his hair, trying desperately to convince himself that the conclusion he was coming to was wrong. It looked like she was gone—permanently.

His head swam as this thought pounded through his brain. "Stop this!" he commanded himself. "You're being an ass. There's got to be a logical explanation and you just have to figure out what it is."

But he couldn't seem to quell the cold knife of dread that was slicing through him. Turning around in a circle, he suddenly spied an envelope sitting on Rachel's desk. He rushed over to look at it, his heart sinking when he saw that it was addressed to him in Rachel's handwriting. Grabbing it off the desk, he peered anxiously at the postmark, gasping when he saw the letter had been written almost two months previously and had been sent from Boston.

With shaking hands, he ripped it open, unfolding the single sheet of stationary. Taking a deep breath, he began reading.

As his eyes travelled down the page, his lips thinned and his face suffused with color. Reaching the bottom, he crumpled the paper in his hand, threw back his head and let out a bellow of pain and frustration. Beside himself, he whirled around, looking for something on which to vent his anger. Scooping up a bottle of tincture of iodine, he hurled it at the wall, feeling a little better as it shattered against the wall, its liquid contents running down in vivid red streaks.

Snatching the next bottle off the shelf, he raised it over his head, preparing to throw it, but, slowly lowered it again. It would prove nothing to destroy Rachel's office. At that moment, all he wanted to do was hurt her as badly as she had hurt him, but ruining this room would do nothing. She wouldn't even know he'd done it.

Wearily setting the antiseptic bottle back on the shelf, he sank into her desk chair, dropping his head into his hands. Gone! She was gone! How could she do this to him? How could she write that she thought he didn't love her, didn't trust her, didn't want her! The only thing that had sustained him during the past two hellish months of chasing Brady was the thought that when he finally succeeded in catching him, he could come home to Rachel. Come home and spend the rest of his life loving her.

He wanted to trumpet to the whole town that they'd been marred since last October. Hell, he'd post their damn marriage certificate on the jail wall if that's what it took to convince the non-believers. And then, if Rachel wanted to, he'd marry her again in the biggest, fanciest, most lavish wedding Stone Creek had ever seen!

But, he thought angrily, Rachel had obviously decided he wasn't worth waiting for. And, judging from the March postmark on her letter, she hadn't wasted any time in fleeing.

Having, by now, worked himself back into a full-blown fury, Seth lunged out of the chair and started for the door. "We'll just see about this, madam," he snarled. Tearing down the hall, he almost ripped the back door off it hinges as he rushed out of his house.

Mounting again, he gathered the reins and started down the street toward Cynthia Fulbright's. If anyone knew where Rachel was, she would, and, even if he had to shake it out of her, she was going to tell him. If Rachel wanted a divorce, as her brief letter indicated then she was going to tell him to his face, by God!

It was Wednesday afternoon and, as usual, Cynthia was entertaining the First Methodist Church Ladies' Sewing Circle. The little group was comprised of Cynthia, Betsy, Jeanette, and five other ladies from the church who met once a week to sew clothing for the children at the orphanage in Wichita. The ladies were happily engrossed in baby clothes and friendly gossip when the tranquil atmosphere was suddenly shattered by a furious pounding at the front door. In perfect unison, the eight women jumped in fright, looking at each other in astonishment.

Leaping to her feet, Cynthia hurried toward the door, but, before she even got there, Seth burst into her front hall.

Cynthia's hand flew to her chest as she saw the huge, dirty, bearded man facing her. "Sheriff!" she gasped, "I didn't know you were back."

"Where is she, Cynthia?"

"Ah, I have guests just now and I think, perhaps, that we should—"

"I won't keep you," Seth interrupted. "Where is she?"

Before Cynthia could think of a suitable reply to calm the distraught, furious man, Betsy, Jeanette, and the other ladies appeared in the hallway, looking at them curiously.

Cynthia whirled around to face her guests, saying quickly, "I'll be with you in just a moment, ladies, if you'd care to go back into the parlor."

But Betsy was not about to be dismissed. Puffing herself up with the pompous righteousness for which she was duly famous, she sailed down the hall toward them.

"I beg your pardon, Sheriff Wellesley, but don't you think you're dressed a little inappropriately for making calls?"

"I haven't come to call, Mrs. Fulbright," Seth gritted out. "I've come to ask Cynthia a simple question and if she will just answer me, I'll be on my way." Belatedly remembering his manners, he whipped his hat off his head and nodded to the ladies who still stood gawking at the other end of the hall. "Good afternoon, ladies. Please excuse my appearance and my intrusion."

Dirty or not, Seth Wellesley was still Seth Wellesley and the good ladies of the First Methodist Church instantly forgave him, nodding and smiling in greeting.

"Mother Fulbright," Cynthia said beseechingly, "if you will please excuse us for a moment—"

"Absolutely not!" Betsy huffed. Stepping in front of Cynthia, she looked up at Seth and said, "State your business, Sheriff, and then please, take your leave."

Seth threw an exasperated look at Cynthia, but said politely, "I've come to inquire whether Cynthia might know the whereabouts of Dr. Hayes."

"Dr. Hayes!" Betsy gasped, "why, I never! Of all the bad taste! That you would intrude on our privacy to ask for news of your cast-off paramour is—is absolutely reprehensible!"

Seth had had enough. This day that he had been looking forward to for months was quickly turning into a nightmare and he was well past the limits of his patience. "Cast-off paramour!" he thundered. "Why you pompous old bat! The *lady* whom you are calling my 'cast-off paramour' happens to be my *wife,* and if it wasn't for you and the other old biddies in this town, she would be here right now!"

Down the hall, five jaws dropped and there was a collective gasp as the ladies grasped what Seth had just said.

Betsy threw them a shaming look, especially Lorraine Hensley who spontaneously blurted, "Congratulations, Sheriff!"

Whirling back on Seth, Betsy commanded, "You will leave this house at once, Sheriff, and I will try very hard to forget your inexcusable rudeness."

"Oh, no he won't," Cynthia declared, giving her mother-in-law a look that dared her to argue. "This is *my* home and the sheriff is welcome here at any time."

Turning to Seth, she put her arm through his and said, "Let's go out to the kitchen for a moment."

"Thank you," Seth nodded. They hurried down the hall, quickly passing the group of tittering, giggling women who were now chorusing their best wishes.

Seth breathed a sigh of relief when the kitchen door closed behind them. "Please accept my apologies," he said contritely. "Your mother-in-law is right. My outburst *was* inexcusable."

Cynthia grinned. "Sheriff, by this time tomorrow, every woman in this town will think your 'outburst' is the most romantic thing that's ever happened in Stone Creek. Now, what makes you think I know where Rachel is?"

"Do you?" he asked, his voice tense. "Please tell me. I'm ready to lose my mind."

"Yes, I do know," she smiled, "and although I promised Rachel I wouldn't tell you, I'm going to break my word. If you're willing to announce to the Ladies' Sewing Circle that you and Rachel are married, then the least I can do is tell you what I know."

"Where *is* she?" Seth repeated, his voice pleading.

"She's at your brother Stuart's house."

"In Boston?" Seth's look was incredulous. "What is she doing there? I found a letter she'd sent me back in March, but all it said was that she was leaving Amelia with my sister, Paula, and that I wasn't to contact her. I know that Paula was in Boston last fall, but I figured that she would have gone home to Durango by now."

"Maybe she has," Cynthia conceded. "I don't know. But, I had a letter from Rachel just last week, and she's still in Marblehead."

"How is she?" he asked quietly.

Cynthia paused for a moment, wondering if she should tell him about Rachel's pregnancy. Quickly deciding that was Rachel's news to share, she answered simply, "She's fine. Lonely, but fine."

Seth blew out a long, relieved breath, then looked at Cynthia curiously. "Did you know Rachel was planning to leave me?"

"No," she answered honestly. "I knew nothing at all until I read Paula's telegram."

"What telegram? My sister sent you a telegram?"

Cynthia looked down at her feet in embarrassment. "Well, actually, she sent it to you—but I read it."

Seth frowned.

"I'm sorry, Sheriff, I really am. It was sent in care of me since Paula knew that you weren't here and I thought—well, I was afraid that something terrible might have happened, so I opened it."

Seth nodded, accepting her explanation. "So Rachel's in Boston. How about Amelia? Has anyone happened to mention where my daughter is?" He winced, suddenly realizing what he'd just divulged.

"It's all right," Cynthia assured him. "I know all about Amelia."

"Is there anything you don't know, Cynthia?"

"Rachel is my best friend," she offered in an attempt to appease him. "She confided a lot to me."

"Did you know before today that we were married?"

"Yes," she admitted. "But, I can assure you, no one else did."

"Well, thank you for that. Do you still have my telegram?"

"Of course." She walked over to a small desk and opened a drawer. Handing him the wire, she asked, "Are you going to Boston?"

"On the next train," he assured her.

With a satisfied nod, Cynthia walked toward her back door. "Why don't you go out this way?" she suggested. "It will save you from running the gauntlet again."

"Thanks," Seth smiled, tucking the telegram into his pocket. He started out the door but then turned back,

335

impulsively putting his arms around Cynthia. "I know I'm dirty and I probably stink to high heaven, but thank you. You're a wonderful friend."

And, then, Seth Wellesley treated Cynthia Fulbright to the most heart-stopping kiss she'd ever received in her life.

Long after he'd ridden out of her yard, she stood holding on to the edge of the sink and staring after him. She'd always thought that Rachel was the luckiest woman in the world. Now, she knew first hand that she had been right.

Rubbing a finger lightly over her lips, Cynthia sighed dreamily. Then, giggling at her own foolishness, she pushed open her kitchen door, wondering how in the world she was going to explain the afternoon's events to the ladies of the First Methodist Church Sewing Circle.

Chapter Thirty

"All right, all right, I'm coming!"

Stuart Wellesley hurried down the staircase of his magnificent home, tying his bathrobe around his waist and muttering imprecations about people beating on other people's front doors at five o'clock in the morning.

He strode across the inlaid marble foyer and pulled the bolt back, preparing to give a proper dressing down to whomever was standing on the other side.

But, when the door swung open and he saw who his early morning caller was, his scowl dissolved into the signature Wellesley grin. "Well, you old son of a gun. It's about time you got here!"

Pulling his brother into the house, Stuart gave him a hearty hug. "How long has it been, Seth? Three years?"

"About that," Seth nodded. "You look good, Stu — for an old codger."

"Still an arrogant puppy, aren't you?" Stuart laughed. "But, it's good to see you anyway. We'd about given up on you. Did you finally get over your mad and decide to come collect your belongings?"

Seth frowned. "Actually, I came as soon as I could. And I wasn't mad until I got home last week after two months on the trail and found that my 'belongings' weren't where I left them. Tell me, are they here?"

"Absolutely. Both of them are upstairs sleeping like babies."

"Thank God," Seth sighed, closing his eyes in relief. "And what about Paula? Is baby sister still here too? I want to see my new nephew."

"Hate to disappoint you, but you're out of luck on that one," Stuart advised him. She and Luke went back to Durango about a month ago."

"Damn! I was hoping to see her. Oh well, Rachel and I will still have to make a trip to Durango, I guess."

Stuart threw Seth a startled look, wondering if it was possible that he didn't know about Rachel's condition. "Well, that may have to wait for a bit," he said meaningfully.

But Seth missed the implication behind his brother's words as he took his first real look around. "Quite a place you've got here, Stu," he chuckled. "Think it's big enough?"

"Hey," Stuart defended, "with all the relatives who keep coming to visit, we need all the space we can get!"

"Well, I'm here to take a couple of those relatives off your hands," Seth laughed. "But I sure appreciate everything you've done."

"Anytime, little brother. Now, how about if you and I go see if we can rustle up some breakfast? I doubt if Cook is up yet, but I think I can remember how to fry bacon and eggs."

"Sounds good, but I want to see Rachel right away."

"And you will, my boy, you will! But, you can't think to rouse the poor darling at this ungodly hour. She'll never forgive you. Besides, you want to wash up and shave first, don't you?"

Seth nodded reluctantly. "Guess you're right. It is pretty early, isn't it? It's going to be enough of a shock for her to see me here. I guess it would be unfair of me to surprise her when she's half asleep."

"Oh, I think she's going to give as good as she'll get

338

in the shock department," Stuart chortled. "But, I definitely don't think five a.m. is the appropriate time to get reacquainted."

"What do you mean?" Seth asked. "What has she done that's going to shock me? She hasn't filed that damn divorce petition, has she? If she has, by God, I'll—"

"Calm down, Seth. I can assure you, Rachel hasn't filed any divorce petitions. But, I might as well warn you, you're not exactly in her good graces."

"Well, she's not in mine either," Seth retorted sourly. "She's the one who walked out and she's got some explaining to do before I take her back."

To Seth's surprise, Stuart broke out in hearty laughter. "Glad you're here, boy, glad you're here! Now, let's eat. I'm starved!"

Rachel stretched lazily and rubbed her hand across her huge stomach. How could anyone be so big at six months? she thought irritably. At this rate, by the time she actually gave birth to the child, he'd probably he half grown!

Heaving herself up to a sitting position, she looked down at her belly and shook her head. "If your father wasn't such a big ox, I wouldn't look like this," she complained. As if in answer to this slur against his sire, the baby kicked her, causing her to grimace in discomfort. "Please don't start this before breakfast!" she pleaded, then smiled and rose awkwardly from the bed.

She walked over to her dressing table and pulled a brush through her hair, looking at the small clock and noting that it wasn't even seven o'clock yet. "To think I used to sleep until ten," she sighed, "and on my stomach, too! Well, come on, kid, let's go downstairs and get us fed."

Pulling on a loose, flowing robe, she tied the sash

under her heavy breasts and walked out of her bedroom, hearing what sounded like men's voices coming from the dining room. Who could be here at this time of the morning? She carefully made her way down the stairs, gripping the handrail for balance. When she arrived safely at the bottom, she headed for the dining room, intending to peek in and see if she dare interrupt long enough to fix a plate.

But what she saw when she peeked around the corner brought her to a dead stop. For a moment, she thought she might faint and she clutched the doorjamb for support. He was here—just as big and blond and handsome as she remembered. A thousand emotions flitted across her face as she stood and stared dumbly at her husband: joy, relief, longing—and absolute fury.

Seth saw Rachel at the same moment as she saw him. His eyes swept over her and he felt his heart stop. She was pregnant! No, not just pregnant—PREGNANT! How was it possible that that small, delicate body could expand so much? My God, when had this happened and WHY DIDN'T HE KNOW ABOUT IT? He lurched to his feet, his eyes bulging.

Rachel watched the emotions flashing across his expressive face—joy, relief, longing—and absolute fury. Then, before either of them could collect themselves enough to utter a word, she spun around and marched out of the room.

Seth gaped after her in disbelief, then turned accusing eyes on his brother. Stuart shrugged, unperturbed by his brother's murderous scowl. "Told you she had a surprise for you," he said smugly, lighting a cigar. Drawing deeply on it, he emitted a stream of fragrant smoke and added, "If I were you, I'd tread softly, boy."

"Tread softly!" Seth bellowed, "you just watch how softly I tread!" And with that, he threw his napkin down on the table, and bolted out of the room.

Stuart leaned back in his chair and waited for the

340

fireworks to begin. He had no doubt there was going to be a picture-rattling explosion at any moment, but he was unconcerned. He'd never seen two people more in love than Seth and Rachel and he was confident they'd work things out. He certainly hoped so, because knowing them as well as she did, he knew neither of them would be fit to live with if they didn't!

Seth caught Rachel on the stairs, grabbing her elbow to steady her as she whirled on him. "Let's go pack your bags," he said in a deceptively soft voice. "We're going home today."

"That's what you think, Sheriff," she spat, wrenching her arm away and continuing up the staircase.

Seth was one step behind her all the way to her room and neatly blocked her attempt to close the door in his face.

With a groan of frustration, Rachel pulled the door open again, realizing that in his present mood, he'd probably kick it down, even if she could manage to get it closed and locked, which she doubted.

"I don't want to see you," she hissed, trying hard to hold on to her temper so she wouldn't rouse the entire household.

Seth felt no such compunction. "Well, you're going to see me, lady," he shouted. "And, what's more, you're coming home now! My son is going to be born in my house!"

Seth's comment about a son took a little wind out of Rachel's sails. She turned on her heel and walked into the bedroom. "Quit yelling," she commanded. "There are people sleeping."

"I don't give a good God damn what people are doing," Seth retorted, but he lowered his voice. Rachel was standing with her back to him and rather than try to turn her toward him, he merely walked around her. "Why didn't you let me know you were having a baby?" he demanded.

341

"Oh, and just how was I supposed to do that?" she countered, again turning away from him.

He calmly circled her again, effectively thwarting her attempt to give him a cold shoulder. "You could have written me."

"Where? From what I've heard, you haven't been in Stone Creek since March."

He had the good grace to look abashed. "That's true," he conceded, "but, as far along as you are, you must have known before either of us left Stone Creek. Why didn't you tell me then?"

"I didn't think it was any of your business," she snapped.

"What?" he exploded, the tenuous hold he had on his temper crumbling. "What the hell are you talking about? You're my wife!"

"Am I?" she said, her voice cracking slightly. "I certainly wouldn't have known it from the amount of attention you paid to me after Christmas!"

Seth jammed his hands in his pockets and took a deep breath, trying hard to be reasonable. "Rachel, you're the one who said you wanted nothing more to do with me after Christmas. If memory serves, you accused me of being an outlaw and then ordered me out of your life! Our estrangement was your idea, not mine."

"It was wrong of me to accuse you of being an outlaw," she admitted, "and I'm sorry. But why do you suppose I came to that conclusion?" She assumed a self-righteous expression which would have done Betsy Fulbright proud.

"I don't have the faintest idea," Seth answered honestly. "I've never been able to figure that one out."

"Well, I'll be happy to explain it to you. I thought you were an outlaw because you had so much money and you'd never tell me where you got it. I assumed, wrongly I admit, that you must be stealing it."

"You never considered that I might have inherited it?" he asked.

"Well, no," she admitted. "Heirs to great fortunes usually live in houses like this one." She made a sweeping gesture that encompassed the sumptuous chamber where they stood. "They don't live out on the Kansas prairie and work themselves to the bone protecting some little no-account town from outlaws."

"This one does," Seth shrugged. "The money never meant anything to me. I didn't care whether I had it or not."

"That's not true," Rachel disagreed. "You seemed to enjoy spending it well enough. Look at the diamonds you bought me."

"I like the way diamonds look on you. They set off your hair."

"And what about your beautiful house?"

"That was for Amelia."

All of his answers sounded so plausible that Rachel found herself suddenly at a loss. Furious with herself for letting his logic get the better of her, she finally snapped, "But, as far as my insisting on an estrangement, the money had nothing to do with it. The whole town thought I was your whore and you didn't care enough about my feelings to set them straight! Did you really think I'd be willing to continue slipping you in and out of my bed with the entire town watching us?"

"Let's not start on that again," Seth said. "You know why I felt I couldn't admit to our marriage. But that's all changed now."

"Why? Did you and your outlaw friend—and don't try to tell me he wasn't one—make your 'big score'?"

"He wasn't an outlaw!" Seth thundered. "The man you saw me with that day was my brother, Nathan! If you'd seen his face, you'd know the truth of it. We look like twins!"

For a moment, Rachel was silent, trying to digest

this incredible bit of information. "Why didn't you tell me that at the time?" she asked.

"Because I couldn't! Nate used to be a Texas Ranger and when I couldn't get to Brady on my own, I wrote him and asked him for help. That man, who you keep accusing of being an outlaw, left his wife and children and risked his life so I wouldn't have to fear for yours and Amelia's anymore. He and I set a trap where he infiltrated Brady's gang and set them up. I had to protect his cover. I couldn't tell you who he was!"

"Because you didn't trust me, right?" Rachel asked, her eyes filled with pain and guilt.

"Of course I trusted you, but the fewer people who knew, the better. Besides," he added, "I thought if you knew what we were planning, you'd try to stop me."

Rachel looked at him for a long moment; then shook her head. "All of this doesn't change the fact that you've never really trusted me. You've always held on to your secrets. Paula told me it's just your nature and that I'd just have to learn to accept it, but I can't live like that."

Seth blew out a long, exasperated breath. "I keep trying to tell you, Rachel, that's over! I got him. I got Brady! It's all over, do you understand? We can tell the whole damn world we're married if you want to."

Rachel sighed and sank down wearily on an exquisite velvet fainting couch. "I'm happy for you, Seth. I know what it meant to you to catch Brady, but, it's too late for us."

"What the hell are you talking about?" he demanded, his voice again rising in frustration. "It's just beginning for us!"

Rachel shook her head. "I want a divorce."

"No."

"Why perpetuate this?" she asked, tears gathering in her eyes. "We're ill suited and you know it. By the way, did you kill Brady?"

Seth's eyes flared with anger at her veiled insult. "As

a matter of fact, no! I even had the chance to, but something stopped me. And you know what that something was?"

"I have no idea."

"My wife. I knew it would please her if I put aside my, what did she call it, my 'barbarous ways', and brought him in for trial instead of gunning him down like he deserved."

Rachel didn't look up. She knew if she did, she'd crumble. "You did the right thing, Seth," she said quietly. "It does please me."

Seth dropped to his knees and gently grasped her by her shoulders. "Rachel, look at me." He waited a moment, but when she refused to meet his eyes, he added, "Please."

Biting her lip in an effort to stem the tears, she raised her eyes to his.

"I love you," he said simply.

"I know."

"Then what is the problem here?"

Again, she didn't answer and, suddenly, his heart dropped into his stomach as he realized what she must be trying to tell him. In a voice barely above a whisper, he said, "You don't love me, do you?"

Rachel looked at him, willing herself not to leap into his arms and confess what she really felt. "Oh, Seth —" she began, but before she could get another word out, he leaped to his feet.

"That's it, isn't it? After all this — my God, after *all* this, you don't love me. Maybe you never did! Maybe you just thought it would be fun to be the one woman in Stone Creek who knew what the handsome sheriff looked like with his pants off. How he kissed and made love. Is that it, Rachel? Did you want to be the woman who brought the sheriff to his knees? Because, if that was your goal, lady, then all I can say is, congratulations. You achieved it."

Without waiting for a response, he walked out of the room, down the stairs, and out of the house.

"Seth, you look terrible. Have you slept at all in the past week?"

Seth smiled tiredly at Claire as she sat down across the table from him at the Atlantic Restaurant.

"Not much," he admitted, "but it doesn't matter. I booked a compartment on the train. I can sleep all the way back to Kansas."

"You're really going, then?" Claire asked, snapping her napkin open and placing it across her lap.

"Yes. I don't see any reason to stay. It's obvious she doesn't want me."

"You're wrong. She hasn't left her room since the day you saw her. She's miserable."

Seth shrugged. "What else can I do? I've waited around a whole week, hoping she'd come to her senses and send me a message."

"Maybe you should come back to the house and try to reason with her again."

"No," he said adamantly. "I won't beg her. I said everything there was to say last Saturday and she made it clear that she didn't care. It's over between us, and the sooner we both admit that and get on with our lives, the happier we'll both be."

"But, what about Amelia and the baby?"

Seth took a drink from a large glass of bourbon which sat in front of him. "The circuit judge is due in Stone Creek in a month or so. When he gets there, I can bring Brady to trial. As soon as that's over, I'll come back for Amelia."

"So you are going to keep her with you?"

"Yes. She's my daughter and, more than anything, I want her to know that. She belongs with me."

"But Seth, do you think you can raise a little girl alone?"

346

"I'll manage."

"And the baby?" Claire prodded.

He closed his eyes for a moment as if the pain was too great to bear. "I don't know. I'm sure Rachel will go back to New York once he's born. We'll just have to come to some agreement that allows me to visit occasionally. Rachel will probably remarry eventually so I want to get something down on paper that allows me clear rights to see him. I don't want him growing up thinking somebody else is his pa."

"Oh, Seth," Claire moaned. "Surely there's some way you two can work this out!"

Seth shook his head. "No, there isn't."

"Do you still love her?" she asked.

"Do I still love her?" he repeated bitterly. "Claire, I've loved her since the day I met her and I'll love her the day I die, but, so what? It doesn't mean a thing when it isn't returned."

Their conversation was interrupted by an impeccably clad waiter approaching the table to take their order. After he left, Claire leaned back in her chair and stared at her brother-in-law speculatively.

"How long do you think Brady's trial will take?" she asked, keeping her voice light and conversational.

"Hard to know," Seth answered, picking up a roll and buttering it. "With his reputation and my testimony, probably only a couple of days. The hard thing's going to be finding an impartial jury."

"So, when do you figure the trial will be over?"

Seth looked at her curiously, wondering why she cared, but mentally toted up the time and said, "Late July, probably."

"Then, you think you'll be back to get Amelia the first part of August?"

"Sounds about right," he nodded.

"Well," she mused, "the baby's due mid-August . . ."

Seth paused with his roll halfway to his mouth, finally grasping her point. "I know, Claire. I already thought about that."

"Good," she smiled, reaching across and taking his hand. "I'm so sorry about all of this, Seth. I wish there was something Stuart and I could do. We both love you very much."

"Thanks, Claire." A shadow of a smile tilted his lips. "I knew that, but it's good to hear. I need all the love I can get right now."

Chapter Thirty-one

Rachel writhed in agony as another contraction wrenched her exhausted body.

"Breathe deeply, Mrs. Wellesley," the doctor instructed. "You're doing fine. Just a few more like that one and you'll be holding your baby in your arms."

"I hope so," Rachel panted as she sucked in her breath against the next pain.

"Now, push!" the doctor commanded. "Push again! We're almost there."

Claire slipped out of the bedroom, hurrying over to where Stuart stood across the hall. "Did you find Seth?" she whispered.

"Yes," he confirmed, "he's downstairs."

"Thank goodness!"

"I caught him just as he was getting off the train."

"Why didn't he come last week?" she questioned. "He almost missed this!"

"He said Brady's trial didn't end till last Thursday. He caught the first train Friday morning. Anyway, it doesn't matter. He's here now, so he made it in time."

A loud newborn squall suddenly erupted from the other side of the bedroom door. *"Just* in time," Claire laughed. "Wait a minute till I find out who we have in there and then you can go down and tell him the big news."

She disappeared back into the bedroom, returning a few minutes later with a huge smile on her face. "Tell Seth he has a son—a big, lusty boy with a full head of dark hair just like Rachel's."

"Ethan." Stuart grinned.

"What?"

"Seth has his Ethan."

At Claire's bewildered look, he explained. "Seth told me on the way over here that if the baby was a boy, he wanted to name him Ethan."

Claire frowned. "Then Seth better march himself right up those stairs and tell his wife that because I doubt that she knows he has any preferences."

"I'll do my best," Stuart said doubtfully and headed down the staircase.

He walked into the parlor, grinning at his brother who looked like he'd just fought a war—and lost. "You'd think you had just been through ten hours of labor," he teased.

Seth failed to see the humor in Stuart's good-natured ribbing. "Is it over?" he asked anxiously. "Is she okay?"

Stuart walked over and pounded his brother on the back. "Yes, it's over and she's fine. And you, my boy, have a fine, strapping son."

An expression of sheer joy crossed Seth's face and he dropped onto the sofa, unsure that his legs would support him. "A son . . ." he repeated happily. Then, abruptly, his expression changed, becoming resentful. "A son . . . whom I can't even see."

Stuart scowled at his younger brother. "Quit acting like an ass," he ordered. "Nobody says you can't see him. He's in the bedroom at the top of those stairs. All you have to do is put aside your damn pride and go up there." At the quick, negative shake of Seth's head, Stuart added, "Your wife's up there too and she's just gone through ten hours of hell to give you the most precious gift in the world. It might be nice if you thanked her."

"I'm sure I'm the last person she wants to see," Seth muttered bitterly.

"What the hell is wrong with you?" Stuart shouted, his temper exploding. "That little girl just gave birth to your son!"

"That little girl, as you so affectionately call her, hasn't so much as written me in three months!" Seth returned just as angrily.

"You served her with a God damn divorce petition when she was seven months pregnant! What did you expect her to do? Send you a thank you note?"

"I expected her to sign it!" Seth lashed out. "She's the one who told me she wanted it!"

Stuart took a deep breath, clamping down on his temper and lowering his voice. "Seth, if you and Rachel would just talk things over, you could clear up this whole ridiculous situation. Now why don't you go upstairs, tell her you're sorry, tell her you love her, and see what happens? You do still love her, don't you?"

"Of course I love her," Seth snapped. "I've always loved her. But, I told her all that in May and her answer was that she wanted a divorce! I'm not going to beg her, Stu."

Stuart threw up his hands in defeat. "Fine. Do whatever you want to. But, if you want to see your son, you're going to have to go to Rachel's room to do it. I'm not allowing anyone in this house to bring him down here to you, and that's final!" Spinning on his heel, Stuart strode out of the room, angrily slamming the door behind him.

* * *

"He's here? Now?" Rachel's eyes widened incredulously as she stared at Claire.

"He's been here for the last three days," Claire confessed.

"Three days? You mean he got here the day Ethan was born?"

Claire nodded.

"But, why?"

"I don't know why. Why don't you ask him?"

Rachel shook her head, but then asked, "Did he really ask to see me?"

Claire nodded again and walked over to pull open the drapes, allowing the warm August sunshine to stream into the room. "Yes, he really did. Now sit up and I'll fix your hair so you look presentable."

"What will I say to him?" Rachel fretted as she pushed herself into a sitting position. "Oh, Claire, I don't think I'm up to this."

"Of course you are." Claire's voice brooked no further argument. Sitting on the edge of the bed, she quickly unbraided Rachel's hair and began running the hairbrush through the thick, dark tresses. "Do you want me to re-braid your hair?" she asked.

"No." Rachel shook her head. "Leave it loose for now."

Claire smiled behind Rachel's back, knowing that only a woman who was trying to please a man would leave her hair unbound while confined to bed. As she continued brushing, she said casually, "How did you decide on the name Ethan?"

Rachel felt herself blush and was glad that Claire couldn't see her face. "Oh, I don't know," she answered, trying to keep her voice from betraying her. "It's a name I've always admired."

"Does Seth like it too?" Claire asked, the rhythmic stroking of the brush continuing.

"I . . . I don't know," Rachel stammered. "It seems like he might have mentioned once that it was a name he favored."

Claire's knowing smile spread into a full fledged grin. "Okay, you're done," she said, springing off the bed and turning toward the dressing table so Rachel wouldn't see her grin. "Pinch your cheeks to give them a little color while I tell Seth you're ready to receive."

The next few minutes crawled by in an agony of anticipation. Rachel heard Seth's heavy tread coming up the stairs, but the footsteps slowed as they neared the bedroom door. When his shadow finally fell across the carpet, she didn't know where to look. She darted a quick, desperate glance around the room, hoping to find something she could focus on, but, when she heard Seth clear his throat, she swiveled around and met him eye to eye. Her heart stopped, and then began wildly pounding as she stared into the face she had despaired of ever seeing again.

Seth was equally tongue tied as he stared back at her. After a long, agonizing silence, he nodded and said simply, "Rachel."

Rachel's heart dropped like a stone. She didn't know what kind of greeting she had been expecting, but surely not just a simple statement of her name. Nodding back, she answered in kind. "Seth."

Another silence.

"How are you feeling?" he asked, his voice detached and polite.

"Remarkably well, thank you."

"Good. I'm glad you're recovering so quickly."

Rachel tried hard to smile, but it came out a strained grimace that didn't reach her eyes. "If you want to see the baby, he's right over there in the cradle," she offered.

Seth nodded curtly and walked over to where his son lay sleeping. His heart contracted as he gazed at the baby. This was his child—his son—and yet, this might be the only time he'd see him before the boy was old enough to go visiting without his mother.

"Have you decided on a name?" he asked, his back still to Rachel.

"Yes," she murmured, "I've named him Ethan."

The vice around Seth's chest tightened. Unable to speak for fear of disgracing himself by breaking down in front of her, he simply nodded. Another endless silence passed until he finally got control of his emotions enough to say, "He looks a lot like you."

"It's just his hair," Rachel answered quickly. "Actually, I think he looks like you. He has your mouth and jaw."

Seth squeezed his eyes shut. *His* mouth . . . *his* jaw . . . *his* son . . . *his* wife. God, *why* couldn't they work this out? Whirling around to face her, he blurted in an anguished voice, "Rachel—"

But she steeled herself against him, knowing that if she let him go any further, she'd start to cry. He served you with a divorce petition, she thought desperately. *He served you with a divorce petition.* The thought drummed through her head like a litany as she struggled to ignore the pleading note in his voice.

"Have you seen Amelia?" she asked quickly.

Seth blew out a long breath, absorbing her rejection like a punch in the stomach. "Yes."

"She's really growing, isn't she?"

His lips thinned, knowing from Rachel's cool, impersonal tone that there was no hope for a reconciliation between them. He might as well drive the final wedge. "That's something I want to talk to you about," he said. "I'm taking Lia back to Kansas with me when I leave next week."

354

It was Rachel's turn to feel like she'd been gut punched. "No! You can't!"

Blind anger welled up in Seth and he turned on her in a fury. "Oh, yes I can! Lia's mine, not yours, and I'm taking her home. You may plan to steal my son from me, but you're not taking my daughter too!"

Rachel stared at him in mute shock, horrified that that's what he thought she was trying to do.

"I told you in May," he continued, his voice rising with all the anger and pain he'd suppressed for so long, "I caught Brady. His trial is over and they've probably already hanged him. I don't know. I didn't stay to watch. But, he's not a threat to Amelia any longer so she's coming home with me where she belongs! I've sired three children and I'll be damned if I'm going to be robbed of all of them!"

"Amelia doesn't even know you're her father!" Rachel shouted, pushing herself further up against the pillows as she readied herself for battle.

"Well, I *am* her father and it's high time she was told!" Seth shouted back. "One thing's for sure. You're not her mother and you're not keeping her!"

"She's better off with me!"

"Like hell she is!" he yelled, moving toward the bed. "As soon as you're rid of me, you'll probably marry some snobby Eastern doctor and the two of you will send her off to some snobby school and teach her to be just as snobby as you are! Well, I won't have it! She's mine and I'm going to raise her the way I see fit!"

"And who's going to be a mother to her?" Rachel demanded. "Etta Lawrence?"

Seth blinked in surprise. He hadn't given Etta so much as a thought in months. "Yeah, maybe," he countered, not caring if his words hurt her. "I think she'd be a good one. But, that's my business, not yours."

Tears stung the back of Rachel's eyes as she realized that what he said was true. She had no right to demand that he leave Amelia with her. Biting her lip hard to keep from crying, she whispered, "All right. Take her back to your precious Stone Creek — to your precious Etta and your precious Betsy Fulbright. I'm sure Betsy will love it. Hearing yet another story about who Amelia really is should give her and Diane Hagen enough fodder to keep them gossiping for the next ten years."

"I've told you before, I don't give a damn what those old harridans gossip about!"

"Oh, I know that!" Rachel sneered. "Your not giving a damn about what people think and say almost ruined my life. Thank God I had the sense to get out before you let them finish the job!"

"Me!" he thundered, looming over her. "If you'd held your ground and not acted so God damn guilty, the whole thing would have died down and disappeared!"

Rachel glared up at him. "And if you'd stood behind me and admitted to our marriage, the whole thing would have never gotten as far as it did! The old harridans would have known I was your wife instead of thinking I was your whore!"

They were now shouting in earnest and their angry voices roused the sleeping baby. With a wail of protest, Ethan loudly voiced his objections, causing both of his parents to immediately clamp their mouths shut and turn toward him in chagrin.

"Now look what you've done!" Rachel hissed. "Give him to me, please, and then leave."

Seth walked over to the cradle and bent down to gingerly pick up the baby. For the briefest moment,

356

he held his son close, then carefully retraced his steps and set him in Rachel's arms. "I'm not leaving," he said flatly. "We're not through discussing this."

Rachel sighed and closed her eyes. "Oh, Seth," she said tiredly, "we're not 'discussing' anything. And I think it's perfectly obvious that we've long since said everything we have to say to each other."

"I'm not ready to leave yet," he reiterated stubbornly.

"Well, you're going to have to because I have to feed Ethan."

"So what? It's not like I've never seen your breasts before." At Rachel's indignant frown, he added, "Have you ever thought that maybe, just maybe, I might enjoy watching my wife suckle my son?"

His intimate confession took Rachel so completely off guard that for a moment, she almost relented. But her anger reasserted itself when she saw the challenge in his eyes. In her haughtiest voice, she said, "As much as I might like to, I can't change the past. But, since I'm soon to be your *former* wife, I can assure you that you will never see my breasts again—for any reason. Now, please leave!"

Seth's face was mottled with rage and his hands clenched at his sides. "How could I ever have loved you?" he demanded through gritted teeth.

Rachel gasped, the pain of his words making her feel ill. But, refusing to allow him the last word, she answered, "I don't think you ever did."

Seth looked down at her, his anger dissolving as his eyes clouded over with sorrow. With a weary shake of his head, he walked slowly over to the bedroom door. Turning back one last time, he gazed at his wife and son. Then, in a voice so soft that she almost didn't hear him, he said, "Goodbye, Rachel."

* * *

Amelia stood and glared at Seth, a mulish expression on her face. "I don't want to go unless Auntie Rachel goes too."

"But, honey," Seth sighed, trying again to reason with his obstinate daughter, "I keep trying to tell you, Auntie Rachel has to stay here with baby Ethan."

"Then, why can't we stay here too?"

"Because I have to go back to Kansas and you have to go with me."

"Why?"

Seth was nearing his wits end. This conversation had been going around in circles for the last ten minutes and he was getting nowhere. He hadn't intended to tell Amelia today that he was her father, but, suddenly, he realized it might be the only way to convince her to leave with him. "Come here, sweetie, and sit on my lap," he invited. "I want to tell you something."

Obediently, Amelia walked across her bedroom and climbed up on her father's lap, looping her little arm around his neck.

"Amelia, do you know who I am?"

"Sure," she nodded. "You're Seth, the sheriff."

Seth smiled, despite himself.

"But, honey, I'm more than that to you. I'm . . . I'm your father."

"I know," she answered promptly.

Seth was momentarily speechless. "You know?" he gasped when he could finally speak again. "How do you know?"

"Auntie Rachel told me."

"WHAT? When!"

"Christmas. She said my father was downstairs and you were there. So, you must be my father."

Seth gaped at his daughter in complete astonishment. He had been standing at the top of the stairs on Christmas morning when Rachel had slipped and told Amelia her father was there, but neither of them realized that the child had believed her.

"Why didn't you ever say anything?" Seth questioned.

Amelia shrugged and hopped off his lap, skipping across the room to pick up a doll. "Can I call you 'Daddy'?"

"Yes," Seth answered, his throat feeling tight, "you can."

Amelia nodded happily. "And I can call Auntie Rachel 'Mommy'."

Seth gulped, swallowing hard. "Well, no, honey, you can't do that. Auntie Rachel isn't your mommy."

"Yes, she is," Amelia said positively.

"No, Lia, she isn't. Your mommy is in heaven."

Amelia nodded. "I know—with the angels. She's my 'heaven Mommy'. But, Auntie Rachel is my mommy too. She's my 'here Mommy'."

Seth was aghast at Amelia's simple logic. She was right. Rachel *was* her mommy, just as surely as if she'd given birth to her. It took every bit of courage he could muster to ask the next question. "Lia, would you rather stay here with Auntie Rachel or go back to Stone Creek with me?"

"Stay here," she answered without hesitation. "But, I want you to stay too."

"I can't do that. I have to go back."

"Okay," she nodded agreeably. "But promise you'll come visit me?"

Looking into his daughter's uplifted face, Seth felt his heart breaking. "I promise," he whispered.

Amelia giggled happily and climbed up beside him, giving him a wet, smacking kiss on his cheek. Then, she jumped down and headed for the door.

Pulling it open, she chirped, "Bye, Daddy," and disappeared down the hall.

Seth stared after her for a long time, then wearily dropped his head on to the back of the chair. He was going back to Kansas alone. For the second time in his life, he'd lost everything.

Chapter Thirty-two

"Did you enjoy the soiree, dear?"

Rachel looked over at Claire who sat next to her in the luxurious carriage. "Yes," she smiled politely. "Deborah Hite always gives a lovely party."

"I noticed David Jackson never left your side."

"I noticed that too," Rachel said wryly. "Wouldn't all the good and proper men of Marblehead be shocked if they knew I wasn't your widowed cousin but, rather, a divorced woman? They'd all drop their suits so fast it would make my head swim!"

"You're not a divorced woman yet," Claire pointed out.

"No," Rachel sighed. "And I can't understand what's taking so long. I signed and sent the divorce papers to Seth four months ago. You'd think I would have heard something by now."

"Maybe he hasn't filed them yet. Have you heard anything at all from him?"

"Not a word." Rachel stared straight ahead. "He writes Amelia every week, but there's never any message for me in the letters."

A long silence ensued, then Claire said casually, "Stuart and I had a letter from him last week."

Rachel's head snapped around. "Oh?"

"Yes. He said everything is fine with him and that the weather there is as foul as it is here."

"Anything else?" Rachel asked hopefully.

"He asked a lot of questions about the baby." Claire's voice trailed off.

"But, nothing about me, right?"

"No, dear," Claire admitted regretfully, "nothing about you."

Rachel quickly turned her face away, staring blindly out the window at the miserable, wet night. She blinked back the tears that, as usual, rose unbidden whenever she thought of her husband. And she rarely thought of anything else. Every time she looked at Ethan, she saw Seth. The baby was now four months old and every day he seemed to develop more and more of his father's characteristics. Even his smile was Seth's. Looking at her son was a constant reminder of her shattered dreams, tearing at her heart till, at times, she didn't think she could stand the pain.

The carriage pulled up in front of the brightly lit house and the women alighted, hurrying through the cold, driving rain into the sanctuary of the warm foyer. As they pulled off their wet coats, Claire said, "Thank you for going with me tonight, Rachel. I really didn't want to go alone, and with Stuart too busy to attend, I thought I was going to have to beg off at the last minute. I appreciate you coming to my rescue."

Rachel smiled at her sister-in-law. "I was happy to do it, Claire. And I . . ." There was a slight hesitation. "I enjoyed myself too."

Sure you did, Claire thought dryly.

At that moment, Edward, the butler, came bustling into the foyer, apologizing for not being in attendance when they arrived. He hurriedly took their coats and as they started up the staircase, called, "Oh, Dr. Wellesley, I almost forgot. A letter arrived from Kansas for you today. I took the liberty of putting it on your bureau."

Rachel's heart leaped into her throat, but she paused

362

in her ascent up the stairs and said calmly, "Thank you, Edward." Then, gathering up her sweeping satin skirts, she continued up the stairs as fast as decorum allowed. Once she was out of sight on the upper gallery, she sped into her room, barely taking time to push the door closed before she grabbed the thick envelope off the dresser. Her heart sank as she stared at the handwriting. The letter was from Cynthia, not Seth. The two women corresponded regularly and although Rachel enjoyed Cynthia's long, chatty letters, her friend never wrote a word about Seth. With a disappointed sigh, Rachel sat down on the edge of her bed and ripped the envelope open, withdrawing several sheets of paper. The first two pages were filled with the usual tidbits about the weather and the children, along with the news that Cynthia was expecting another baby. Rachel smiled, knowing that her friend wanted a large family and happy that her wish was coming true with such regularity.

As she shifted the sheets and began reading the third page, her breath suddenly caught in her throat. Her eyes raced down the paper, then flicked back up to the top, her lips thinning ominously. She slowly re-read the sheet, digesting every word as a combination of anger, jealousy and hurt warred within her.

Every time I write you, Rachel, there are so many questions I want to ask, but I'm afraid of upsetting you. I guess this time I'll take my chances because I just can't keep quiet any longer.

I don't know if you know this, but before Seth went East last spring, he told everyone in town that you two were married. It was such fun for me to see Betsy's and Diane's faces when they found out! Then, when he left in May, we all thought you'd come back with him. When you didn't, everyone wondered why. Several people were bold

363

enough to ask Seth why you had stayed in Massachusetts, but all he said was that he expected you back soon. However, when people tried to pin him down, he'd never commit to when. Then, when you still hadn't returned by the time winter set in, people really began speculating. I know I shouldn't ask this since it's really none of my business, but are you two still married? Because, if you are, there's a couple of things you should know. If you've separated permanently, feel free to skip the next section and forgive me for sticking my nose in where it doesn't belong.

First of all, Seth has started drinking. I know every man overindulges once in a while, but, Rachel, he's drinking heavily and he doesn't even try to hide it. He spends most evenings at Rosie's Saloon and you know what kind of place that is! Everyone has noticed how terrible he looks and some people are saying that he's changed so much in the last few months that they're not going to vote for him in the next election. I have to believe that something is bothering him terribly since I've known him for five years and I've never seen him act like this.

You might not even care about the next thing I'm going to say and, personally, I hope you don't. Please believe that it gives me no pleasure to tell you this and I've debated for weeks whether I should. I'm still not sure whether I'm doing the right thing, but here it is. Seth has started seeing Etta Lawrence again. Not often, I don't think, but enough that people are talking about them and Etta looks like the cat that swallowed the canary. If you two have formally separated, then, of course, there's nothing wrong with what Seth is doing. But, if you're still married . . . well, I just know that if it was me, I'd be back here on the first train, if for no other reason than to have the distinct pleasure of pulling Etta's hair out by the roots!

The letter ended with Cynthia's heartfelt hope that Rachel would not resent her interference and many pleas for her to write back soon. There was also a postscript telling her that the town had finally given up waiting for her to return and hired a new doctor. A man.

Rachel re-read the letter four times, then set it aside and burst into furious tears. So, that damn Etta Lawrence was sashaying around Stone Creek with her husband, was she?

Well, we'll just see about that, Rachel thought angrily, leaping off the bed and pulling her trunks out of the closet.

"You can't have it both ways, Seth Wellesley," she raged, throwing clothes willy-nilly into a trunk. "We're going to have this out once and for all. You file the divorce papers and then you can do anything you please. But, until then, you're not crawling into bed with anybody but me if I have anything to say about it!"

Rachel suddenly ceased her furious pacing, realizing what she'd just said. She closed her eyes, still grasping two chemises and a corset, as the thought of climbing into bed with Seth made her weak in the knees. She collapsed on the bed, finally admitting to herself what she wanted — and didn't want. She didn't want to stay in Massachusetts. She didn't want to attend Deborah Hite's stuffy soirees. She didn't want David Jackson hovering solicitously at her elbow. *She wanted her husband!* And, by God, she was going back to Kansas to get him!

With a joyous whoop, she tossed the undergarments in the air and spun around in a circle, arms outstretched, head thrown back.

"Watch out, Etta Lawrence!" she sang out gleefully to the empty room. "Mrs. Seth Wellesley is coming home!"

Claire extinguished the kerosene lamp and slipped into bed. Snuggling up to her dozing husband, she whispered, "Stu, do you think Rachel is doing the right thing going back to Kansas?"

"I think she's doing exactly the right thing," Stuart murmured sleepily.

"What do you suppose made her decide so abruptly?"

"Must have been something in the letter she got from that friend of hers."

"Yes, but what?"

With a sigh, Stuart sat up and lit a candle, realizing that he wasn't going to be allowed to go to sleep any time soon. Settling back into the pillows and drawing Claire up next to him, he said, "I don't know what was in the letter, love. I didn't read it. But something set her off, that's for sure. She's been whipping around this house in a frenzy for three days now."

"I just hope she's not going back for the wrong reasons," Claire fretted.

"I don't care what her reasons are," Stuart chuckled. "The important thing is that she's going. It's obvious she and Seth still love each other and I'm just happy that one of them has finally come to their senses."

Lifting her head off Stuart's shoulder, Claire looked at him earnestly. "Do you think we should wire Seth and let him know she's coming?"

"Absolutely not! If Rachel wanted him to know, she would have wired him herself. No, I think that something's going on in Stone Creek that Rachel thinks warrants a surprise visit. It's not our place to interfere."

"Well, maybe you're right," Claire said doubtfully, lying back down and running an idle hand across her husband's muscular chest, "but, I'm certainly going to miss her—and those darling children too. I just don't know what I'm going to do without Ethan! I didn't realize how much I missed having a baby in the house until he was born."

Stuart turned incredulous eyes on his wife. "Claire, please tell me that you're not hinting at what I think you're hinting at."

"Oh, Stuart," she sighed, lightly dragging a long, tapered nail across his nipple, "wouldn't you like to have just one more?"

Stuart grasped his wife's hand, stilling her provocative play. "Sweetheart, I'm forty-three and you're thirty-six! Don't you think we're a bit long in the tooth to be thinking about adding to our family? Besides, we already have five children and Andrew is only four years old!"

"I know," Claire whispered, planting feathery kisses on his neck. "He's already four. Before you know it, he'll be grown and gone."

Stuart sighed. After fifteen years of marriage, he knew when he was beaten and, with a groan of surrender, he pulled Claire over on top of him. "All right, you vixen, come here," he rasped, his voice low and husky. "If you want another baby, I guess I'll just have to give you one. I never could deny you anything . . ."

Chapter Thirty-three

Rachel had never been so frightened in her life. In fact, as the train pulled to a wheezing stop in front of the tiny Stone Creek station, she didn't know if she had the courage to get off. But, looking over at Amelia's bright, expectant face, she knew she had no choice. With a determined smile, she rose from her seat, cradling Ethan in one arm and taking Amelia's hand. "Come on, honey, we're home."

Emerging into the dusky, winter twilight, she drew a deep breath of the frigid December air and looked around hopefully for Arthur Brown, proprietor of Stone Creek's only cab. Despite the freezing temperatures and the lateness of the hour, she spotted him sitting stoically atop his wagon next to the station. She hurried toward him, hailing him as he looked up in astonishment.

"Mrs. Wellesley!" he shouted in greeting, jumping down from the high seat. "Wasn't expectin' to see you!" His curious gaze settled on the baby in her arms, then flicked back up to her face. "Is the sheriff meetin' you?"

"Ah, no," Rachel stammered, embarrassed that she had to admit Seth didn't know of her arrival. "I wonder if you could take me to my house?"

Arthur's eyebrows rose slightly, but noting Rachel's flaming face, he said simply, "Sure thing. Let's get you and these children out of this weather."

They loaded Rachel's trunks into the back of the

wagon and pulled away from the station, but, when they reached Main Street, Arthur pulled to a stop and turned toward her. "Uh, which house do you mean, ma'am?"

For a brief moment, Rachel didn't know what he meant, then, realizing that he didn't know if she wanted to go to Seth's or the little house she had once rented, she said, "To Sheriff Wellesley's, please," and hurriedly turned her face away.

With a quick nod, Arthur wheeled his horse to the right and proceeded down Main Street toward Elm. Since it was close to dinnertime, the streets were nearly deserted, a fact for which Rachel was profoundly grateful.

They pulled into Seth's yard and Rachel looked anxiously at the house, releasing a sigh of relief when she saw lights from within. She hadn't thought about what she would do if Seth wasn't home, and she was very glad that she wasn't going to be faced with that dilemma.

Seth heard a wagon pulling into the yard and rose from the kitchen table. "Wonder who that could be?"

"I can't imagine," Etta Lawrence replied, rising also. "Are you expecting someone?"

"No." He shook his head. "Who'd come calling on a cold night like this?" Pushing through the kitchen door, he walked down the hall and looked out the front window into the rapidly gathering darkness.

His heart slammed against his ribs and he grabbed for the door frame as his knees threatened to buckle. For an endless moment he stood frozen, staring out the window in disbelief. It wasn't until he heard Etta's sharply indrawn breath as she walked up next to him and peered out also that he moved. Turning to meet her stricken gaze, he found his voice enough to say, "Move out of the way so I can open the door."

Mechanically, Etta took a step sideways, wishing, with all her heart, that Seth wouldn't open the door.

He had no more than snapped the lock and turned the knob when the door was suddenly flung open from the opposite side and Amelia launched herself against her father's legs. "Daddy!" she shrieked gleefully. "Daddy, we're home!"

Seth reached down and scooped his daughter into his arms, not even noticing that the color had drained from Etta's face.

"Hello, sweetheart," he greeted her, whirling in a circle as he hugged her close. "Lord, have you grown!"

"Yes," Amelia agreed, enthusiastically hugging him around the neck. "I'm big now." Then, wiggling to get down, she demanded, "I want to see my bedroom. Are my dollies still here?"

Reluctantly, Seth set her on her feet and watched her tear up the stairs. Turning back toward the door, his heart suddenly skipped a beat as he came face to face with Rachel.

She stood on the porch, clutching the baby, and for a long moment neither of them said anything. Etta stood to one side, silently watching the couple, her heart sinking like a stone as she saw the myriad of emotions crossing their faces. Surprise, trepidation, and anger were reflected, but even more noticeable were desire, longing, and, Etta admitted bitterly, love.

The moment dragged on endlessly as the strange threesome stood in suspended silence. Finally, Etta drew a deep breath and said, "For heaven's sake, Seth, step aside so Dr. Hayes can come in out of the cold."

Rachel suddenly gathered her wits and threw Etta a furious glare. "It's Dr. *Wellesley,* if you don't mind." A great wave of despair washed over Etta as she realized that with that one statement, the battle lines had again been drawn.

Seth had still not said a word. The entire scene was like a tableau from a bad melodrama and he was utterly at a loss as to what to say — or to whom.

Rachel, however, was girded up by blinding anger.

Stepping into the foyer, she thrust Ethan at her husband. "Will you take him a minute, please, so I can remove my boots?"

Seth dumbly accepted the baby, and, looking down at the tiny face, finally seemed to realize who he held. "Ethan . . ." he breathed, eagerly unwrapping the heavy quilt the baby was wrapped in and taking a long, searching look at his son. "He's so big," he murmured, more to himself than to the women.

Rachel pulled off her boots and said curtly, "Yes, well, he's almost five months old now. He's also wet, hungry and exhausted." Reaching out to reclaim her son, she said, "If you don't mind, I'll take him upstairs and tend to him."

Seth reluctantly handed the baby back to her and without another glance at either him or Etta, Rachel started up the staircase.

"Second door on the right," Seth called after her.

Without turning, Rachel nodded and continued on her way. When she'd disappeared into the darkness at the top of the stairs, Seth blew out a long breath and turned toward Etta. "I think I'd better take you home."

Dropping her eyes to the floor, Etta nodded miserably. "What does this mean, Seth?" she asked quietly. "Did you know she was coming?"

"No! And I don't know what it means. But, I damn well mean to find out."

Etta looked up at him, her eyes bright with the tears she was trying to fight. "Will you come see me tomorrow?"

"I'll try," Seth said shortly, taking her coat off the rack by the door and handing it to her, "but don't count on me."

"Will she be staying here with you?" Etta pursued, hating herself for the way her voice trembled.

"I don't know!" Seth answered impatiently, shrugging into his heavy parka. "I don't know anything right now."

Etta nodded again and walked dejectedly out the front

door, wondering, as she stepped on to the porch, if she'd ever enter this house again.

Rachel walked down the upstairs hall and turned into the bedroom Seth had directed her to. It was one of several unused bedrooms and had been nearly devoid of furniture the last time she'd been in the house. The room was situated next to the master bedroom and she had often thought that it was ideally suited for a nursery.

The door was closed and Rachel pushed it open, pausing to light a lamp which she remembered stood on a small stand next to the door. The wick flared, casting a soft light over the room's interior and as she looked around, she gasped in astonishment. The bedroom had been completely redecorated and was now, indeed, a nursery. The walls had been painted pale blue and a thick, Aubusson carpet covered the highly polished, wooden floor. An ornately carved cradle sat against a wall and a four-drawer bureau had been added. In one corner was a large Bentwood rocking chair with plush cushions covering the seat and back. The chair was currently occupied by a small rag doll dressed in boy's clothing.

Rachel bit her lip as her gaze swept the warm, cozy room. It was obvious that a lot of loving thought had gone into the furnishing of this nursery and some of the initial anger she had felt after finding Etta Lawrence in the house evaporated.

Gently laying Ethan in the cradle, she turned back toward the door, intending to go downstairs and get his valise. But, as she walked across the room, she noticed a table against the far wall covered with neatly folded stacks of sparkling white diapers. A wave of guilt engulfed her as she stared at the diapers. What must it have been like for Seth to prepare this room and then never have it occupied? No wonder he kept the door closed! Curiously, she walked over to the bureau and pulled open the top drawer. As she had somehow known it would, the drawer contained rows of tiny clothes. Shirts, sleeping sacks, and light blankets seemed to stare accusingly back at her, crisp and bright in their unused newness.

Plucking a sleeping sack off the top of a pile, Rachel hurriedly closed the drawer. She walked over to the table and snatched up one of the clean diapers, then returned to the baby.

She was midway through feeding him when she heard Seth come in downstairs. She held her breath, waiting for him to appear in the doorway, but released it with a gusty sigh when she heard Amelia clatter down the stairs and the two of them go into the kitchen.

An hour later, she had both children tucked in bed and knew she could no longer delay facing her husband. But, what was she going to say to him? All the way across the country, Rachel had dreamed of Seth's reaction to her arrival. She had pictured him with arms open and happiness wreathing his face when he found her and his children on his doorstep. The reality of his cold welcome and Etta Lawrence's presence had been like a slap in the face and Rachel had been sorely tempted to get back into Arthur Brown's wagon and return to the station. But, as she had sat in the plush rocker, feeding her son and gazing around the luxurious nursery her husband had so lovingly prepared, she had finally admitted that leaving was the last thing she wanted to do. This was her home, Seth was her husband and, whatever it took on her part, she wanted it to remain that way.

As she slowly descended the stairs, Claire's parting words came back to her. "You've hurt him badly," Claire had said, "and if you want him back, it's going to be up to you to mend the rift."

Well, Rachel meant to mend it, and if that meant begging his forgiveness, she'd do it.

Seth was in the kitchen, sitting at the table and staring into an untouched cup of coffee. Rachel knew he heard her as she came through the door, but he didn't look up. Walking quietly over to the stove, she poured herself a cup of the strong brew and sat down at the table across from him.

Several minutes ticked by with neither of them saying a word. All the poignant pleas that Rachel had mentally rehearsed flew out of her head and she seemed unable to put two lucid thoughts together as she sat and blindly stared at Seth's bowed head.

Finally, when the tension between them had grown to such proportions that she was ready to scream, he raised his head and gave her a hard look. "What are you doing here?"

Rachel was totally unprepared for the cold accusation in his tone and merely stared at him speechlessly.

"I said, what are you doing here?" he repeated.

"I — I've come back."

"Why?"

Her apprehension grew. "Because — because you're my husband, and this is my home."

"I'm not your husband," he said flatly.

"What?" she gasped. "Do you mean we're divorced?"

"Close."

"But, it's not final, right? It can still be called off?"

"We're not calling it off."

Rachel was suddenly very, very frightened. This cold, disinterested man was not what she had expected and she didn't have the slightest idea how to approach him. She had expected anger, expected he might want to punish her for the hurt she had inflicted on him, but this . . . this was far worse than anger. As the silence between them lengthened, it suddenly dawned on her that her worst fears were being realized. Seth simply no longer cared.

"I . . . I thought you'd be glad to see your children."

"I *am* glad to see my children." His voice trailed off and what he left unsaid hit her like a fist in the chest.

"I want to stay in Stone Creek," she whispered, tears choking her voice and making it almost impossible to talk.

Seth shrugged indifferently. "That's your prerogative.

374

You're free to live anywhere you want to. I can't stop you."

"But you would if you could, wouldn't you?"

The rage he was trying so hard to control suddenly erupted and Seth leaped to his feet, turning on her in a fury.

"You're God damned right I would!" he shouted. "I want you out of my life, do you understand me? I don't want you in my house, in my town, anywhere near me. I don't want to see you, I don't want to talk to you, I don't want to think about you! Why did you come back here? *Why?*"

Rachel stared up into his enraged face and knew, with crystal clarity, that all was lost. There was something close to hatred in his eyes. The kind of steely hatred that had brought seasoned killers to their knees when confronted by him. Only a moment ago, she had wished he would become angry, but he was now in a rage so terrifying in its intensity that she found herself too intimidated to even answer him.

"I asked you a question, madam," he repeated. "Why did you come back here?"

"Because I love you!" she blurted.

Seth gaped at her for a moment and, although she would have doubted it possible, his face became even angrier. "Love me!" he bellowed. "LOVE ME! Lady, you don't know the meaning of the word! How dare you come waltzing into my house, calmly telling me you're back and that you love me. Did you think that was going to make everything all right between us? Well, you've got another think coming!"

"Seth —" she interrupted.

"No!" he countered, halting her words. "Don't say anything, Rachel. It's way too late for explanations."

"Seth, *please*," Rachel sobbed, burying her head in her hands, "I know I've been wrong, but if you'd just give us another chance . . ."

Seth threw his head back and squeezed his eyes shut,

struggling to bring his temper under control. Finally, he dropped into the chair next to her, saying quietly, "Rachel, look at me." When she didn't respond, he grabbed her hands, forcing them away from her face. "I said, look at me, damn it! And listen to what I'm telling you."

Raising her tear-stained face, Rachel nodded weakly.

Satisfied that he had her attention, Seth said, "I wanted to die last summer when you told me you wanted a divorce. I figured if I couldn't have you, I didn't even want to live. But, no matter how little I cared about myself, I kept on living and, finally, I realized I had to start rebuilding my life. Without you. Do you understand what I'm saying? WITHOUT YOU! Now you come here and tell me that you've decided you want me again. Well, that's no longer an option, lady, because I'm over you. Do you hear me?" He gave her hands a rough shake. "I'M OVER YOU!"

Rachel nodded miserably, realizing that he meant what he said and that there really was no hope for them.

"Now," Seth continued, rising and walking over to the sink where he stood with his back to her, "since both children are already in bed, you may spend the night here. But, tomorrow, I want you gone. I don't care if you stay in Stone Creek, go back to Boston, go to New York, or go to Timbucktu, but I want you gone. Do you understand?" He turned and looked at her, waiting for a response.

"Yes," she whispered, standing up on shaky legs. "I understand perfectly."

And, turning, Rachel walked out of the kitchen and climbed slowly up the stairs.

Chapter Thirty-four

The baby was crying again. With an exhausted sigh, Rachel opened her eyes and threw back the covers of the bed she was sharing with Amelia. This was the third time Ethan had been up since she'd gone to bed and it was barely past two. She knew he couldn't be hungry since he was long past night feedings, but, perhaps, if she offered him her breast, it would put him to sleep again.

Poor little boy, she thought as she trudged down the hall toward the nursery, he's having as bad a night as I am. Maybe she'd just take him to bed with her. It might be a little crowded with her, Amelia, and Ethan all in one bed, but if it would allow her to sleep the rest of the night, it would be worth it.

She started through the nursery door, but came to an abrupt halt, quickly backing into the shadows so she wouldn't be seen.

Seth was sitting in the rocker, cuddling his son against him as he murmured something Rachel couldn't hear. A fire burned merrily where he had stoked up the glowing coals and the serene beauty of the man and the baby in the flickering light made her heart wrench painfully.

Careful to stay deep in the shadows, Rachel crept closer to the door, hoping to hear what Seth was saying to their son.

". . . and you've got to stop this nonsense, now. You're warm, you're safe, you're dry, and it's time to get a little shut-eye. Your mama's tired, your pa's tired, and you must be tired too. So just shut your eyes and give it up, little man."

Tears started down Rachel's cheeks as she listened to Seth croon to the baby. Hastily wiping her eyes to clear her vision, she saw him lean his head back against the chair and close his eyes.

"Oh, Ethan, Ethan," he sighed, "where did I go wrong? All I ever wanted was for you and Lia and your mama and me to be a family. That doesn't seem like so much to ask. Tell me, little boy, where did I fail? I loved her—God, how I loved her. And, you know what? I really think she loved me too. So, how did this happen?"

Gazing down at the baby who was now dozing, Seth smiled. "You're not giving me any answers, Ethan. I thought for sure you'd be able to tell me what I should do, but, you're no help at all. Do you think maybe if I admitted to her that I still love her, there'd be any chance for us?"

He waited as if expecting the baby to respond, the tenderness in his expression so poignant that Rachel clapped her hand over her mouth to keep from crying out loud.

"So, you think it's worth another try, eh?" Seth said, nodding at Ethan as if the baby had just imparted his considered opinion. "Gonna be pretty rough, though, after tonight. I said some terrible things to her down in that kitchen. Told some terrible lies. Even told her I didn't love her anymore. But, damn it all, she made me so mad that I just said anything I could think of that would hurt her." Seth paused. "I know that was a stupid mistake," he admitted. "Now, I just have to figure out how to correct it, if that's even possible."

Looking down at the baby, Seth smiled ruefully. "Your pa's a fool sometimes, boy. But, for your sake and

Lia's—and mine, I'll see if I can't right things in the morning."

Ethan was now sound asleep, his tiny head lolling against his father's bare chest where Seth's heavy woolen robe gaped open.

"Okay, come on, baby boy," Seth crooned, getting slowly to his feet. "Let's give this sleeping thing another try."

Padding across the bedroom, he carefully laid the baby in the cradle, stooping to tuck a beautiful cashmere blanket around him. "By the way, Ethan," he whispered, straightening, "thanks for the advice."

Rachel stood outside the door, transfixed by the scene unfolding in front of her. She unabashedly wept at the gentle love her husband was bestowing on their son, realizing that she would do anything—ANYTHING—to put their marriage back together. But, she didn't want to wait until morning. She wanted to settle things now. What they needed was a little intimacy—a little physical closeness to help break down the barriers they'd built against each other. Without pausing to think about the chance she was taking, Rachel flew down the hall, disappearing into Seth's room just as he came out of Ethan's.

Deep in thought, Seth walked silently down the dark hall and into his room. Pulling off his heavy robe, he sat down, naked, on the edge of the bed, dropping his head into his hands as he tried to figure out a way to reconcile with his wife. But he was too exhausted to think clearly and, finally, he gave up and lay down, pulling the quilt over him.

Immediately, he felt her against him and sat bolt upright, sucking in his breath. "Rachel?"

"Yes?" came the soft reply.

For a moment, his voice hardened. "What are you doing in here?"

Rachel slowly sat up. She had shed her nightgown

and was as naked as he. Pressing her chest against his back, she put her arms around his neck and whispered, "I heard you talking to Ethan."

"You heard?" he said, his voice becoming husky as he reacted to her nudity.

"Um hmmm," she whispered. "And you know what?"

"What?" he rasped.

"I don't want you to try to make things right with me in the morning."

Seth's shoulders stiffened and he tried to pull away, but Rachel wouldn't release her hold.

"Then, what the hell —"

"Because," she interrupted, her voice softly caressing, "you don't have anything to apologize for. I'm the one who wants to apologize and I want to do it right now."

Seth turned his head, unable to see her in the dark, but knowing her lips were a whisper away from his.

"I love you, Seth," she breathed, brushing her lips against his. "Please forgive me. Please —"

With a groan, Seth twisted around, wrapping his arms around her and pulling her close as his mouth devoured her like a starving man at a feast. His kisses fell everywhere — her forehead, eyes, nose, chin. He kissed away the tears that were trickling down her cheeks, then lowered his mouth to cover hers. Rachel's lips parted as she welcomed his caress, and with a moan of pleasure, Seth bent her backward till they lay with his body partially covering hers.

"I love you," he murmured hoarsely, his lips tracing the column of her throat. "I love you. I love you. I love you."

"Oh, Seth," Rachel murmured, gently stroking his thick, tawny hair. "I love you too. More than you could possibly know. Can you ever forgive me?"

"Shh . . ." he commanded, moving to cover her more fully and letting her feel his rising passion. "It's behind us now."

"But," Rachel whispered, unconsciously pressing her hips against his as she reacted to his arousal.

"Don't talk," he muttered, his hand feathering down her stomach until his fingers glided into the soft nest at the juncture of her thighs. "Just love me."

Rachel gasped at the erotic sensations flowing over her. She raised her hips to her husband's gently questing hand, then convulsed with the first blush of ecstasy as his fingers slipped easily inside her.

Wanting to return the pleasure, she reached down, gently encircling him with cool fingers. He moaned, the long starved fires of passion quickly igniting into an inferno of need.

Rising above her, he pressed into her welcoming warmth, sighing with an ecstasy he had thought never to know again.

Giving her a searing kiss, he sought love's rhythm until, together, they found heaven. It was a perfect moment—a merging of two bodies completely attuned by love and two souls who, at long last, were at peace with each other.

As their hearts slowed and their breathing calmed, Seth pulled Rachel over on top of him. Still intimately joined, he whispered, "It's been so long . . ."

"I know," she sighed drowsily, "almost a year."

"I didn't hurt you, did I?"

"No. Remember, I've had a baby."

"I know," he chuckled, kissing the top of her head where it lay against his chest, "my baby. By the way, did I thank you for him?"

"No," she giggled, "but, better late than never."

"Next time," he promised, tipping her chin up and softly kissing her lips. "Next time, I'll be right there with you so I can thank you properly at the proper time."

"I'm going to hold you to that," Rachel smiled.

"I just hope it'll be soon," he whispered provocatively.

"Hope what will be soon?"

"Another baby."

"Oh . . ." she answered, her eyes widening as she felt him harden within her. Raising her eyes to his, she threw him a delicious look. "At this rate, you may get your wish sooner than you think."

"Hope so," he muttered throatily, giving her a heated look as he again rolled her beneath him. "It's my fondest wish to fill this big house up with our babies."

And, though he didn't know it, at that very moment, Seth Wellesley's fondest wish was being fulfilled.

Epilogue

It was barely six o'clock the following morning when Seth heard someone beating on the back door.

Disentangling himself from where he and Rachel lay entwined, he sat up irritably.

"Who could be here at this time of the morning?" Rachel murmured sleepily.

"I don't know," he growled, swinging his long legs over the side of the bed, "but, it better be a matter of life or death." He pulled on his robe and stomped down the stairs, Rachel following a few steps behind him.

"It's someone at my office door," she said in surprise as they walked into the kitchen.

Striding angrily through the little bedroom and into Rachel's office, Seth yanked open the door scowling at the man who stood meekly on the other side.

"Sorry to bother you so early, Sheriff. I'm looking for your wife."

Rachel peeked over Seth's shoulder to see Hank Johnson standing on the stoop, his hat in his hand. "Hello, Mr. Johnson. May I help you?"

With an embarrassed glance at Rachel's sleeping attire, Hank said quickly, "Art Brown told me last night that you were back, Doc, and I'm sure glad to see you. Looks like you got here just in the nick of time."

Becoming concerned, Rachel stepped in front of Seth

and put her hand on Hank's arm. "What's wrong, Mr. Johnson?"

Hank hurried over to his wagon and lifted his old collie out of the back. "Well, you see, Doctor," he panted as he staggered toward the door, "old Jess here needs your services again. She's so big this time, I think she may break her record. I'm countin' on ten."

Rachel glanced over her shoulder at Seth, but he just rolled his eyes and shrugged. Then, looking back into Hank Johnson's hopeful face, she broke into a peal of delighted laughter. "Okay, Mr. Johnson, bring the lady in and let's get down to work!"